IMMORTAL BASTARD

THE ORDER OF VAMPIRES

LYDIA MICHAELS

READ ALONG WITH THE AUDIOBOOK!

Find Immortal Bastard and the rest of The Order of Vampires series on Audible!

CONTENT WARNING

Sensitive readers can check tropes and triggers at
www.LydiaMichaelsBooks.com

DEDICATION

To my beautiful husband, Mike, who spent his entire vacation watching me sweat this book. Thank you for understanding when I crept out of bed at two in the morning to write, and for letting me work long into the night. Thank you for all the silly interruptions and cocktails and cuddles when I needed them most. Thank you for tolerating my addiction and always supporting my dreams. Thank you for so many late-night trips to get me ice cream, the only comfort I wanted when my brain could not write one more word. And thank you for loving all of me in my most chaotic, stressful form + those extra ten fluffy pounds said ice cream gave. You are an unparalleled man and the love of my life—a true mate in every sense of the word. I'm so glad I claimed you twenty-seven years ago when I had the chance. I never would have recovered if you got away.

CHAPTER 1

$\mathcal{D}$elilah's pulse pumped with the beat of the bass as she entered the downtown club, Tribeca. Wired from a long day at the studio, she needed to let go and release some steam. It had been a trying fucking week.

Her skin itched from her new ink. This one was simple. A red thread tied around her wrist like a reminder of something she'd already forgotten. The ink was so thin and delicate, the skin had already started to heal.

She wasn't sure what the tattoo symbolized or what compelled her to permanently mark her skin with such a whimsical thing. She only knew that she woke up three weeks ago with the impression that she was forgetting something important—something that hinted at impending doom, or endless possibility—she wasn't really sure because, ironically, she couldn't remember what it was she'd been trying not to forget.

She got to work, tattooing her wrist that morning. Three weeks later and she couldn't shake the sense of déjà vu that followed every time she glanced at it.

Maybe it was a lost dream or something silly that gave her such an implacable yet familiar feeling. It didn't matter. Half of her tattoos had no meaning anyway. But this one... It itched more than usual, like it was purposely refusing to be forgotten.

Pain exploded in her foot and she nearly swallowed her tongue. *"Do you mind?"* she barked as a three-hundred-pound rhino stepped on the toe of her Mary Jane.

"Sorry." The drunk asshole stumbled into the wall.

This place was going to shit. It used to have an air of exclusivity. Now, anyone could get in.

Her luck had been the shitty precedent of her shittier fucking mood. It hadn't sunk in yet that her bad fortune had turned around and she was no longer in danger of being evicted. But, man, it had come close.

A lesser woman might have resorted to selling blowjobs in order to make ends meet. Rock bottom was a few floors above the bedrock where her finances had plummeted this month. Thankfully, a new client showed up just in the nick of time and saved her ass from one of two things—eviction or working out her rent under her fat, heaving prick of a landlord.

Delilah shivered, perishing the thought. She'd never resort to selling her body to make ends meet, but she loved her shop and the thought had crossed her mind in a dark moment of desperation. The tattoo parlor was her baby. Yes, sometimes babies grow up to become failures that suck the ever-living life out of a person, but she wasn't ready to quit on her baby just yet. Skin Deep still had a few good months left.

Sooner or later, she'd have to make a move. She needed a career change. Or a miracle. People just weren't spending money on tattoos like they used to now that the economy was in the shitter. Chances were, she'd be back in this destitute situation again next month when she needed to scrounge up rent money and pay her bills.

The crowd blocking the bar bottlenecked toward the bathrooms and the rancid scent of beer and piss had her crinkling her nose. She seriously needed to find a better hangout. Pushing her way through a group of towering men, she squeezed her way closer to the bar.

"Where'd you come from, cutie?" a guy asked, helping himself to her personal space.

"Touch me and you lose a hand."

He held up his palms in surrender and laughed, like she was rude for not welcoming a stranger's grubby paws on her. If only men knew what it was like to live in a world where predators assumed an open invitation to grope them at will. She edged up another two steps, escaping the odor of sweat and cheap drugstore cologne.

She could easily let one of the surrounding men buy her a drink, but tonight was on her dollar. She fucking earned it and didn't feel like dealing with anyone's bullshit.

It wasn't just her shop that suffered. Everyone felt the pinch as prices skyrocketed, and customer service became a thing of the past. Groceries alone could break a person, so she understood why her shop had grown so quiet.

People didn't blow money on body art unless they had substantial money to waste. And her shop, unfortunately, wasn't located in a wealthy part of town—unless one considered dilapidated bowling alleys and foreclosed, vacant storefronts posh.

Her guardian angel, a shitty fucking angel at best, must have pulled some last-second strings when those college sorority sisters stumbled in last night. Nothing like tipsy customers with purses full of *Daddy's* money and a hankering for some regrettable work. Three fucking tramp stamps later and Delilah would live to fight another day.

Still nowhere close to making rent this morning, she'd been sure Skin Deep's doors would close for good. Then another dope showed up requesting a declaration of love inked permanently into his arm. It was the curse of any relationship, but Delilah didn't tell him that. She happily tattooed the name *Debbie* into his bicep and took the money for the job.

It had been a slow day, one where she up-charged every service not spelled out on their menu, and she'd barely made any progress. The few random customers helped but weren't enough to keep Delilah's greasy landlord off her ass.

Desperation and panic truly set in as the streets grew quiet and the shop shut down for the night. Until, lo and behold, in walked a man asking for not only an enormous piece of Christ on the cross going up his spine but an entire sleeve as well.

Can you say down payment?

The man, a beautiful, chiseled work of art, left two grand in cash as a deposit, saving her ass and making it possible for Delilah to breathe without pinching anxiety for the first time in weeks. She'd been so convinced her shop was dead, her change in fortune still hadn't fully sunk in.

Things had gotten so bad, she'd hardly slept from the stress of it all. Her worry about her mounting debt and the cost of operating Skin Deep left her constantly tense and unsure of what to do. But now, she had work. The kind of work that would take weeks to finish and cover at least a few months of rent.

She'd had to temporarily lay off her staff in hopes of salvaging some much-needed money for the bills, but even that seemed too little too late. At least now, she had a client to hold her over for a while.

As soon as she got the cash down payment tonight, she wrote a check to her douchebag landlord and caught up with the utility companies. A stack of sealed envelopes waited on her counter for the postman as sweet relief slowly settled in.

Post-stress-euphoria pushed her to the bar directly after closing. She needed to celebrate— or intoxicate. Adrenaline had driven her past burnout and rubbed the last of her nerves raw. She might have the rent handled, but her anxiety was still jacked up from the panic. She needed to blow off steam.

Pushing through the remaining throng blocking the bar, Delilah growled as an over-bearded hipster made eyes at her and lifted his IPA. *Not now, puppy.* She wanted nothing to do with the juvenile college crowd that dominated their town.

Frowning, as some tit cut in front of her, Delilah elbowed her way up to the bar. Tribeca needed more servers. The wench working the tap played favorites and struggled to keep up with orders. Waving a twenty did nothing to flag down a drink.

One quick skim of the packed club, and Delilah assumed her friends weren't coming. No shock there. But she still suffered a pinch of disappointment all the same. Of course, her friends were mostly her employees. It made sense that they might be a little bent over the recent downsizing, but Delilah hoped they could still keep things cool.

After letting her staff go—a call she'd been forced to make due to economic hardship—her social life grew more and more isolated. She didn't want to examine the loneliness creeping over her too closely. Her life was not a fucking Instagram reel of inspiring boss lady posts. *Hashtag goal-getter! Hashtag boss babe! Hashtag fuck off.*

Owning a business was hard, lonely work and when the chips were down, people bailed to worry about themselves, even though she'd constantly worried about taking care of everyone else. Fuck Lance and McGuire if they couldn't come out and celebrate with her. She didn't need their commentary anyway. It wasn't hard to find someone else to keep her entertained—someone better than those two Lurch-looking motherfuckers.

Waiting for the bartender to get to her, Delilah glanced at her newest piece popping against the inside of her wrist, reminding her of... *nothing.* She really thought the memory would have come to her by now.

She loved being a tattoo artist, loved the adrenaline rush of marking herself with something new, loved the bite of pain that slowly numbed out as the needle pegged over her skin. She also loved inflicting a little of that pain. It helped release some of the inner bitch that built up over her early adult years.

She based her life on a simple philosophy of

you get what you get. People waste too many years trying to fit some shitty mold proper society valued when the majority of the world was broken and struggling just like her. Fuck society. Fuck the rules. And fuck anyone who tried to lump her into a group. She valued individuality above all else.

She would never survive working some crappy nine-to-five job, knee-deep in paperwork, scrimping by making small talk with co-workers she hated just to appear pleasant. Nope. Put her in that fishbowl and it would only be a matter of time before she snapped.

When clients were on her table, she was in charge, just as she liked it. With minimal tolerance for stupid people and no patience for entitlement, she called the shots and worked for herself. Yeah, it was hard and there wasn't always money when she needed it, but she managed to make ends meet each month. So far, so good, as long as she didn't let the stress get to her.

"Can I get some fucking service?" she yelled, her voice lost in the din of the crowd as the pulsating music rattled her bones.

Some would say she had anger issues, but that was crap. She was a very nice person to those who deserved it.

Stealthily digging her elbow in the ribs of some stool hog, she leaned over and whistled at the bartender. The acrid smell of booze, sweat, and sex tickled her nose as her eyes adjusted to the blue strobe lights flickering throughout the club.

The chick lifted a pencil-thin brow and proceeded to ignore Delilah. Whatever. It was her tip.

"It looks like someone spilled a crayon box on you," the stool hog next to her commented, his gaze roaming over Delilah's skin without invitation.

Great. Another insightful boomer who thought it was appropriate to share his unwanted, outdated opinions and hang out in a club with a clientele three generations younger. These judgmental relics were all the same. They still used fax machines, misogyny, and Facebook.

She tried not to look directly at him because guys like this mistook basic eye contact for a rapt audience. The moment they thought they had someone's attention, the offensive jokes would start. *No, thank you.*

If she could just get her drink she'd get out of his way. Impatiently tapping her nail on the lacquered bar, she waited for the bartender to take her order.

"Let me ask you something," Stool Hog continued, swiveling to fully face her with his protruding gut.

Delilah angled her eyeballs in his direction without moving her head. That was all he was getting.

"What would make a pretty young girl like yourself cover your skin in all that crap?"

Here we go... "I like it."

"I don't understand why women do that to themselves. A woman's body is a work of art."

Turning completely, she eyed her annoying companion. "I don't understand why men who aren't starring in a 1970's porn flick have mustaches, but that didn't make you shave that caterpillar off your face or toss out that dead cat of a toupee you're trying to pass off as hair, did it? To each his own."

"Oh, you're one of *them*." He stilled then laughed. "You'll regret those tattoos, just wait."

"Thanks for the prophecy, Nostradamus." She leaned over the bar and yelled, "Can I *please* get some service?"

"Imagine what you'll look like when you're old and wrinkled."

Her molars locked. "I'm guessing I'd probably look something like everyone else that age, but prettier and more interesting."

He chuckled as if they were friends. "You're a feisty little thing."

The bartender finally made her way over. Delilah stood on the foot-rail and shouted, "Can I get a red-headed slut and a Guinness?"

With a nod, she rushed off to fill the order and Delilah anxiously waited, hoping to slam her shot, grab her beer, and get the hell away from google-eyed-boomer. Gazing straight ahead, her knee bounced as her foot balanced on the lowest rung of the stool.

"You know," Stool Hog started again. "There

are laser treatments now. You could get them removed."

Mother. Fucker. This guy didn't know when to stop.

"You could probably find one in the area—"

"Look," she snapped, cutting off any more of his pedantic bullshit. "If my tattoos bother you so much, maybe you should find someone else to ogle. I don't remember asking for your fucking opinion or even sending you a signal that I was remotely interested in what you thought. Look at me and look at you. You're older than my dad. No wonder you don't get it."

"You've got quite a mouth on you."

"And I bite."

"I bet." His gaze dropped and he leaned in, moving to touch her, but she jerked back.

"Hands off, dude. Find yourself a geriatric center and have some pudding with people your own age."

"That's the problem with you young people—"

"How about you shut the fuck up about things you're too fucking closed-minded to understand, and let me order my goddamn drink in peace?"

He scowled. It should have been enough to end any further dialogue, but the dickhead was enslaved by his ego and couldn't resist hearing himself talk. "I was just going to say—"

"I believe you were saying goodnight," a deep voice cut off Stool Hog's response, and Delilah stilled as the fine hairs on her neck lifted with awareness as the new ink on her wrist tingled.

She slowly rotated her body to look up. Holy shit. Her mouth fell open as she gaped at the gorgeous man. Tall, with dark wavy brown hair, a strong jaw, a straight nose, and bright crystalline eyes lined with thick, dark lashes stared back at her.

Come to mama.

The boomer also pivoted. "This is a private conversation."

That stunning face locked on the boomer, his eyes brimming with unflinching promise. How could anyone so menacing also be so damn beautiful? "The lady asked you to leave her in peace, did she not?"

Stool Hog glared at the intruder. "What are you, her keeper?"

"Yes."

That one word hit like a punch, knocking the wind out of her as heat tingled through her veins. Every muscle in her body went weak. Heat consumed her blood and her thighs pressed tight. She'd never seen the man before in her life, yet his classically beautiful face fit her definition of perfect so well, he seemed familiar as if he were literally the man of her dreams.

Wow, she silently mouthed, wondering what a man like that might do with a few extra hours and her naked body sprawled beneath him. Visions of entangled, sweaty limbs filled her mind. Mouths licking, bodies writhing, muscles contracting…

His glare snapped from Stool Hog to her and his nostrils flared. Was he having the same chemical response? Picturing the same sinful scene? Something in his intense stare told her he was.

Fuck the drink. This tall glass of water was better than anything the bar was serving. Yes, she definitely could see herself riding his face and wearing his cum before dawn.

His hand shot out, possessively curling around her shoulder, doing that thing when guys see a woman in trouble with a creeper and act like they know her.

She smiled and fluttered her lashes up at him, enjoying his possessive hold even if it was total bullshit. *My hero…*

His grip tightened on her bare shoulder, once again implying his interest. The strobe lights flashed against his catlike eyes and she frowned at the inhuman shape of his pupils. Was he wearing contacts?

"Look, buddy—"

"I'm not your buddy." Mr. Gorgeous corrected the forgotten pest to her left.

He spoke with an accent, thick and heavy, hopefully like his cock.

Stool Hog took a disgruntled stance and started to rise. "We were having a perfectly nice conversation until—"

His words abruptly cut off as if they were

physically trapped in his throat. Before he could lumber his fat ass off his seat, Mr. Gorgeous ordered him to rethink his next move. "Do not speak another word about her if you wish to keep your tongue. Get up and walk away. *Now.*"

Was this guy with the mafia? He delivered that threat with chilling assuredness as if he would not hesitate one millisecond to cut out the boomer's tongue. It should have been a red flag, but if Delilah had a flag, she'd use it to mop up the mess that was now soaking her panties.

Who the hell was this guy?

Like a puppet on a string, the older man silently rose from the stool and ambled away, forgetting his cocktail and appearing as unsure as a lost child.

Delilah gaped at the now empty seat as the beautiful man slid more into view. Lean, carved muscle, not an ounce of fat on him. Talk about a brick shit house. No wonder the other guy didn't put up a fight. This ripped Adonis could annihilate most men in one swing.

When he met her hungry stare with his own, she preened. Yup, she literally tittered like a giddy little schoolgirl as butterflies or some other cheesy romantic shit tickled her core. The swooning sensation was so intense she broke eye contact and fidgeted awkwardly. She couldn't recall ever responding to a man in such a way.

"You do not have to be nervous around me, little one."

A hundred fantasies raced through her head

in the span of that glance, several starring her as the disobedient student in a short plaid skirt while he held a wooden ruler in that firm—*holy shit those were some big hands.* Her body melted, heat sinking deeper into her stomach and ruining her panties once and for all.

"Where are you from?" There was something old world about him. Maybe he was from an obscure place she never thought to visit like Bulgaria or Estonia.

"I'm originally from Portugal." He scowled as he scanned the bar.

Was he looking for something? Maybe looking for someone. Delilah wanted his full attention so she leaned forward, trying to monopolize his view with what was likely the most desperate smile she'd ever given a man.

His menacing presence left no room for misinterpretation. He stood beside her like a bodyguard, assuring no other men would approach, but also appearing very put out by their surroundings.

"Do you get out much?" she asked, teasing him.

He didn't laugh or smile. He just continued scanning the bar as if looking for threats. Okay, maybe this was a little weird.

"You're not safe in a place of such ill repute." His hand protectively pressed into her back.

She laughed and looked around, wondering if this was some sort of prank. "Did Lance and McGuire send you here to fuck with me?" He was pretty enough to be an actor.

His scowl deepened. "Who?"

"Lance and…" Her words faded as he moved closer, showing no recognition. "Never mind."

Another wave of patrons crowded the bar and bumped her seat. He turned and growled something threatening in another language. The group of patrons immediately backed off and gave them space.

Talk about territorial foreplay. No one had ever laid such an indisputable, nonverbal claim. She liked it. From his starched collar down to his booted feet, the man was all power and inarguable influence. She took pity on anyone who dared to tell him no.

She wanted—no, needed—him to hit on her so she could deny him just to see how he'd react. Visions of hot flesh flashed through her mind as she imagined pushing him to the brink of losing his self-control and seeing what really lay beneath that gruff exterior. Would he hold her down? Make her beg? She wanted all the possibilities.

He looked at her again, the black of his eyes swallowing the silver. "Are you waiting for something?" His graveled voice tinged with impatience as those strange eyes made a slow perusal of her body.

"Just my drink."

Another man approached, this one college-age. As he attempted to claim the unoccupied stool, Captain Handsome pants twisted and growled, "Leave."

The younger man didn't flinch as he reversed and obeyed the command. The beautifully intense man had an indisputable air of authority. Everything about the territorial bastard called to her on some baser, carnal level.

"You have many admirers here."

"Hardly." She snorted.

He leaned closer and his cologne intoxicated her every breath, a mixture of earthy masculinity and savage authority. "I know what these men are thinking, little one." His warm breath teased the delicate shell of her ear and she shivered. "Their minds are full of sin. You're not safe here."

"Um, it's cool. I know how to keep the creepers at bay. But I appreciate you stepping in like you did." She pivoted to fully face him. "Did you want to sit?" Flirtatiously waving a hand at the vacant stool, she suggestively lifted a shoulder under her cherry-red, rockabilly dress as she batted her eyes.

He didn't smile back. Rather, his gaze swept over her and he scowled. His obvious disapproval played into her fantasies—unless that look meant he didn't find her attractive.

The heat in her belly faded as he continued to study her in a way that triggered an edge of uncertainty. His bright eyes hooded and shadowed as his condemning frown grew. Maybe she misread his interest.

She couldn't recall ever finding a man so appealing that his opinion of her would carry so much weight. She didn't like how much she wanted him to find her attractive. Since when was she desperate for other people's approval?

"Your skin is…"

Great, another critic. She sighed and turned her attention back to the bar. If he wasn't interested, why the hell did he interfere?

She sighed, irritated by her own desperate desire for a man's approval. Shoving away her purely hormonal response to a good looking guy, she grabbed her phone. Okay, fine, he was a fucking god, but she didn't like being attracted to someone who obviously disapproved of her. She spent enough time in her life being someone else's regrettable circumstance.

She didn't need judgement. She was just lonely and horny. There were way less complicated men around to help her remedy that.

Her drinks arrived just in time. Tossing a ten on the bar, she flung back the shot, swallowed the tart fiery liquid, and gave her Bettie Page-styled black hair a flip.

Time to move on.

Grabbing the pilsner of beer, she ignored Captain Yummy Pants and moved to find a new place to lurk. When he caught her wrist, the dark frothy beer sloshed and almost fell out of her hand.

Her glare narrowed on Mr. Mixed Message. Pretty or not, she wasn't down for mind games. "Dude, did I give you the impression that you could touch me?"

He unclutched her arm but the sensation of

his firm grip remained. "I've made you uncomfortable."

Her day had been too long to put in this sort of work. "It's cool. I was leaving."

He blocked her escape with his body, his broad shoulders sheltering her view. "Allow me to sit with you."

The formality of his speech had to be the result of a language barrier. Was that German? He'd said he was originally from Portugal, but maybe he was an army brat who moved around a lot.

It didn't matter anyway, since his initial interest now resonated like disdain. She was definitely attracted to him but also aware of the warning chill teasing up her spine.

Sometimes men wanted her but didn't like her. Men often saw her as a Freudian rebellion that went against their mother's version of the perfect woman. She could be that for them—she liked being the bad girl that unleashed a good boy's fantasies—but not for a man like this. This guy was dangerous. The question was, how dangerous?

"What's your deal?" she asked, point blank.

"You mistake my curiosity for criticism. I was merely taking in your beauty. Where I'm from, females don't look like you."

She frowned, unsure if she should be insulted. "And where is that?" His stilted English was decent enough that she believed he lived in America, just not from anywhere around here.

"I live somewhere very different from this city."

Intrigue battled with warning bells. She wasn't sure if he was giving *who's your daddy* vibes or serial killer ones. When she fully met his mercurial stare, her heart slammed into an erratic tempo that jerked her whole system out of whack.

He held her eye contact and lifted a finger at the bar. The preoccupied bartender rushed over as if he was the most important customer there.

"What can I get you?"

Whoever he was, people obeyed his command without question. "Scotch," he said, without taking his eyes off her.

Interesting.

He was very, 'It was the butler in the study with the wrench' sophisticated. Indisputable eloquence wrapped him in luxury, but his clothes were rather plain. Just black slacks and a button down, yet there was something seasoned about him. Classic. Monochromatic. Timeless. People eagerly obeyed him.

Was he a celebrity? Maybe the owner of the club? Everyone noticed him but no one had the balls to look directly at him. It was like he was used to hiding in plain sight. She needed more information.

"Soooo," she said, swiveling on her stool. "You come here often?"

His stare dropped quickly to her breasts, almost dispassionately, as if he were disappointed, but determined all the same. The mixed signals were giving her whiplash. Was he interested or not?

He lowered to the stool, never taking his stare off of her. "You're very interesting to me."

Well, that was *something*, she supposed. She preferred directness but didn't know him well enough to determine if his words were sincere.

"I speak the truth." He leaned closer to talk over the pounding music. The scent of his skin and clothing was the perfect combination of masculine virility and slow-aged patience. She bet he spent hundreds of dollars on one little bottle.

She cupped her beer with both hands so not to fidget.

"Your pulse is racing."

No shit. Horny and nervous wasn't a desirable baseline. "It's been a long day."

"You can relax now, little one. You never have to be nervous around me."

She met his stare as calm washed over her. It was the strangest eye fuck she'd ever experienced. Should she be turned on or cautious? At the moment, she was both—but not nervous. Not anymore. It was like his words instantly soothed her, and she could relax even when her mind didn't know or trust this man. Weird.

He spoke over the thrumming music. "What's your name?"

"Delilah. Delilah Starling."

His dark brows lifted as he studied her. "In

the Old Testament, Delilah betrays Samson to his enemies."

That was a new one. As an agnostic, she didn't do Bibles, so she had no response. "How about you?"

"Pardon?"

"Your name…"

"I'm Christian Schrock."

"Are you in town on business or something?"

"Yes. Business."

"And what is it you do, Christian Schrock?" In her head, she sang The Name Game to commit his name to memory. *Schrock, Schrock, bo bock, banana fana fo fock! Bet you got a big old cock, Christian Schrah-ock.*

"I'm a farmer."

She snorted. "A *farmer*?" That was unexpected. "Like Old McDonald?"

"Who?"

"You know… *A chick, chick here, and a chick, chick there*?" She pictured him on a tractor in a straw hat. Nope. He looked too much like a foreign drug lord for her to conjure a believable image of him working a farm. "You should really come up with a better cover if you expect people to buy it."

His scowl was a mix of indignation and wounded shock. "You're accusing me of lying, Delilah?"

Her name rolled off his tongue like distant, soothing thunder. "Come on, Chris, you and I both know you're not a farmer."

"My name's Christian. Not Chris."

Touchy much? This guy was all formality. "Sorry, *Christian.* You're going to have to sell that farmer in the dell image a little harder if you expect people to buy it." She plucked a business card out of her bra and slid it in front of him.

He frowned at the action and read the card. "What is this?"

"That's proof that I own the tattoo shop around the corner. You got a farmer's card, *Christian?*"

"I do not."

She turned over his hands noting the soft skin and lack of callouses. The only reason anyone would make up a lie like that would be to cover something big. Her money was on mob ties.

"You really should come up with something more convincing."

"I prefer the truth."

"Right…" She pulled out her phone to show him her Instagram page. "Is your farm on The Gram?"

His frown deepened.

"Let me guess, you're off the grid."

"Our farm is very private, yes."

He was really sticking to the lie. She turned her attention toward locking him in as a client. "Do you have any ink?" When he looked at her in confusion, she clarified, "Tattoos."

"I do not."

The thought of working on such a perfect

canvas filled her with inspiration. Pictures of this guy's body on her page would get serious traffic. Just the glimpse of his forearms peeking out from under his cuffed sleeves told her his body was a chiseled work of art—combined with her talent, she could make him a total masterpiece.

"Here's some of my work." She scrolled slowly, offering her phone to him, but he made no move to take it.

He arched an eyebrow and slipped her business card into his pocket. "You paint tattoos on strangers' bodies?"

"I use instruments a little tougher than paintbrushes."

His gaze coasted over the stars wrapped around her hand, the fresh red thread tied at her wrist, the leopard print traveling up the curve of her shoulder, and the little devil sitting on her other one. "You have so many," he said, merely making an honest observation.

"Did you ever think about getting any?"

His lips parted but he hesitated. His answer faded as he asked, "You said your shop's nearby?"

"Yup, right down the block." Was he interested? "I have some openings next week if you—"

"I'll be gone by then."

"Oh. Well, I could probably squeeze you in—"

"Tonight."

His insistence surprised her. "Tonight?"

"Yes. You'll take me there now."

"It's after hours." Was this really happening? Her recent bout of poverty turned her into an instant capitalist. "I'd have to charge—"

"I'll pay whatever the fee. But we should go now. I'm running out of time."

His sense of urgency motivated her more than anything else. She chugged the last of her beer and slid the empty glass onto the bar. "Let's go."

Her body tingled as he followed her toward the exit. Each time she looked back, her gaze crawled over his impeccable build.

As they walked, her mind crunched numbers, wondering how much she could get away with charging him on some late-night art. Being an entrepreneur meant she had to drive her business like it was stolen, so her mind was on money first, but once she took care of that, she planned to focus on pleasure.

The thought of touching his bare skin sent her into a tailspin. A kaleidoscope of kinky images ran through her head and hardened her nipples as his warm palm pressed into her lower back. His more than six-foot frame towered over her.

She rarely fucked men impetuously, but this guy broke the laws of the ordinary, so she found herself making extraordinary decisions no matter how reckless. Maybe that was part of the lure. There was something undeniably dangerous about him, and she wanted to find out what.

They walked in silence, the cool night air stripping away any remnants of the stagnant humidity of the club. His steps measured one for every three clicks of her Mary Jane's. The weight of his hand burned through the back of her dress, his fingers wide enough to span her waist.

Desire swirled with anticipation in her belly. The quiet ones were always the wild ones. "Do you have an idea about what kind of tattoo you want?"

He didn't answer right away. "Do you work with a lot of male clients?"

He seemed really preoccupied with her male customers. She hoped she didn't misread the situation. It would be a crushing blow to women everywhere if this chiseled Adonis turned out to be gay. "Most of my customers are men."

"And how long do you work on them?"

She shrugged. "Depends on what they get. People ask for all kinds of wild shit. The more intricate, the longer it takes."

"You swear too much."

She frowned and laughed. "You some kind of minister, too?"

"I told you, I'm just a farmer."

"Right."

He glanced at her exposed arms. "How many tattoos do you have?"

"They sort of blend together at this point. I've been in the chair at least fifty times."

Turning the corner, Skin Deep came into view. "Here we are."

Removing the key from her purse, she unlocked the metal caging over the door. It slid up with a slow rolling rumble. Opening the glass door, she held it for him as her fingers flipped the light switch.

Christian scanned the decorated walls as he stepped inside. Nothing in his expression gave away his thoughts. In the bright lights of the store, he looked even more gorgeous than before. Arousal teased as she imagined him sliding inside of her.

He drew in an audible breath and abruptly faced her. She stilled, the strangest notion raising the hairs on her arms. Was she in danger?

Oddly, she still wasn't nervous. The energy between them crackled as he looked at her through intensely hooded eyes. She needed a moment to gather her thoughts and check her tools.

"I'll, uh, get my portfolio so you can get some ideas."

He took a slow step toward her, closing the distance. "We both know I didn't come here for a tattoo, Delilah."

She swallowed, her head angling back as she looked up at him. "You didn't?"

He slowly shook his head. "Don't play coy. Your body betrays you. Your heart rate's accelerating and your eyes are dilated." Then he did something no man had ever done in her presence before. He tipped back his head, shutting his eyes, as he sniffed the air, long and slow. "And you're aroused."

Did he just smell her vagina? What the fuck…

Uncertainty unraveled inside of her and she took a step back. Why had she brought him here?

"Easy, little one," he said softly in that placating voice. "There's no need for unease."

And just like that, her jittery trepidation calmed and a placid peace washed over her as if someone hooked her up to an IV of heavily soothing drugs. His words should not have lulled her, yet she felt cocooned in a state of trustful bliss.

"Okay," she said in an embarrassingly dopey voice.

"I prefer when you're calm."

Was he asking or pointing out the obvious? She should've been alarmed by the uncharacteristic sense of tranquility, but she was too damn chill at the moment to care.

Her brow pinched. "This doesn't make sense. I don't know you, yet I feel incredibly peaceful in your presence."

"Perhaps your instincts recognize me as someone trustworthy."

That didn't sound right, but it felt right. Weird.

She studied his intent expression under the clinical lights of the studio. He had one of those faces that were hard to put an age to. He could've been in his late twenties just as easily as he could've been in his early forties. He was definitely older than her twenty-nine years.

Her gaze traveled down his front to the substantial bulge between his hips. Adrenaline pumped through her veins, her mind wavering between sensuality and uncertainty.

Reaching forward, he stroked a jet-black tendril of her hair and she leaned into the caress. "I enjoy it when you look at me like that, Delilah."

Shallow, jagged breaths filled her lungs as the energy of the room thickened and her body tightened. Instinctively, she knew he was a predator and the world was his prey. So why wasn't she scared?

She wanted him inside of her. But she also didn't want to get murdered and chopped up into little colorful pieces. "I have cameras outside. If you hurt me, I've got your face on file."

"I could never hurt you. I desire something else entirely."

Every muscle in her body relaxed. "Something?" Even the inflection of her voice was subdued as if the odd sense of calm affected her vocal cords as well.

"Yes. I desire *you*." His hand slid from her hair to the back of her neck, tipping her head back. "I want to taste every inch of you. Do you understand?"

She nodded slowly and that was all the permission he needed.

His mouth slammed over hers, warm and

demanding, and her heart rate spiked, but she still wasn't scared. Her hands gripped his broad shoulders. This felt right. She couldn't explain it, but her body seemed to recognize his, as if they'd done this a thousand times before.

Backing her against the wall, his arms coiled around her waist, lifting her off the ground. Wreathing his neck, her fingers slid through his hair as his mouth delivered an onslaught of passion.

The crinkle of wall art under her back reminded her where they were. She tore her mouth from his and looked out the wide storefront window. It was nighttime, but the shop was lit up like a fucking Christmas tree.

"In the back," she panted as he kissed his way down her shoulder.

His dominant touch ignited a fire inside of her. Every press of his hard body to hers filled her with the burning desire to get him naked.

Large, strong hands gripped her ass, as her legs wrapped around his waist. His thick erection pressed hard into her core. He carried her toward the back.

"Wait!" She reached into the big fishbowl on the counter, snatching a purple Skin Deep condom from the ones she ordered for promotional purposes.

As if he knew exactly where to go, he took her to one of the rooms with a reclining chair she used for piercings. As soon as the cool leather of the seat hit her back, his mouth was on hers again.

Her fingers nimbly sought the buttons on his shirt, but she couldn't find them. The fabric was coarser than expected.

"Rip it," he growled, mouth against her throat.

Not needing to be told twice, her fists yanked the fabric open. Her palms collided with hard, masculine muscle wrapped in hot, unmarked flesh. He roughly tugged at the dainty cap sleeve of her dress. She twisted her arms, withdrawing them from the fabric.

He yanked down the cups of her bra. Cool air teased her puckering flesh. Ripping his mouth from hers, he stilled, one knee wedged between her thighs. "What have you done to yourself, Delilah?"

Glancing down at her exposed breasts, the glint of the overhead lights reflected in her nipple rings. Her arm lifted to cover her breasts, but he caught her wrist, forcing her to remain in a vulnerable position as he studied her.

She couldn't decipher his expression. "You don't like it?"

He swallowed, his Adam's apple shifting slowly under his tanned, shadowed jaw. "Does it pain you?"

"Not anymore. But...I don't mind a little pain."

His gaze was transfixed on the twin silver hoops. Gently, he traced the ring, moving the tiny ball and engorging her nipples all the more. She moaned and his hungry gaze flashed to hers. "Why would you do this to your body?"

"Because I like the way it looks and, well, they feel good."

"How could this feel good?"

"The sensitivity makes me more responsive."

His head tilted, and his attention snagged on her neck. He brushed her hair away from her shoulders and ran a fingertip up her throat and frowned. "What is this?"

Her hand lifted to her neck, cupping her skin to hide the tattoo. *Damn young adult books!* Although it was only two tiny dots with a trickle of crimson, it was one of her most re-grettable tattoos. "That…is the mark of a childish phase."

"Phase?"

She could explain that dumb tattoos hap-pened and this was one of hers. The result of too much paranormal fiction, a bottle of rum, and the pressure of impressionable friends. "It's a vampire bite," she mumbled, em-barrassed.

He stiffened. "I beg your pardon?"

Here she was, pierced tits and tattoos out while he used words like *pardon*. But she re-fused to pretend she was someone else. "I was drunk when I got it."

He cupped her breast. "*Who* did this to you?"

"I got them pierced when we were in Florida for senior week. The place probably isn't even there anymore."

"Male or female?"

What did that matter? She had to think back to recall such irrelevant details. "It was a guy."

He looked away, a low growl rumbling from his chest. "I want to see all of you."

She hesitated. Was he planning on inspecting every inch of her the way he inspected her nipples? It was unsettling to have anyone look at her so closely.

He stood, catching her hand and pulling her to her feet. "Remove your dress."

Tugged from the white leather chair, she hesitated. What kind of kink was this? She liked the edge of uncertainty but wasn't sure about his endgame. "Why?"

"Because I asked."

She cocked her head. He didn't ask. He commanded. And he was going to have to give her something more.

"Your body's a work of art, Delilah. It was designed for worship and I plan to honor every inch of you."

Good enough. The dress fell from her chest, snagging at her hips.

"Keep going. I want to see all of you."

His gentle command had her sex pulsing. The slow buzz of the zipper loosened the material as her insides clenched with desire. The dress fell to the floor, leaving her standing before him in nothing more than a thong, Mary Janes, and her painted skin.

His breath labored. No words in her vocabulary could describe the intense look on his face. Desire. Longing. Hunger. Lust. They all came up short. No one had ever looked at her that way.

"Men gave you these markings?"

Again, with the men. "Some were done by women."

He circled her slowly, dragging a fingertip from her left shoulder to her right as he inspected every inch of her tattooed flesh. Chills raced down her spine as he outlined the tree of life. He caressed the swell of her hip, his touch dipping under the elastic of her panties. With a quick snap, the material fell to her ankles and her breath hitched.

He dropped to his haunches and kissed the spattering of monarch butterflies taking flight over her thigh, his face only inches from her sex. Her insides quivered as liquid fire pooled at her core.

Dragging his face to her stomach, his eyes closed as his nose tickled her flesh, lighter than a feather's touch. "You're so much more exotic than I ever imagined."

He framed her hips reverently as if her body were a sacrament. His thumb traced the adorned silhouette of Mother Nature above her sex and drifted lower, pausing when he discovered another piercing peeking from beneath the soft hair at her apex.

He looked up at her, startled. "You have one here, too?" His words fanned over her flesh as his thumb gently grazed her clit.

She sucked in a sharp breath. "That one's especially sensitive."

Holding her stare, he leaned forward. She whimpered as his tongue traced over the piercing, sliding into her as his grip tightened on her hips.

Heart hammering, her nails dug into the thick muscle of his shoulders and she widened her stance, gasping when his tongue penetrated deeply. A metal tray clattered to the ground as he lifted her, depositing her once more on the chair.

His mouth dropped between her thighs as he pressed her legs wide, spreading her and making a feast of her body. She cried out in pleasure as his tongue stabbed into her sex. He touched her with animal-like instinct, growling as he tasted her. Holding her with vicious possession, he licked her clit and ate her pussy. The first wave of euphoria tumbled into something bigger. Pleasure ripped through her, fast and overwhelming, and she screamed in ecstasy.

Fuck, fuck, fuck! The orgasm rolled through her like a wave of fire.

His relentless mouth plundered her tender body as he wrenched her thighs wider. Her muscles had no time to adapt to the onslaught of pleasure once the spasms began. She cried out, begging for more as he fervently teased her piercing with his wicked tongue, driving her to a riotous climax.

Her body gushed and trembled as chills rolled into blinding spasms, each one igniting another flow of pleasure that overshadowed any orgasm she'd had before. In a dizzying blur, he pinned her to the chair and kissed her hard on the mouth, sharing her taste as his tongue swept over hers.

She shoved the condom into his hand. "Here."

He growled, taking it, then flipping her onto her stomach and hitching her hips to meet his height. Everything happened so fast. She wasn't sure how he undressed so quickly. Hot flesh pressed into the backs of her thighs. His touch disappeared, replaced by the thick, probing tip of his cock.

Her body stretched to accommodate him —*Holy Mother* he was big. She grunted as he shoved into her body in one fluid motion, deep and hard, giving her no chance to adjust to his massive size.

"Jesus."

His grunt of satisfaction spoke of sheer arrogance. His hands gripped her hips, holding her in place as if he wanted her to experience all of him—his size, his strength, his complete possession of her in that moment. She'd never felt so full.

His palm coasted up her spine and fisted in her hair. "I have you now, little one."

A tremor of unease spiked inside of her, the sense of calm unraveling. He slowly withdrew and thrust into her, hard and unforgiving. Her body shivered, a guttural moan falling from her lips as he filled her again. He took her like a true alpha, holding her neck and hair, pinning her for his use and pleasure.

There was fear, but also gratification like nothing she'd experienced before. His possession was a welcomed drug. It had been too long since she'd been with a man and this man was unlike any past lover she'd had. Releasing her tension, she embraced the moment.

He pounded into her with limitless stamina. Her body slickened with sweat. Pleasure peaked, suspended on an endless plateau of ecstasy as he drove her higher and higher to that climactic precipice once more.

The slap of their skin and their breathy cries played like an erotic symphony. He brought her to another climax but didn't stop there. Riding her hard and leaving her weak, he greedily took what her body could offer. She didn't mind when he fucked her like a rag doll. Nor did she mind when he cupped her throat. It felt incredible, so no matter how much he took from her, she couldn't call him a selfish lover, but deep down she sensed he could be a cold-hearted bastard when he chose.

She liked that dangerous edge, enjoyed knowing something animalistic hid under his sophisticated, well-mannered surface. As her body softened with fatigue, he held her close, never letting their connection sever—not until he had his fill.

She submissively gave herself over to him, falling into his control as he continued to pound into her body and grope her with possessive entitlement. Sweat and arousal left her thighs sticky. She was spent and unsure how much longer she could carry on like this. Marathon fucking was fun, but this had to be some sort of a record.

His wide hand spanned the front of her stomach, urging her to rise to her knees. Her eyes closed as her head lulled to his shoulder. Her strength had depleted. She needed to rest. If not for his muscular arms wrapped around her, she would have fallen on her face.

Hips thrusting, he brushed her hair away and softly kissed her throat. "Your body fits mine perfectly."

She could only sigh an incoherent murmur at this point. The fact that she was still somewhat upright was impressive. But he was being very sweet, whispering praise into her ear as he kissed her neck and licked over her steady pulse.

"Just relax, little one. I have you now."

Her ear pressed into her shoulder, giving him full access to her neck as he licked and kissed. He sent a thrill of shivers down her spine and she laughed. "That tickles."

His hold tightened, and she suddenly found it difficult to move. Frowning, she draped her arm over his, noting the way his muscles corded tightly around her ribcage.

She grunted when he thrust into her, filling her to the hilt, and holding himself deep inside of her body. "Christian…" Roped with swollen veins, his forearm pinned her to him, making it difficult to draw in a full breath.

"It will all be over soon."

"You're holding me too tight." She tried to dislodge the arm under her ribs, but he only tightened his grip as a sharp sting pierced her flesh. *"Ouch!"*

Something punctured her neck and she jerked, but he held her in an unbreakable grip as his cock pulsed inside of her. What was it? One of her tools? A gun? A needle? Pliers?

Something wasn't right. She struggled to break his hold, but it only tightened, crushing her body to his as he grunted and sucked at her throat, soothing the sting.

His hold on her intensified and she flinched, his jaw locked over her, biting hard enough to draw blood. True fear chased up her spine followed by an unfamiliar bolt of ecstasy. Her mouth opened on a silent scream, her body tightening and twisting in a mix of pain, pleasure, and horror.

What was he doing to her? Panic mounted and she slapped at his unbreakable grip. "Wait—"

"Hush, *pintura.* It was always going to end this way."

The moment he lifted his mouth to speak, blood raced down her shoulder, forming a river of red between her breasts as rivulets cascaded over the sinew of his arm. "Get off of me!"

He covered her mouth, muffling her cries. "It's already begun, little one. You must let me finish."

Heat trickled down her stomach. Blood. It was fucking blood! There was so much and she was certain it was all hers. Why had she been so stupid?

"Please!" Her hysterical plea was lost against the tight grip of his hand covering her mouth.

Her breath beat against his fingers and her muzzled scream was lost. Eyes wide, she watched in horror as a hot flood of blood trailed down her breasts and thighs, spattering over the white leather chair and pooling at her knees.

Realizing he must have cut her throat, her panic doubled and tears gathered in her eyes. She fought, but his hold was unbreakable.

Then his hand pulled away and she screamed, evacuating every breath from her lungs. His forearm covered her gaping mouth, hot copper burned her tongue and she choked on the unmistakable taste of blood.

"Drink."

Gagging and struggling, she tried to break free and shove his arm away. Tried to scream. His hold was so tight, so constricting, she could barely breathe.

"You must swallow, Delilah! Be calm and do as I say."

Fatigue slammed into her, nearly knocking her out, but her throat instinctively swallowed, much like an infant nursing at a mother's breast. Her sluggish thoughts slowed and her fear muted. She became estranged from her panic.

His hips flexed, his body still inside of hers.

She detached—from herself, from him, from all the inexplicable.

A low purr emanated from his chest. She sensed his deep satisfaction but would likely die before ever understanding what would push a man to do this to her.

How much blood had she lost?

He was killing her. She could feel the life-sapping from her body.

Why?

It was the only thought she could hold.

Why? Why would he do this to her?

Then a calm blackness moved in like a quiet storm darkening the light into shadows that stretched across her peripheral.

Tears spilled from her eyes, but she no longer fought him. His hold loosened, but it was too late. She was too weak.

"Hush now, *pintura*. I have you."

Tears leaked from her unblinking eyes as she unwillingly lost her grip on reality. She hated him, but she hated herself more for trusting a stranger.

Then, even her hate became too much to bear so she had no choice but to let it go. Sweet surrender engulfed her and there was no more fear, no more pain. She was finished. Empty. Depleted. Over.

His grip on her throat loosened and she weakly gagged. He covered her mouth, his thumb petting softly over her lips. "Shh…You must keep it down, Delilah."

Blood settled like tar into her stomach. She

swayed with queasiness, revolted by the way he stroked her. The room turned on end as he cradled her body to his, no longer inside her. Thoughts fragmented into partial syllables she couldn't string together.

Her vision blurred with more unshed tears.

Weak. She was so weak.

Soft hums whispered in the dark shadows of her fading conscience. Blinking up at the hard angles of his face, she sensed a strange tenderness.

"Why?" she rasped, a steady stream of tears leaking from her eyes as she lay broken, battered, and bloodstained in his arms.

He held her the way a parent might hold and comfort a child. "Because you are mine."

She shivered, her body numb and cold. Her heart struggled to beat. It was too much.

Her breathing slowed and her body chilled as the last of her straining muscles gave out. Her lashes lowered. She dropped into nothingness as the blackness swallowed her.

No more pain. No more fear.

Peace.

CHAPTER 2

The reverberation of the distant school bell woke Dane from a dead sleep. The bright sky painted a blue backdrop as he glanced out the loft window. "Shit." He shot out of bed, tripping over the tangle of sheets and pillows that had fallen to the floor.

Maggie lifted her head and a mess of tumbled gold curls fell over her eyes. "Where are you running off to?"

Dane shoved his legs into his pants and hoisted up the suspenders. "There's a council meeting today."

She laughed and flopped back onto the bed with disinterest. "And why would that concern you?"

Her bare breasts tempted him to rethink his schedule. No. This meeting was important. He shoved the thought of having her one more time away. There would be plenty of chances for that later.

Dane wasn't permitted to actually enter Council Hall, but he'd learned ways to push the limitations and stay informed. As an outsider, eavesdropping from the Safe House sometimes seemed the only way to stay in control of anything around here. A trusted friend had taught him that.

Stuffing his feet into his boots, he searched for his hat. "They're discussing vital topics today that could affect my sister. I don't want to miss it."

She sat up from the bed with interest in her eyes. "Will they discuss the witch?"

"I don't know and I don't care what they decide to do with that wicked girl. My only concern is Cybil."

"Is she wicked, though?" Maggie wondered aloud. "They say Brother Jonas burnt down her house first—killed her aunt."

Dane rolled his eyes. "She's evil."

Too many nights had passed when he'd visited his sister Cybil's cell only to have that horrid witch chatter on and on about what she planned to do to all of them. Well, Dane wasn't like the rest of them, so he didn't appreciate being lumped into her revenge schemes.

The witch's taunting became so irritating he eventually asked the bishop to move her cell. Now, at least, she was far enough away that he didn't have to look at her when he visited Cybil each night.

Maggie's soft pink smile twisted with intrigue. "I think she's a concubine to the elders."

"I wouldn't be surprised." He brushed a quick kiss on her cheek. "I have to run."

"Will I see you tonight?" she called, as he rushed down the loft ladder. "I'm making stew. I can bring you leftovers."

He paused at the door of the barn, considering the day. Tonight dinner was at Cain and Destiny's, which meant Gracie would definitely be there. "I can't tonight."

Her head poked out from the opening of the loft. Even from far above he could read her disappointment. "Let me guess, supper with the Hartzlers?"

Despite the frail lineage shown in his bloodlines, the Hartzlers were the closest thing to family he had left. If not for Cain bringing them to the farm, he'd probably be homeless and Cybil would have been sent off to live in foster care under the eyes of the state.

But she would be alive.

He shoved the chilling regret away, refusing to admit his sister's life was over, even though everyone else on the farm seemed to whisper as much.

He didn't dwell on alternate realities like that. What was once a fear now sounded like a great comfort, after the hell he and his sister had lived through. Maybe Cybil would have been bullied or even cried herself to sleep for a few months in foster care, but she would have adjusted to that sort of life, just as he'd adjusted to life on an Amish farm.

Now, she had no life. Just an endless existence caged in a one-room cell with a dirt floor. Next to the monster that started it all.

"I have to go," he said, rushing out the door.

Dane's sole purpose, aside from watching over his sister and ensuring no harm came to her, whittled down to seeing that monster destroyed. Isaiah Hartzler was an abomination, a feral, vicious, dangerous behemoth beast that needed to be put down. It wasn't enough to simply kill him. Dane wanted to see him suffer. He wanted to stand by and watch as maggots ate away his eyes and fire burned away his skin.

The fucking vampire was immortal, of course, so any damage would eventually repair, but that was fine. Dane was more concerned with his suffering anyway. He wanted—no, *needed*—Isaiah to suffer for his crimes—again and again and again until the son of a bitch begged for death.

But he deserved no mercy. Just as Isaiah had shown his mother and countless other innocent women none.

Emerald fields dappled the distance like a patchwork quilt as hand-drawn tills stood forgotten, the earth and soil of rotation fields only partially churned for the next season while other fields bloomed with life as they approached the repetitive harvest. Seasons echoed and marked the passing of time here like a clock bell.

The consistent cycle could be a comfort as much as an annoyance. He sometimes missed the days when he would wake up and grab his phone, check the time, and see what trouble his friends got into overnight. They all assumed he was a dead runaway by now, so the temptation of going back to a place where he'd once had friends was no more promising than chasing a sky full of clouds. It was a fantasy he'd never touch.

He didn't belong in that world anymore. And he'd been on the farm for so many years he didn't trust his memories of how life used to be. The mind had a way of glorifying what it couldn't have. Life was no easier out there than it was in here, surrounded by a bunch of blood-thirsty Amish immortals he'd never fully trust.

If he stared hard enough, just past the line of forest trees and countless acres of plain Amish homes, he'd see hints of modern civilization. While he couldn't quite make out the smoke-stacks, there was always a smudge of pollution dirtying the sky in the far east where the re-fineries were located.

The Order was one of the oldest and, while their numbers were not as impressive as some, the land was large. Not much had changed since the farm was founded in the mid-seven-teen-hundreds, as was the case with many Amish farms. But unlike those other orders, where members lived, worked, and died, the faces here never changed.

He walked quickly, cutting through the

meadow where a waterwheel pumped steadily. Teams of horses dragged plows, kicking up dust in the distance as small groups of women busied themselves with tasks for the day ahead.

Always in groups. Children traveled in packs of three or more and the women tended to huddle over their work with cheery smiles and dispositions as they spoke on subjects that interested them. The men labored in the fields, steering horses all day and making repairs, while the females prepared meals and refreshments in between chores, to see to their needs.

No one cared about Dane's needs. Like the reclusive, roaming rooster he sometimes spotted wandering the farm, he was alone.

Maggie helped curb the endless isolation that often choked him awake at night. She scratched an itch and gave him someone to talk to besides the Hartzlers or his half-crazed sister, but she would never be the one he wanted to close his days beside.

Passing the one-room schoolhouse, he knew the desks were full by the abandoned boots and metal lunch pails gathered in the shade of the front porch. Mornings on the farm passed in a whirlwind of busy activities. Laundry already hung from the lines and quilts dried over railings.

Unlike the others, he did not spend his life following the Bible and a plow, so he didn't wake with the dawn. Dane sometimes helped with harvesting tobacco, but he mostly worked at the market in town, selling cakes, pies, meats, and other Amish wares to the English.

Having grown up in the modern world, he didn't mind the noise and startling pace as much as the others, but the longer he lived within the quiet tranquility of the farm, the more draining he found modern society. Many shunned the English, but Dane liked having an excuse to travel back and forth. It reminded him of who he was and assured he'd never get too comfortable in a place he didn't belong. But lately, after working the market, he found himself anxious to return to the peaceful quiet of the farm.

The bishop had suggested he work the market as a way of bringing in money. Dane had no family, so his only possessions were the clothes on his back and whatever gifts he accumulated through the generosity of others. He appreciated the pay and it felt good to have a purpose.

As he passed the seed mill, sacks of grain filled the beds of several wagons, but no one hooked the grain or hoisted the sacks. While women gathered around tables, picking beans and mending clothes, all the male equipment sat abandoned.

Whenever meetings took place, an eerie emptiness overwhelmed the farm. Within the orderly confines of the wide open land, beyond the idyllic impression stolen at first glance, there hid an oppressive truth. Time turned with every season, as life was reborn, again and again, but the reality hardly changed.

Unaltered by modernization or society's progressive views, oppression thrived in The Order. Conformity was total and orderliness was demanded and upheld by strict tradition. Those who disobeyed faced consequences. But unlike other Amish sects, members were rarely shunned. Those that wished to live a different life could leave, but those who stayed were required to obey. Anyone who violated The Order's laws would suffer. Some were punished, while the worst of them were executed.

He didn't know much about such things, but he'd heard whispers and knew that it happened. Immortals were sturdy, age-defying creatures without the limitations of disease or deterioration, but they could die. And Dane was on his way to discovering how.

"Good morning, Brother Dane!" Sister Abigail appeared from under the shade of an outbuilding carrying a wooden peel used for lifting fresh bread in and out of the Dutch oven.

"Morning, Abby."

"It's a beautiful day." She smiled, adding to the pleasantness.

"It is."

Setting the long wooden peel against the brick wall, she dusted off her hands in her apron and slowly approached. "Have you eaten?"

Her friendliness assured her father, Elder Abraham, had gone to the meeting. The scent of freshly baked bread was too tempting to ignore. "I have not."

Typically, the immortal females ignored him. They noticed him, covering their mouths as their eyes followed him like a sideshow and their lips whispered about his piss-poor lineage, but they rarely spoke directly to him. Abigail, however, was different. She always had time to say hello and ask how his day was going.

She was one of the oldest on the farm, but there remained a youthful innocence about her. Cain once told him her mother died on the journey over and her father had never been the same. Abraham ruled Abigail's life with a tight fist, and she'd dutifully followed his rule the way a God-fearing, obedient daughter should, according to The Order.

She was sheltered but kind and good at heart. While others whispered about him when he'd first arrived, she befriended him and often brought him apples and stories about the farm. That all ended when her father found out, but whenever Abraham wasn't around, she made a point to talk to him.

"Well, you have to eat, don't you?" Abigail's sweet smile often reminded him of the prettiest ornament on a Christmas tree. His eyes couldn't help but watch her mouth and, whenever she smiled, he felt an overwhelming sense of comfort, much like he remembered feeling when he was a boy. To him, she represented a welcoming sense of home.

"This one's still hot." She reached into her apron and removed a tea towel. "I'll wrap it for you so it doesn't burn your hands."

Burns were not a concern to immortals and her sensitivity further validated her awareness of his differences, but there was no malice in her offering, only kind consideration.

"Thanks."

She winked and tore a loaf in half, wrapping the still-steaming bread, fresh from the brick oven. "I'll simply tell Father I got hungry, which isn't a lie. I do nibble from time to time." She laughed.

He wondered at Abraham's strictness. If the man was controlling enough to involve himself with the daily count of rolls, he definitely needed a hobby. Eventually, Abigail was bound to get married. Then what would her father do?

Dane accepted the warm, wrapped bread. "I appreciate it." The soft inside smelled of grain and honey while the crusty outside still held the smoky scent of the brick oven. He plucked a piece off and popped it in his mouth, savoring the delicious way the flavors burst over his tongue.

"I love the bread here."

She cocked her head. "Did they not have bread where you're from?"

"They do," he said, stuffing his mouth with a larger piece and covering his gaping hole with his hands when the hot dough burnt his tongue. "But nothing like this. It's already sliced and wrapped in plastic."

"Homemade is always best. If you come back this way later, I'll leave another loaf for you with a jar of honey we just harvested."

"Are you sure?" He didn't want to get her in trouble.

She nodded. "Father will work late tonight, on account of the meeting today, so it shouldn't be an issue. He's there now."

"That's where I'm headed."

"But you're not…allowed"

He laughed at her surprise. "Don't worry. They won't let me in, but I like to sit outside."

She smiled. "You and Sister Adriel. I don't know how she manages that. The elders discourage loitering and *forbid* females from eavesdropping on male business."

Because the more sheltered and repressed the females were, the more ignorant they remained of their human rights. It was a battle Dane didn't have the strength to champion and one that would quickly get him exiled from the farm.

"Sister Adriel gets away with lingering around the hall because she's the bishop's closest friend."

"How scandalous." Abigail smirked. Looking over her shoulder to assure no one approached, she whispered, "She's mated, you know."

Gossip, no matter how prohibited, would never be extinct.

Abigail did not know that his bloodline connected directly to the Schrock line, which was why Sister Adriel had taken him under her wing. His mother's journals mentioned Adriel Schrock's mate, a Cerberus Maddox, and Dane's blood tests had linked him to Adriel's son, Christian Schrock. According to the bishop, he and Christian were half-brothers, but they shared no affection as such.

The elder was a miserable bastard who kept to himself. When Cybil's life was on trial, Christian had been one of the first to suggest she be executed. He said it was the most merciful option, but Dane disagreed. The Order had limited knowledge about situations like Cybil's. Her transition was not sanctioned by God and therefore left her deranged.

But there was something left of her in that cell. He sensed it most while she slept. She was his sister. His only true family no matter what the blood tests said. For all they knew, Cybil might also be Christian's sibling, but due to her condition, the results of her bloodwork were muddled by some unidentified pathogen that clouded the labs.

Christian Schrock was a cold, heartless bastard Dane would never view as any sort of family. In all reality, his mother, Adriel, should be the one sitting on The Elder's Council representing the Schrock line, but she was a female and such things were prohibited.

While most men disdained Adriel's fierce disregard for man-made laws, Dane admired her and felt a sense of loyalty to the ancient female.

"You shouldn't speak of such things," he said to Abigail.

She appeared instantly contrite. "I didn't mean…" Regret and worry flashed in her eyes. "I'm sorry. That was cruel of me."

He frowned at her overreaction, recognizing her fear of any sort of backlash. "I won't tell anyone. I just meant that Adriel is a good person, and I don't like when others talk about her."

"Of course. She's your friend. I don't know why I'd presume you wouldn't know of such things. I wasn't judging, you know? I was only passing along information."

Something Abigail had done since the beginning with him. "I know. I'll never betray your trust, Abby." He appreciated all the secrets she shared in the past.

As an outsider, he wasn't someone the others felt pressed to inform. And because of Abigail, words like half-breed, boy, mortal, English, misfit, and orphan no longer affected him.

Her worry abated and a gentle smile curved her lips. "I trust you too," she whispered, stepping closer.

He matched her smile but mirrored her step with a step back. Unlike the other unmarried and unmated immortals on the farm, Abigail was not permitted to socialize after service on Sundays. She'd attend the three-hour sermon like the rest, but after the meal, she always returned home with her father.

Bishop King had warned Dane to keep his distance, as Abraham would not want his daughter risking her virtue on a male who was not her true called mate and, therefore, would disapprove of Abigail associating with someone of mortal blood.

That much was made clear the day Abby missed service. Dane had gone to visit her that evening, only to find her suffering, her immortal flesh struggling to recover from several lashes her father had given her that morning after finding a small hand-sewn favor Abby planned to give Dane at service.

They were friends. That was all.

"I have to get going."

Her fingers twisted in her apron. "Of course. Don't forget to stop by later. I'll leave the bread and honey on the bricks for you."

"Thanks."

Pocketing what remained of the wrapped treat, he raced down the hill toward the Safe House. Like many of the old homes on the farm, the bishop's house had undergone additions over time, the biggest being the extension of the hall where the elders met.

Compared to the other homes, the Safe House was a fortress. Behind the large, white colonial, a long stone antechamber extended tunneling into what could best be described as a courtroom.

On the other end, offices and medical testing facilities were situated. The offices were frequently occupied by elders, but the labs had little function. Once in a while the bishop would compel a mortal doctor to the site and order tests performed. That was how they discovered Dane's bloodline, but once the tests concluded, the modernized rooms were cleaned and closed off, not to be discussed or visited again unless ordered by The Council.

None of that was of interest to him. Dane only cared about the laws imposed by The Council and what lie beneath Council Hall.

As he approached, a droning hymn sung by the males of The Order seeped from the open windows. A stone-carved sign, crumbling at the corners and faded by time, marked the entrance to the Safe House with an illegible script. The eroded Germanic text included a psalm and the identifying numbers of the biblical verse.

Dane took the porch steps two at a time and rushed inside. Black hats littered the corridor, occupying every peg on the wall and taking up every inch of surface space on the empty tables and benches. As expected, Adriel sat quietly on the bench outside of Council Hall, dutifully stitching her needlework.

He smirked at her clever conformity. Females were not permitted to wear patterns or fancy embroidery, but they were often encouraged to busy their idle hands stitching Bible verses, one of the few permitted decorations allowed in Amish homes. Whenever there was a council meeting, Adriel's hands worked tirelessly on a new verse. And, as she worked, she listened.

He sat beside her on the bench and she gave him a disapproving glance for his tardy entrance. "*Unabbeditlich*, you stink of bread and sex."

"Sorry."

She twisted the embroidery hoop and pulled the needle slowly through the fabric. "I recognize Magdalene's scent, but who else do I smell?"

"Abigail. She gave me some bread."

"Is that all?"

He shot her a warning glance. "Yes. We're friends."

"Best to keep it that way. Abraham's quite possessive of her time."

"I know."

The dull hum of masculine voices ceased and the meeting began. Through the wall, he could make out their words, thanks to his improved diet of Magdalene's blood. His senses had never been sharper, but they would never be what Adriel's or the full-bred immortals' were.

He squinted and cocked his head as he focused on the muffled words coming from the other side of the wall. "What did he say?"

She waved a hand. "They're still in the tiresome stage of complimenting each other and boasting their great contributions." She rolled her eyes and shook her head. "However, would they make it more than a day without having their fragile egos stroked?"

Dane chuckled, appreciating Adriel's disdain and dry wit. Unlike the other females, she wore her fiery red hair short under her bonnet.

According to the Amish, a female's hair was her glory and to be covered at all times outside of the house. When he'd first caught sight of Adriel's hair, he'd been shocked. Cain later told him her shorn locks were a sign of rebellion, a slap in the face of the elders who wrote the laws.

Immortal bodies maintained a natural standard of optimal health and beauty. Regardless of age, they all looked to be around their mid to late twenties and in the prime of their lives. While the hair on their heads seemed to grow past their shoulders, other hair never appeared. He assumed it had to do with evolution and a gift for self-regulating body temperature.

When he'd first slept with Maggie, she told him the others did not have hair between their legs or under their arms. It was why, unlike other Amish orders, their sect did not grow beards. Maggie only had hair on her private parts because she was a half-breed like him.

For Adriel to keep her hair short, she needed to cut it regularly. That sort of ongoing defiance did not go unnoticed and probably would have been punished if not for her son's seat on The Council and her close friendship with the bishop. Despite the covering, he still glimpsed wisps of red sneaking out from below the trim of her bonnet.

She bounced her leg impatiently, one bare foot peeking out from below her dress. He wasn't sure if the shoeless trend was an Amish thing or an immortal thing, but the females tended to go barefoot during most of the warm months.

"You seem tense," He said, sensing something was bothering her.

"Christian's not here."

Dane frowned. It wasn't like her son to miss a meeting. "Where is he?"

"I'm not sure. The most peculiar thing happened this morning. I stopped by his house to deliver eggs and every room was empty. The stove was cold and the windows were all shut."

"Did he go into town?"

"Why close the windows in this heat if he was only taking a trip to town?" She pressed her lips tight. "He went somewhere, but no one seems to know where."

"The bishop?"

"Eleazar assumed he was on the farm." She stopped stitching and dropped her needlepoint into her lap, cocking her head curiously. "He built an indoor washroom."

When the Hartzlers rebuilt their home after the fire they had also built one. It was rather sophisticated compared to the outhouses others used, but still archaic compared to the modern amenities Dane had grown up with. The Hartzlers had a copper-lined, self-heating bathtub connected to its own wood stove and a pull-chain latrine that drained down to the old privy.

"Maybe he got tired of walking outside."

Dane's house didn't have modern plumbing and shitting in the winter on a cold seat was a literal pain in the ass.

"He's suddenly going to change his habits after three-hundred years? No, I know my son. He likes consistency and loathes modern technology. Something's going on."

He chuckled. "Installing an indoor toilet isn't exactly what I'd call modern technology, Adriel."

"It is for Christian. He's up to something. He never misses a meeting."

Many of the elders despised modernization and vilified any whiff of progressive thinking because they feared future headstrong generations being overrun by the lure of contemporary amenities and loose morals. Not to say the Amish weren't innovative. They were incredibly clever and had mastered many conveniences without the use of electricity. Ice houses, root cellars, and cold streams for example, all helped preserve the food needed for survival throughout every changing season.

Morality was not a condition of immortality, but immortality was a condition of this specific Amish order. Very few exceptions were made outside of the mortals brought here by their called mates. Those people were always transitioned—converted into immortals—but that trick only worked on humans pre-ordained by God or some other such paranormal magic.

He never would have believed vampires existed, until he saw one murder his mother in the woods. The Order wasn't *vampire*, but they could become so if they ignored the calling of their god. Some immortals lived five hundred years before receiving a call. Some died before ever making it that far.

The farm kept them safe. Although immortality implied eternal life, accidents happened. Dane was trying to figure out what kind of accident could kill an immortal because the one locked in the cell below needed to die. Not his sister, of course, but the one who killed his mother.

"We now move to the discussion of Isaiah Hartzler." Speak of the devil.

Dane sat up and listened through the wall as another male delivered a report. "It's been seven hundred seventy-two days since Brother Isaiah entered captivity. He shows faint signs of aging, but his astonishing strength remains unchanged. Since reinforcing the cell bars and fashioning chains, he shows fewer signs of aggression but he's still gravely dangerous."

Voices mumbled as conversation broke out. Dane didn't need the recap the way others might. He knew exactly when that bastard came to the farm. It had been two years, one month, twelve days, and—he pulled out his windable pocket watch—eleven hours. In his opinion, the fucker had stayed long enough.

David, the bishop's right hand, took the brunt of Isaiah's last attack, but even that didn't convince the elders to end him. Dane had been visiting Cybil at the time. The horrific sight had tortured him for weeks, triggering old night-mares of his mother's limp, gutted body and his sister's last screams. He then decided that he wouldn't kill Isaiah until he had a sure-proof plan.

The vicious prick was ancient, his already impressive strength reinforced by decades of adrenaline-laced human blood. Dane knew his first attempt would be his last. He'd either avenge his mother and kill the vile beast or die trying.

"Get that foolish plan out of your head," Adriel hissed. "Bands of elders have tried and failed what you're considering. It took decades just to capture him. Be content with knowing no other women will be harmed."

"That's not enough." He hissed back, adamantly married to his plan.

They all mourned the lives lost at the hands of Isaiah, but no one really saw those women as anything more than statistics. Humans were less valuable to them. And even among their species, females were little more than property. The human women Isiah killed died because they were lower on the food chain, and, there-fore, prey. To immortals, it was just nature doing what nature does.

Just as a lion has the natural right to take down a gazelle, immortals had the right to de-vour mortals. Only The Order forbade such practices, but they were not the norm. Ac-cording to Cain, immortals roamed the entire earth, and very few ever stopped to consider morality when hunger struck.

Social order was only loosely maintained by their Christian faith here on the farm. It amazed Dane how much the immortals on the farm abided such constraints. Cain seemed the only male brave enough to disregard The Order's threats, but he always claimed to be a bit of a black sheep.

Isaiah was considered a full-fledged vampire, a term saved for those intoxicated by human blood and driven by bloodlust. According to The Order, *vampire* was a derogatory, offensive word, but Dane knew they all had it in them. Even sweet, beautiful Gracie possessed a darkness that could kill, which she had done when the witches attacked her father.

The moment his thoughts turned to Gracie his pulse quickened. What was she doing right now? He missed the days he could wander into her kitchen, and she'd happily offer him a piece of pie. Gracie was an incredible cook, but he never visited for the pie.

Adriel scoffed, her head turning from her work so she could eye him with an incredulous stare. "With Abigail's bread in your pocket and the scent of Magdalene still on your breath, one might say you have enough females in your life."

He grimaced, wishing Adriel would stay out of his head. "She's different."

There was no need to specify who *she* was. Adriel read his mind and saw his deepest fantasies. What he did with Maggie and what he shared with Abigail was nothing compared to the love he felt for Grace Hartzler. From her magnificent dark hair to her dulcet laugh, she fulfilled every inch of what he deemed feminine perfection.

"Must we?" Adriel grumbled. "Bad enough I have to suffer through the self-important thoughts of every male in The Order, but do I need to suffer through your ongoing romanticized fantasies of what will never be?"

"You could just stop eavesdropping on my thoughts."

"You know as well as I that some things cannot be controlled."

Dane, like Adriel, often gleaned unwanted details from people's minds, but his telepathy was limited to young, unguarded minds. Most immortals were blank to him, including the children. Despite their innocence, the young immortals on the farm only spoke and thought in Pennsylvania Dutch.

Cain once explained to him that the language barrier was another form of protection from the outside world. Children were less disciplined. Speaking Dutch created another layer of protection in case the children made youthful mistakes and spoke of their species in mixed company. Only once they were school-age and old enough to understand the importance of secrecy and consequence, did they learn to speak, read, and write in English.

Adriel grumbled. "I still recall when Christian went through puberty. He was obsessed with watching the animals rut, and I frequently found him pleasuring himself when he was supposed to be doing his chores."

"I really wish I didn't know that."

"It lasted decades. I had to threaten to sew the panel of his broadfall pants shut."

"Please stop." He couldn't prevent the horrifying image of Christian whacking off from blasting like a Broadway show centerstage in his head.

"Yes, it was much like that."

He shot her a look and snapped, "Thanks, now I'm going to picture that every time I see him."

She shrugged and returned to her needlework. "That's because, like most twenty-something boys, your mind is filled with sin."

A ruckus erupted from Council Hall and they both ceased whispering to better hear what was being said. Dane scowled as he tried to focus on their heavily accented words. "Who are they talking about?"

"I believe Jonas. Poor, Ezekiel. He's been through so much."

"Retrieve the witch!" someone yelled and the double doors of Council Hall opened.

Adriel's gaze dropped to her needlepoint as David stepped into the hall. As soon as he spotted Dane, he scowled. "What are you doing here, boy?"

"He brought me a piece of bread. I was hungry."

Dane quickly fished the bread out of his pocket and handed it to Adriel. David frowned.

"He shouldn't be here. Neither should you."

She set down her hoop and slowly stood, meeting the other immortal's challenging stare. "Careful, David. I'm your elder, and as such, you will not rebuke me."

His eyes narrowed. "Sit down, Sister Adriel. Your son shirked his duties today so he's not here to defend your presence. It's indecent for a female—"

"I do not need my son to come to my defense. I'm perfectly capable of taking care of myself. Now, why don't you run off and do your elders' bidding before *someone* gets angry."

"Willful female," he growled and marched off to the cellar door.

Adriel sat down and handed him back the tea towel of bread. "I can't say I'm completely distraught over the loss of his arm. If Isaiah was going to hurt someone, I suppose David was a good choice."

Dane also disliked the smug immortal, but he didn't think he deserved to have his arm ripped off. A stump had grown back, but the ordeal would probably scar the male for life.

Minutes later, the basement doors opened and the witch, Juniper, was hauled past them. Mouth muzzled, eyes blindfolded, and hands tied, she didn't pose much of a threat, but the girl had done her fair share of damage.

"He looks like he could use a hand," Adriel

muttered under her breath, snickering at her own joke.

Dane watched David steer Juniper into Council Hall as she blindly dragged her feet and feebly struggled. She was a small thing and her resistance was futile.

The witch's audible, labored breathing spoke of fear, as did her muffled outcry. Two years in a cell would humble anyone, but the rage that simmered under her surface was plain to see.

When she'd come to the farm and attacked Jonas with black magic and burned down the Hartzler's house, Gracie had killed Juniper's aunt and last living relative.

The fire had been retribution, apparently, for one Jonas had started at the witches' house. A fire that killed Juniper's other aunt. Dane, having no family left, aside from his deranged sister, could empathize, but he spared no sympathy for the witch who could be better described as a bitch.

Jonas was sick, possibly dying because of whatever spell the witches cast. Attacking the first son of Elder Ezekiel Hartzler was not a crime the elders took lightly. And without Jonas able to speak, no decision had been made as to the witch's future. They were hoping she might reverse the spell in time.

Gracie had warned Dane to keep his distance, but before the witch's cell had been moved to the other end of the hall, she'd been imprisoned beside Cybil. He had no choice but to see her every night when he visited his sister.

At first, she seemed pitiful and harmless, an ignorant accomplice to her aunt's crime, but over time he realized Gracie was right. The witch was more powerful than she let on. She couldn't be compelled and could tolerate endless hours of what the elders called examination, which was more like an interrogation.

Though he had not personally witnessed the witch being tortured or mistreated, he often overheard her weeping in her cell, and sometimes suspected the immortal males of taking advantage of her captivity like Magdalene suggested.

More shouting erupted from the other side of the wall and Dane winced. "What are they doing with her?"

"They're examining her. It will continue until they agree on a punishment for her crime, which won't happen until we see the extent of Jonas's suffering."

Jonas was going to die. Dane sensed it in his gut. Every day he grew sicker and struggled to communicate, but never spoke a word. His life had transformed into endless suffering since the witches got ahold of him. If they wanted to show mercy, he deserved a quick death.

"Careful, my friend," Adriel whispered. "Thoughts like that will get you shunned or worse."

She was right, so he didn't think long on the subject. He turned his ear back to Council Hall where several voices shouted. Over time, fewer and fewer of the males saw a reason to destroy the witch, another indicator that they found a use for keeping her locked up below.

"Can you read her?" he asked Adriel.

"The plebe? I suppose, but I have no interest." She looked at him in confusion. "She's mortal and roughly your age, can't you?"

He'd tried several times, but she had him blocked. "It's like there's a forcefield around her mind. I sense that I could read her, but she's doing something to stop me."

"Witches. Never trust them."

"So long as she's gagged and bound, her magic remains inaccessible," a male voice yelled. "See how she can't protect herself when there's pain?"

"Animals," Adriel hissed, shutting her eyes as the muffled moans of the witch wailed through the wall.

"What are they doing to her?"

"Burning her feet." She held her breath as the shouting grew. "They stopped, now. She'll be fine after the healer tends to her."

"Barbaric."

"She tried to burn one of us alive, Dane. They would be justified to do much worse if they chose."

"So much for Christian forgiveness."

A cold chuckle passed her lips. "You're smarter than that."

He was. They might live an Amish life and worship their God through the words of the

Bible, favoring verses that justified chastisement and discipline, but they also did things that weren't Christian at all. Things that took place in the silent hours of the night under covered mouths and clenched eyes.

First and foremost, they were predators, enslaved by their animal instincts and loyal to their impulses. Immortals reveled in the hunt. They lived with an ever-present lust for blood and loved to flaunt their dominance over others. The elders had come here to curb such impulses and find a more domestic way of life, which they had, but they would never change what they were. Inside every immortal hid a vicious vampire, and the problem with vampires was that they lived forever.

The doors opened and two males dragged Juniper out. Her bare feet were charred and blistered at the souls and her head hung weakly between her shoulders, her arms still bound tightly behind her back.

Dane's jaw clenched. He didn't like the girl, but no one deserved that sort of mistreatment. Aside from what she'd done to Jonas, which he truly believed was the workings of her older aunt, her only other crime was taunting him and making Gracie cry.

The meeting sounded as though it were concluding, and he no longer wanted to sit there. The two immortal males returned from the basement empty-handed.

Dane stood. "I'm leaving. Let me know if I miss anything important."

Adriel nodded, her gaze focused on her work as she carefully pulled the needle through the material. "I will. If you see my son, tell him I was looking for him."

He took the long corridor to the cellar entrance. Far beyond what appeared to be an old forgotten basement hid another door that led to the cells below.

Cybil wouldn't be awake this early in the day because she followed a nocturnal schedule since the change, but he detoured into the basement anyway. The witch's soft weeping could be heard from the stairs.

He slowly followed the sound to the first cell and frowned at the way they left her. Curled on her side, her blistered feet peeking from her chemise, her neck and face hardly on the cot, but her body too weak to change positions. She reminded him of a broken swan, the kind kings would admire only to destroy and eat in the end.

The iron muzzle covering her mouth, otherwise called a scold's bridle, was a medieval device used to silence and shame difficult women during the sixteenth century. It secured to the face with a metal frame that encircled the back of the head and suppressed the tongue with a flat lead that was inserted into the mouth, locked in place by a small key.

He'd read about such things in high school when they learned about the Salem witch trials, but the horrific devices weren't just intended for witches. They were originally created for rude and troublesome wives and applied mostly by husbands.

Her whimpered cries tore at him and he struggled to leave her in such pain. Glancing back at the door, he assumed the meeting could take several more minutes to conclude. A chain rattled from the far end of the corridor where Cybil slept and Isaiah prowled, no doubt woken by the foot traffic on this end of the hall.

"Hey," he whispered, and the witch stilled.

Her head couldn't turn very far under the weight of the bridle but her silence implied she heard him. With her eyes covered as they were, she wouldn't know who spoke.

"It's Dane," he hissed, keeping his voice low. "I...I want to help you, but you have to promise not to do anything bad."

A small whimper escaped her throat and he quietly slipped the keys from the peg on the wall. The door to her cell opened with a creak and he crept inside. Looking back over his shoulder to make sure no one was coming, he pulled the metal door partially closed.

"I swear to God, if you try to pull anything I'll never help you again." He pocketed the keys and crept close to the cot. "I'm going to move your head. Relax."

She winced the moment he touched her. The bridle was awkward and heavy, forcing her neck to bend at an uncomfortable angle. Her arms were bound behind her back so she had little control over her upper body.

He propped the weight of her head up with

a threadbare blanket and helped her shift to a less strenuous position. The material of her underclothes was thick enough to protect her modesty, but not enough to hide how thin and frail she'd become.

He carefully loosened the knot of her blindfold and uncovered her eyes. She blinked up at him with a glassy stare. Her eyes squinted at the dim glow of the lanterns several feet away outside of her cell.

"I'm not gonna hurt you." Removing the bread from his pocket, he showed it to her. "For later." He stuffed the bread between her cot and the wall then retrieved the pitcher and basin from the floor. "The water will help your feet."

He pushed her chemise up to her shins and frowned. The souls of her feet had looked worse when he saw them upstairs, but maybe his mind exaggerated the damage. They were blistered, but not nearly as bad as he'd initially thought.

He used the tea towel to soak up some water and gently pressed the cool rag over her injured feet. She sucked a sharp breath in through her nose and winced, her muffled cry tugging at his heart.

"Sorry." Carefully, he cleaned away the dirt. "It doesn't look like it'll get infected, but you'll want to keep them clean."

He stilled when he looked up at her to read her eyes and saw a tear escape. No one deserved this.

He didn't have much time, so he carefully

focused on tending to her feet and tried not to waste time thinking about circumstances outside of his control. When he had done all he could do, he returned the basin and pitcher to the floor. He wanted to shred the towel and wrap her feet for protection, but then they would know someone had been inside her cell.

He couldn't risk getting caught breaking the rules, not when the consequence might include losing his basement privileges. He felt bad for the witch, but nothing would keep him from looking after his sister.

"That's all I can do. Their healer will visit you. When he does, he'll probably bandage your feet so you can walk."

He didn't know why they burned her but figured it was to test her abilities. They'd done other things to try to trigger her magic, such as cutting her skin and binding her hands in metal mitts. He was beginning to doubt if she'd ever had any magic at all.

She was like him, from the modern outside world and educated by a regular school system, so she likely understood how witch trials went. Knowledge could be a terrifying thing and he took pity on her.

"If you just give them what they want, they'd probably show you mercy. They're Amish." He didn't trust his own advice. "They just want you to help Jonas. Nothing will bring your aunts back, but you can save yourself. Just help him."

She stared up at him with a hardened glare. He thought about Isaiah. Dane would never help the monster that killed his mother, so how could he expect her to help the one that killed her aunts?

"You know how witch trials end."

The lines of her scowl softened with acceptance. No matter her pain, she seemed resolved to see this through.

"Stubborn."

He'd always assumed the victims back in the day were just regular women accused of being witches because they were too seductive or too interested in modern medicine. Some were simply punished for actions meant to protect themselves from greater harm. Witch or not, most cases ended in the tragic death of a tortured innocent. Many of those unnecessary deaths included unimaginable suffering.

A mark on her shin caught his eye and he returned to her side. Frowning at the dark bruise, he bent to lift her chemise. She whimpered and he stilled, catching the fear in her watchful eyes.

"I won't hurt you. I promise."

She instinctively kicked when he lifted her chemise again, but the motion only irritated her injured feet. He'd seen enough anyway and covered her legs again.

The bruises were in the shape of large hands and traveled to her inner thighs. As he'd assumed, she'd had some visitors.

"If you truly are a witch, why don't you punish them?"

Another tear rolled from her eye. He

couldn't let this stand. Someone had to tell the elders what was happening.

"I'll say something to the bishop. He'll put a stop to it." He could see she had little hope in his plan, so he assured her, "He's good. They call him honorable."

"Have you lost your mind?"

Dane sprang off the cot and shot to his feet. Cain stood at the door of the cell, scowling at him. "They burned her."

"I know. Get out of there." Dane rushed forward and Cain caught him by the back of the shirt. "Keys."

He fished the key out of his pocket. "She needs a healer."

"There's no way Adam's letting Anna come down here." Cain snatched the dingy blindfold off the floor and shook it out. "Should have thought about that when you tried to kill our father," he told Juniper, just before covering her eyes.

Her muffled outcry did no good.

"She needs bandages."

Cain backed out of the cell and locked the door. "You need to understand your limits." He shoved Dane in the chest, pushing him into the adjacent wall. "I get that you've had a taste of Magdalene and you're coming to embrace the benefits of blood, but you're still half mortal. What would you have done if she used magic on you?"

"She can't. If she could, she would have used it on whatever son of a bitch did that to her feet. It's been two years, Cain, and she hasn't shown us any proof that she's an actual witch. Maybe it's time to admit the one who did that to your father is dead."

He shook his head. "She might not have actively participated in the spell, but her aunt used her presence to harness more power. It's in their blood, Dane. She's dangerous."

"She's just a girl!"

"She's no more a girl than you're a boy. When will you learn that things aren't as simple as they seem? Especially here. You should know better by now."

Chains rattled from the cell at the end of the hall. "I'm so sick of the double standards. You save your mercy for the least deserving and show cruelty to those who are incapable of protecting themselves. How is that living in the light?"

Cain's hand pressed into his shoulder and his head shook with regret. "There's no light here, Dane. There hasn't been in some time. If you were smart, you'd keep working until you saved up enough money and go start over somewhere else."

He shoved away his touch. "I can't leave Cybil. You know I won't."

"She's never going to be well."

"You don't know that!" He moved to push him, but Cain caught his arms, restraining him.

"I know that your life is worth more than this. My father only intended for you to be here a short time. You're an adult now and you should be doing more than passing your nights with a female you don't love. You'll lose a hundred years standing vigil outside of Cybil's cell —assuming you have that many to spare."

"Let go." He jerked his arms free and glared at him. "She's all I have left."

"She's not the Cybil we knew. The sister you loved is gone. And my sister..." He sighed. "Gracie is never going to stop waiting for her called mate to come. That can't be you."

His stare jerked to the wall as his vision blurred with unshed tears of frustration. "What if he never comes? What if she spends her life waiting for something that never happens?"

"That's her choice to make."

Sick of this place, sick of staring at the same stone walls, he turned and marched up the stairs and out the door. The placement of the sun told him it was nearly noon. Adjusting his hat, he headed toward the Hartzler's land.

The males were back to work, harvesting, steering the cattle across the pasture, and driving the plows. Females worked the pump, filling pitchers with cool water as they prepared to deliver the males their cold mid-day meal. Annalise would likely be in the woodshop with Adam, so he headed that way.

As he stepped into the barn he nearly collided with Gracie, who was on her way out. "Gracie."

"Dane," she said sharply, then looked away and scowled. "What are you doing here?"

"I'm looking for Anna."

"She's not here."

The wood shop wasn't a place Gracie usually hung out. "Where is everyone? Are you alone?"

"Not that it's any of your business, but Adam's making me a cabinet for my dishes. I was checking on his progress."

Amish women had a strange fixation with dishes and clocks. Because such things were functional, he supposed they were one of the few ways they got to show off something that would otherwise be considered fancy.

"Can I see it?"

She huffed but turned back into the barn to show him. Adam's tools were scattered about, but no one else was in the barn.

The cabinet was more of a hutch, tall and wide. He could picture her decorating it with her favorite things and that made him smile.

"It's nice," he said, truly admiring Adam's fine craftsmanship.

She admired the drawers and the paneling with unmistakable pride. It was rare to see her covet such things. He liked the way her fingers traced each detail, touching the raw wood almost sensually.

Her hand fisted and she scoffed. "What is wrong with you?"

"Huh?" Too late, he realized he wasn't guarding his thoughts.

Shaking her head, she snapped, "I can smell her all over you." She sniffed and drew back. "And someone else." When he took a step forward, she mirrored it with a step back. "Don't."

He scowled. "I didn't do anything."

"Well, you sure thought about it. And with her stench all over you!"

Her words only triggered another vision, this one a memory of Magdalene last night, except he wanted to see Gracie in his bed, so his brain naturally transposed the image. She shoved him and he banged into the hutch, whacking his elbow. "Ow!"

"Pig!" She pivoted and stomped out of the wood shop.

Adam appeared, looking back as his sister stormed off. "I see you two are up to your usual antics. Did you need something?"

Dane sighed. "I need a favor, from your wife."

He stilled. "What kind of favor?"

"The witch—"

"No."

"She's hurt—"

"I said no."

"They burned her, Adam."

"She tried to burn my father alive."

Frustrated, he snapped, "You're an empath! Where the hell's your compassion?"

Adam pinched the bridge of his nose and finally gave him his full attention. "I was there, in the meeting today. It was terrible."

"Why didn't you stop them?"

"What kind of authority do you think I have?" Removing his hat, he swept a hand over his hair. "Some want her executed, others want her kept alive. It's an ongoing debate and my opinion has little to do with the outcome."

"They're doing more than burning her. She has bruises all over her body."

He frowned. "How do you know?"

"I saw her…when I was visiting Cybil."

Adam eyed him skeptically. "Talk to Eleazar. If the bishop permits Anna to visit her and provides the necessary precautions, I'll allow her to go. But I intend to accompany her."

"Go where?"

They both turned and found Annalise holding a tray of food at the entrance to the barn. "*Ainsicht*," Adam said, moving to greet his wife with a kiss. "We were just talking about you."

"So I assumed, until I heard the word *allow*." She looked at Dane and smirked. "Sometimes Adam forgets that I'm my own person, capable of making my own decisions. What did you need, Dane?"

"The witch—"

"Absolutely not." Cain glared from the door. "I told you to leave her out of it."

"Out of what?" Anna asked.

Cain shoved off the wall and entered the barn. "Caring for the plebe. Her feet are injured and Dane stupidly thinks you'll risk your own safety to care for someone who tried to kill our father."

"What happened to her feet?"

"Nothing," both brothers snapped.

"They burned them!"

"*What?*" Anna's face contorted in horror. "*Who?*"

"The Council," Dane explained.

"*Why?*"

"To see if she would use magic."

"That's barbaric! What is this, the Salem witch trials? Adam, you have to do something!"

Her husband rubbed his temples.

"Does anyone care that this woman tried to kill our father?" Cain barked.

"She's barely an adult, Cain. Show some compassion," Anna snapped back.

"All right, enough." Adam held up his hands, defusing the debate. "Anna, I will speak to Eleazar and request that he let you examine the girl, but only in my presence and the presence of other guards."

"I can't believe they burned her," Anna muttered.

"That's not all they did to her."

"Enough," Adam snapped, his eyes darkening with unspoken threats.

"What else did they do?" Anna turned to him, but he hesitated. "Dane? Tell me."

Both Adam and Cain glared at him. But Anna wasn't like the other females on the farm. She was originally mortal. She wasn't sheltered. She'd heard worse things on the evening news.

"Someone's using her body."

"For wha—*Oh, my God.*"

"Annalise, language!"

"Not now, Adam." She looked up at Dane. "Are you saying someone raped her?"

"I don't know. But she has bruises up to her thighs."

Cain shook his head. "Let's just walk through this. You three clowns go marching into the bishop's office demanding guards and entrance into the witch's cell. Our dear sister, Larissa, will sense something's up and no doubt get involved, leaving Eleazar no choice but to grant your request, despite his better judgment."

"She's not dangerous," Dane argued, prepared to admit that he'd been in her cell only minutes prior and no harm came to him.

Cain held up a silencing hand. "Then Dane will make the accusation of sexual assault and what will be the next question?"

"How does Dane know her thighs are bruised?" Adam asked, like a true Scooby Doo detective.

"Exactly. And Dane will say…?"

Adam and Anna turned to Dane. He held open his palms. "Why do I have to say anything?"

"Because everyone will want an explanation as to how you know what the witch's thighs look like." Cain sniffed. "You stink of multiple females, so who's to say you didn't touch her."

"*I didn't!*"

Cain arched a brow. "You washed her feet."

"Well, I didn't hurt her. I wouldn't. They can look in my memories."

"He has a point," Adam agreed.

"Well, we have to say something," Anna argued. "If someone is hurting that poor child, we have to help her."

"She's not a child," Cain reminded. "She's an adult witch—a homicidal one at that."

None of this mattered. Dane didn't want to waste any more time bullshitting with Velma, Freddy, and Shag. "I'm going to talk to Eleazar."

"I'm going with you," Anna insisted, rushing after him.

"Not without me," Adam ordered, following closely behind.

Cain threw up his hands in frustration. "Well, I guess I'll just wait here." He grabbed Adam's sandwich and took a bite then yelled, "She tried to kill our father!"

CHAPTER 3

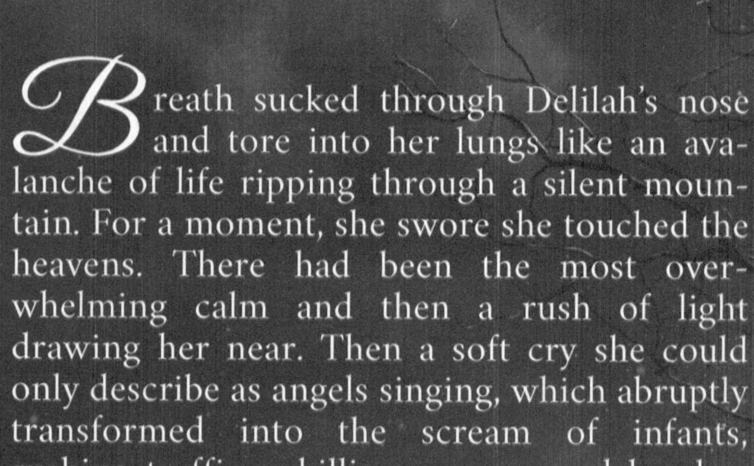

*B*reath sucked through Delilah's nose and tore into her lungs like an avalanche of life ripping through a silent mountain. For a moment, she swore she touched the heavens. There had been the most overwhelming calm and then a rush of light drawing her near. Then a soft cry she could only describe as angels singing, which abruptly transformed into the scream of infants, rushing traffic, a billion prayers, and her hyperventilating lungs seeking air where there was none. No gravity, no physical form, no reality to hold onto. Just space. Not even time. And then she was being ripped back through the blackness, fighting her way back into her physical form as if suffering some sort of backward birth.

Her chest stretched painfully on a vocal gasp and sweet, hydrating oxygen bathed her lungs. Air never tasted so good or burned so much.

Panting, she jackknifed upward and covered her face, dizzier than a time traveler. How much had she had to drink? She must've blacked out, yet her body felt fine. No lingering headache. No nausea. Just the burning in her lungs and a hollow ache in her stomach, which probably explained why her equilibrium felt off. She dry heaved, closing her eyes and searching for balance.

Slowly, the burn in her chest eased and the world stopped spinning. She wiggled her shoulders, taking inventory of her usual aches and pains. The pinched nerve in her back didn't stab like a shiv in a prison fight for once.

"You are awake."

Stranger danger. Her eyes flashed open and she stilled. Where the fuck was she, and who the hell—

She gasped. Her memories came hurtling back and she sprang to her feet, her legs unsteady on the mattress as she scrambled as far away from that sick fuck as she could manage.

"*Am I fucking dead?*" she screamed.

"There's no need for salty language—"

"*What the fucking fuck!*" Having the stability of a kid on a moon bounce, she wobbled and gripped the headboard. Her free hand inspected her body, frantically feeling her neck and shoulders for injury, certain he'd stabbed her. "Where am I?"

Was this a kidnapping? Her gaze zipped

around the bare room. Absolutely no memory of coming here voluntarily. She touched her face, arms, hips, stomach, thighs, vagina, toes. Where the hell were her clothes?

He took a step closer.

"Stay back!" she snapped, holding out an unsteady arm, unsure how she could possibly protect herself against a man that size. "Where are my fucking clothes?"

He scowled at her. "No more foul language, Delilah."

"Go fuck yourself!" She drew in another burning breath and screamed, *"Help!"*

Shaking his head, he crossed to a dresser in the corner, moving with such agility and grace, it was as if he walked on air.

Her eyes twitched. In the corner, a tiny spider slept on a web. Her focus zeroed in and she counted all eight of its legs then frowned. What the fuck? The thing was smaller than a pencil tip, but she had no problem seeing every detail of its miniature body from ten feet away.

A motored vehicle passed in the distance and her ear followed the sound, her gaze darting to the window. Her mind tracked the distant rumble, certain the car was miles away, yet she heard the engine, scented the exhaust, and even detected the music playing from the speakers.

Was that T-Swift?

She frowned at the faint trail of cigarette smoke.

He opened a drawer, the rattle of wood

louder than a wrecking ball. Gripping her ears, she hunched down and flinched. Maybe she *was* hungover—or drugged. That made more sense.

"You're experiencing heightened sensory. You'll adapt in a minute or two. Just relax."

The last time he told her to relax, he slit her throat open. "What did you do to me?"

He moved past the window and she hissed. Sunlight pierced her corneas and she covered her eyes. Squinting, she zeroed in on the dust motes drifting through the air and every fiber of woven thread sewn into the curtain.

She counted the exit points. One door, two windows. Somehow, she knew they were on the second floor. A shirt and hat hung from pegs on the wall. Was there time to steal clothes or should she run naked?

He poured liquid from a pitcher, the trickle of water interfering with her perception of other sounds. As soon as he stopped filling the glass she could once again hear the trill of insects chirping outside and the birds calling from the trees. There was way too much nature to be the city. Wherever they were, it wasn't near home.

"Drink this."

Shifting into a praying mantis slash Daniel son *Karate Kid* pose, she bared her teeth. "Don't come any closer!"

"I'm only offering you water—"

"Ha! You think I'm stupid?" She kicked the cup out of his hand. The metal dish clattered to the ground.

His eyebrow arched, triggering a strange memory she couldn't place. Pushing the sense of déjà vu away, she kicked the air again, warning him back.

"Perhaps I should remind you that you're naked."

"You think that's going to stop me, you fucking psycho? I'll go Hannibal on your ass if you get any closer. I want my clothes and a phone. *Now.*"

He sighed and took a step closer. She hissed then clapped her hands over her mouth. *Hissing? Really?* She wasn't feeling like herself.

Retrieving a black shirt from the dresser, he extended his arm. "You may wear this."

Hesitantly, she snatched the garment out of his hand with more force than intended. He kept his back to her as she unraveled the fabric and held it up. It wasn't a shirt, but a dress, a hideous, plain, frock-like dress.

Instinctively, she knew this was the first step of brainwashing. The bad guys always stripped their victims down and took away all signs of individuality. "This isn't mine. Where are my clothes?"

"I'm giving it to you. Consider it yours."

"I don't want it. I prefer pants."

He scoffed. "I think not."

Her eyes narrowed. "Oh, do you? Do you *think not?* We aren't in bloody London! And I'm not wearing some cult frock from one of your medieval fantasies. I want a fucking pair of pants, and I want my phone!"

His mercury irises flashed like blue light-ning. Under such a threatening glare, her bravado abandoned her, but she forced herself not to show fear.

"I've asked you to refrain from such foul language. I won't ask again."

She wanted to snap, *or what*, but she also didn't want to find out what the *what* was. Huffing, she yanked the drab sack he was trying to pass off as clothing over her head.

His mouth formed a flat line as his stare did a quick assessment of her. "We need to speak, Delilah."

"Yeah, okay, let's start with where the hell am I? What the fuck did you do to me? And where the hell are my real clothes?"

"Control your tongue. My patience wears thin."

"Your patience? Hello..." She shoved a thumb against her chest. "I'm here against my will. Your patience can eat a dick."

A growl rolled through the room like thun-der. "Last warning, *pintura.* Mind your tongue."

Pintura? She locked her jaw so her teeth didn't chatter. Name-changing was another sign of brainwashing. She saw it on an episode of *60 Minutes.*

As tempting as it was to tell him to fuck off, she couldn't stop thinking about the girl from Silence of the Lambs that Buffalo Bill trapped in the well. If this guy asked her to rub lotion on her skin, she was going to lose her shit.

Who knew how crazy he was? If she didn't

actually watch her mouth, he might end up cutting out her tongue. Who would look for her? Gran and Pop, dead. Lance and McGuire, gone. She was fucked. True fear settled in and she whimpered.

"May we speak now?"

Sarcasm was her first defense whenever she was scared, but in this case, saying the wrong thing could get her killed.

"Talk," she barked.

He frowned, silently studying her. Was he waiting for an engraved invitation?

"Well?"

He drew in a deep breath and sighed, dragging the chair in the corner of the room closer to the bed. He straddled it, crossing his arms over the back. The thickly corded muscles she had found so attractive now terrified her. His broad shoulders bunched under the crisp black linen of his shirt.

The bastard was probably going to sell her to *some sex trafficking ring.* Her stomach lurched at the thought.

"Are you planning on standing up there through our discussion?"

Sitting on the bed put her at a disadvantage. He was bigger in every way. She could at least give the illusion that she was taller. "Yes."

He pinched the bridge of his nose. "I can see this is going to be a trial. You're in Lancaster, Pennsylvania."

"*Pennsylvania!*" How had he brought her all the way from Detroit without getting caught?

"How long did I sleep?" He definitely drugged her.

"Not long. I told you I lived on a farm. This is my land."

Great. He probably had a whole cartel out in the barn and women chained up in every stable. "Why did you bring me here?"

"We'll get to that."

"How about you tell me now, asshole?"

"My name is Christian. Use it."

Her legs trembled from strain. She'd been crouching on the bed for too long and hunger pains were cutting through her empty stomach. She was going to lose it in a second if she didn't get some answers.

"Sit," he ordered. "You're trembling."

"I'm fine." She wasn't.

"Your body's under stress. I give you my word, I won't come near you."

Cautiously, she lowered her butt to the farthest corner of the bed. "I'm sitting because *I* want to, not because you told me to."

"Very well." He cleared his throat. "There are some rules I expect you to be mindful of now that you're here. You will use clean language at all times. You will dress appropriately, like the other females on the farm, and you will not speak to any males outside of my presence. I'll have a bonnet and apron brought to you as soon as I can. I expect you to behave like a modest God-fearing woman now that you're here."

Annnnnd that was the straw that choked the

chauvinistic camel. "Are you freaking nuts? I'm not staying here. I'm certainly not going to conform to whatever fantasy compound shit you have in your head. And as far as Christian modesty goes, that went out the window when you choked me out with your dick still buried inside of me."

"That's not what happened."

"My memory says otherwise."

"You're not injured. As a matter of fact, you're healthier than you've ever been. Sometimes human memories can be misleading. How do you feel now? Is your throat sore? Do you have any scrapes or cuts? If I wanted to kill you, you'd be dead. But you're very much alive and well."

She didn't know how to respond to that. He was technically right on most counts, but... "I know you did something to me."

"It's my God-given duty to protect you. You need to trust me in all things, Delilah."

Right. "Let's get something clear. Your god is not mine, and I will never trust you again."

"You will—"

"The fuck I will. And FYI, I don't have a modest bone in my body, so as far as modesty goes, mine's gone. There's no domesticating me. I'm as feral as they come, so how about you let me walk out of here, and I won't go for the jugular when I press charges against your psychotic ass. Sound good, fuck face?"

Her body hurled back and she screamed as his hulking frame pinned her down. *"I will not be spoken to with such disrespect.* This is my home. You belong to me. And you will behave like an obedient female or there will be consequences."

True fear gripped her as she trembled under his weight. No level of sarcasm could save her now. And without that go-to coping skill, she was just a terrified little girl in the hands of an unpredictable maniac.

"Tell me you understand. Say it. Say, I understand, Christian."

Her heart thundered in her ears. Frightened beyond measure, she nodded, but her voice had dried up like a mollusk. He waited for her to speak.

"I understand, Christian," she croaked, and the threat in his eyes vanished, his composure returning as he eased off of her.

Terrified, she curled into a ball and sucked in a jagged breath. She, once again, had no control. Too many painful memories triggered at once. She shoved them back, compartmentalizing each one with a mental slam. She remembered what her therapist had said. Be present. Wall. Door. Dresser. Window. But no sense of safety came.

"I wish no negativity between us, Delilah. We must deal with what's happened and move forward."

The bastard was insane. All that mattered now was that she stay alive.

Brushing a wrinkle out of his shirt, he moved toward the door. "This is your home now. You need to accept that. The harder you fight me, the more difficult this transition will be for you."

A tear rolled from her eyes. This was not actually happening. She didn't know what he wanted from her, but she was certain there had been some sort of mistake.

"Relinquish your English ways, and I'll help you as much as possible. Disrespect me, and you will not like the result. You should see me as your partner now. I'm here to help you and protect you."

No words came. None of this made sense. She simply shivered and held her knees close to her chest, terrified that this room might be the last place she ever visited.

"We Amish live a simpler life than you're used to, but it's a good life. You will see."

Did he say Amish? Like buggies and Bibles and shit? Oh, hell no. She sat up and wiped her eyes. "Christian…" That was his name, right? "I think you got the wrong girl."

"You're the one. There's no mistaking you for anyone else. You're my true called mate."

"What?"

"You're a divination of God. He chooses the other half of our souls, and he chose you for me."

Oh, this was bad. "You think I was chosen for you by some sort of divine intervention?"

"I know you were. I saw you in my dreams. We are one. Two halves of God's perfect design."

This was getting worse by the minute. She

didn't know how to reason with a crazy person. Should she play along or use logic? She decided to cut him off at the source. "But I'm agnostic."

He stilled. "You can't be."

She leaned forward with wide eyes, unsure how to debate his outright refusal. "But I am."

"No. We're Anabaptist Christians."

"There is no we. There's you and then there's me."

He shook his head. "I will study the Bible with you and you'll learn."

Dear God... "You can't force faith on other people."

"No force. Enlightenment. You'll see."

"No!" she snapped. This wasn't happening. "I'm me. I won't change who I am. I'm not going to conform, no matter what you say or do. Do you understand me?" She never felt so passionately about religion, but her entire being felt under attack, and she had to salvage some part of herself. Jabbing a finger at her chest, she said, "You can't change what's deep inside a person."

He frowned and cocked his head. "Agnostic. What does it mean?"

She could have been a hundred things. Jewish, Muslim, Hindu, a witch. No matter what she believed, it wasn't his place to judge. "It means I'm nothing. I don't believe in religion."

He frowned. "Religion exists whether you believe in it or not."

"Well, a person's practice typically requires

faith. You can't force someone to believe in something they don't."

"Then how do you explain your being here."

"Um, you kidnapped me."

"Not here. But *here*—existing on this planet."

Did he want the whole *Big Bang Theory* theme song? She sucked in a long breath and belted out, *"Our whole universe was in a hot dense state then nearly fourteen million years ago expansion started—"*

"Wait." He held up his hand.

"Oh, you know it. Good. Then you get it."

"I understand you're different, Delilah. But I'm not sure you're grasping just how special you are. You're a miracle. *My* miracle."

Maybe it would be best to save her energy until he went to sleep. There was no negotiating with terrorists and no reasoning with fanatics. "If I'm such a miracle, why are you trying to change me?"

"Not change. Refine."

Yeah, because that was different.

He paced, his long legs eating up the length of the room in only a few strides. His rolled-up sleeves exposed the corded muscle that flexed as his fingers forked through his wavy brown hair. "I will not have a disobedient wife."

"Whoa." She scooted forward. "*Wife?*"

He faced her. "You're my mate. Of course, we will marry."

Her annoyance trumped her fear when he said dumb shit like that. "Uh, Christian, darling, you have to ask."

He frowned, no longer pacing. "Pardon?"

"Marriage is another one of those pesky personal choices that can't be dictated. You can't force someone to marry you. You have to ask."

His head cocked as if he never heard of such a concept. "Will you be my wife?"

"No!"

He drew back, his look of surprise comical. "But you're my mate."

"See, you say mate and I think Animal Planet. You're not so good with the lady talk, Christian."

"Mates are predestined partners. We only have but one for all eternity. I've waited lifetimes to find you. You're my mate, Delilah. Marriage or no marriage, what we are to each other is bigger than any legal contract or vow. I'm not letting you go."

She remembered an article she read in the last issue of *Tat* about how to deal with crazy, stalker exes, but her head hurt and she couldn't concentrate with all the intrusive noise. For a farm, it was an ungodly loud place.

Insects chortled through the thin walls as animals brayed from every direction. Leaves rustled as if a hurricane were on its way. And her stomach was really starting to ache. She jammed her fist into her side and rubbed her brow.

Huh, that pimple finally went away.

"You're hungry."

As much as she despised the idea of accepting food from him, she needed to think and that meant getting something in her stomach. "Do you have crackers or something?"

"Crackers are what you crave?"

"I'll take anything. How about an apple? Pop-tart? Something quick and small. I'm a vegetarian, so—"

"Delilah, sweet—"

"Unless you want me to call you one nut, please refrain from using the cutesy pet names. Especially ones that don't fit me."

His jaw ticked. "You'll find your tastes adapting here on the farm. Your needs can no longer be met by vegetables alone."

She rolled her eyes. "Why does every carnivore think meat is the only source of protein? Trust me, my diet's just fine. I just need something to—" A cramp grabbed hold of her stomach and she doubled over in pain.

Christian was by her side in a second, rubbing her back.

"Ew!" She shouldered him off. "Don't touch me."

"Delilah, you must feed. Your body's been through a lot in the last eight hours. You need to feed in order to sustain your energy."

She gritted her teeth and breathed through the overwhelming pain twisting her stomach, fearing she would retch from the discomfort. On an empty stomach, puking would only bring more pain. She fucking hated throwing up so she swallowed back the urge.

Grumbling, she glared up at him. "What did you give me?"

"This is all part of it. You need to feed."

A ceaseless thumping came from his chest. *Thump-thump. Thump-thump. Thump-thump.*

She rolled to her side and moaned in agony, hand clamping over her mouth as her gums and face radiated with a sharp ache she couldn't fathom. What was happening to her?

He continued to stroke her hair. "Your body's changing, *pintura*."

She swatted his hand away, but he swatted back, pulling her onto his lap. *Thump-thump. Thump-thump. Thump-thump.* "You must listen to your instincts. What are they telling you?"

"Stranger danger," she groaned, doubling over with an agonizing moan. "Let go of me, you psycho."

"I cannot help you if you refuse to take this seriously." *Thump-thump. Thump-thump. Thump-thump.*

"Oh, believe me," she gritted. "I'm taking this very, serious—*ah!*" The sharp cramp overwhelmed her.

"Enough." He pulled her close, turning her face to his shoulder. Her vision blurred as though she were looking through someone else's prescription glasses. *Thump-thump. Thump-thump. Thump-thump.* God, he smelled good.

The pain in her mouth returned and she whimpered miserably. Unable to take any more, she snapped, "What the fuck is that thumping?"

Christian growled and cradled her head, turning her face toward his neck. "Open your mouth."

She didn't understand why it was so easy to obey his command when everything inside of her wanted to do the opposite. Her lips parted and her eyes zeroed in on the thin flutter below his jaw.

Thump-thump. Thump-thump. Thump-thump. His flesh skipped with every jump of his pulse. The tempo doubled. *Thump. Thump. Thump. Thump. Thump.*

In a gravelly voice, Christian whispered, "That's it, *pintura,* take what you need from your mate."

His fingers tangled in her hair, not pulling but guiding, urging her closer. The press of her nose to his skin awoke something inside of her. It was a fire, all-consuming and impossible to resist. A guttural moan, almost sexual, broke through the pain as she dragged her tongue over his pulse.

Her mouth yawned wide and there was a snap. She struck like a snake and he twitched slightly, forcing himself to remain still.

Warm and satisfying, hot nectar flowed over her tongue and she drank deeply. A strange purring came from deep within her chest. It trailed down her throat and hit her belly like the first rain over the desert.

Her body shifted and her lashes lowered, as

her mind fell into a dreamlike state where she no longer existed. Instinct took over. Angling to take more, she climbed fully onto Christian's lap and his strong hands gripped her hips.

Her body rocked as sensations filled her. Having never done drugs heavier than weed and some magic mushrooms, she had nothing to compare it to. But she imagined the effect might be similar to amphetamines or crack cocaine. She could feel everything, the follicles of her hair growing, the beds of her nails strengthening, the heavy pounding of her heart, the delicious contraction of her sex. It was all connected.

She moaned and he echoed her pleasure, pulling her closer so her knees fit perfectly to either side of his hips. The bulge of his arousal pressed against her heated core, right where she needed pressure most. His hand fisted in her hair and she rode him, her orgasm building—

Her brain screeched to a sudden halt as self-awareness doused her like a frigid bucket of ice water. She ripped her mouth away, flinging her body off of his. Her back hit the wall and she stared in wide-eyed horror.

He grunted and cupped his neck. Blood seeped through his fingers and she screamed.

"Do not panic," he shouted over her screams.

She swiped a hand over her glossy mouth and pulled her fingers away with a horrified whimper. Crimson blood stained her flesh. She bolted for the door, but he reached it first.

"No!"

She dodged his grasp, ran to the corner, and caught her reflection in the glass of the window. Her chin and lips were smeared with his blood and she had fangs. *Fucking fangs!* She screamed and raced to the window, wanting to shatter the image and escape before someone died, fully prepared to hurl herself through the glass.

"Stop!" He caught her shoulders and shook her hard enough to rattle her teeth. She was no longer sure who was in the greatest danger. "*Pintura*, you must calm down—"

"*Stay away from me! You're bleeding!*" She hated him, but never wanted to hurt anyone. She just wanted him to let her go. She needed to call the cops. "What did you give me?" She had to be on drugs. This had to be some terrible acid trip. "Help! *Somebody help me!*"

He roughly shook her again. "Delilah! Hush!"

She whimpered, tears welling in her eyes. She didn't know what was happening to her. It was like her body was no longer her own.

His hold on her gentled and he pulled her stiff body close, pressing her ear to his chest. It was then she understood the thumping had been the pounding of his heart.

"Hush, now," he whispered.

She trembled under his touch, incapable of softening as he attempted to soothe her.

"Be calm, *pintura,* it's all right. Everything is all right."

Shock took over and she shivered, her panic drifting to the back corner of her mind as a sort of numbness took hold. He carried her back to the bed and laid her down. She blinked at the plain walls and ceiling, salvaging whatever was left of her sanity. Her brain moved under a fog of subconsciousness.

He wiped her mouth with a damp cloth. She watched him as if in a trance and said nothing.

When her face was clean, he tucked her under the covers. "You must rest, little one. Sleep will do you well."

She was going to die here. Inexplicable confusion convinced her that some memories had been moved or implanted because her actions were not her own, and the timeline she had to work with didn't make sense. Was she some sort of government experiment, in some strange incubation period where they stripped away her past habits and conditioned her for a new life?

She tried to scream, but there was a disconnect between her brain and vocal cords. She couldn't push through the weighted calm, even when her brain knew she should be panicking. She never felt so out of control of her own autonomy, so frightened, so certain she was not herself, but trapped in her body—or a body that felt almost like her own.

His fingers tucked a strand of hair behind

her ear and he looked down at her, concern weighing heavily in his eyes. "Rest, little one."

Giving in to his command, her mind shut down. She surrendered to the oblivion of sleep with the lingering hope that this was all a terrible dream and when she awoke, the nightmare would be over.

CHAPTER 4

$\mathcal{C}$onsumed by concern, Christian paced, worried for his mate's well-being. The female was nothing like he expected. Since the start of his symptoms, he accepted his inevitable fate and set out to conquer the challenges ahead with absolute determination. But claiming his mate had been an absolute disaster.

He didn't regret keeping his calling to himself. He was an elder. He knew how such things worked. The outcome was inescapable and the risks were great, so he moved with haste and did what was necessary.

"You mustn't fight God's will, little one," he'd whispered softly, wiping away the last of his blood from her lips as she stared up at him, her mind in some sort of shock that kept even her most unguarded thoughts quiet and at bay.

Whenever he sensed her conscience waking,

she would mentally push her attention to objects in the room, mentally listing each one. *Chair. Pitcher. Curtain. Hat.* He suspected it was some sort of coping mechanism.

She was terrified, of him, but also of things he'd yet to discover in her memories. Someone had hurt her and he wanted to know who.

He winced, considering his actions. He'd hurt her. Having never shared any sort of emotional attachment to another, he wasn't expecting this deep-rooted self-doubt or irrational need to please her. No. He would not go down that road of regrets and possibilities. He'd made his decision and the messy deed was done. It was for her own good, end of story. If he'd waited and tried to reason with her, they might have run out of time and run into real problems.

Her even heartbeat assured she was calm. He quietly observed her, finally able to let this new reality settle in.

Her beauty—when she wasn't screaming like a banshee or swearing like a heathen—was unmatched. Her soft, lily-white flesh against her long, dark lashes gave her the look of an antique doll. The marks on her body were unexpected, as he hadn't noticed such markings in his dreams, but he was coming to like them.

She had a vibrancy about her that was all her own. It was sinful to enjoy such showiness, but in private, between only the two of them, there could be no sin.

The trauma of her transition would pass,

and soon she would see the gift they'd been given. Never one to hem and haw with nonsense, he could not regret attaining her so quickly. She was his mate and that was the end of it. She would come to love him in time.

It had been a long three weeks and he was glad to see the hunt come to an end. After suffering the first dream and recovering from such a dizzying experience, he found his equilibrium and prepared for a long and draining chase. He would not rest until he found her, and he hadn't rested. Not once.

His mind had been focused and his intent unbending. When he finally laid eyes on her, he was consumed. The undeniable rightness of her existence fit into him like a missing piece. Feeding from her, mating, completing the bond, it had been an unmatched experience he only wished she could have appreciated as much as he.

The dreams were vivid but disorienting. Often, he would indulge in copious amounts of alcohol and tonics to help him sleep longer. She came to him like a jigsaw, piece by piece, until he was able to form a true picture of her in his mind.

Three weeks later, and here they were.

Her lashes finally lowered and her breathing tapered off to a slow ebb and flow. Occasionally, her brow pinched and she'd whimper. He tried to soothe her with his touch, but even in slumber, she recoiled from his affection.

A restless moan escaped, drawing his concern. He'd never been so in tune with another creature, or so consumed by the aching need to see to her comfort. It was a bit of an inconvenience he hoped to adapt to over time, but something told him his feelings for her would only grow. How would he ever bear such unrelenting worry, especially when she refused to accept his guidance?

She trembled viciously. Humans were delicate and prone to shock. She was no longer human, but some habits might take time to overcome. The transition could be a lot for a female to process if not properly prepared. Perhaps he could have done more to ready her.

No. Had he warned her in any way, he would have invited complications. They couldn't afford delays. Mating was a life-or-death situation and, as an elder, he'd witnessed too many catastrophes come from equivocating the inevitable. It was best to see the deed through with haste and move forward once the danger was over at a calmer pace.

He knew that, so why did he feel so guilty?

Again she shivered. The soft, mews of distress coming from her alarmed him. He didn't understand why her nervous system would respond so temperamentally hours after the transition.

He supposed a good deal of her response was mental. Was she dreaming? He'd thought the dreams would end after the bond, but perhaps they continued for mates. There was no guidebook for this sort of thing. He'd also presumed she'd recognize him at first sight, but she did not.

His fingers brushed over her pulse. Perhaps she feigned sleep. "Do you not recognize me, little one?"

The pinch of her brow deepened but she didn't answer. He would give her time.

She was a tempting female, one who awoke his carnal desires like no other, but she was also so much more than that. She was *his.*

While she slept, he examined the markings on her body. The Amish did not waste time on such distractions, but distracted he was. Every detail, every unique accent, he wanted to touch and study. He desired to learn every inch of her and every thought behind each adorned decoration she'd chosen for her skin.

He grinned, thinking how misleadingly calm she appeared in sleep. When awake, she was a tornado of pride, stirring with explosive emotions too large for such a delicate frame. Courageous and strong yet also fragile and vulnerable.

Already, he was coming to understand her. His feisty mate did not like showing her softer sides, but he sensed her hidden vulnerabilities all the same. As her mate, it was his duty to know all of her weaknesses so that he may serve and protect her. He would be her strength just as she would be his.

Her confidence would develop once she understood the gifts of immortality. These brief moments of uncertainty would grow further and further apart as she realized the gift they'd been given.

Stroking her porcelain cheek, he tried to convey how much he cared for her and how deeply he ached to love and protect her. She, again, recoiled from his touch, her face pinching and her pulse quickening.

"Do not hate me, little—"

"Fuck off." She rolled to her side, tucking her face into the pillows and hiding behind her dark hair.

Her mouth was indeed a problem. Foul language would not be tolerated among their people. She would acclimate in time. He could be patient, but he feared her anger might lead to public humiliation. His own insecurities roused at the thought.

Growing up in torment, named the bastard Schrock by his peers due to his father's absence and his mother's hard-headed manner, had been a long and torturous experience. He'd combatted others' cruelty with an air of indifference, but the scars were there.

His position as an elder allowed him a measure of ambivalence that served him well over the centuries. But finding his mate had opened a gate of emotions and a dam had been broken, flooding his heart with not only hope and joy but fears and worry. Having Delilah meant he now had something to lose, and he'd yet to figure out the best way to manage such vulnerability.

The sooner she conformed to their simple

lifestyle, the sooner his concerns would be laid to rest. He believed in traditional Amish values and expected his mate to uphold such time-honored convictions.

She certainly was a brazen female. But with time and discipline, she would learn to control her impulsivity and tongue. Deep down, he believed her a docile kitten, one who hid razor-sharp fangs and claws.

A soft sniff caught his ear, and he sensed her emotional turmoil. "We should discuss what's happened, Delilah."

She muttered a response that made no sense to his ears. Either her slang went beyond his translation skills or she was still in shock.

He studied her with a perplexed frown. He did not expect her to reject him so completely. She had been very agreeable at first meeting, but that connection crumbled the moment he started the bonding.

Her disappointment was understandable, but she needed to hear him out. Had he not done what he'd done, he would have died. Others could have died. And she would have gone on living a life that was not her destiny.

"I know you feel betrayed, but I would never intentionally harm you."

His words fell into the deafening quiet with hardly a ripple of response. She'd been lying in silence for so long he was coming to miss her fury.

From what he understood, feeding after transitioning was a natural occurrence. Mates naturally took to the vein directly after waking from transition. Why would the natural act of taking his blood overwhelm her to this degree?

"Do you find me so repulsive you cannot look at me?"

He touched the back of his fingers to her bare, tattooed shoulder and she jerked away. He shoved down his anger, reminding himself that she was also angry, rightfully so. In time she would understand that his actions were the only course. God had decided their fate long ago.

"This despair will pass, little one. There should be no hostility between called mates. I understand you're upset about your current circumstances, but it's best that we focus on the future. The past cannot be undone."

Her fingers tightened on the pillow pulled over her head until her fists cracked. "You don't know shit about how I feel."

He sighed. At least she was speaking.

Drawing the curtains to block out the afternoon sun, he removed his shirt. This was not the homecoming he anticipated. Exhausted after weeks of hunting her, he needed rest.

When he eased onto the bed beside her, she stiffened. "You'll learn to accept my presence over time."

Pretending space could exist between them was a waste of energy. Mates needed each other, not just to feed, but to thrive. He pulled her stiff body to his and rested his head on the pillows.

Several minutes later, his mind started to drift, as did his sneaky mate. First, she slipped her toes out from beneath the covers, angling only her lower leg toward the floor. Christian kept his body relaxed and eyes closed, curious to see how far she would go.

She carefully lifted his arm off of her torso and curled it around a pillow, as if the synthetic sack of fluff felt remotely similar to her warm body. His mate obviously decided he was a fool with the intellect of a tree stump.

She slithered lower, bending and sliding out from under the covers until she crouched on the floor. Stealthily, she tiptoed toward the door, her hand reaching for the metal handle. He watched her from under his lashes, amused and curious. The latch gave way and the hinge creaked.

Her back pressed to the wall, her breathing silent. Slipping through the narrowest crack, she slunk into the hall. He rolled his eyes.

His ears traced her steps down the staircase and to the front door. He would have no issue tracking her, but it was daylight, so others would likely spot her and that would result in arduous questions and unwanted attention.

After decades of publicly suffering the abandonment of his father, he could not stomach the thought of a mate on the run. The taunts would be too familiar for him to tolerate.

The knob of the front door clicked and her soft footfalls sprinted down the porch. The erratic tremor of her racing heart called to him. It always would now that they were bound. If only the foolish female understood he was the absolute last male she needed to fear, she'd see she had no cause to run.

Her bare feet beat against the earth, slipping over the dewy grass as labored breath rushed from her lungs, more out of habit than necessity. Her behavior proved she had yet to understand what she'd become, as she was still carrying on as if she had the limitations of a human. If she wanted to, she could run faster than a modern vehicle and leap beyond the trees, but her mortal memories limited her. That was probably best, being that he would eventually have to catch up to her and bring her back home.

He used their mental link to see what she saw. Reaching the tree line, she paused, likely confused by her surroundings and unsure which direction was closer to English civilization. There were acres to travel before she'd reach a highway or public road.

She cut across the field leading to the stone barn and then broke into a dead run. Her heartbeat kept pace for nearly a mile, then her feet slowed and he grinned, sensing she was catching on to her new gifts and realizing her stamina could only be defined as inhuman.

Enough playing around. It was time to retrieve her.

Christian threw back the covers and stood. Sliding on his shirt, he prepared for another battle, knowing she wouldn't come easily.

She was nearing the edge of his property line, a good several acres from his home, but nothing he couldn't cross in under a minute. His mind reached for hers, sending a casual brush she likely wouldn't recognize yet, but he liked that they shared a mental thread and he could reach her that way.

The moment his mind caressed hers, she staggered to a stop and he sensed her confusion, even detected that she wanted to ask if the mental brush had been him, but stubborn independence kept her worry to herself. Then she bolted, pushing her limits and running full speed toward the border.

Christian cursed, rushing out the door and after her.

The scent of smoke he detected in her mind acted as a sharp implication that she was about to be in the company of another. Christian raced over the field toward the old barn, just as his mate spotted the young male.

"Help me!" she cried before Christian could intercede. "Please!"

Thankfully, it was only Dane, a mortal half-breed with limited knowledge of their kind. His circumstances left him loyal to The Order, but Christian trusted no male in the presence of his mate. Even this one, who also happened to be his half-brother.

"I'm being held captive by a psychopath, and I need to use a phone!"

Startled by her outburst, Dane jumped back from where he'd been cutting wood. "Who are you?" Eyes wide, he blinked at her ragged attire. "Where did you get that dress?"

"My name's Delilah and I need help! I don't have much time! Please! A phone!"

Christian sighed and crossed the property line. This was exactly what he wanted to avoid. He should have never allowed her so much freedom.

"Who are you? How did you get here?"

"Please! I just want to go home. Some crazy asshole kidnapped me, and I think I've been drugged—"

"Someone drugged you?"

"Yes!" She closed the distance, and Christian had heard enough.

"Delilah," he snapped as she reached out to grab Dane.

She spun away from him and held up her hands in a protective motion, backing toward the barn. "Stay away from me. I'm going home. I don't want any trouble. I just want to leave peacefully." Her voice cracked and she started to cry. "Please. You have to let me go."

Dane met his stare. "Yours?"

"Mine." Christian took a slow step forward then turned his attention back to his frantic mate. "This is your home, now."

"No." She shook her head, rejecting his claim. "No. You can't just keep me here. I have a life and a business and friends—"

"You're acting hysterical."

"*Fuck you! Of course, I'm hysterical!* You're holding me on a fucking farm against my will!"

Dane snickered.

The male was more mortal than anything else, and closer to his mate's age than Christian. Territorial possessiveness ripped through him, and he found himself standing between the two, trusting neither.

"Enough," Christian snapped. "Dane, this doesn't concern you."

"Um...You're on my land."

Technically, it was The Order's land, but the barn had been abandoned and the boy had been granted permission to stay there. "Regardless, I'll thank you to keep this to yourself."

He eyed them suspiciously. "Why all the secrecy?"

Delilah bolted, but Christian caught her arm before she made it one full step.

"No!" She jerked wildly, but his grip was unbreakable. "Please help me! He's crazy! You have to help me!"

She bucked like a wild bronco and, due to her newfound immortal strength, Christian had to truly exert himself to detain her. *"Settle yourself!"*

She bit him and he hissed.

"Vicious female!" His arm pinned down her flailing hands and he fisted her hair, forcing her head back so she would not harm him or herself. "Be still." The compulsion forced her muscles to stiffen.

"Looks like love," Dane joked.

"Mind your tongue, mortal."

The boy raised a brow. Humiliation burned

at the back of Christian's neck. She was making a spectacle of both of them.

"You're hurting me!" He wasn't, but her dramatic cry lured Dane closer.

Christian shot him a threatening look and bared his teeth, making it clear that any interference on the matter of him and his mate would not be tolerated. The young man had been around long enough to understand their laws and immediately backed up, choosing to ignore Delilah's hysterical pleas and listen to Christian's warning growl.

Dane shook his head. "I see she's experienced your full, ruthless charm."

Christian snarled, not appreciating his snide commentary. Half-brother or not, there was no love lost between them. The boy didn't belong on the farm, and it was against Christian's recommendation that the bishop allowed him and his mute sister to stay—a sister who was now deranged and would likely need to be put down after her unlawful transition.

Irritated, he dragged his mate away from the barn, unsure how to convince her that she could not carry on in such a manner. "This behavior is unacceptable." In time, she would appreciate having an adamant male who was as resolute and enduring as he.

Dane called after him, "Your mother's looking for you, by the way."

The last thing he needed to think about during a time like this was his mother.

The moment the compulsion wore off,

Delilah kicked her legs out, flinging her feet off the ground and swinging her head toward his face. He hauled her back, this time hoisting her onto his shoulder.

"*Oomph!* Put me down!" She kicked and screamed, raining punches onto his back.

"You're behaving like a feral cat." Christian lugged her back to the house.

Eventually, Delilah's frantic kicking gave way to feeble swats and pitiful pleading. "Please, don't do this. I have no money."

"I don't want money."

"Then what? Are you going to kill me? Sell me? I'll run. I'll never stop fighting you."

"Your life is incredibly important to me, *pintura*. Once you calm down, I'll explain our situation, but first, you must settle yourself."

She squirmed and elbowed him in the kidney. He grunted, but refused to let her go.

"Put. Me. Down."

Growing tired of her endless opposition, he doubled his pace. Once in the house, he slammed the front door and locked it. Taking her back upstairs to the bedroom, he deposited her on the bed. She immediately sprang forward, but he pointed a finger at her and gave an unbreakable command.

"*Stay!*"

"*I'm not a fucking dog!*"

He lunged forward, losing his patience. "I grow tired of your filthy language and insolence. Sit down and be silent."

She dropped her weight onto the bed. Her

jaw trembled, and he immediately wanted to apologize but thought it might be better to show strength at the moment. Still, he silently relieved her of any compulsion, preferring that she follow his command out of honor and respect rather than force.

"Do not move from that bed." He'd never known a female could have such a filthy mouth.

He left the room and slammed the door, swinging out his hand at the last moment to compel the latch to lock. Her footsteps rushed after him, followed by her heavy pounding on the wood. "Let me out of here!"

He tipped his head back, surprised to find a strange crick in his neck. Was that tension?

He debated what to do with her. A wooden door was no obstacle for an immortal and she would soon realize that.

The pounding stopped and he listened as drawers opened and closed. She rummaged through his personal belongings, pacing and banging on the walls, slamming into his furniture and throwing items against the door.

When his patience wore thin, he yanked the knob. Delilah blinked up at him, the metal doorknob, now detached from the hardware, filled her fist. Beveled grooves and imprints from her palm marked the walls. She hurled the doorknob at him and he ducked.

"You're breaking my house."

She kicked the dresser and it slammed into the adjacent wall. "Let me out of here."

"I will when I have your word you'll behave yourself."

She snatched his hat off the floor. "I'll shred it," she threatened. "I'll destroy everything you own unless you let me go."

He chuckled, amused that she assumed her value was equivalent to that of a hat or a house or any other possession he might claim. "There are countless hats in the world, *pintura,* but only one of you."

Panting, she dropped the hat to the floor and stomped on the crown with her bare foot, crushing the shape. The motion jostled her loose breast under her gown, and he found himself distracted.

Recalling the way her nipples wore metal rings, his mind drifted to a wild fantasy, which was all he could enjoy at the moment with her despising him as she did. His body hardened and he took a step forward, tapping the underside of her chin with his finger as she glared up at him and seethed.

"It's just a hat."

She scoffed and smacked his hand away. "Do me a favor and keep your hands to yourself." She paced toward the window and stilled.

He followed her stare. Buggies passed in the distance and children cloaked in Amish attire scampered, pushing kick scooters toward the schoolhouse. Dust kicked up from a field as an enormous horse-drawn wagon traveled south.

"I'm in hell."

Her disturbing assessment concerned him.

"This is different from what you know, I'm sure, but it's no hell."

She shot a thumb toward the window and sneered at him. "There are six Clydesdales pulling an Amish dude across a field like he's in a beer commercial, but no beer. I'm trapped in an Amish apocalypse."

"Are you thirsty?"

"No, I'm not thirsty, you moron! I want to leave." She glanced back out the window and scoffed again. "Here's to you, Miss Amish drug lord hostage," she mumbled then sang the words, *"Real American heroes..."*

Her face dropped into her hands, a startling shift from her bravado. A whimper slipped through her fingers and the ever-present ache he felt to soothe her doubled.

"Why me?" she cried. "You could have chosen anyone."

"I didn't choose you, little one, God did."

She rolled her bleary eyes and glared at him with palpable disdain. "Just stop." Looking around the simple room she'd ransacked, she flung out her hands in frustration. "Look at me. I don't belong here."

"You're my mate. You belong with me."

"Oh, my God," she moaned. "You have to chill with that."

"I only speak the truth, *pintura—*"

"Delilah! My name is *Delilah."*

"Delilah," he corrected, wishing there was something he could offer her to make this passage easier on her. "What do you need that I can provide right now?"

"My freedom."

"Something else."

Her lips pursed. "A bathroom would be nice."

That he could do. "Follow me."

She followed him down the long hall to the water closet. Lighting the lantern hanging from the wall, he stepped back, proud to show off the basin and pump he'd built. The latrine allowed for modernized plumbing tucked within a discrete wooden chest.

She glanced at him questioningly. "You want me to pee in a box?"

"It's not a box. It's a toilet."

"It's medieval."

He stepped into the water closet, and she immediately backed up, the small space hardly large enough for two individuals. With a huff, he lifted the square wooden lid exposing a round porcelain seat. "It is a toilet, sufficient to meet your needs."

He pulled the chain demonstrating how the mechanism drained and flushed. Considering how primitive some Amish houses on the farm were, he'd imagined she'd be pleased he arranged such amenities for her arrival.

"Lovely. Get out."

Her disappointment displeased him in unexpected ways, especially when he'd gone through such great pains to see to her comfort.

"If your aim is to injure me with your withering disregard, you have succeeded."

She gaped at him. "Are you kidding me? Hello? You brought me here against my will. I still haven't figured out what you've done to me, but I know it's bad and I'm starting to think it's irreversible. If my *words* hurt you, tough shit. That's all I got. You, on the other hand… You're a monster."

Again, she wounded him. At a loss, he backed out of the water closet and shut the door.

There was no cost for common courtesy, but apparently, it was the price he'd pay for taking her life, which she still didn't realize he'd done. Then there was the gift of immortality. Would she see that differently as well?

The toilet flushed and she opened the door, appearing surprised to find him waiting for her. "Don't you have other women to abduct or a field to plow?"

"Perhaps we could agree on a truce where we set aside the nasty commentary for an hour."

"Not likely. If you wanted a more agreeable hostage, you should have kidnapped a submissive masochist or maybe someone into cottage core off-the-grid living. Now, if you don't mind, I need a sink. I just peed in a box."

Her brashness was unparalleled.

He led her to the kitchen and waited as she washed her hands. The sound of another person in his home after centuries of silence was an oddity in and of itself, but the reoccurring reminder that she was his mate was surreal and thrilling and crushing. The cosmic twist of her hatred pricked at his insecurities and he feared if he didn't break down her dislike soon, her cruel disregard would build a callus around his heart.

He wanted to please her but had already failed. If only there were some sort of an olive branch or sign of goodwill he could offer her, something to make her feel safe and ensure that she trusted him. He realized now, nothing about Delilah would be as simple as he'd hoped.

After drying her hands, she turned and bowed her head. "What now, master?"

His body stilled. It was the first time she'd addressed him with any sort of respect, yet she was clearly being facetious. His head understood that but his heart did not. His cock twitched at such demure compliance. But it was all a lie. Artifice meant to mock him. His lust quickly shifted to anger.

Grit scraped beneath his boots on the wood-planked floor as he closed the distance between them and tipped up her chin, forcing her to look at him. The sexual tension they shared hadn't vanished, it had only been obstructed by his actions.

He stared hard into her eyes. His intent to punish her with the inescapable truth. Their connection would last an eternity. Their bond was unbreakable, and he wanted to cruelly remind her of that. Overwhelmed by the sudden burst of malice, he blew out a breath, searching desperately for calm.

She trembled under his touch and tried to look away, but he wouldn't allow it. Her rejection stung, deeply wounding him in ways that had him questioning everything.

Holding her jaw tight, he put his mouth close to hers. "One day, you'll crave gratifying me more than anything else. You'll easily put my needs before your own and honor me with unquestionable devotion. Mark my words, little one. This is just the beginning of life as you know it. I've watched many conform to the *unthinkable*." He glanced down at all her tattoos, each one a cry for individuality. "You're no different than any of the females who have come before."

He released her jaw and turned away. Let her despise him. She already did.

Her hands slapped into his back, shoving him forward and he spun, catching her wrists before she hit him again. "We do not act in violence toward one another."

Her anger charged the air between them as she bared her teeth. No matter how her fury consumed her, she would never be able to deny their chemistry. They were as connected as the cosmos, as reliant on each other as the moon and the earth. Like the pull of the tides, she would always gravitate toward him, just as he would suffer the same relentless pull to her.

Yet, she scorned him. She forced her expression to remain blank but he heard the increased tempo of her heartbeat, saw the dilation of her pupils. His nostrils flared as he breathed in the faint scent of her arousal.

Hunger punched through him. "You mean to mock me by masquerading as demure. You're hoping to get a rise out of me, to force some sort of response." The corner of his mouth curved into a half-grin. "Careful what you wish for, little one."

Her eyes narrowed on him and her heart hammered in her chest. Under the plain fabric of her chemise, her nipples tightened into sharp pebbles.

His head lowered, leaning closer until they shared the same breath. "Your mind and your body are in discord, it seems. I could help you."

Her full lips parted when she understood what he offered. He only needed a chance to show her what they shared. Then she would see. Once she understood there was no use in fighting their connection, she would lay down her anger and they could move past this nasty introduction.

He closed the distance, sensing her defenses soften, then she slammed her knee into his groin.

Pain exploded in his crotch and stomach, knocking the wind out of him as he doubled over and grunted. Gritting his teeth, he lunged for her, snatching the back of her frock and dragging her to him as she once more tried to run away.

"We *do not* hit, Delilah." He breathed through clenched teeth as the pain subsided.

"And I don't kiss Amish psychos!"

"I'm your mate."

"You kidnapped me, you delusional fuck!"

He shifted her in his arms, holding her shoulders tight and forcing her to face him. "This is the last warning I'll give. You will not speak to me in such a disrespectful manner. I'm an elder and your mate. You will respect me as a female is expected to respect her husband."

"I will never—"

"You will do as you're told!" he snapped, losing patience. "This isn't English society! Your life is bound to mine and, as such, so is your honor! If you can't obey such simple requests, I'll confine and discipline you as I see fit." Gripping her arm, he dragged her toward the stairs. "You will learn to behave."

For a split second, he believed he was making headway, and then she sprang. Claws scraped down his face and his body hit the wall. She yanked his hair and screamed in his ear, biting and hitting like a hellcat on fire.

She was surviving on his blood and consequently stronger than most, but not stronger than him. He caught her wrist and slammed her into the adjacent wall, demanding her attention. *"Enough."*

She struggled, but he subdued her with his mind.

"Do not make me take away your free will.

I'm giving you a choice. Take it, or I will choose for you."

"I'll fight you."

"No, you won't. Do not test me, Delilah. I have methods you couldn't even conceive. One way or another, you will accept the life I'm trying to give you. No part of me will ever give up on us. Of that, you have my solemn vow."

"I hate you."

Her words cut deep, but he accepted it was the only truth she knew in that moment.

The tension vanished from her body and her fists softened. He loosened his grip. When it appeared she was ready to cooperate, he released her.

"Very good." His scalp and face stung from her attack but there had been minimal damage. "I assume you're hungry."

Her gaze remained downcast and her mouth stayed shut. The echo of her last words still stabbed deep.

"Come." He took her hand and led her back to the kitchen. "Have a seat."

She abided his command and lowered into a chair, her motions robotic and her expression devoid of any emotion. It was as if he had placed her under compulsion, which he had not, specifically because he had no desire to pass time with her in such a comatose state. Earlier, he'd calmed her sympathetic nervous system so she would stop attacking him, but now she maintained the calm on her own.

He wanted to get to know her, understand

her. But when she wasn't fighting him with words or fists, she was beating him with silence. Presenting her a human comfort, he made her a sandwich and waited for her to eat, but she didn't touch his offering.

Prepared to wait her out, he sat in the chair across from her, wondering who she was under all that anger and ferocity. Was she a fair hand in the kitchen? After nearly three hundred years of preparing his own meals, he welcomed the prospect of having a mate to cook for him.

He'd hoped to teach her the way of their traditions before introducing her to his mother, a revolutionary female who frequently disregarded the beliefs of the elders, but that outcome was appearing less likely with each passing hour. If he couldn't convince Delilah to conform to their Amish ways, there would be no persuading her after she met Adriel.

His rebellious mother was a force of nature. She would be all too pleased to learn that his mate was equally, if not more, independent than she herself.

He wasn't asking for subservience. He merely desired compromise. Delilah's obedience was a temporary request, only until she understood their culture and laws. His governance was only meant to protect her. He had no lasting desire to control her.

Fearing his mother might encourage Delilah's defiance, he worried he'd have to keep his mate confined longer than intended. He loved and respected his mother, but she had a habit of complicating matters with her progressive views.

Some would argue advancement was Adriel's birthright, as the matriarch of the Schrock line. But The Order did not recognize female authority, so the position of elder became his responsibility the moment he came of age.

Nudging the plate forward, he once again prompted his mate to eat. "Food will help."

How could he hold so much influence as an elder yet have no control over his mate? He'd occupied a seat on The Council for more than two and a half centuries. He could certainly manage one female. But he had his doubts about navigating two, so it was best he kept his mother and mate separated until he had matters more under control.

"Try to eat," he suggested gently.

Her hunger beat at him. Providing actual food would be easier than forcing her to feed, but would not be enough to sustain her long term.

He was coming to recognize all the ways they were connected. The familiarity of her needs mingling with his own came so naturally, he struggled to recall how his mind had worked before the calling, when her needs were absent from his thinking. His every instinct pushed him to provide her every comfort and desire.

Come to think of it, now that he'd experienced the chemistry between mates firsthand, he wasn't clear how his parents had parted. Mated immortals shared an unbreakable link.

Glancing at Delilah's untouched plate, he asked, "Do you not care for the sandwich?"

She pushed the plate away, her tearful eyes looking up at him. "I don't eat meat."

Ah, yes, she believed she was a vegetarian. He'd forgotten, mostly because it was as absurd to consider an immortal herbivore as it was to imagine a vegetarian lion. Immortals were on top of the food chain. Of course, they ate meat.

For Delilah's sake, at least The Order observed specific moral laws when it came to how and when they fed. Not all immortals adhered to societal rules, let alone a society as stringent as the Amish.

The untamed portion of their species had no qualms about feeding from the vein of humans whenever hunger struck. But no matter what god one prayed to or what law or order they followed, every immortal needed one thing—blood.

Now that she was immortal, she would never survive without blood or protein. Their biological makeup, immortality, and rapid healing cells demanded certain sources of fuel.

"Delilah," he said calmly, choosing his words carefully. "We're Amish. Our lives are sustained by the animals on the farm."

Her face twitched with disgust and her complexion paled. "That's barbaric."

It wasn't barbaric. They treated their livestock extremely well compared to modern

American agricultural standards. In Europe, there were no such restrictions on immortals. Their kind simply fed off the hoof, drinking from human victims whenever hunger struck. Here, mates fed from each other, while the males doubled their blood intake, feeding from the animals whenever necessary, but never taking a life in exchange for blood.

Yes, they ate meat. But most of their kind relied on feeding, hardly consuming half the animal protein some diets required. They did not take any living creature's life lightly, and all of God's creations were treated with great respect and honor.

The Order forbade them to consume human blood due to its potency. Exceptions were only made in emergency cases. Humans carried a mix of dangerous synthetics and antibiotics in their blood, therefore, their adrenaline could hit like a drug. Immortals often became addicted to the intense flavor and intoxicating rush, sometimes accidentally draining donors to the point of death. The Order believed in a much more tempered way of survival.

She stared at the table, sandwich untouched. Her hunger gnawed at him. She'd barely taken his blood earlier and needed sustenance. It was his duty to keep her safe and healthy above all else.

He carried her plate to the sink and dumped the sandwich into the rubbish bin. In the pantry, he retrieved a jar of homemade peanut butter and jam from the last berry harvest.

"Do you prefer grape or berry?"

She glanced over her shoulder. The glassy sheen in her eyes gave him pause. He placed the jars on the dry sink and crossed the room, crouching at her side.

"Tell me how to make this easier for you. I can't bear the sight of tears in your eyes. I'd much prefer your sharp tongue and disdain if it's a choice between my pain and yours."

"Grape," she rasped.

He waited, hoping she'd say more, but nodded when she remained silent. Perhaps her tears were of relief. A small battle won, when she learned she had options and would not have to abandon all of her values. Did she also realize he would do anything to prevent her a moment's suffering?

He rose to prepare her another sandwich. Maybe there were ways around the vegetarian issue after all.

This time, when he placed it in front of her, she attacked it with ravenous zeal. In less than a minute, only crumbs remained. He poured her a glass of milk to wash it down.

He ached for her acceptance, desperately wanting her approval in a way he'd never desired anyone's approval before. It felt very good to please her.

She glanced at the glass then met his stare. "Do you have any juice?"

Thrilled her guard was lowering, and they were speaking in civilized tones, he pulled a jar of cider down from the shelf and filled a glass for her. She drank heavily, guzzling half the offering and washing down the sandwich. She must have been starving indeed.

When she finished, she leaned back in the chair and patted her flat belly. The press of her decorated nipples showed through the material of her shift and he found himself recalling how the metal gauges felt in his mouth.

"Would you like a bath?"

Her gaze snapped to his face and she scowled, their alliance gone without a trace. "Alone?"

That hadn't been what he'd offered, but he supposed he hadn't fully expressed his desires. She clearly wasn't suffering the attraction he'd been combatting in that moment.

"Yes, alone. Of course."

She nodded.

"Follow me." He didn't want her to run away again, so he held out his hand. She looked at the offering and walked past him.

"Where?"

He sighed. So much for their alliance. "The bedroom."

He set a kettle over the fire and she watched him work as she waited quietly on the edge of the bed. There were methods for heated tubs using coal and copper wire, but he hadn't had time to build such amenities. It was a choice between an indoor latrine or a self-heating tub, and he thought she'd appreciate the latrine more, especially during the colder months.

"Eventually, we'll have a faster system," he

said, pouring another kettle of steaming water into the copper tub. He stirred in some fragrant oils to help her relax and placed a towel on a chair beside the basin, with a hunk of soap for washing.

"That should be warm enough. If the water chills, you can add more from the kettle."

She trailed a tattooed finger through the water. Crossing to the door, she held it open to him.

"I'll leave you to bathing then."

Her gaze followed him in an almost entrapping sense. Dark lashes framed her watchful eyes as her mouth curved ever so slightly with the hint of a smile. Alas, they were forming a truce.

"Is there anything else you need, *pintura?*" His voice turned gravelly as the image of her naked body soaking in the tub filled his mind.

Her dainty fingers curled around the thick edge of the open door. His chest filled with a much-needed breath as the scent of lavender mingled with her familiar fragrance. She smiled at him sweetly, and he drew closer, a magnetic pull luring him in.

Then the door slammed in his face.

Right. So, she was still upset about being taken and held against her will.

Every couple had challenges.

CHAPTER 5

As Delilah washed, she noticed several things that were not quite normal. Her fingernails, which she always kept clipped short for work because they easily split and cracked, were strong and peeking past the tips of her fingers. Also, the scar she'd had on her knee since eighth grade when she fell off a dirt bike was gone. Most alarming, though, was her tattoo, the one of a ladybug over her knuckle, the one she'd gotten before all the others when she was just a girl, was fading. She'd have to touch it up as soon as she got back to her shop.

Like a feather, something tickled at the edge of her mind, irritating, and begging to be investigated. Some deeply buried part of her conscience that favored self-preservation and sanity told her not to examine those nagging instincts too closely.

She needed to cope with her circumstances

and focus on escape. She could process the trauma of whatever was happening to her later.

Not wanting her fear to overwhelm her, she concentrated hard to avoid the most upsetting of her thoughts, repeating several commands like affirmations.

Don't pay attention to the psycho on the other side of the door.

Try not to dwell on the big gaping hole in your memory.

Don't think about him choking you—while he fucked you.

And what happened earlier...

Oh God...

Shame reared its ugly head and she submerged under the water, screaming in frustration.

She focused only on what she could handle, temporarily ignoring the sense that something absolutely terrible happened to her, something that went deeper than a kidnapping and assault.

She rose from under the suds and stared at her hands. No hangnails. No scars.

She searched her body, noting the tightness of her skin over lean muscle. There were no creases or dry patches. Not an ounce of blubber, not a dent of cellulite, and not a single mosquito bite when she knew damn well she got lit up last week at a bonfire party.

Dragging her sharpest fingernail across the back of her hand, she watched as flesh peeled back like pulp leaving a raw scrape in her soft skin. Seconds later, the mark was gone.

"What the fuck?"

The water grew cold, but she was reluctant to get out, not wanting to face Christian again. So confused about what he did to her and what he expected of her, she feared moving. If she stayed very still, perhaps she could stop time, stop this nightmare from continuing.

The man was destined for disappointment. She wasn't staying. It was just a matter of escaping and getting to a phone.

His mixed signals baffled her as he flip-flopped between kind and cruel. Didn't he realize as soon as she was safe, she'd go to the police? She had no loyalty to him and wouldn't hesitate when it came to seeking justice. She hated him. Yet sometimes he watched her as if he wanted, more than anything in the world, for her to like him. That sort of insecurity was a complete contradiction to his default setting of arrogant controlling asshole.

Earlier, when she'd yelled at him, he actually looked hurt. Well, what did he expect? He kidnapped her. They weren't friends.

And damn her for being such a waif of a cliché, because she *had* liked him on some level. And part of her, despite everything he'd done to her, still lusted for him.

She sank into the tub again, so disgusted with herself that she thought she deserved to drown. What sort of modern woman did she represent if she still fell for that pull-your-hair playground bullshit?

There was something seriously wrong with

her because he did way worse than pull her hair. And damn her to hell, because the moment she thought of him pulling her hair a bolt of desire spiked through her, deflating her fury.

She must still be on drugs. That was the only explanation. He probably put something in the juice or her food.

When her lungs pinched and burned for air, she broke through the surface and gasped for breath. She needed to think. Even Achilles had a weak spot.

She caught glimpses of Christian's vulnerability earlier, pretty sure she could use that to her advantage. Maybe she could stab him or something if it came down to it. How far was she willing to go for her escape?

The jerk took her against her will and drugged her. That should kill any soft feelings. He was an asshole and now her enemy. She needed to work past her pacifist nature and do whatever it took to get out of there.

Sure, she couldn't eat anything with a face and always hit the brakes for turtles and birds, but she could stab a man. Last night—which felt like last month—he'd stabbed her. Hadn't he?

Her hand examined her neck, once again finding no evidence of the assault. Where had the blood come from? The skin wasn't even tender but she flinched as unwanted memories rushed at her. Then she thought about earlier when she'd...

Her stomach turned and knotted. What exactly had she done?

Her mouth watered and her stomach swilled, pushing the contents up. With nowhere to puke, she rushed to stand from the tub and covered her mouth.

Don't think about it. It was just kissing.

But she knew it was more. She'd tasted him. Not his kiss. Not the sweat on his skin. She'd tasted *him. Metallic* and warm, sharp like a penny.

Her stomach revolted and she shivered.

Keep it the fuck down... Shutting her eyes, she forced her insides to calm as she repeatedly swallowed. Spiking only when intrusive thoughts slipped past her guard.

Blood...

It was blood...

Her shoulders jerked as she fought her reflexes. *It's over! Chair. Fireplace. Bed. Window. Bed. Christian's body. Bed. Blood...*

The nausea faded and something else took hold. Something darker and deeper. A strong hunger that had nothing to do with food. Her cravings shifted into something altogether distracting as images flashed through her mind.

Bed. Bodies entwined. Lips. Teeth. Hands. Christian. Christian's throat...

She slipped back into the water with a shiver, her hands clenched at her ears as she tried to stop the visions from assaulting her. *Muscled flesh. Tongues. Sweat. Fingers. Mouths. Breasts. Blood...*

Ignoring the intrusive thoughts, she sloshed the cool water over her thighs with pruned fingers. He was probably waiting at the door. The longer she stayed the more confused she felt. She needed to leave—tonight.

Maybe she could reason with him. Maybe she could convince him to let her go if she cooperated and pretended to like him. She could play it off as if their relationship could work. It wouldn't, of course, on account of all the drugging and kidnapping red flags, but she could lie.

If she planned to escape, she needed to learn her surroundings and form a plan. She couldn't let her fear paralyze her. No more wasting time.

With a sigh, she stood. Water rushed from her skin as she wrapped herself in the towel. Glaring at the rag of a dress he'd offered her before, she decided to find some pants. And shoes if she planned to make it more than a mile.

The door stood ajar and unlocked. She smirked, glad she'd broken the knob, but then her brow furrowed. More inexplicable memories came to mind, namely her superhuman strength.

When he'd locked her in the room she'd torn it apart, denting the walls and throwing furniture with the ease of tossing a whiffle ball. Her strength must have been triggered by an adrenaline rush linked to fear and rage, sort of like when moms lift cars to save a child.

Padding softly to the door, she searched the hall. *Nada.* Was she finally alone?

Quietly, she slipped back into the room and searched the spilled drawers. Lifting a freshly laundered white chemise and a pair of pillow-case underwear she scowled.

Commando it is.

The next drawer contained shirts and pants. The pants were loose, but she found suspenders and they did the trick. A thick-bristled brush sat next to the pitcher of water on the wash-stand. Perching on the edge of the bed, she brushed her damp hair.

"Delilah?" She flinched when he knocked at the door.

There was no need to respond as he let him-self into the room. She glared, grateful she al-ready dressed. He too had washed up. His dark, damp hair slicked back behind his ears and his face appeared freshly cleaned. Narrowing her eyes, she scowled at him. So pretty, so unfair, so completely psychotic.

"Did you not see the gown—"

"Yeah, I'm not wearing that."

His lips pressed together. "I'm working on getting more clothing for you so you have op-tions, but it takes time to stitch them."

She planned to be gone by then.

"There are straight pins in the box on the dresser for your hair. That will have to do until I locate a bonnet." He retrieved the small wooden box. Opening it up, he showed her sev-eral shiny, sharp pins.

"Those aren't for hair."

"These are what the females use."

"For what, lobotomies? I'm not putting sewing pins in my head."

He snapped the box closed. "Every female on the farm pins their braids. You can choose the style of braids, but your hair cannot stay loose. It's a reflection of morals."

"Well, I didn't choose to be here, so I guess I'll just keep my hair nice and loose—like my morals, which, by the way, you took no issue with last night when you were shoving your cock inside of me."

He stilled and for once, she couldn't read his expression. Unsure if he wanted to throttle her or kiss her, she backed up.

Shit. She was messing this all up. She was supposed to cooperate and lure him into trusting her. She needed to cut the snark and play nice, but her resentment kept getting in the way.

"Delilah, I want us to understand one another."

"That would be great. Can we start with why you brought me here and why you're dressing me up like Amish Barbie?"

"Our kind does not do well with waiting. My circumstances were urgent and there was no use delaying the inevitable."

Was he talking about the Amish? One would think they'd be incredibly patient, what with having to wait for things to heat over a flame and churning butter and such shit.

She needed to make it believable. Softening her glare, she tried to reason with him. "That's no excuse for the way you've treated me. I'm not an object you can just take. I'm a human being. I have a business to run. People will be looking for me. I have responsibilities."

"What people?"

"Friends. Clients. I have a life, Christian. I want to go home."

He looked sad for a moment and then his expression hardened. "You cannot leave. Ever. Your life is here now. This is where you'll live. I'm sorry if you're unhappy, but that will fade. The sooner you accept your reality, the faster your heart will heal. God teaches us to forgive even the worst of men. Eventually, you will forgive me—"

"No," she snapped. His unbending refusal to hear reason infuriated her.

"No?"

Fuck this. If he wouldn't meet her halfway, she saw no reason to play nice. "I'm not going to just roll over and let you decide my life for me. What you're doing is against the law. I'll fight you to my last breath if I have to. And if you force me to stay here, I'll never forgive you. I'll hate you with every fiber of my being and make your life a living hell."

"That's not an option."

"Oh really? Do you plan to keep me on drugs? How do you intend to make me stay? You aren't armed. Will you beat me into submission with your hands? Let's go, tough guy." She jumped off the bed, crowding him until he backed up a step. "Bring it." She poked his shoulder.

"You're getting hostile again."

"Yeah, turns out lavender oil and bubble baths only go so far when I'm being forced to do things against my will." Another poke.

"Do not test me, Delilah."

She got in his face. "You keep saying that, but I think you're just a full-of-shit hypocrite. Which is it, Christian? Are you a God-fearing man who knows right from wrong, or do you only lean on your faith when it can be weaponized to control others? Huh?" She shoved him, harder this time, and he staggered back. "Which is it? Will you hit a woman? Tie me down so I can't leave? Torture me until you break my will to run? What's the big fucking plan?" He'd already gotten physical, but she had no memory of him actually striking her. "Come on, tough guy. Try to stop me."

He just stood there. Maybe it was that easy. She only had to look her fears directly in the eye and march the fuck out of there.

She scoffed. "Exactly what I thought." Pivoting, she looked at the door, but Christian was already there. She did a double take, looking back at the empty space where he stood a second ago. "How...?"

"You cannot leave." He blocked the door.

It was the drugs. It had to be the drugs. Her eyes were playing tricks on her. She blinked and shook her head.

"Look, if you're afraid I'll tell someone about what you did, I won't." That was a lie. "But only if you let me go right now. I just want to get back to my life. I have a shop to run and friends that will be worried."

"You can't survive out there anymore. Things are different now. You must remain here where I can protect you."

"Protect me from what? Kidnappers? Give me a break. I know about the Amish. No resistance. Forgiveness. And no violence. Get out of my way."

She pushed him and he grabbed her. Instinctively, she raised her hand to slap him but he caught her wrist in an unbreakable grip. "There is no violence because our values are strong, and we have a devout faith in God. But do not ever mistake me for weak."

Her molars locked. "Let. Go."

"I've waited an eternity for you, Delilah. I'll never let you go. On that, I would stake my life, my existence, and my faith. Do not take my graciousness for granted. I may be Amish, but there are greater powers that control my instincts, forces that you would be wise to respect."

It was in his eyes, something unnamable and terrifying. Something that told her he could snap her like a twig. Something that promised, when push came to shove, he would always have his way.

Hopeless emotion welled up inside of her with the dizzying effect of a funhouse. There was no way out. The bite of tears had her lashes flickering and her throat constricting. "Christian, please, you have to let me go."

His jaw twitched and his nostrils flared. "I would give you almost anything. I'd lay my life down for yours. But I can't give you that."

A tear tripped down her cheek. "Why?" She'd likely ask that until the day he killed her.

"I cannot kill you, *pintura*. My nature forbids it."

Startled that he'd guessed her thoughts, her breath hitched. Or had she been so upset she'd spoken the thought out loud?

"You need to trust me."

"Trust is earned."

"Then give me the chance to earn it."

She hated him.

"You may hate me now, but in time—"

"How are you doing that?" Was she still high? Talking out loud without realizing it? Or was she just that transparent?

"Sometimes we communicate without words."

This was more than body language. He'd read her specific thoughts more than once. She frowned at him. *Can you hear me? Brown. Thirteen. Shovel. Ostrich.*

He sighed and loosened his hold on her wrist. "Brown. Thirteen. Shovel. Ostrich."

She stumbled back. "What the fuck?"

"Language, Delilah."

"You're reading my mind. That's fucking nuts."

"It's not as unusual as you might think. You're broadcasting. It's common when emotions run high." He glanced at the bed. "I can tell you how I do it, maybe even teach you to do it as well *if* you'll sit and listen to what I have to say."

She rubbed her arms and paced. "Fine, but you stay over there." She pointed to the chair.

Once they were both seated, he only stared at her. She had finally agreed to listen, and he had nothing to say.

She held out her arms. "Well?"

"I arrived in America in 1737."

Her thoughts screeched to a halt. Her wide eyes blinked at him. *Great. More lies.*

"I only speak the truth. We arrived on a ship called *The Charming Nancy*. My name's on the records if you need proof. I, along with several others in The Order, were passengers."

Realizing he was serious, she eyed him with caution. This was not a stable man. "That's impossible."

"Your society knows only what we allow them to know. Your understanding of mortality is a limiting belief, ignorant of our kind."

She looked at his young features and strong build. "You traveled through time?"

"No. Time holds little significance to our species."

Did he say species? She frowned and fanned out her hands. "I'm lost."

"I was eight years old when I came to America."

"In 1737," she clarified, wanting to get every ridiculous detail straight.

"Yes. I'm two-hundred-ninety-five years old."

"Riiiiight."

He remained silent, his chest slowly rising and falling with each breath as he studied her. "Sarcasm is an English form of irony we don't use."

"Good for you."

His eyes narrowed. "I'm aware you're mocking me."

"Oh. I was worried you wouldn't notice."

"More sarcasm."

"Oh, I'm sorry."

He did not look pleased. "You're free to go *if* you can make it out the door in ten seconds."

All thoughts of teasing him vanished as she did a double take. "Seriously? Just like that?"

"Six seconds."

She bolted off the bed, but the moment her feet hit the floor he was out of his chair, blocking the door. How had he gotten there before her?

"Time's up." He smirked.

"You lied."

"No, you failed. How does it feel to be mocked?"

Confused by how fast he crossed the room, she considered her options. "Do it again. Give me another chance."

"I'm afraid not. I've made my point."

Frustration bubbled, forming a lump in her throat and tears filled her eyes. "That you're an asshole? Yeah, great job. So much for earning my trust."

He drew in a deep breath and exhaled loudly. "You may not trust me, but I'm going to trust you with everything I'm about to share."

She shook her head and walked back to her side of the room. "I don't care about anything you have to say. I just want you out of my life."

"Look at me."

"Fuck off."

"Delilah, *look*."

With a sniff, she wiped her nose and turned, prepared to unleash on him. "Why the hell would I—*Jesus!*" She stumbled back, pressing her shoulders into the far wall. His dilated eyes glowed silver, and his hands splayed with talon-like claws. But his teeth...*his fucking teeth...*

"I'm not going to hurt you."

She whimpered, feeling about as safe as anyone would with a wild animal in the room. His fangs curved sharply, lethal like a lion's. His claws were razor thick and long. But his eyes. There was nothing human about his eyes as they illuminated the room with an eerie, alien glow. "What are you?"

"You already know."

Her head shook in denial. But his beauty alone made the possibility believable.

No. There was no such thing as vampires. It was drugs. He'd done something to the bath or the sandwich or the juice.

"I haven't given you any tonics or drugs. Not once."

His claws retracted and she sucked in a breath, slightly relieved. But his eyes remained an inhuman shade of silver, glowing like the moon.

Her hand drifted to her neck. She knew. He was right. She knew exactly what he was, but she didn't want to admit it because that would make her as crazy as him. "Did you bite me?"

"I had no choice. If I didn't complete the bond, I would have turned. People would have died—myself included."

She looked down at her hands as they trembled. Did he...make her like him? She covered her mouth and dry heaved.

"Do not panic, little one."

"What did you do to me?" Her words came out in a croak. She finally faced her memories, piecing all the confusing parts together in a way that made irrevocable sense but shouldn't.

Her head shook and she gripped her temples, refusing to accept his bullshit. But her memories were unraveling. It was all there. Nowhere left to compartmentalize the truth once she looked it dead in the eye.

She was losing her shit. This wasn't real. "There's no such thing as vampires."

"There are, but that's not what I am. I'm... immortal. And now, so are you."

Time slowed and there was a loud crack as the earth snapped right off its axis. Up was suddenly down. Fiction was fact. And she was trapped in some Alice in Wonderland Amish nightmare with a fucking vampire who tried to eat her.

"That's not what happened."

She twitched, sensing him in her head but unsure how to get him out. They had sex. He drank her blood. Was she now under his spell? Every vampire movie and novel she'd ever come across had different rules. What was real and what was fake?

Again, her gaze dropped to her trembling hands. *Claws.* All she had to do was think it and her nails sharpened and grew. She sucked in a horrified breath. "You bastard."

"You're not the first to make such an accusation."

It was more than sex. She knew it when it was happening, and now she knew why. *Fuck, fuck, fuck!*

"When I found you, I claimed you, and now you're mine. Forever. I made you like me because that was your destiny. It was always going to be the two of us, Delilah. We were torn from the same soul and have been incomplete up until now."

She shook her head. "No. I'm only twenty-nine. You found the wrong woman." She no longer wanted to escape the room or house. She wanted to escape her own skin.

"I found exactly who I was meant to find. You're my mate, my true calling, the other half of my soul. It just took you longer to get here."

She couldn't breathe. Her heart was going to beat out of her chest.

"You know what we are now. You see why I could never hurt you. Should anything happen to you, my purpose on this earth would be lost. I exist for you and you alone."

She glanced around the room, her collection of overwhelming memories in this place only added up to one day. How was that possible? How long would it take to live out an eternity here?

Too many uncertainties assured she'd stick around. She didn't understand any of this. Ignorant and scared, she had no choice but to rely on his help—when he was the monster that did this to her in the first place.

"And the Amish thing?"

"It allows us to hide in plain sight and keep outsiders at bay. The farm provides privacy and safety, which you'll come to cherish. It's not safe out there for our kind. We're hunted. Some have even been tortured and enslaved. Very few now believe we exist, thanks to our ability to stay safely removed and isolated."

She was not like him. She couldn't be. How would she survive? "I can't drink..." Her stomach rebelled at the thought of blood.

"You already have."

She swayed, once again fighting back the urge to throw up. The truth was there, but every muscle in her body tightened, fighting with hard refusal to accept it. She couldn't acknowledge what she'd done. What he'd done to her. What they did together.

Doubling over, she held her knees and tried

to breathe. The contents of her stomach threatened to rise. She fought back the rushing pressure of bile, her mouth filling with saliva as her shoulders tensed, and she moaned. "Oh, God…"

"We feed from the animals, Delilah, so no life is harmed. You'll feed from me, your mate, when you're in need. Just like before, it'll be pleasurable. Instinct will guide you. Try not to overthink it."

Her stomach roiled. After years of being a vegetarian, the thought of ingesting any animal byproduct sickened her. She was going to starve to death. Could an immortal die? Obviously, there were ways they were hunted.

"Death is not an option. Immortality has limits, but I will not let you die."

"Even if I'd rather die than live like this?"

How could he do this to her? How could he take her choice away? Movies and books hadn't prepared her. There was always a choice. Bella had a choice. Louis had a choice, become a vampire or another one of Lestat's victims. Hell, even annoying Elena Gilbert had options. Was there a cure? Could it be reversed?

"Do not trust fiction. I'll teach you everything you need to know."

"After the fact."

"This is where we are now. Forget everything you knew before. The sun will not affect you. Garlic is safe. Crucifixes are beautiful. And holy water won't burn. Legends of nocturnal lifestyles are false, except in the rare case when one is called, but even that's temporary and not anything you'll ever have to worry about now that I've claimed you."

"Is there a way to undo it?"

He shook his head. "Our bond's eternal. I'm yours and you are mine."

Her back slid down the wall, the fight washed out of her, and she had nothing left. He had her. Where else could she go? She didn't know how to live. Didn't know how to die. He'd sentenced her to an eternity by his side.

"I hate you." The quiet venom of her words only underscored the edge of her resentment. The full extent of her outrage would take lifetimes to communicate properly. Lifetimes she now had.

It would take more than an eternity for her to forgive him for what he'd done.

CHAPTER 6

$\mathcal{I}$t had been two days since Delilah spoke to him, and her last words were nothing he wished to remember. She hated him. Not only did she despise him, but she also entertained thoughts of punishing him. Everything from manipulation to disembowelment. Her ideas on torture were extremely grim for a female who refused to eat anything with a face.

She only moved when she absolutely needed to. But, even then, she fought her reflexes with stubborn paralysis. If not for her unguarded emotions, her discomfort would have been undetectable. She refused to eat, refused to feed, and stubbornly refused to acknowledge him.

Only when she couldn't escape her needs did she visit the washroom. Then her still silence continued.

She was as headstrong as an ox, starving herself and forcing such foolish silence only to spite him. Well, he had waited centuries for her, he could certainly wait her out a few more days until she realized her stubbornness was futile.

He made her several peanut butter and jam sandwiches, fruit, freshly squeezed juice, cookies, and anything else he could find that fit her preferred diet. She touched none of it, and now her little hunger strike was costing them both.

They'd become so in sync he suffered the same ravenous cravings. The relentless hunger pains and symptoms of malnutrition were driving him mad, but they weren't his to feed. Only her actions could satisfy the beast that haunted them both, and she refused, perhaps more so because she was coming to understand her suffering also punished him.

Dark circles underscored her eyes, deepened by her jutting cheekbones. He tried coaxing her to drink water, but she ignored every request. When he pressed a cup to her mouth, she stared blankly in that catatonic trance and let the liquid spill down her chin. All the while her thoughts viciously attacking him with every foul-mouthed English vulgarity she knew.

He'd been surviving off distilled blood, not yet comfortable with leaving her alone, but his rations were running low. Hours passed where he only counted her breaths, and even then, he suspected she held them to punish him.

The silence had become deafening. A steady mental combat of will, where one of them would have to surrender eventually. He had nothing to surrender. His actions could not be undone at this point. If only she would compromise to make this easier on both of them.

A floorboard creaked behind him and he pivoted, hissing protectively and guarding his mate.

"I see it's true then."

Startled to find the bishop in his house, he retracted his fangs. "Eleazar."

"I've been standing here for a full minute. What's wrong with you?"

Christian exhaled. He was starving, that was what was wrong. "I was distracted in thought. Come." He gestured toward the connecting room.

"You missed a council meeting. Your mother was concerned."

His mother. He was surprised she hadn't come to visit him herself. Then he realized the half-breed, Dane, likely told her about Delilah.

He grimaced. "No doubt that's what brought you here."

A passive puppeteer who orchestrated many events without a trace, his mother played the bishop well. Of course she'd have him come here to investigate the situation for her. That way she could feign disinterest while also passively making her disappointment known.

Not that she would be unhappy about his mating. On the contrary, she'd be thrilled. But she would be disappointed that Christian hadn't confided in her. She'd take his secrecy as a personal slight, claiming him cold and hateful for intentionally leaving her out of such a monumental life event.

He sighed. She'd show up eventually, but not before gaining a bit of information first. If anything, his mother liked to be prepared.

"How long have you had her here, Christian?"

"Four days."

"And things are…"

It was not the bishop's business to ask, certainly not his right to know. But Christian knew he was inquiring as a friend.

"Not well." Glancing at his catatonic mate who watched the bishop like a statue, Christian pushed a hand through his hair, setting it on end as his neck burned. "I'm afraid the situation is worsening by the day if you want the truth."

Eleazar's silent observation spoke volumes. As the most powerful immortal on the farm, over half a millennia-old, the bishop had the power to look into Christian's or Delilah's mind and see anything he wanted to know.

Eleazar frowned. "She's transitioned, yet…"

Christian grimaced. "The bonding was swift. I didn't want to chance…complications."

"I see."

"I realize now, a little patience might have benefited both of us." He hoped Delilah heard the sincerity of his words. The admission was made for her benefit more than anything else.

Eleazar switched from English to Dutch. "Modern mortal females are different, Christian. They like their independence and tend to be much more free-spirited than the females of The Order."

"I realize that also," Christian also transitioned to their native language.

"How old is your female?"

"Just under thirty years."

He frowned, studying Delilah and no doubt reading some of her memories.

"She came to me willingly," Christian explained. "I took nothing she didn't offer."

"Except her life."

His head lowered in shame. "Yes."

Once the calling had begun, Christian could not shake the fear of turning *feeish*. What had become of his once close friend, Isaiah, was an abomination. He did not want to risk the same fate.

Eleazar placed a comforting hand on his shoulder. "What's done is done, brother. Rest easy. You're both through the transition and safe."

Safe but not happy.

"I've been alone too long. I'm not sure I know how to do this." Only because he was certain Delilah did not understand their version of Pennsylvania Dutch did Christian confide such personal information to his trusted friend.

"Nonsense. Resolutions will come in time. You must be patient."

"She hates me. I assumed there was no point in delaying the inevitable, but perhaps I was wrong."

"Perhaps. But there's no undoing what's

been done and, now you're in no danger of becoming *feeish*."

"Yes, but I have an angry female on my hands, which may be more hazardous."

The bishop cocked his head and cleared his throat, drawing back his telepathic inspection. "How are you tolerating her hunger?"

Eleazar was so perceptive, it didn't surprise Christian that he could sense such internal agony. Delilah had been starving herself for days. He had no idea how far she would go to punish him, but he already forgave her for whatever suffering may come. She was angry. Rightly so. However she needed to process her pain, he would process it with her as one.

"She needs time."

"She needs food and fluids, Christian."

"I've already forced enough on her."

"You would be saving her from suffering. It's your duty to protect her."

"I'm aware of my duty and my right to run my home as I see fit."

Family law forbade an outsider from commenting on any couple's private conduct, whether married or mated. He believed she would eventually make the right choice. He just hoped she didn't wait too long.

Eleazar held up his palms. "Fair enough. But might I suggest compulsion? She wouldn't have to know."

"How often do you lie to Larissa?"

The bishop grimaced. "You have a point.

"I'm hoping, in time, she comes to me

willingly."

Truth be told, immortals could go without nutrition for decades. He hoped she'd come to him before her body shut down to preserve energy. Desiccation was painful, and he wasn't sure he could respect her choice if she took this self-harm that far. It could take a century or more for an immortal to actually starve to the point of death. She couldn't possibly be that willful.

"Very well." The bishop returned to the front door. "I'll let you get back to your mate. Congratulations, my friend."

"Thank you." Christian walked the bishop out, his heart consumed with worry and his spirits too low to feel deserving of any praise.

Once back inside, he faced the den reluctantly. With a sigh, he slowly crossed the threshold. Delilah remained exactly where he left her, eyes closed but not asleep.

If they were companions, he'd tell her immortals could sense such things, but at the moment they seemed more like enemies, so he kept his knowledge to himself. Their mental link was the only connection they shared, and he did not want to lose that as well.

The purple hue of her pale skin only slightly concerned him. Immortals often paled when they needed to feed.

What he couldn't comprehend was the change to her hair. The jet-black strands had lightened to chestnut hues, reminding him more of his dreams than the female he'd found in a bar. Perhaps these shifts in hair color were residual adjustments from her transition. He didn't believe two days of hunger would cause such changes.

"Delilah?"

She didn't move, but her heart rate and blood pressure assured she was awake.

"That was our bishop. News of your arrival has spread."

He decided not to bother her with warnings of his mother's impending visit. It was hardly dusk, but he was ready for the day to end.

"I'll take you upstairs." As always, she stiffened the moment he touched her, but she didn't object when he lifted her to his chest.

He carried her upstairs and lay her on his bed. Memories of how he anticipated this first week taunted him. She absolutely detested him. And, to be honest, he wasn't sure he deserved anything less than her animosity.

"Sleep now, little one." He pressed a kiss to her forehead and reclined next to her on the bed.

The ache of her hunger gnawed at his insides. At this point, ingesting any sustenance would cause her pain. He could sense her overwhelming fatigue, and his heart ached.

Every instinct demanded he tend to her needs and take away her discomfort, but her physical symptoms were only an indicator of the emotional damage he'd done.

His knuckle grazed her arm and her dainty fingers balled into a tight fist. "I'm sorry I've disappointed you, *pintura*. I'll make this right. I promise." He had to believe, in time, she'd forgive him and see the beauty of an immortal bond.

Several minutes later, her knuckles unclenched and her heart rate slowed. She was finally asleep.

He shut his eyes and pressed into her mind. No thoughts. No dreams. She dozed exactly as the rest of the immortal race slept.

The bishop's words echoed in his mind. The ache of hunger battled with his desire to do right by her. But what was right? Should he respect her decision to starve herself or protect her from pain? This foolish starvation would change nothing. The pain was unnecessary.

The more he thought about her hunger strike, the more frustrated he grew. Perhaps forcing her hand would prove she had nothing to fear. She'd understand that feeding was a pleasant, intimate exchange that most immortals valued above all other physical interactions.

Unsure if his offered comfort was merciful or if he was making another grave mistake, he pushed deep into her psyche and took hold of her free will, cradling her close to his chest. Her head lolled as his fingers swept her hair away from her face. Unable to stop himself, he pressed a kiss to the corner of her mouth.

"I ache for your forgiveness so that we may make a happy life together."

He simply held her for a moment, enjoying the novelty of the weight of her body in his arms. He needed to earn her forgiveness, but first, he needed her trust. Only then, would he win her love. What he was considering would delay that trust, but also speed them toward acceptance.

A sharp pinch came from deep within. Another hunger pain, followed by a long, gargling growl as air worked through her intestines. She softly moaned, her face tightening in agony as she slept.

The hunger symptoms he could manage, but her suffering he couldn't bear. Expecting him to leave her in such agony when there was a simple solution was as absurd as asking a fish to fly or a bird to swim. Impossible.

Perhaps her stubbornness outmatched his will, because when another sharp cramp took hold, his resolution not to interfere crumbled. She would never accept her new life if she didn't find peace. There was truly no cause for this unnecessary misery, and he wanted it to stop. He wanted her comfort and happiness above all else.

His fingers moved to the collar of his shirt and he hesitated, knowing this was not the way one earned another's trust. But perhaps he could prove to her that she was capable of the unthinkable and the obstacles were only in her head.

Needing the intimate contact, he removed his shirt. It would have been easier to feed her from his wrist, but he wanted to hold her skin to skin. He was a selfish bastard.

He shifted her close to his neck and cupped the back of her head. Slicing his throat with a sharp nail, he whispered, "Take from me what you need, *pintura*. Feed from your mate until your hunger is gone."

He drew in a sharp breath as her little teeth latched onto his skin instinctually. His body immediately hardened at her suckling. She drew from his vein much like a sleeping babe feeds for survival, proving her repulsion to blood was strictly psychological.

Her physical instincts and hunger drove her enough that she required no compulsion to feed, he merely held the command for her to sleep.

He gripped her hip as her thighs pressed tight. He tried to still her rocking motions as her body chased additional friction. It was common for mates to bond when they fed and her immortal blood hungered for such a connection—as did his. He wanted to give her what she craved, but knew—deep down—she would not want that, so he tensed and held his breath, trying not to draw any satisfaction from the way her body gyrated against his.

There was no denying how much he wanted her. She was the other half of his soul, the light to his darkness, the answer to his prayers. Denying himself access to her body was a sort of masochistic torture he hadn't anticipated, but more than anything, he wanted to be the mate she deserved, the mate she wanted.

He believed himself an honorable male and

deeply craved her to see him as such, despite their rocky start. He would not take from her what she did not consciously offer. But he would always provide for her and protect her, no matter what she believed she needed and no matter how much she hated him.

Unfortunately, his body was not aligned with his thinking and the longer she pulled from his vein the more his cock hardened. She drew his release closer to the surface with each precious sip of his blood.

"Delilah…" He breathed, pressing his lips into her shoulder and forcing his mouth to remain closed.

Unconscious of her actions, she greedily took from his vein, the result of not feeding properly for days. Ecstasy, a natural consequence of feeding, amplified his pleasure through the link they shared. Soon enough he'd have a mess of his own to clean.

Her body responded to the sensual process, and he could scent her arousal, hear her quiet purr. He ached to meet those carnal needs as well, but he would not—not until she came to him willingly of sound mind.

Mating was their most sacred vow. The act went hand in hand with feeding, and while he did not touch her in any lustful manner, her moans increased and her muscles tightened until her body finally climaxed. To his shame, his release naturally followed.

Her delicate finish was innocent and affirming, reminding him that much patience was needed on his part. He traced a finger over her hair, in awe of her perfect ear, as she continued to gently feed.

"That's right, little one. Let me take care of all your needs."

Fragile tremors shook her body as she remained asleep. This was what she did to him. She stripped him down until he was defenseless against her beauty and touch, leaving him with the mess of a young male in his lap.

The desire to earn her trust and true, conscious affection carved a hole in his heart. A jagged breath escaped and he shivered as her tongue reflexively closed the puncture wound at his neck, another natural instinct that came to her as effortlessly as breathing.

Reluctantly, he lowered her back to the bed. She showed no adverse response to the blood. On the contrary, her flesh was once again rosy and her eyes no longer appeared sunken in.

A droplet of his blood remained on the curve of her lower lip. Leaning down, he licked away the trace. She sighed and he groaned, forcing himself to leave the bed and clean away the mess he'd made of himself. When he returned, she lay exactly as he left her.

She was a portrait of perfection. A masterpiece. His *pintura*. He paused in the doorway, gratitude overwhelming him as he breathed in the image of her sleeping soundly on his bed. Then her eyes flashed open wide—fully dilated —and he knew he was in trouble.

CHAPTER 7

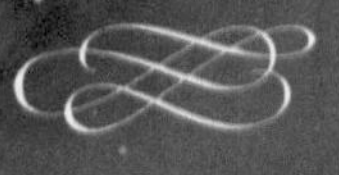

$\mathcal{H}$e was watching her. She sensed him before seeing him, could feel him admiring her while she slept. Her eyes flicked open, finding his tall form filling the doorway. Her blood boiled.

Him. He did this.

The lethargic shock that overtook her these past few days had abated. In its place seethed an uncontainable rage.

A low growl broke the near silence, the uncharacteristic rumble coming from her throat. Beneath the primal snarling, she heard the insects crawling under the foundation of the house, the flap of birds' wings overhead, the snap of a branch, and the snick of a matchstick catching flame. She could scent the sulfur burning, feel the tingle of the sunlight damaging her skin through the glass of the window, and taste a strange copper tang on her tongue.

She glared at him, pouring every bit of hatred into her gaze.

"You're awake."

She sensed his surprise and a trace of something else. Fear? Uncertainty? Good. He should be afraid.

Time stretched and yawned within every passing second, moving slower than usual as her mind gathered and stored every transient detail. Baring her teeth, she panted through her fury, her muscles vibrating with the urge to wound him. He did this to her.

She frowned, unsure how such seething ferocity could live inside of her. She was a pacifist, an animal rights activist. Of course, she liked animals better than people. Most people sucked. But she never suffered any inclination to harm another. Until *him*... She wanted to claw his eyes out, rip his hair out in hunks, bite into his throat, and tear open his flesh.

Her insides twitched with awareness. A tingle of unwelcome arousal zipped through her core, angering her all the more.

She frowned, because in light of everything else it seemed a weird time to feel horny. *Must be a vampire thing.*

Her jaw shifted and she dragged her tongue over the sharp edge of her teeth, stilling when she discovered the lengthened tip of her incisor. Fangs. Yup. They were real.

"Do you feel better now that you've...slept?"

Grateful sleep didn't require a coffin or being underground with creepy crawlers and spiders, she mentally nodded but made no motion that would give him the satisfaction of acknowledgment. But she did feel better. Incredible actually.

He took a step forward and she hissed like a cornered cat. Another vampire trait, she supposed.

Did she have powers? Could she turn into a bat? Fly? Maybe she could turn into a butterfly or—*ooh!*—a unicorn. *Pretty!* Or, no, *ooh,* a dragon! If vampires were real, dragons had to have existed at some point in time, too.

Visions of burning him to ash filled her mind. She'd like to light him up like Kings Landing. She pictured doing just that, fiery dragon breath exploding out of her and engulfing him in pain. *Burn, motherfucker!*

He grimaced and mentally withdrew from her head. Served him right for trespassing in her thoughts.

Stay the fuck out of my head!

"Delilah—"

Her eyes snapped back to him. *Bad man.* The hissing seemed a natural response to his proximity. Maybe there was some cat in her after all because she felt rather feral at the moment.

He took another step, and she sprang to her feet, knees bent, arms spread, ready to attack. Her hands splayed wide like talons as she panted through her bared teeth. Holy shit, she felt strong, like she could move a mountain. *Bad. Ass.*

She flexed her arms and rolled her shoulders testing her newfound strength. Limber and loose. Like she could really fuck him up. Her eyes zeroed in on his throat.

Christian took a cautious step back and held out a calming hand. She sniffed the air, somehow recognizing the scent of his uncertainty, enjoying the fact that she made him nervous. Feeling as reliable as a loose fucking cannon full of God-knew-what kind of mystical gunpowder, she recognized that she could blow at any moment. Apparently, so did he.

Her eyes dared him to make a move.

"I'm not your enemy, little one."

Nothing about her felt little at that moment. Her senses cataloged every element from the wind on the house to the earth rotating on its axis. Her body calibrated with the heat of the sun and her mind knew exactly how far she'd have to travel to reach water. She was a Goddess, tapping into all of nature's beautiful powers.

He slid his foot one-eighth of an inch toward her, and she sprang to the other side of the room, dizzy from moving so fast.

"Stay back or I'll attack," she warned, a courtesy he didn't deserve, but she preferred to avoid contact altogether.

Still holding his hands in a gesture of peace, he spoke slowly, "I don't want to hurt you, Delilah. I only wish to check on you."

"You're not my caretaker."

"But I am."

"Did they teach you to say that shit in captor

school?" Her anger seethed like a building fire in her lungs. "Sorry to disappoint, but I'm not the Stockholm's type."

"I only want to mend this rift between us. If you could simply forgive me, we could move forward. I could show you around the farm, and you would see it's not so bad here."

The thought of leaving the house held promise. "Show me around?"

"Yes, at least give you a tour to the Schrock property lines. The Order's land is enormous, divided between all the families. Being that it's only my mother and I, and now you, occupying our parcel, our land's rather spacious and underdeveloped. We have an open spread."

She didn't want to be included in his *we*. She could run away. She'd only need a distraction—

"If you run, I will catch you, *pintura*. I am much older and faster."

Her eyes narrowed. He didn't know the extent of her strength. He couldn't feel the power coursing through her veins. Maybe she was different, special. Her muscles bunched and vibrated with the urge to move as indescribable energy buzzed through every nerve.

"Your new strength will bring many gifts, but my age will always put me at an advantage. I'm stronger with many disciplines you have yet to learn. With time and practice, your abilities will improve. I'm happy to teach you if you'll allow me."

Anything you can do, I can do better. I can do anything better than you...Arrogant much?

He viewed himself as her superior and spoke as if he hoped to be her master. Not likely.

"I don't wish to master you. I only wish to help you. Your ability to protect yourself is important to me. Trust that I don't want to suppress your autonomy. I want you to embrace your full potential and grasp the tremendous gift I've given you."

I, I, I, I! Fuuuuuuuuck you, you Amish, sheep fucking vampire.

He growled and his eyes flashed silver.

Aww, poor widdle Dwacula. If he refused to get out of her head, she'd make her thoughts as inhospitable and unwelcoming as possible. She wanted him to suffer.

Am I not the obedient woman you hoped for? However will I learn my place, master?

His nostrils flared, and his fists clenched at his side.

He may be stronger, but she was no weakling. She would not be mastered.

The potency of her vehemence intoxicated her. Newfound strength pumped through her veins like heroin. Fuck him, and fuck his farm. If anything, maybe she'd meet a better mate, now that he brought her here.

Like a crack of thunder, a growl snapped from his throat, and he sprang, grabbing her by the shoulders faster than she could draw breath. She raked her claws down his face and he knocked her to the ground.

Snapping her teeth at him like a rabid dog,

she tried to bite him. Snarls rent the air as they clawed at each other. Growls ripped from her throat in place of screams. They tussled, rolling over the planked floor, biting and scratching, hissing like animals.

Once he had her pinned to the ground, he snapped, *"Enough!"*

She tasted blood and took inventory of her body as she panted. Not a single scratch marred her skin. All the damage had been her doing, enough blood that it dripped from his face and pooled on her chest.

She thrashed and growled, arching up to bite him, but he maintained control, slamming her back down and demanding her submission. Outmatched, her fury subdued.

His expression bore no tells of anger, only hurt. He was injured. Bleeding. But it was not her delinquent behavior that upset him. It was her determination to hurt him.

She'd succeeded.

Shame overwhelmed her as she took in the damage she'd done. What was happening to her? She wasn't a cruel person. She certainly wasn't a violent one. The surface damage was only the start of his pain.

Swells of emotion bombarded her. He craved her compassion, her approval, and her rejection injured him more than any physical wound ever could.

"Stop," she whispered. "You're trying to make me feel bad."

"I'm doing no such thing."

But he was. She had an empathetic link to his feelings and they were killing her. "Knock it off. I feel you inside of me."

His hold loosened. "I'm hardly touching you."

But he was in her. There. With her thoughts. Present in every nerve. Stroking parts of her she couldn't picture from places she didn't know how to locate.

A strange scent met her nose. *Arousal.* Hers and his.

Shifting under his hulking build, she tested his hold on her. She was hardly restrained, yet he'd tamed her with little effort as he straddled and pinned her to the floor. A purring growl murmured from both of them.

"Get off of me."

"Do you think I can't detect your desire, little one? I know what you want. Your stubbornness is costing you."

She struggled beneath him but he didn't budge. The hard press of his arousal weighed on her stomach. She recalled how deeply he'd filled her the last time he was inside of her.

"You're doing this on purpose."

"No. I'm doing nothing. Everything you're feeling is your own body trying to communicate a need. You should listen."

Her jaw locked and her thighs pressed tight, her sex practically weeping for him to take her.

"My body's yours, Delilah. I freely offer whatever you need." He looked down at her like he planned to consume her, and she resented the effect his desire had on her.

She wanted to be strong. Powerful. Independent and in no need of him whatsoever.

Then she noticed the deep gouge by his eye. Concern tore at her heart when she realized how deeply she'd cut him. Ashamed, she tried to roll away but, again, he held her down.

"It'll heal. Your distance wounds me more than anything else."

How, after everything he'd done to her, could he still cause such an unwelcome ache in her heart? She didn't want to feel sorry for him or attracted to him or anything else. She only wanted to be rid of him, but even the brief thought of leaving him spiked a terrible sense of panic inside of her. How could she possibly feel so many contradicting things for someone she hated?

Fuck, desire was literally building and burning in her loins. *Loins!* What the fuck did that even mean?

"We're one, *pintura.* Your needs are mine, just as mine are yours. Your pleasure's my pleasure. Your hunger my hunger. It's futile to fight such a connection. There's no severing what God has forged, so why not accept it and stop fighting what your body so obviously needs?"

She didn't want to hear about his God. When he wrapped their circumstances up in some biblical bow, it excused him, placing all accountability on some cosmic force. But this was his doing, his fault. She hated that he'd done this to her without giving her a choice, and if she stopped fighting him it would be too much like she was giving up on herself.

Life as she knew it was gone. Her shop, her friends… Would she ever see Lance and McGuire again? They were the only family she had. He took them from her. He took everything from her.

And now she wanted to hurt him. "I don't need anything from you."

The gash at his eye stopped trickling blood, the wound sealing shut without a stitch or even a tissue to stop the wound from gushing. "You'll always need me, *pintura,* and I you."

She glared up at him. "Do you think you're the only warm body—"

He growled and jerked her knees wide, shifting quickly to stretch them around his thighs as he pressed the bulge of his cock against her sex. "I'll warn you now, the males of our species are extremely territorial with their mates. You do *not* want to anger the beast that hides within."

"I'm not afraid of you," she rasped, voice trembling.

"When it comes to you and other males, you should be. I'll kill any male who thinks to lay a finger on you."

"Not so virtuous now, are you?"

"I warned you, I'm an immortal before all else, and there is nothing more sacred than an immortal's bond to his mate."

But an addiction to someone was not the

same as love. If he truly cared about her, he would let her go. She almost said as much, but that would start the whole cycle over of how he couldn't live without her so he couldn't let her go, and blah, blah, blah… They were going in circles.

This argument was endless and making her head ache. "Get off."

"Is that what you truly wish?" The wounds on his flesh had closed, the skin mended as if it were never torn. His voice turned to gravel and the scent of his desire intensified. "I could give you what you really want, *pintura*. I could make the ache disappear."

Her breath caught and her sex clenched. The temptation was real. But her stubborn refusal to cooperate forbade her from accepting his offer, no matter how much it enticed her.

Part of her wished he would just take what he wanted and take the damn choice out of her hands.

Wait… No. That was all wrong.

She didn't want him. He was an asshole. So, if he could just shove himself inside of her—

No, no, no! What the fuck was wrong with her? No sex. He was evil. Gross. Horrible. She hated him. Hated everything about him.

Well, there were some appealing parts. But most of him was crap. "

He ground his cock against her and she moaned before she could stop herself, softening right under his horrific touch. Where were these raging hormones were coming from?

Clueless about immortals and ovulation, she could only assume this was one more vampire thing.

Her lips pressed tight to prevent any sort of begging from accidentally slipping out. Bending low, he dragged his nose up her throat and whispered, "All of your frustration could go away if you just say the word."

A whimper filled her throat. He wouldn't break her.

The thick weight of his cock nudged her sex through the thin fabric of her chemise. She was slick and ready for him. Starved and needy.

"I…" She squinched her face tight.

"Say it," he dared, licking up her throat and nibbling her ear. "Try to tell me you don't want me inside of you."

She wouldn't. Couldn't. It was like there was some sort of truth serum controlling her vocal cords.

He shifted her wrists, transferring her arms above her head in an unbreakable grip. With his free hand, he fisted the front of her chemise and stared at her.

Her breath quickened. She wanted him to tear the barrier away and give her what she needed. Just take it so she didn't have to be the weak one to give up her position and surrender.

"If it must be this way, so be it." The material pulled tight and her desperation mounted. "Last chance, Delilah. Tell me no."

She said nothing as her mind screamed *do it!*

The fabric tore open with one hard tug, exposing her bare breasts and amping up her desire. His hot palm cupped her possessively, his thumb tracing over the ball of her piercing and teasing her flesh into a taught and needy point. She arched into his hold, a deep moan escaping her throat, as she silently begged for his mouth on her.

Her body was such a traitor!

"I hate you." Unsure if she was speaking to him or herself, she closed her eyes and let him have his way. He captured her pierced nipple, sucking forcefully as heat pulled at her core.

He was right. There was no use fighting him. But that didn't assuage her guilt.

Her conscience relentlessly beat at her, shaming her and disrupting whatever pleasure he tried to give. She couldn't stand on two sides of an argument. Where was her self-respect? This man ruined her life, and she was giving herself to him without a fight.

"Look at me, Delilah."

When she opened her eyes, tears blurred her vision. His hold on her gentled and he caressed her cheek. It was too much, too intimate. A tear fell and she closed her eyes, turning away.

He caught her face in a delicate grip and said, "No. Your pain is my pain. There's no hiding it. And why should you, when I'm responsible for so much of your sorrow?"

She didn't want his sweet apologies or his remorse. She wasn't ready to forgive him. She just wanted him to distract her from this forced reality long enough for her to find her strength again.

"Sweet, beautiful Delilah. You're entitled to feel everything you're feeling. There's no shame or secrets between mates."

Her head shook. This wasn't what she'd wanted. He'd used his body to get close to her, and now he was turning everything around. She searched for her anger, but it had faded into mist. He'd done the unthinkable. He didn't deserve forgiveness. So why was her resolve weakening?

"I'll spend eternity making amends to you, *pintura.* I swear it, by my God and whatever deity you choose. Let that be my most sacred vow to you."

"Please stop…" She just wanted to hate him. He was her enemy.

"I'm never your enemy, Delilah. I've lived nearly three centuries and made a lot of mistakes, but hurting you is by far my greatest regret. Taking away your choice was an inexcusable oversight. I didn't think about your dignity or how deeply my high-handedness would violate your independence. It was a terrible, selfish mistake with a far-reaching consequence that has hurt you deeply, and I am truly sorry for that."

Sadness enveloped her. His apology was a balm to her heart but it did not reverse his actions. Her situation would not go away tomorrow or the next.

"You regret hurting me, but not the result?"

He didn't need to say anything. She understood, no matter how much he regretted upsetting her, how deeply he hated the consequences of his actions, he would only do the same thing again if he had the choice.

"How is that supposed to make things better?"

He lowered his forehead to her chest, chastised and weak with shame. "I don't know."

Quietly, he slid off of her and helped her right her clothes as best she could. The gown was torn beyond fixing, so she drew the edges together like a robe.

They were a mess, sitting on the floor, covered in blood, neither looking at the other. "I won't be some old-fashioned wife-mate, or whatever the right term is. I hate uniformity. The idea of wearing the same clothes as everyone else guts me. I can't live like this, Christian."

"You're immortal now. You can survive almost anything."

"I mean mentally. I'll die inside. Do you want that?"

He looked at her through a glassy stare and rasped, "No."

"Can we go somewhere else?"

He hesitated and she sensed he was hiding something. "Other immortals aren't like us. The risk is too great. It's why we fled centuries ago. They're lawless and dangerous, even to their own kind. There is no loyalty. Here, we're safe."

Because there was nothing. Life would be a

monotonous cycle of boring obligations. Her individuality was already getting stripped away after only a few days.

"I can learn to accept the immortal stuff, but I don't know that I'll ever accept living an Amish life."

"Then we'll break the rules. Whatever I have to do to get you to willingly stay. My sole duty is to protect you. It's safest here. I'll do what I must."

"What rules?"

"Ribbons for your hair instead of pins. The bonnet is necessary to protect us from the suspicions of outsiders, but while you're in the house, I'll make an exception. My mother frequently removes hers."

His offer was sweet, but a far cry from the life she lived four days ago. "I need more than ribbons, Christian."

"I could introduce you to the new transitions—females, around your age. They were mortal too. I heard that one male allows his mate to listen to music. She has a device that plays records. And Dane, my half-brother, he's part mortal."

"The guy from the other day?"

"Yes."

"He's not like the rest of you?"

He shook his head. "No. But his genealogy leads us to believe that he has a connection to my father."

"Can't you just ask your dad?"

His expression shuttered. The fact that he

would gate-keep anything when he was asking so much of her hurt.

"It's very obvious when you're keeping something from me."

"My father is not a member of The Order. I was raised by my mother alone."

Was that why he flinched when she called him a bastard? "Wait. I thought mates couldn't live apart." She waited for him to explain how his parents could separate, but he remained silent. "Christian?"

"I don't have an explanation for you. All I know is that I won't let you go, *pintura.* Perhaps our bond is stronger."

She decided to choose her battles and let the topic of his parents drop for now, but she intended to get some answers. "I don't want to hear any chauvinistic garbage. If we're truly connected, half of each other's soul, then we're equals."

"Yes."

"I want some pants." Before he could object, she said, "I have two legs just like you. Why should I have to wear dresses?"

"You had a dress on when we met."

"That was different. That was sexy."

He chuckled. "I find it difficult to believe you wouldn't look sexy in a proper gown. You're an incredibly beautiful female, *pintura.*"

Heat bloomed on her cheeks. If she could ignore the guilt, shame, and the sense that she was betraying herself by softening to him, she found a much needed sense of relief. It felt good to let down her guard and just talk. Her body was tense and tired of fighting. Maybe this was just a temporary truce, but it was one she desperately needed.

"What's *pintura*?"

He glanced away, color now tinging his face. "It's Portuguese." His finger traced over the lotus tattoo on her arm. "It means painting."

Well, didn't that fill her with the warm and fuzzies? "Oh."

"When I first saw you, I thought... *She's a masterpiece.*"

Fighting a grin, she kept her head down and gently elbowed him. "Thanks."

"It was an honest observation."

Her emotions were all over the place. She took a deep breath and tried to compose herself. "So, can I do any cool tricks like fly or turn into stuff?"

He chuckled. "I'm afraid not. I told you most legends were nonsense."

"Well, what good is being a vampire then?"

"The proper term is immortal. Vampires are...different."

"How so?"

"They're dangerous. They lack self-control."

"The immortals that aren't Amish, are they vampires?"

"Some. Vampires are *feeish*. Called, but unanswered. They drink from the veins of mortals who are not their true mates, and an addiction begins. It mutates the mind. Bodies are drained and... Many tragedies have occurred over the centuries. We formed The Order to prevent such barbarism. Our soul belief is that immortals must answer the call to God, because bonding with a mate is our most sacred act. It is our purpose."

"*We?*"

He frowned, then said, "I told you I came over on the Charming Nancy. I'm considered an elder, and I sit on The Council."

"You mean you make the laws?"

"I enforce them, yes. But I do so because I believe in our way of life, Delilah. I don't recall much about my youth, but I've heard tales of those lawless times. There are elders here much older than I."

"Can the old guys turn into stuff?"

"The *old guys?*" He chuckled, "We *old guys* possess many honed disciplines, but there are also young immortals who have impressive gifts as well."

"Like?"

His hand lowered and rested on the floor, his palm turning up and his fingers opening. He waited for her to take the offering. Only when she set her hand in his did he continue. "There's telekinesis, telepathic touch, scent memory, tracking, fear inducement, projecting hallucinations, the ability to drain another's energy or provoke paralysis, gravitation, and a few others."

"Holy shit."

He glanced at her, and she felt a mental stroke, sort of like a featherlight touch across her mind, and she knew he was reprimanding her for her language.

"Is that how you do that?"

"What we share, that internal communication, is a result of our bond. Disciplines are slightly different."

"What can you do?"

He buttoned up.

"Seriously? You're not gonna tell me?"

"I only hesitate out of habit. It's not wise to share your abilities."

"Even with your mate?"

His eyes darkened and in a hoarse whisper, he said, "No, with your mate you share everything."

She waited, but he divulged nothing. "Well?"

"Are you my mate, Delilah?"

She withdrew her hand from his. "You set me up for that."

"My intent wasn't malicious. I only want to know how you think of me."

She lifted a shoulder and shrugged. Breaking the intense eye contact, she plucked at her finger, pulling a piece of skin back until it bled. The flesh sewed back together right before her eyes. *Freaky.*

"No one could ever love you as much as your mate, *pintura.*"

"Don't say things like that. You don't know me well enough to love me or to even decide if I'm lovable. I'm still pissed at you. I don't know if I'll ever fully forgive you for taking away my life. All of my friends..." Her vision blurred. "My apartment…" Her voice broke. "My shop."

A tear slipped past her lashes, and this time when he pulled her close to comfort her, she allowed it. Despite him being the cause of her heartache, he also seemed the greatest comfort. For reasons she couldn't comprehend, hugging Christian felt better than hugging anyone else —and that royally pissed her off.

"You're allowed to be angry with me, little one. I'm angry with myself."

There was no easy solution, no escaping her new reality. No going back to the way things were.

She was some mutated genetic thing that she didn't understand. And she was going to have to drink blood. Her stomach lurched and she sobbed into his shoulder, using his shirt as a rag for her snot and tears. He at least owed her that much.

"I'll make this right, Delilah. Somehow, I will make this bearable for you."

She sniffled and nodded but could think of no solution after everything he'd explained. He stole from her. He stole everything. Nothing could reverse his crime, especially because while he may regret the consequences, he didn't regret his actual actions.

He kissed the top of her head. "I think we—" His words cut off abruptly and he tensed.

She looked up at him. "What's wrong?"

"It's my—" A thunderous pounding rattled the front door. "—mother."

She jolted upright. "Your mother's here?"

The banging rattled the walls, and he scrambled to his feet, helping her off the floor. "Yes. I'm sorry. I need to let her in before she breaks our house."

"What should I do?"

She'd never seen him so frantic. "There are clean shifts in the drawer. Please, wait here until I have a chance to speak to her."

It was strange how easy it was to obey him. He was there and then he wasn't. She was completely alone. Her gaze went to the dresser, then the window, then the door.

CHAPTER 8

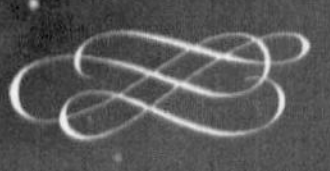

Christian yanked open the front door, and his mother burst in like a fast-moving storm cloud. She flung off her bonnet and tossed it on the table in the hall.

"*Four days?* Four days you've had your mate here, and you didn't tell me? I had to find out from Eleazar! What kind of son doesn't tell his mother he's been *called?*"

"Mother, I—"

"All of you males are the same, thinking only of yourself. Did it ever occur to you that I might *want* to meet this woman who will be joining our family for eternity? That I might have some parting words for you before you complete the bond?"

He flushed, mindful of the floor creaking overhead. "You do realize my age."

"You're still my son." She pointed a sharp

finger toward the second floor. "And that female will be my daughter. We're to be a family, and I will not have you denying my seat as matriarch. I find it incredibly selfish that you would hide her away all for yourself!"

"Are you finished?"

"I don't even know her name! You never even mentioned you were dreaming! When did you become so deceptive?"

"Mother—"

"I raised you better than that. Families are supposed to—"

"Hi."

His mother stilled and turned toward the stairs. Delilah stood at the top wearing a chemise and his baggy black shirt tied at the waist.

"Oh." His mother smiled. "I'm Adriel, Christian's mother."

"I'm Delilah."

She was a vision, a rebellious heathen, and he wanted to take her right there on the stairs. Pin her down as she tussled wildly beneath him, only calming when he slid into her. He would be the only male to tame her.

His body hardened and his mouth curved upward at the sight of the dark, insubordinate waves falling around her face and shoulders.

"Christian, control yourself," his mother scolded then softened her voice. "Delilah, won't you come down and sit with me while I visit?"

She glanced at him and hesitated. Her face

was clean, unlike his own, and despite her attire, there seemed a demure air about her he hadn't noticed before.

He gave her a slight nod and she took a slow step forward. "Sorry about the way I'm dressed—"

"Nonsense, you're at home. You should be able to wear whatever makes you comfortable."

Delilah smiled. It was perhaps the most beautiful smile in the entire world. Her relief was evident, and Christian appreciated his mother's ability to put her at ease.

When Delilah reached the lowest step, his mother took her hands and smiled. "Well, look at you." She glanced back at Christian. "Lovely." Then she frowned. "Why are you such a mess?"

If he had known she planned to visit he would have had a chance to clean himself up. "We had a mishap."

His mother's eyes narrowed on the dried blood marking his face. She looked back at his mate and studied her for injuries, but found none. She grinned. "You're a fighter. Good. The males around here need to be challenged."

They entered the den and sat. Typically, the female of the house would bring refreshments, but that would all come in time. Reluctant to leave his mother alone with his mate, he made no such offer.

"Christian, I'm thirsty," his mother said pointedly.

"Mother—"

She raised a sharp red eyebrow, barring any further argument. Right.

He stood. "Delilah, would you like to give me a hand?"

"We're visiting. I'm sure you can manage on your own."

His mother could be an unflinching and intimidating female. Concerned for Delilah, he pressed into her mind and sensed insecurity. Leaning down he kissed the top of her head. "I'll be right back."

He quickly went to the kitchen and gathered glasses and a pitcher.

"How do you like the farm so far, child?"

"I haven't really been out much."

Christian hurried to clean his face with a damp cloth.

"It's been four days. Surely Christian's shown you around the land by now."

"I haven't been permitted to leave."

"Permitted?"

Cursing under his breath he quickly lifted the tray and rushed back into the den. His feminist mother looked irate.

"Christian, why has Delilah not been *permitted* to leave the house?"

Flustered, he filled a glass of water and handed it to his mate. Then shoved another in his mother's direction, nearly splashing it over the rim. "Your water, Mother."

"Perhaps if you offered her proper attire, she wouldn't feel so restricted to the house."

"We've hardly had time—"

"Pish! Don't feed me that pile of manure. We can build a barn in a day. I'm certain we can clothe one tiny female in less."

"My concern was completing the bond and getting her here safely."

"Yes, yes, you males must always claim what's yours lest someone else come along and steal it." She shook her head and tsked. "Don't be like your father." She lifted the pitcher and filled a glass.

His patience stretched thin, and he lowered his voice, "I'm nothing like him."

He filled another glass and handed it to Delilah. "You're thirsty, *pintura*. Drink." He gave a slight nudge of compulsion to avoid any argument in front of his mother. His mate still couldn't perceive such subtle influences and she was near dehydration. The water was necessary.

His mother raised a brow, studying them, as she sipped from a glass. "It seems to me—"

"Remember yourself, Mother. I'm not Eleazar, and this is not Council Hall. This is my home. My family."

She drew back. "Am I not a part of this family?"

Tension sizzled between them. She knew family law prohibited her from meddling in their affairs, yet she did so anyway, spoiled by Eleazar's endless indulgence of her progressive views.

"Christian," Delilah set down her empty

glass, interrupting the tense moment. "I think your mother—"

"My mother needs to remember her place and that I am not a boy. I'm the head of this family and an elder of The Order."

Adriel scoffed. "And what am I, Christian?"

The female had too much pride for her own good. "You're a guest in my home."

She bolted to her feet. "I'm your mother, the cause of your existence, and I deserve some respect."

He leaned closer, lowering his voice to a growl. "You're making a spectacle. You intentionally forget your place to make my life more challenging. I do not need additional obstacles right now."

"Yes, *Let the woman learn in silence with all subjection.*"

He recognized the verse. "Quoting scripture only further validates my point. You're upsetting my mate."

He sensed Delilah's unease as the tension thickened.

Adriel bristled and stepped back. "Well then, I believe our visit is over. My apologies for any upset I might have caused, Delilah."

"Oh, it's really fine—"

"I'll walk you out." Christian caught her arm, steering her toward the front door. Jaw locked, he growled, "You will not turn my home into a place of rebellion."

His mother yanked her arm free from his grip and glared at him. "The Bible is a book,

Christian. It's full of stories. *This* is reality. If you want a love that can survive an eternity, then you need to look outside those dusty pages and see with your heart."

He understood she only meant to advise him, but she humiliated him as well. Just as she'd done countless times in his youth when she carried on, preaching against the word of God until the elders ordered her disciplined with a rod, an act that brought shame not just to her but to their family.

He would not allow her to turn his mating into another uprising. "This is my home. You won't return until you're ready to respect my rules."

"And which rules will they be? Will she bring forth your children in sorrow, as the Good Book says? *'Thy be thy husband's desire, and he shall rule over thee'*, is that how you imagine your reign as master and mate?"

Seething, his jaw locked. Had any other elder heard such blasphemous talk, she would have been whipped again.

"The bishop's tolerance of your endless defiance has spoiled you. Speak out of turn in my house again, and I will report your actions to The Council." He pointed toward the other room where Delilah waited. "That is my *mate*. It was one thing when your rebellious ways embarrassed me, but I will not let you hurt her with this nonsense. Do you understand?"

She glared up at him, grave indignation rolling off of her in waves. "I understand."

He snatched the bonnet from the table and handed it to her. "Your *kapp*."

She looked down at the offensive accessory with palpable disdain. It was a symbol of submission, and her retrieval of the item a display of obedience.

Whenever his mother had been reprimanded in the past, she'd been disciplined in Council Hall, publicly flogged before the elders and males, and he'd been forced to watch so that he understood there could be no mercy when it came to protecting their ways, even against the slightest uprising.

His mother never cried. She would watch the elders in silence, blocking her thoughts as the lashes rained down, but her eyes said everything. No matter how many times they tried to discipline her, she would never be like the other dutiful females on the farm.

Her rebellious reputation impacted him in many negative ways over the centuries, branding their family as outcasts for years on end. He would not allow her actions to ostracize Delilah as well. While he'd adapted to a reclusive life, his mate would need more. She deserved more, and he would see that she got it.

His mother's shorn red hair disappeared under the bonnet and she lifted her chin. "You will let me say my piece before I go."

This quarrelsome behavior was confusing for his mate. He just wanted her gone. Steering her onto the front porch, he said, "Speak."

"Any fool can claim a female, Christian. But it

takes a male of honor to claim someone's heart. Do not make the same mistakes your father made or you will find yourself alone. Try to consider how foreign this must be to her. Everything you do has a direct effect on your relationship and her trust. You'll always be bigger, stronger, older, and more powerful. If that's not assurance enough for your ego, that's *your* issue, not hers. Relationships require compromise. If you don't bend, I *promise* the bond you share with her will break. God controls many things, but a female's will is her own."

"I don't want you involving yourself—"

She held up a hand. "Yes, you were perfectly clear in your dressing down of me. Just remember this, we have but one mate in this life. I hope your experience is better than mine."

She was gone before he could muster a response and that was probably for the best.

His mother had no qualms when it came to judging others but ambivalently kept her own shameful past hidden from view. She might have experience and sage advice, but she also had a habit of projecting. He was not his father. How could he be, when he had no memory of the male?

He entered the house and found Delilah slinking up the stairs. "Where are you going?"

She tensed but didn't pivot.

"Delilah?"

When she faced him, her expression wore a riot of emotion. "You didn't have to talk to her like that."

He frowned. "It's not appropriate for her—or anyone for that matter—to interfere in the affairs of a mated couple. There are laws."

She sighed. "Christian, I don't have parents. My grandmother raised me, and she passed away when I was twenty. So many times in my life, I wished I had just one parent to go to when I was confused or scared."

"I'm not a seventeen-year-old child," he reminded.

"No, but you'll always be her son. Maybe at your age you don't feel the need for guidance. Maybe it's a cultural difference I don't understand, but I think she was only trying to help. And to be honest, I wanted her help. You can't be my only source of knowledge around here or I'll never catch up. I don't like gatekeepers, and I don't like the way you just spoke to your mother."

"You're disappointed." His desperation to have her see him in a favorable light had him rethinking his words and actions.

"I'm a lot of things—mostly, I'm confused and scared."

Fearful he might have been too rigid with his mother, he crossed the foyer to comfort his mate, but she held up a staying hand.

"I just want to be alone right now."

Her rejection sank through him like cold poison constricting his veins. There was no deceit in her mind, only mental fatigue and worry. "There's no need to worry."

"That's where you're wrong. You should be worried too, Christian."

A prickle of fear teased up his spine. "Why?"

"Because I'm me and you're you. No matter what brought us to this point, I don't belong here."

CHAPTER 9

$\mathcal{A}$driel paced in front of the bishop's grand fireplace, venting her fury. "You didn't hear him, Eleazar. He reminded me so much of his father, so absolute and arrogant."

"Adriel, you should not have interfered. You know that. Family law states—"

"You males and your family law! I am so tired of hearing that used as an excuse. How can you even justify such rubbish after learning what Silus did to your wife?"

The bishop's eyes narrowed and his mouth formed a hard line across his face. "Christian is not Cerberus or Silus," he growled. "I know what my wife suffered, and I corrected the situation, much like I fixed yours. Do not mention his name again in my house."

"I'm sorry. You're right." She should not have brought up such a fresh and painful subject involving his new mate. She was angry and scared for her son. "But what if Christian's more like his father than we realized?"

"Your son is a good and honorable male, Adriel. He's done nothing to make me believe otherwise. If he's struggling, it's only because he's finding his way. There are centuries between him and his mate. Of course, it will take time. He's adjusting."

"He hasn't let her leave the house."

"Because she tried to run."

"And why do you think that is?"

"I understand you're only trying to help and you care for the young female's well-being, but do you honestly believe your son would harm his mate?"

She recalled the blood on her son's temple and the way his mate deferred to him so meekly. The young female had markings on her hands that told Adriel she was of a modern time. Her behavior didn't match her appearance, but the blood covering her son might explain why.

"Not all men possess limitless patience, Eleazar."

"He's not Cerberus. You raised him. Believe me, his bullheadedness is of your line, not his father's. He will not hurt his mate."

"How can you be so sure?"

Her mind traveled back a lifetime, to a place she would never forget, a place that existed long before they arrived in the colonies and made their pilgrimage from Philadelphia, a journey she never assumed she'd live to see.

Three hundred years later, she still feared she was in the calm before the storm and her mate would eventually find her.

"You're letting fear influence your thinking, Adriel. Perhaps you should pray."

While the steadiness of prayer could center her at times, it would not help her son. These initial moments between mates were crucial and delicate. "He needs guidance."

"Do you also plan to hold his prick whenever they copulate? Really, Adriel, Christian's three centuries old."

Centuries could not dull the shock of what Cerberus had done to her. She shivered at the memory of her mate's palm striking her down, his heavy fists hammering into her, and the ruthless crush of his manhood tearing into tender, virginal places.

"Only a male could find humor in such things." She turned and sniffed. "There's a fire in that girl. I sensed it. Christian might have banked the flames of her impetuous nature, but she's a far cry from the domesticity he was expecting."

"They all are."

"Your situation's different. You're the bishop, and your mate was born immortal."

"That does not excuse me from shock. My wife and I share a four-and-a-half-century age gap. I performed her baptism. Believe me, she was not what I expected."

"But you were pleased. What if Christian isn't happy with God's choice?"

"When the dreams started, I refused to accept her as the other half of my soul. I assumed there had to be some sort of mistake. But I was the mistaken one. Larissa's my perfect match and the other half of my soul. She challenges me in ways I need to be challenged, and I do the same for her."

She studied him for a long moment, noting all the ways he'd mellowed since mating with the young female. "You're less irritable since bonding."

He raised a brow, not commenting on the obvious reasons why that might be, but he also said, "Larissa has convinced me that I am not needed everywhere at once."

She chuckled. "But however will you maintain your omnipotent authority, Eleazar?"

"Very amusing, Adriel. In truth, it's been... peaceful. When I shut the world out, my evenings belong to my family alone. They deserve my full attention, and I'm finding I truly enjoy spending my evenings alone with my daughter and mate. The Order is large and some nights the intrusive noise can be endless. Now that I've gotten into the habit of turning down my sensory in the evenings, I'm able to focus on what matters most—my family. We're...happy."

"Then I'm happy for you. As a mother, you have to understand why I want the same for my son."

"Have faith. Christian and Delilah will realize the perfection of their bond in time."

It was a nice fantasy he painted, one of flawless divination, but if that were always true, how did he explain the cruelty she experienced at the hands of her called mate?

Moving to the window, she stared off in the direction of her family's land. "I want them to be happy."

"Happiness is an American notion that has nothing to do with survival and procreation."

She glared at him over her shoulder. "Shut up."

He chuckled. "Adriel, they will find their way. Give them time and a little grace."

She thought of her son's gentle side. It had been a long time since he showed any sort of susceptibility. Like his father, Christian despised appearing weak. "Love is vulnerable. It weakens us and leaves us open to pain and injury."

Her mind went to her mate. The cruel bastard had meant to punish her for reasons she still didn't understand, conditions far beyond her control. He never loved her, but he believed he owned her and he resented the meager care she required.

"Christian's stronger than you realize, Adriel. He might be the youngest elder on The Council, but he's patient and wise beyond his years. Give them space to work through their trials. Have faith that you raised an honorable male. I say this to you, not because you're my friend, but because Christian is also one of my most trusted confidants. I would not assign such a label to someone I didn't trust to act honorably in all things."

Her eyes closed. Eleazar was right. Her son was a male of honor and morality. He would not cross that line.

So much past trauma had come to the surface since discovering Dane was Christian's half-brother. Adriel struggled to take comfort in the illusions that once made her feel safe. And her worry for her own safety was infecting her thinking. "Has there been any word from your informants overseas?"

"Nothing yet."

She wrung her hands in her apron. "He's not there. I can feel it in my bones. I sense his closeness."

"He's had centuries to consider his actions. Perhaps he's learned his lesson."

She shivered, recalling the way her mate screamed when they tore off his limbs. Those horrific howls had haunted her for a hundred years. It had been a long time since the memories stopped, but since learning of Dane's heritage, she'd been on edge.

"It weakens me to guard my thoughts so diligently." She feared letting down her guard for even a second, unsure how close Cerberus was to her at any moment. "If he finds that mental thread, he'll find me." Perhaps he already had. Dane was of her mate's seed and the boy never lived more than ninety miles from the farm.

"The Order will protect you," Eleazar reminded, but she'd heard similar promises before.

"If he finds me, I can only hope he kills me once and for all. I'll never live through that again." She couldn't.

"He won't find you." More empty promises.

Two centuries older than Eleazar, Cer had abilities far beyond any other immortal of that time. Matings were not so organized in those days. There were no ledgers of record, no ceremonies of commitment. Once males were called, they hunted and took what was rightfully theirs without question.

Adriel dreamt of her mate years before he laid claim to her life. The dreams were clear but sporadic. Sometimes months would pass without a single vision. She'd resented the time it took him to find her, but looking back she wished it had taken longer.

Once Cerberus claimed her, she never saw her family again. She'd give anything to have those final moments back, but they were long gone, lost in time, and faded beyond recognition from her memory.

Recalling Cerberus's long wavy hair and piercing amber eyes, she shivered. Adriel had been such an idealistic and gullible girl, so naive to the oppression of claimed females during those times.

She'd anticipated her mate's arrival with great hope. Foolishly fluttering about the village, woolgathering, she anxiously waited for her true mate to arrive, thinking she was better than the other females, privileged beyond measure because God had chosen her for such a fine-looking male. He was to be her greatest love, her savior, and her purpose until the end of time.

"Adriel, come down from there and help me with your brothers," the echo of her mother's call brought a faded vision of the woman who raised her.

Though she couldn't recall the color of her mother's hair or the shape of her face, Adriel remembered the impatience in her voice and the cries of the squalling babes perched on each hip. The children were her siblings, but she had no memories of their names. She was lucky to recall her own name after all she'd endured during that time.

She looked once more toward the open horizon and sighed. "Coming, Mommá."

Lowering from the crossbeam of the thatched roof where she'd been knotting hay into the straw gable, Adriel's feet landed on the dirt ground with barely a sound. She'd been mending the roof since the dreams began, expecting the sight of her mate any day.

Often, she'd imagine him riding into their village on horseback, hair wild and windblown. He'd dismount and come to her, relieved and pleased as he claimed what was his with a passionate kiss.

But it had been a fortnight and there was still no sign of him. She feared for his life, worrying he'd run into some ill-fated trouble on his journey to reach her.

Two winters passed, and the dreams continued. But her hope had withered into worry. Perhaps he'd been displeased or detained. God would not be so cruel as to tease her with an unfulfillable fate. After waiting more than a century for the call, those years had been slow and torturous. She became obsessed with meeting her destiny. If only she'd known...

Then one night, he jerked her from sleep. "Get up, girl."

She woke with a startled gasp "Is it you?" She rose from her pallet, sweeping the mass of red curls from her face.

"Dress and so we may be gone."

She glanced beyond the clay wall where her parents slept soundly. Her two brothers curled together like puppies beside her, peacefully, and her five sisters scattered about the floor on makeshift cots made of hay and horse hair. "I must wake my family. They've waited for you—"

Her grabbed her roughly, as if shaking sense into her. "Are you daft, girl? I said make haste." He shoved her toward the door.

Not used to being spoken to in such an abrupt manner, Adriel dressed, deliberately trying to wake the others without speaking. Surely, he did not mean for her to leave her family without a proper goodbye.

After tying her shift, she reached for a basket of items she'd packed months ago and he smacked the belongings out of her hand, knocking the contents to the floor. "You'll have no need for such trappings."

A horrible weight settled in her stomach as he led her from the cottage, the dark shadows of night obscuring their path as her home disappeared from view. She had yet to even braid her hair. He'd given her too much time and then no time at all.

Wanting to cry out to her family to wake them, she looked back as he yanked her toward his horse. She was his to claim, and she did not wish to anger him before even learning his name.

He was her future now. They could visit her family once they completed the bond and settled into a life of their own. But the abrupt exit from the only life she'd ever known was an emotional one.

Tears welled in her eyes, but she fought them back, not wanting him to think her the kind of girl to give in to nonsense. But she was innocent, and her young heart had filled her head with promises that were destined to be broken.

How foolish she'd been to think they might return to the cliffs after mating to celebrate their union. How naive to believe the bonding of two souls would be pleasant.

The heavy vapor from the snout of his steed cut through the cold and she shivered, but her mate offered no comfort as he hoisted her onto the horse. The dark inky sky offered little light as he held her body to his, absconding her into the endless night.

Clouds crossed the moon in silence, tossing eerie shadows over the unfamiliar landscape. After countless miles, they stopped. She assumed they'd rest, but he only made a quick adjustment to the packs, relieved himself and ordered her to do the same, then commanded her to get back on the horse.

Her legs ached and her clothes were damp from the rain. She shivered, frozen to the bone and in need of shelter. "I cannot go any further. It's nearly dawn. We've been riding all night."

"I will not have a helpless mate. Get on the beast. Now."

Her damp shift clung to her trembling body, her bare legs stiff and refusing to move. "The sun will—"

Pain exploded in her cheek. The blow knocked her to the muddy ground, her weak body twisting and her face burning from the force of his open palm.

Her fingers curled into the rain-pocked soil as she spit, unsure if he'd knocked teeth loose. She would never forget the pungent scent of earth and grass against the metallic flavor of her own blood.

It was the taste of shock.

He'd caught her by surprise. For the rest of her life, she'd exist on the edge of anticipation, never quite sure what he was fully capable of, never wanting to suffer the extent of his total cruelty.

Contrite, she rose to her feet and kept her head down.

Without assisting her, he adjusted the saddle-bags. "I have no patience for idleness. Get on the bloody horse."

Adriel's legs wobbled, and her heart pounded erratically. This monster held no resemblance to the hero of her dreams.

Once she seated herself, he climbed up behind her. His thighs swallowed her and his broad chest formed a hard wall at her back. He himself was a prison and she'd never forget the sight of his enormous hands gripping the leather reins in front of her, hands that could break her.

As far as males were concerned, Adriel's understanding only went as far as her father and brothers.

Observing her mate's great size diminished the illusion of her father's magnitude. Her da had always been a looming presence, but he was nothing compared to the cruel giant stealing her away.

Hooves pounded across the wet earth, the quick gallop decapitating her past from her present like a sawing blade separating time. They traveled at a grueling pace for a full day, into the following night. She'd fallen asleep from pure exhaustion, only to be awoken when he yanked her down from the horse.

He took his rights that evening, in an open field with no shelter and barely a word to acknowledge that she was a living-breathing being.

Her cries did not go ignored. Whimpers were rewarded with more cruelty as he ordered her to keep quiet, brutally covering her mouth and viciously cleaving into her. His crushing weight was nothing compared to the paralyzing dread that pulverized whatever hope she held for their courtship.

His possessive claim was clear. She was his to do with as he pleased and he would not tolerate any show of frailty when it came to meeting his needs. He was her master and she, his servant. A slab of meat on the bone, for him to chew up and toss away.

"Open your mouth," he ordered, tearing into his own wrist.

She obediently did as he said and he shoved his wrist between her lips, stretching her jaw.

"Swallow it." Moonlight glinted off his fangs as he glared down at her. "More."

His manhood stabbed into her, pinning her in place as she stared up at him with wide eyes.

"That's enough," he snapped, ripping his arm

away and yanking her off the ground. He fisted her hair, jerking her head aside, as long fangs impaled her throat, and he gorged himself on her blood, drinking until she was dizzy and weak.

She took no pleasure from the act. And when he was finished, he left her trembling in the dirt with her shift pushed up to her waist, blood, mud, and his seed covering her thighs.

She watched the sunrise through silent tears. Under the golden rays of dawn, she counted her bruises, but there was little time to rest or heal.

They traveled for days, riding long into the night. When they stopped for food, he always ate first, saving only his scraps for her, tossing them in her direction as if she were less than a dog.

At night, he would take her body and blood again, slaking his hunger and forgetting to feed her. She feared his touch so much, she didn't mind the hunger pains. But as her body became more battered and malnourished, the longer the bruises took to heal and the weaker she became.

Gentleness drifted out of her world with the force of a tornado. He claimed her body whenever the mood struck and only spoke to her in clipped commands. The moon had waxed and waned, and she still didn't know his name.

He was a beast without a conscience or care for her well-being. When they found lodging, he would sleep for days but never let her out of his grip. And if she disturbed his rest, he'd punish her by rutting into her again.

Some nights he'd grow frustrated with her weakness, but rather than strengthen her with his blood, he'd throw her to the ground. "You lay there!" he'd yell if she tried to get up. "Move and I'll break your legs."

Naked and shivering on the floor, she cowered, grateful when he disappeared to find a mortal whore at the pub below. He'd bring the women back to their bed and make her watch as he took them, showing he was capable of gentleness and affirming that he intentionally showed her none.

It was clear he despised her. The mortal women would coo and smile for their coin, and many times he drained them of life before they were paid. The bodies sometimes rotted for days before he removed them, and she swore their sins left ghosts behind to haunt her for not intervening.

She felt responsible for their deaths. Her conscience couldn't bear the mounting tally of souls they left behind in each village. Sometimes, she suffered his harsh treatment longer than her frail body could endure, simply to save those she could.

The legends of loyalty between called mates were false. He held a limitless disdain for her, proven by his dishonor every day. He never looked kindly on her or spoke with any sort of affection. She lived with a steady ache between her thighs that never had time to heal, flesh that was often more blue than pink, a hunger that never abated, and an unmendable crack within her heart.

She forgot what it was to smile, losing all sense of time and place. She no longer cared where they were going. They never stopped moving.

She tried to remember the soft, clean scent of her baby brother's hair, but as more time passed, those surreal memories began to fade. After several years of him only calling her girl, she found it difficult to recall her own name.

They settled only to move on again, over and over, their untethered existence withered away her sense of self like moths chewing through the fabric of time. She cooked, laundered his clothing, and darned his socks, but no amount of servitude won his favor. She lived in her thoughts, but her mind grew darker every day.

When they finally reached the kingdom of Leon, they settled and he declared it their home, but stillness did not suit him. His pensive stare watched her as if he finally had time to consider that she might be more than an object to serve his needs.

One night, while chewing his food, he dissected her with his eyes. "Why do you not speak, girl?"

Afraid to answer and terrified to stay silent, her unused voice stammered out of her, scratchy and dry. "I... have nothing to say."

"Say your name."

It had been so long, the word did not come easily to mind. "A-Adriel."

He grunted, licking the bits of meat from his fingers and watching her with ill intent. Soon, he would be inside of her, crushing her with his weight and holding her down as she internally screamed. He did not need her name for that, so she didn't see why he asked.

But she wanted his. She needed a word to curse when it came time for her revenge. "W-what... should I...call you?"

His brow lifted, as if surprised she did not know

his title, and then he nodded. "I am Cerberus Maddox."

"Cerberus Maddox," she repeated, testing the word with her tongue. They hardly spoke and she didn't want to forget it.

He pointed to his chest. "Cer," pronouncing the title like sir.

"Cer," she repeated, hoping to satisfy him and earn his kindness.

He pushed his plate aside and opened his knees, reaching into his clothes. "Take off your frock and come here."

Not once did he speak her name after that, so she never understood why he'd asked for it.

They remained in Portugal for several decades, and over time, Adriel settled in. Seeing those of her kind on occasion stirred an insufferable ache for home. But this was her home now.

One afternoon, she spotted a male immortal with hair blacker than a raven's wing and obsidian eyes watching her while she washed clothes. He looked at her—into her—as if he could somehow see the whole of her misery.

Whenever Cer left, she waited for the dark-haired male to return, desperately wanting another look at him. When he finally appeared, she was taken aback by his beauty. His stare pulled her in like the moon draws the tide and she found herself captivated and calmed by his presence.

Who was he and why did he watch her in such a way?

Eleazar.

The name intruded into her mind, jarring her into a fearful state of distress.

Do not fear. I mean you no harm.

Her breath caught. Her mouth framed the word, Eleazar, repeating it without sound. It became a mantra she mentally thought whenever she wanted to escape her reality. For a time, she wondered if he was her destiny, and the life she'd been suffering had been a terrible mistake.

Day after day, he traveled by, always pausing across the thoroughfare and meeting her stare. She didn't know how she could hear him in her thoughts or why she felt so intrigued by him, but something inside of her believed he came to her for a reason.

What's your name, girl?

She recoiled at the term girl, afraid he might know Cerberus, but he quickly confronted her fears.

I only want your name, friend.

She hadn't realized she could communicate in such a way with other immortals. Cer always kept his thoughts closed off to her.

I am Adriel, *she thought, unsure if he would understand her.*

Adriel. *The sound of her name in his voice was a pouring rain after a long drought.*

Her breath hitched and she recalled what hope felt like. She trusted he would continue to visit, continue to speak to her this way, and be her friend.

"What did I tell you about standing by that window?"

Startled to learn Cer had returned, Adriel pivoted, throwing her back to the window so not to ex-

pose her friend. He jerked her away from the wall and threw her to the floor.

"Learn a new trick today, girl?"

Although he did not move a muscle, the house shook. The fire flickered and pottery fell as his menacing scowl darkened.

"How dare you let another male into your head?"

She shook with fear. Where had he come from? How had he known? He grabbed her roughly, throwing her into the table. Plates and bowls shattered to the ground, and he yanked her up only to haul her across the room and throw her down again.

Her head hit the hearth and blood seeped into her eyes. He dragged her up by her hair and shoved her down on the table, pushing up her shift.

"You belong to me." Fabric tore as he wrenched her legs apart. "Your body is mine." Fisting her hair, he slammed her face into the wood. "I own every part of you." Jerking her head close to his mouth, he hissed, "Your mind belongs to me." He shoved her forward, entering her with the brutal intention to punish her. "Your quim. Your thoughts. Your servitude. You're mine, girl. Mine! How dare you let another male speak to you so intimately." His fist came down with bludgeoning force. "Filthy whore!"

Pain engulfed her from the blow as an unseen hand clamped down on her throat. She gasped for air and tried to scream but he strangled her into silence.

"Can't talk now, can you wench?"

Gasping, she choked and clawed at her throat as he brutalized her with relentless force. His vicious attack was beyond any cruelty he'd shown before.

Blood pooled in her eyes as the lack of oxygen burst into apoplexy and her body seized.

If she assumed that was the worst he could possibly do, she was wrong.

After that day, he destroyed whatever was left of her will to live. He delivered a mortal death to her uncountable times, only to bring her back and force her through such torture again.

She never visited the window after that day. Time passed in increments of aching, catatonic consciousness, and battered delirium. She died a hundred deaths at Cer's hand, wishing hopelessly that one time he might waste her completely and life would end.

One evening, as she lay on the dirt floor in a puddle of her own tears and pain, Cer abruptly stood. She flinched and whimpered as he stomped to the door. Her ears had been boxed, making it impossible to hear beyond a muffled whale, but when a lantern spilled and the table splintered behind her she knew trouble had come for them.

Curling into a ball, hoping to be mistaken for dead, she tried to remain calm. Voices roared like thunder as the world fell to pieces around her. She flinched and cried out when gentle hands lifted her from the ground.

"Fica calma, Adriel."

The familiar voice filled her with calm, but her body was too weak to communicate. With her eyes swollen shut and her ears so damaged, she could only trust that the stranger would watch over her.

She awoke in bed, judging the passing of time by

her diminished pain. Her heart shuddered when she opened her eyes and found Cer watching her.

His eyes were blackened sockets and his nose had been broken. He cradled his arm close to his chest as if it had been ripped from the joint. He didn't bother her after that for some time. Together, they watched each other and slept for several days and nights, an unspoken truce between them she did not trust.

When she found the strength to rise, she moved about the home cautiously, keeping to the walls and never stepping within his reach. She dare not grow comfortable in his presence.

It took many nights for him to hit her again and, once he started, he made up for lost time. But the others returned like a band of avenging angels set to rescue her away from that hell.

That was the last night she died at the hands of her mate. He snapped her neck just before the others attacked.

The cool night air chilled her naked skin as gentle arms carried her away. Flinching at the screams in the distance, she only wanted to escape the ugliness of the world.

"Please, let me die."

"Fica calma. *You're safe now."*

Eleazar. He'd come back for her.

Fear choked her as she worried for her friend. Cer would come for her and destroy anyone who tried to stop him. Then he would punish her.

"Easy, friend. He can't hurt you anymore. You have my word and my protection."

She shook, certain Cer would find them. "No." She needed to go back.

"Adriel, you're safe." The lie echoed through her panic. *"Adriel...Adriel? Adriel are you listening to me?"*

Adriel's breath hitched as she blinked at Eleazar, her mind returning from those terrifying memories and taking solace in her safe surroundings and the affirming presence of her dear friend. Only because of his interference was she alive today.

"I apologize, Eleazar. I slipped away for a moment."

"There's no sense in remembering those times."

Her heart pinched. "I'll never forget." It was her duty to remember what that monster was capable of.

The males that rescued her left her mate quartered and buried alive. It would have taken decades for that kind of damage to heal, longer without proper nourishment. And while the males that avenged her believed it would give Cerberus the necessary time to think and repent, she knew him better than anyone. His only thoughts would be toward revenge.

She smiled at Eleazar. "Nor will I forget what you did for me, my friend." *My savior.*

"Leave the past in the past, Adriel."

A year ago, she would have agreed, but now things were different. "My mind will not rest until I'm certain he can't find me."

Dane was proof that Cer was still alive and, once again, strong enough to litter the immortal population with his tainted seed. He likely had several bastards roaming the earth, but she could never consider her son his. Christian was an honorable male. She raised him as her son alone, and Cerberus could not know he existed.

Eleazar was the only one who knew the extent of the evil her mate had put her through. He had nursed her back to health, diligently worked to mend her mind, and taught her many disciplines that made her stronger than most female immortals. He promised her a new life, in a new world.

Eleazar sighed. "Adriel, I know you are frightened. But if Dane's life is any indication, Cerberus has been free for at least two decades and has yet to find you."

"Dane was in Jim Thorpe when we found him, Eleazar. That means Cerberus has been close to here. What if he's simply biding his time?"

"I don't believe that's the case. If he wanted you, he would have collected you by now." Hesitating, he chose his words carefully. "He would know your blood, Adriel. Cerberus is strong. Stronger than any male I've ever met. But no one is unstoppable. We outmatched him before and we'll do it again if need be. You're safe here. This is your home."

"He could surprise us—"

"We'll sense him coming. You forget, when we buried him alive, there were twelve of us. Now, there are hundreds on your side. The Order will protect you."

"Like you've protected that witch downstairs?"

His head snapped up. "Who told you about that?"

"Do you know who it is? Or should I ask, do you know who *they* are?"

His scowl darkened. "Do *you*? You trespass in more minds than I."

She wouldn't apologize for eavesdropping. It was sometimes the only way to protect herself and stay informed. Most of the males preferred to keep the females completely in the dark. "I have my suspicions. The younger males aren't involved. Whoever's hurting that girl is more than capable of guarding his thoughts, that tells me he's at least a century old. Whoever it is, they have to be punished."

"They will be. Regardless of her crimes, the plebe is under our protection."

Their archaic tactics only proved how unsafe females truly were. Not much had changed from when Adriel was young and taken in the middle of the night in the presence of her entire family.

While her Amish lifestyle protected them in terms of privacy, it left them vulnerable in many other ways. "Eleazar, I want a firearm."

He tensed. "No."

"But if I—"

"The answer is no, Adriel, and that is final."

"I am completely helpless here. I—"

"Think of what you're asking. It goes against everything we believe to use a firearm in self-defense. Rifles are for hunting and hunting alone, and our species has no need for such things."

"I've watched you make much bigger concessions, Eleazar. I know you've allowed the new transitions modern comforts that would never be permitted in other sects."

He scoffed. "Those are harmless spoils. Battery-operated musical devices for Annalise and books for Destiny. You're asking for a weapon. It's out of the question."

"I would not use it unless I needed it."

"Weapons wound, Adriel."

"Cerberus wounds!" she snapped. "He's killed me a hundred times before. I won't let him do it again." She couldn't go back to that weakened state of starvation. He was sentencing her to an endless existence ripped between this world and the purgatory where undead immortals go. "You can't leave me defenseless."

"The answer is no. You're not a defenseless child anymore."

"Who is to say any of my disciplines will serve me when I'm running for my life. Would you truly leave me helpless?"

"You're one of the strongest females I know. You will never be helpless again. You're safe here."

"I don't feel safe." Furious that he would not grant her this wish, she stood. "I'm a lamb waiting for slaughter." She wrung her hands. "He's coming for me, Eleazar. I can sense it."

"Adriel, you're giving him power by—"

"No," she snapped. "I give him nothing. He doesn't need me to make him powerful. He's survived more than any elder on this farm. You're right, I'm not a foolish little girl anymore. I'm wise, and I know exactly what an immortal of his age is capable of. I will not stand meekly by, waiting, while he plans his revenge. This time I'll be prepared. And I'll not go calmly into the night."

"Adriel—"

She silenced him with a cold stare. "Mark my words, Eleazar, I will kill him. I'll kill him so there's no possible way that monster can hurt me or anyone else again."

CHAPTER 10

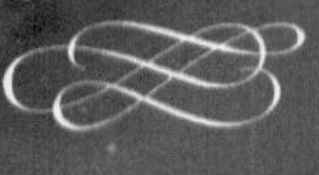

Time didn't pass by unnoticed, it beat over Delilah like a river's tide, shaping her and stripping stains of experience with relentless force. Every gentle lapping stole a piece of her, smoothing her abrasive edges. It didn't hurt as much as she'd expected. It just happened, whether she wanted it to or not.

Inevitable. Christian had claimed it would be so, but she hadn't believed him. She didn't trust him. Yet here she was, adapting and accepting these changes with baffling calm.

Her anger was at odds with the overwhelming threat of acceptance. While she clung to a disgruntled need for retaliation and revenge, another part of her seemed centered and at peace with what was happening.

The new version of herself seemed... cleaner, sharper, healthier, and, for all of those reasons, unrecognizable.

"Ladybug, ladybug, fly away..." she whispered, turning her hand in a golden ray of the setting sun. The small tattoo on her finger was fading at a concerning rate.

The details had vanished leaving a slight blemish on her knuckle. Compared to what it was a day ago, the darkened smear worried her. How many tattoos would she lose? She was afraid to look at her body too closely, afraid she was fading away, disappearing into the ether of time and losing her individuality.

If her identity washed away, would all traces of her existence eventually follow? The permanence of her world didn't matter here. There were powers at play she couldn't comprehend and rules she broke without trying.

Her mind was a mess of chaos, endless spinning vortexes of confusion followed by too many stormy emotions to decipher. She only knew she wasn't happy.

Time alone helped. She needed time to process, and there was so much to digest, she wanted to think things through on her own. Sitting in the privacy of Christian's bedroom, unsure where he'd gone or how long he'd be, she looked at his hat, forgotten on the floor.

Nothing—in terms of possibilities—seemed off the table at this point. Holding her hand out, palm facing the hat, she opened her fingers and held her breath, forcing her energy into her arm, directing all her focus at the crushed hat lying on the floor.

It didn't move.

Disappointed, she blew out a breath. *No Jedi mind tricks.*

She glanced at the door, anticipating his return when she heard a distant creek in the foundation of the house. Perhaps part of her even yearned for his presence, but that couldn't be. She hated him. She was here because of what he'd done to her. He was her enemy.

Her emotions were stronger than usual yet harder to read than ever before. She despised him for doing this to her, yet she recognized a strange connection to him, potent and overwhelming. Her instincts goaded her to trust him, but her mind could not accept what he'd done.

And her heart? The ache was still too tender to evaluate. When she considered all he stole and everything she'd lose because of his selfish actions, the heartbreak consumed her. But just as that overwhelming moment of despair set in, so did unfamiliar relief. Her debt would not follow her here. This could be a fresh start. A do over. Or was it? Was this how anyone would ask to start over? Confusing hope remained tucked away, hidden beneath all the resentment and anger.

She could not possibly harbor gratitude for him, could she? He did this to her, yet some part of her believed she was safe with him, safer than she'd ever been on her own. It made no sense. She preferred to hate him.

Visions of his beautiful face played in her mind, aggravating and thrilling her. Her belly tightened and her eyes narrowed, irritated by her memories of the possessive way he rocked into her earlier that day.

He intended to prove his virility. He had, and now she was deeply torn between attraction and revulsion. Pride forbade her to go easily into the night. She couldn't come this far only to surrender to a man who abducted her and held her against her will.

Yet something baited her to trust him and let him lead. It was an unfamiliar and inexplicable instinct. A complication.

Her mind was changing and that frightened her more than the undeniable evolution taking place throughout her body. Her body was just the packaging. If she lost her mind, she lost all of herself.

Was she losing her mind? What if none of this was real and she was tied up in a padded room and straightjacket somewhere?

Her brain tested every theory from Christian's explanations of legends and fables to the possibility of alternate dimensions. But there was no way of telling which version of the truth was her actual reality.

The sheer volume of new information she needed to process paralyzed her. Incidentally, the overwhelming carnal memories of his body buried inside of hers invigorated her with energy. The itch to have him again burned like a fiery rage, one that grew hotter and hotter with each passing hour.

She craved him like a drug, and like an addict, the effects of not having him started to take a toll. Her skin tingled and her insides pulsed. She paced and worried her lower lip until it bled.

Where was he? She couldn't sense him in her mind. He'd purposely hidden himself from her, and she suffered his absence in ways she shouldn't.

Worrying her hands, she considered that this might be a fight or flight response to the situation. Not knowing where he was or what he was doing filled her with unease. It wasn't personal. She merely wanted to keep an eye on the enemy at all times. He was the enemy. Right?

Or was she actually worried about him? What if something happened to him? What if he abandoned her and she had to figure this stuff out on her own? She'd never make it without his guidance.

Deep instinct promised the moment he returned to her he would bring a sense of calm that could ground her more than any thought or circumstance. Why? How? He was evil. He shouldn't have that kind of power over her psyche.

It wasn't just her psyche. He influenced her entire being. And her body knew it, so her mind wouldn't relent until he soothed this awful tension riding her nerves raw.

She drew in a breath, prepared to call for him, then caught herself. What the hell was she doing? She should be planning her escape. Fuck planning. She should just go.

Glancing at the windows and doors, she questioned which route would be the wisest, only her body felt no compulsion to leave the longer she evaluated her options. There were several escapes, yet ...

Was she actually considering staying here? She could run, find a main road, hitchhike her way into a stranger's car and then—visions of ripping open said stranger's throat flashed through her head and she bit her knuckle.

Dear God, he turned her into a killing machine.

Who knew if she had any self-control? She wouldn't know until she found out. But she didn't want to find out what human jugular tasted like in the process. Her stomach swilled, and she went back to thinking about Christian —a thought less likely to make her vomit.

Once again, she experienced an inexplicable calm at the mere thought of him. Her heart rate dropped and her panic subsided, the chaotic tempo of her blood replaced with a different sort of adrenaline rush.

He was too much man. Too powerful. Too steadfast and determined. Too fixated on having her. Too relentless in his refusal to ne-gotiate what he did not wish to concede. And yet, she remained attracted to him.

How had he worn her down so quickly? He'd cornered her, disarmed her, outmaneu-vered her, and dropped her into an alternate world of sheer confusion. She was outmatched and worn out after just a few days. By the end of the week, he'd probably have the obedient little woman he was hoping for.

The man could make stone malleable. Somehow, he was changing her without fully breaking her. Perhaps that was how he obtained his power. Shatter the victims right from the start so the slightest show of kindness felt like the greatest relief.

Hating that any enemy could have that sort of control over her, her hostile intolerance for the fucker grew. She shoved back any sense of compassion, reminding herself that he ripped her from the world she'd known like a weed plucked from the soil.

Her possessions and friends were nothing to him. Didn't he realize they were everything to her? A cold worry chased through her like a chill. Did her friends even realize she was missing? The guys had sort of ghosted her since she downsized at the shop. Were they truly friends, or merely acquaintances conditionally linked to her life through a job?

As the truth sank in, loneliness consumed her. She had nothing. No one but...Christian.

He wanted her, but she continued to resist. Why?

Then it hit her. He didn't want *her*, per se, he wanted her to fill a role. Well, tough.

She feared if she gave in to him, she'd lose everything. What would be left of her if he got his way? Her eclectic presence was all she had to prove she'd existed in this crazy world, and he was erasing her with terrifying ease and success. She didn't want to lose herself. If she gave in, she'd be giving up on herself just like everyone else had done.

It didn't matter what she wanted in her heart. There was no way to un-ring this bell. She didn't know what the future held, but she knew he'd hold her until the end. But what end?

For an immortal, the end could be a long way away, and she struggled to measure such a length of time, unsure what obstacles his kind faced. If she was ever going to outmatch him, she needed to learn his weaknesses.

Could they regenerate severed limbs? What about decapitation? And suffocation? Could they drown? She had so many questions about life and death, questions she was certain he wouldn't rush to answer.

And why, whenever she pictured harming him, did she suffer a twinge of guilt followed by a soothing caress in the deepest part of her mind? It was like he was there with her, experiencing her chaotic thoughts and weathering the emotional storm with her.

"I know you're listening to me," she said, like a crazy person trapped in an asylum. "I can feel you in my head."

He'd been quietly hiding for hours, but the moment she sensed shame or guilt he chased it with empathy. She didn't want his empathy. What kind of twisted fuck would comfort her for feeling guilty about fantasizing about killing him?

Another stroke along her frontal lobe. She combed a hand over her hair. "Get out of my head! Do you have any idea how off-putting that is?"

Of course he didn't answer.

She'd had lovers in the past where everything revolved around sex and chemistry. This thing with Christian went beyond that. The inexplicable, intense way her body reacted to his, the way her mind catalogued him as familiar when he was still a stranger, the potent need to touch and *mark* him somehow, it overpowered common sense. When it came to him, she had pitiful willpower.

And what did that even mean, *mark him?*

Deep satisfaction that was not her own rolled through her. Some instinctual, animal part of her buzzed with awareness. Her head jerked as her ears and nose actively tried to track him, but he stayed carefully hidden. Silent, like a predator watching its prey and biding its time to attack.

Triggered by the game, she felt the urge to hunt him. She stood, her body taking an agile stance as she prepared to stalk him the way he stalked her.

Instinct directed her actions while she remained fully aware of just how psycho this strange behavior was. Perhaps a padded cell wasn't such a bad idea after all, because as she breathed in the familiar aroma of the house, tracing his scent down to the floor below, she quietly started to purr.

A primal need to rub her body against his—not fuck him per se, actually rub, like a cat seeking attention and affection--drove her harder than any self-preservation ever could. She wanted him to wear her scent and needed to find him for that to happen.

Nearing the door, she considered how crazy she was acting and tried to regain control over her body. She pictured him with another woman, and the purr turned to a growl. Okay, that wasn't the strategy to use. She quickly threw away the thought and squelched the visceral response the image triggered. He was hers as much as she was his. It didn't matter that she fucking hated the bastard.

But did she hate him?

Staggering back from the door, she rushed to the far corner and cowered, gripping her head as she slid down the wall. "What's happening to me?"

Another subtle stroke over her limbic system.

Her spine stiffened as her wild gaze searched the empty bedroom. "Stop. I don't want your comfort!"

Time to toughen up. No more wallowing in self-pity. Fuck his rules and expectations. She didn't need his help. She needed to get the hell out of there and speak to someone who could actually advise her, because she was one-hundred percent positive she was having some sort of mental breakdown.

Paralyzed by indecision, she whimpered from the corner. "Get up," she told herself on an unsteady breath. "Get up and walk out the fucking door."

To hell with her new feline instincts—she'd find someone less scary to rub against.

She could do this. She just had to get up.

But she couldn't. Her panic was too heavy.

Another stroke through her mind and she screamed, raking her hands angrily over her head and messing her hair. "Get out of my head!"

Her breath hitched as a new sensation skipped through her. Fear. But not her own.

She recalled the glint of loneliness she detected whenever he became introspective. No! That was not her problem. Any sensitive side he hid could eat a dick.

She had a life and freedom before he came along. Only an idiot would feel bad for the man holding them captive, and she was no idiot. Fuck him and his fucking farm full of fanged Amish fuckers. She needed to escape while some shred of her true self still remained.

She saw his true colors when he chased out his mother. He was a cold, unfeeling bastard with little patience and extremely stringent expectations. In no universe of mythical anything would she put up with such a chauvinistic prick.

There was no room for hope with a man

like that. People didn't change. And even if he did hide some redeemable traits, a million apologies wouldn't negate the fact that he abducted her and expected her to obey like a domesticated pet. She needed to remember who he was at the bone. And she couldn't forget who she was. She would not let him wash her away.

The door opened and she drew back. She'd let her guard down when she should've been tracking him.

"Such skills take practice. Be patient with yourself, little one. You're only in the infant stages of a transition and you're learning at a rapid rate. It's difficult to discriminate the useful information from the irrelevant."

She resented his calm and patient manner as much as she resented him eavesdropping on her thoughts.

"I know you're upset."

Because he'd been lurking in her mind, not fully disclosing his nearness but always present. So much for privacy. "I asked you to leave me alone."

"We're mated. We're never alone. I'll always be with you. A part of you."

Sometimes, a body rejected a piercing. Delilah had seen it happen. She'd done everything she'd been taught to do, but some bodies saw the intrusion as an infection and naturally pushed it out. She could push him out. If she set her will to the task and focused all of her energy on eradicating all traces of him from her body, she could rid herself of the infection.

He shut the door and sighed. "Delilah, I'm exhausted with the opposition."

He didn't know the first thing about exhaustion. Her combativeness wore her down faster than it could ever fatigue him. She was the one fearing for her life—if she was even technically still alive.

She planned to oppose him on as many things as possible, for the simple principle. She'd make him work for every concession, even the ones she didn't mind. Nothing about this would be easy for him. It was the least she owed herself if she hoped to hold onto a shred of dignity.

"I know you're upset about the way I spoke to my mother, but the woman has spent her entire life attempting to revolutionize the laws that protect her. She was out of line—"

Delilah made a choking sound and gaped at him. "You think this is about your mother?"

"Is it not?"

"You kidnapped me. I could write a book longer than the Bible of all the ways you've wronged me. Your mother doesn't even touch the surface of my first thousand complaints." He was so embedded in his own perspective, the thought of making him see things from her point of view drained her. "I'm thinking of calling it The Asshole Chronicles, *B-T-dubs*."

"Mind your tongue."

"Bite me."

"Don't tempt me."

Her stare jerked to him and her eyes narrowed. "Oh, I bet you'd like that."

"I would."

Energy crackled in the stillness between them and her treasonous body tightened.

He took a slow step closer. "As a matter of fact, I'd like nothing more than to sink my teeth into your flesh—among other things."

His words, paired with that intense silver stare, intoxicated her senses and softened her resolve. Despite her dislike for him, he weakened her desire to disobey by merely existing.

"Y-you just keep your distance." It wasn't fair. Her loyalties should be to herself, yet she physically ached to fulfill his every need and meet his darkest desires. He was a hunger she did not want to feed, an obsession that only grew.

The temptation became inescapable as he held her stare, he took another step closer. "Do you remember how good it felt when I was deep inside of you?"

An intrusive vision of herself sprang to mind. The vision was not her own. It was how he saw her, remembered her during that first encounter, mouth open in the throes of passion as he made her come again and again.

"Stop!"

"But you don't want me to stop, *pintura*. You want me to hoist you off the floor and take you against your protest so you can go on denying what you actually crave. I see your desires. I feel the way your body aches for mine. I smell the sweet honeyed air, rich with the intoxicating fragrance of your arousal. And it's taking every ounce of my self-control not to touch you. If you think it again, I might not be able to restrain myself."

Her traitorous body clenched as more flutters of desire stirred.

"You're picturing it right now, imagining the heavy weight of my cock sinking into you as I bite down on your neck."

"More like the image of circumcising you with a dull, rusty blade."

"You forget how readable you are to me. Your heart's racing because adrenaline's coursing through your veins at the mere thought of my touch. Your body's readying for me as you stew over every truth I share. And its defiance angers you. You can point that outrage at me. I want all of it, *pintura.* There is nothing of yourself that I can't handle. No part of you I don't desire."

"Well, any desire… I mean, *if* I'm feeling…" She didn't have a sharp comeback locked and loaded for once, so she just snapped, "If I'm horny it's not for you, so back off."

He frowned and she heard how dumb her words sounded. Of course, it was for him. He was the sole purpose for her shitty mood and whatever the hell was going on with her body.

Her faculties were in a total uproar at the sight of him, and she had to squirm and clench her thighs together to maintain the slightest composure, which she was quickly losing. "I know you're using mind tricks on me. You're making me feel these things."

"I'm doing no such thing."

Her breath quickened as he took another step closer. Like a cornered animal, she shrank back, searching for an escape while her heart beat against her ribs like a caged hummingbird.

"Passion comes in many forms, Delilah. Your outrage is futile. The bond we share is inescapable. I'm inside of you. I'll always be an irrevocable part of you. If you close your eyes, you'll find me there, with you, deeply embedded in your most secret places. I'll never leave you."

"Go to hell."

"You hate how strong the pull is, but there's no denying it." He lifted his arm, rolling back the sleeve of his crisp white shirt. His claws lengthened. "You can't bear to see me injured." He sliced into his wrist, cutting through delicate tendons and veins.

"Don't!" She sprang to her feet.

"Why? Do you care?"

"No..." Her mind scrambled for a lie. "I just don't like blood."

His eyes narrowed as he considered her statement then his claws retracted. Crimson trickled down his arm, but the flesh already started to heal. "Perhaps a different demonstration then."

He moved to the window and drew back the curtain. "We're on the second story. The fall will likely break a limb or two if I make no effort to land on my feet." He opened the window and pulled himself up to stand on the sill with shocking agility. "Let's find out—"

"*Stop!*" She rushed forward. "You could die."

He shook his head. "Not from a fall. But it would hurt." He glanced out the window at the ground. "I could crack my skull open or break my neck. Perhaps my back."

Her jaw quivered as unease filled her. She didn't want any of those terrible things to happen. "Why are you doing this?"

"You know why—to prove that you have a natural desire to protect me, just as I have a need to protect you. You care about me, Delilah."

Her head shook in denial. "I don't."

He leaned back and flung himself forward.

"*No!* Wait!" She rushed to the window, catching his arm. "*Okay, I care!* Please, just…get away from the window."

He studied her then nodded, hopping off the windowsill. "Do you see now? My pain is as unacceptable to you as yours is to me. Your body recognizes mine. Your soul's naturally carved from mine, a perfect match, the yin to yang, a paradox of polarity so detailed in its finite perfection there's no disputing its rightness. We are irrevocably one, my dear."

Her acceptance wasn't gentle like a gradual tide. It was painful and destructive like a hurricane. The devastation was done. He spoke the truth and nothing could replace all she'd lost. There was no going back.

Twin tears tripped down her face. "Help me," she pleaded, desperately wanting to make sense of too many implausible truths.

He pulled her into his arms and she took shelter in his strength. "It's natural to feel scared, *pintura,* but I'll always be here to protect you."

"I'll never forgive you." She sniffled. "I had a life."

"Careful, little one. Wars are easy to start but extremely difficult to end."

She pushed away from him and wiped her eyes, but the tears kept flowing. "Well, riddle me this, Nostradamus, what happens when a so-called mate refuses to let her other cosmic half touch her?"

"As I said, denial is futile." He pointed to his chest, just below the intersection of his ribs. "It's here, where instinct stems, not the heart or the mind. We have no control over the all-encompassing divination that implanted itself inside of us. It's been there since birth, always germinating, and preparing for the righteous purpose we must fulfill."

If his words were meant to comfort her, they epically failed. She was a holy piece of meat. "So, it has nothing to do with *me* then, just the fact that I'm *'The One'.*" She made air quotes, her detached expression and indifferent attitude the total opposite of the hurt that hid inside.

"You're fulfilling your purpose. As am I."

His words further insulted her as they removed all accountability on his part. He hadn't hit on her because of attraction or desire, she had been a source, an ingredient, a dehumanized puzzle piece he needed so he could form a bigger picture. His apathy landed a lot like rejection, and she hated that his lack of culpability could sting. Not because he'd caused massive upheaval in her life, but because some pathetic part of her wanted him to care —about *her*.

But he didn't. He only cared about his stupid God and their destined bond. And why the hell did she care anyway? He was a psycho. A liar. Not anyone she'd choose.

But how would she survive without him? Even now, despising him as deeply as she did, she scrimmaged with the fear of losing him. Was this Stockholm syndrome?

No, he'd done nothing to endear her. She hated him.

Or did she?

Fuck! He was giving her emotional whiplash.

Every feeling he stirred battled a completely contradicting response. Self-constructed delusions. Artificial symptoms of a link they shared. It meant nothing if they had no real connection and that bothered her. But more than that, it bothered her that it bothered her. She was losing her mind.

"Delilah, there's something I must ask you."

His tone was not taunting or playful, and that scared her. "What?"

"What is…*B-T-dubs?*"

She couldn't help it. She laughed. Her humor was so out of place in that heavy moment that she squealed for breath, tears squeezing from her eyes and a cramp forming in her side. She doubled over, holding her stomach, and let the sound carry her away. It was the perfect outlet.

"Is it a swear I'm not familiar with?"

More laughter poured out of her. The levity of the moment relieved some of the tension, and she was grateful for his curiosity. "It's by the way."

He waited. "By the way…?"

"That's what *B-T-dubs* means—*by the way —B.T.W.*"

His eyes moved as he considered her explanation then he laughed too. It was an endearing sound, one she didn't want to enjoy as deeply as she did.

Their eyes met and they both smiled. The moment softened as time wrapped in an ephemeral cloud—intimate and secure. Just the two of them.

When had he closed the distance? She should step back, but a greater part of her wished to stay. Perhaps she even wished he would come closer.

His hand turned as the backs of his fingers gently trailed down her cheek. The soft pad of his thumb brushed away a tear. "You'll discover there's much to enjoy once you get on with your grief so that we can get on with our lives."

His words knocked the breath out of her and the endearing truce vanished. "Get on with my grief? Is that what you just said to me?"

The mirth in his eyes disappeared when he realized his overstep, but he didn't apologize. "This unnecessary hostility between us has gone on long enough."

"It's been a few days! You stole *my life!*" She shoved his touch away. "And now I'm stuck with you for the rest of my life—which, B-T-dubs, is *eternity,* you insensitive dick!"

His jaw hardened. "Then let's have it."

"Have what?"

He extended his arms as if opening himself up in surrender to a firing squad. "Unburden yourself. Whatever you have to say, I accept. I'll absorb your fury, relieve your fears, comfort your sorrow—"

"I don't want you to do any of that!"

"You don't have to navigate life alone any-more. I'm here to serve and protect you. It's my greatest duty and honor."

She flung the wooden box on the nightstand at him. He dodged the assault and the case smashed into a dozen pieces as silver straight pins rained onto the floor. "Did it ever occur to you that I liked being alone?"

"No," he said succinctly. "Just as it never oc-curred to me that deceit would come so easily to you." His head cocked. "But I don't believe you realize you're lying. I think you've been making these excuses for so long they feel like truth to you. They're familiar, and that familiarity comforts you more than the unknown ever will."

"You don't know shit," she seethed, refusing to show the vulnerability he so precisely exposed.

He crossed the room to stare out the window at the fading sky. This time, if he threatened to jump, she sincerely considered letting him.

His shoulders hunched in a show of fatigue. "The bishop's wife was kind enough to send some gowns over. Had there been civility between us, we could have enjoyed an evening stroll. I now see we're a long way away from that sort of diplomacy and trust."

These were the crumbs meant to manipulate her into cooperation. "You can't buy me."

"I'd never assume to. You're priceless."

"Stop!" She scoffed and held up her hand, looking away from him. "Just...stop. Saying stuff like that only makes me cringe. You don't even know me."

"That doesn't mean I can't comprehend your value."

"I'm not a fucking object! I'm a human being!"

"You're an immortal."

She pivoted, pinning him with a scorching glare. "Wow, you really are clueless. Do yourself a favor and stop talking for a while."

"Or what?" He fully faced her. "You'll eventually tire of waging this unwinnable war. How many more vengeful promises will you make? How many do you honestly think you can keep? You can't hurt me any more than I could hurt you, so when the guilt gnaws away at your insides because you're too stubborn to accept your reality, know that I will suffer with you."

Fury hissed from her pores. "Good. I hope it's excruciating."

"Another lie."

She looked for something else to throw at him, but there was nothing in this simplistic hell hole of a room. Tears stung her eyes as frustration choked her. Disarmed and dejected, she whispered, "Get out."

"No. Distance is not the answer—" The moment he touched her she went ballistic, punching and clawing.

"*I said get out!* I don't want to look at you! I don't want to hear your voice! You make me sick! I hate you! *I hate you!*"

He caught her wrists and stilled her body as the fury built into a volcanic rage. Jerking her arms left then right, she tried to break his hold as she spewed every turbulent thought she had at him.

"You stole my life! You're erasing me!" Crazed and vicious, disdain exploded out of her until she exhausted herself trying to escape his hold. "I hate you," she panted, defeated and out of steam.

He collected her in his arms. "Do you feel better now?"

His lips pressed to her hair as he hugged her tight. She hated how much she relied on his physical bolstering. She ached to collapse into an unconscious heap on the floor, desperate to escape the turmoil overwhelming her, but he forced her to face it. He held her when every part of her felt like breaking, proving his vow never to let her go.

"I promise you, *pintura*, this change will bring more good than evil."

Mentally she wanted to stop fighting, but self-preservation forbade it. With a jolt of impassioned rage, she shoved him and his grip once again tightened.

He met the fire in her eyes with blazing preparedness. In that single, silent glance, he reminded her that he was older, stronger, and determined to get his way.

She despised him. "Fuck. You."

In a dizzying twist, he slammed her back into the wall, pinning her arms over her head and grinding his hard body against hers. "Is that what you want?"

The distraction of his fury felt better than her pain and she shamefully moaned, sinking her weight into him. "Fuck you," she repeated, whispering the words through clenched teeth.

"Your filthy language only makes me think of all the filthy things I want to do to you. Filthy things I *will* do."

Need softened her clenched muscles as he ground his body into her. Any pleasure was defused by an instant chaser of shame.

A gravelly purr emanated from his chest as an intoxicating scent surrounded him, luring her in. Body lax with desire, she slipped further into his hold. Sweet relief threatened to overtake her the closer she came to surrender.

How could the target of her anger dissolve her fury so easily, especially when there had been so much? Tears welled in her eyes. There was something greater than her pride at play. "I'll never stop hating you." She trembled with emotion. Certain that, in the end, she'd only hate herself more for giving in to him.

"Delilah, your hate I can handle. It's your indifference that guts me." His hold gentled and he caressed her cheek.

She shut her eyes, self-loathing making her own traitorous presence unbearable.

"Don't cry, *pintura*. There's no need for this pain and animosity between us. What's done is done. I only want to take care of you now." His face nuzzled into the delicate skin of her throat just below her ear. "Unburden yourself. Let go. Let me take away what grief I can."

Warm lips glided to her pulse, soft and hypnotic. Her body recognized his touch in ways that made no sense, and she relaxed into the comfort of his hold.

"Christian," his name crossed her lips like a solemn vow, an exhalation of a dying breath. "Please."

Kissing her throat, he transferred her wrists into the grasp of one hand. With the other, he delicately raised her chemise and teased her legs apart. "Whatever you need, *pintura*. I am yours."

Tipping her head back, she tried not to hate herself for being so weak. Or perhaps it wasn't her weakness that bothered her at all. Perhaps it was the part of her that couldn't accept she wanted him. That perfidious desire for his touch consumed her, building and expanding inside of her until she could hardly contain it.

"Hold onto me, *pintura*." Releasing her arms, he guided her hold around his neck and lifted her legs, wrapping them around his hips, and she gasped when he pushed into her with complete entitlement as if he owned her. Perhaps he did. She no longer felt like she fully belonged to herself.

His intrusive entrance into her life split her in two. Within such duality, she found value and tranquility in his possessive hold as much as she found discomfort and fear.

His lips found hers. "Feel that?" Slow drugging kisses coaxed her mouth open. "Perfection." He thrust slowly and a sense of completeness washed over her. The sweet surrender washed away her pain so that she could feel free of guilt once more.

Her head fell back on a low moan and his mouth found her ear as he whispered softly to her. "That's it, Delilah. I have you. Trust that I'll always have you."

Lazy, deep strokes filled her as he pressed into her body. Her arms wreathed around his broad shoulders, pulling his face closer. Warm breath washed over her neck. Pressure built and she raked her fingers up the back of his head, her fist knotting in his hair.

Her mouth ached for a split second, and then her lips parted. The sharp tip of her fangs grazed her tongue and she didn't want to think what the change implied. She only wanted to feel.

"More," she breathed, nuzzling her nose along the steady throb of his pulse. "Keep going."

Gentle nips pulled at her delicate flesh and her pulse went wild. "Let me taste you, *pintura.*"

The thought of his face buried between her thighs drove her mad with lust. She wanted that sweet release more than anything. "Yes—"

He struck with startling speed, sinking his teeth into her throat and puncturing an artery. Not at all the tasting she'd envisioned.

With a whimper, she tensed. Her entire nervous system fired off as he pulled greedily from her. Her words locked in her throat, paralyzed by fear.

His bite was strong and unbreakable, the suction of his mouth stretching her insides into something malleable as her heart sped up and her mind panicked. She struggled but he was still inside of her and the combination of his mouth on her vein and his stroking cock drove her to the edge of pleasure where her body could only fall into an all-consuming climax.

It wasn't natural for women to reach such pleasure so quickly. Mentally, she panicked but physically she was in heaven. He suckled as intently as a baby nurses, consumed by the act. If anyone stumbled upon them in such a vulnerable moment, he would be completely helpless to protect himself.

Short of breath, she cried out in pleasure, waves of ecstasy beating over her like the ocean reshapes the shore. As her strength waned, she didn't think about blood or all the things she learned in school about disease. Her mind couldn't go there. She only felt the pleasure of the act. It was unlike anything she'd experienced before. Sinful and dirty yet poetic and right. There was a ritual here, something unwritten that carried through time by tradition alone. She was a part of that bigger picture. A part of him.

They dropped to the bed, their bodies never parting. Possessive and primal. He grunted and shoved deeper, thrusting his hips hard and holding her beneath him. Impaled. Claimed. Owned.

Then he growled, *"Mine,"* deep in her mind, she heard his claim as clearly as if he whispered it into her ear, but she was certain he hadn't. He was inside of her in every possible and impossible way.

That irrefutable claim unlocked something inside of her and a gentle ease took over. Her desire to escape had fled, and she was content to simply let him use her.

He drank deeply, moaning and rocking his hips as something else marked her. She sensed him covering her even where their bodies didn't touch. He was everywhere. On her. In her. Running through her veins.

Finally, he licked the bite and the conclusion of the act left her instantly craving more. "My beautiful *pintura.*" He rolled to his back, taking her with him. Her hair formed a curtain around them. It was perfect until the fading light glinted against the smeared blood on his teeth and she stiffened.

Blood. That was her blood on his fangs. What the hell had they just done? Why would she allow him to do such a thing to her?

Because we are one and the same. She shoved the thought away, immediately rejecting the idea that she, too, was such an abomination.

"Let go of me."

"Easy, *little one*—"

"Don't try to calm me." The connection had severed the moment he stopped drinking from her *and*—*Oh, God*—he drank her blood. Her revulsion sickened her. "Get off of me."

He studied her with caution, obviously reluctant to let her go. "Delilah—"

"Let go. Let go of me right now or I'll scream." She shoved at him and her body was suddenly free. Empty. Her legs tangled in the blankets and she collapsed, rolling to her side. Hiding like a child who wanted to be invisible.

"Delilah."

She sensed his concern, but couldn't handle his worry on top of her own. Her hand blindly explored her neck, but there was no wound.

Not even a trace of spilled blood. She pushed her chemise down over her legs, but there was no retracting what he'd just done. What she'd allowed.

His hand gently touched her back and she flinched. "There's no reason to feel ashamed, little one."

She buried her face in the pillows and covered her ears. "Don't call me that. I'm a grown woman."

"I know you're grown. I don't call you *little one* to slight you, but because I see how innocent you are in all of this."

"Then how can you take advantage of me?"

Her words left him stricken, and his devastation rolled into her so hard and fast it knocked the breath from her lungs. "I would never take advantage of your innocence, Delilah. You're my only light and hope in a world of shadows. My North Star in a black sky. My guiding compass."

"I don't want to be your light or your compass. I just want to be the woman I was before I met you. I can't stomach this... This... *thing* that you made me."

It was as if she could feel the air leave his lungs, feel every trace of warmth siphon from the room. "You don't mean that."

"Don't you get it? This isn't me. I'm just a girl—"

"No." His stern rejection forbid her to belittle her relevance in his predestined world. "You might be a solitary female, but you're much more than *just a girl*. You're all I can see, all that I exist for."

"I don't belong to you, Christian."

"But you do. Just as I belong to you."

They were going in circles again. The relentless hamster wheel exhausted her. So much so, she had no desire to argue. A part of her even felt sorry for rejecting him, and she refused to acknowledge the illogical inclination to comfort him after all he'd done. But the urge existed all the same. "I'm tired."

"You need to feed." Without him explaining, she understood what he wanted.

"I'm not doing that to you."

"Your body needs it, *pintura*."

"I don't care. I just want to sleep."

He hesitated, then brushed a soft hand over her hair. "Very well. Rest now."

It seemed too easy, but she was too mentally and physically exhausted to spare another second of concern. She even allowed him to run his fingers over her hair, the act soothing and peaceful in a way that comforted her as she so desperately needed to be comforted.

"Shut your eyes and sleep, little one." Her lashes lowered with each heavy blink until every muscle in her face relaxed and darkness blanketed her. "I'll take care of you."

His words tugged at something but the smooth sense of relief that washed over her had her quickly forgetting her concerns. With no recollection of actually falling asleep, she glided deeper and deeper into a comfortable rest, aware that the hollow ache in her belly subsided and the gnawing hunger disappeared.

Warm contentment flowed through her and she rested soundly in his arms. Safe. Trusting that he would protect her, even if it meant saving her from herself.

CHAPTER 11

The gown was a disgusting shade of mint green that reminded Delilah of the time she threw up after too many Jell-o shots. The black apron wasn't horrible, but the *Handmaid's Tale* bonnet was not going anywhere near her head. "I'm not wearing this."

Christian sighed. "It's a traditional Amish bonnet."

"Yes," she agreed, pointing at her chest. "And I'm traditionally non-Amish."

The stiff, gauzy atrocity was the epitome of suppression in her mind. It symbolized too much negativity in this day and age. "Men would never wear something so demeaning."

"We wear hats."

"To block the sun. That thing—" She pointed at the offensive bonnet. "Is meant to hide a woman's hair because you people associate hair with vanity and shame. No way am I conforming to such nonsense."

"I think you misunderstand our meaning, *pintura*. We cover our heads because it's proper for prayer. This way, we're always prepared to speak to God."

Her chin dropped to her chest as she stared at him with a Kubrick stare.

He shifted under her upward gaze. "Should I protect my manhood?"

"Good instinct." Only then did she notice the small package wrapped in brown paper that he held in his hand. "What's that?"

"A gift for you." He handed her the lightweight bundle that obviously held something delicate inside.

The flowing script reminded her of an exhibit she once saw of Civil War letters—equally beautiful and chilling as she read, *To Brother Christian's betrothed.* "God, help me."

"*He's* trying."

She stilled and returned her stare to him, catching a glimmer of humor in his eye. "Was that a joke?"

Rather than answer, he turned away and busied himself at the dresser.

She smirked and lowered to the bed with the package.

Maybe it was insane to normalize their situation, but she was tired of having bad days and wanted to try a different approach. Last night had been… enlightening and exhausting.

She'd assumed she'd wake up with an information overload hangover, but she actually woke up feeling fantastic. Wanting to get out of the house and explore, she made a promise to behave. She'd bite her tongue clean off if that's what it took for that to happen. So far, she and Christian had been tolerating each other and managing their circumstances agreeably.

Pulling the jute ribbon from the package, she tried to recall the last time anyone had given her a gift. No tape was used to wrap the bundle, but a tea towel was folded neatly inside the brown paper.

She frowned. Was this more pressure toward a domestic future of servitude? Unfolding the towel, a note fluttered to the floor along with a pile of pink lace. Several modern hairpins scattered across the wood planks.

Confused, she lifted the pink lace and laughed. "Is this traditional Amish as well?"

Christian turned and his eyes widened. "That's…" He scowled. "Was that in the package?"

"Yup." She twirled the hot pink panties around on her finger, loving whatever this was doing to him. "And you said the *bishop's* wife sent this over?"

He muttered something under his breath in a different language.

Delilah retrieved the handwritten note.

Hello friend,
My sisters and I thought these items might be of

some use. The underthings are from Destiny, the pins from myself. Anna has volunteered to find you decent shoes, but first, she needs your size. The females are working on new dresses and aprons so you will have your own. Do you have a preference in color?

We look forward to meeting you in person and becoming great friends. Congratulations on your mating! Welcome to your new home. May the years ahead be filled with happiness and love.

Best wishes,
Larissa King
Wife to Bishop Eleazar King

AN ODD SENSATION settled over her. How had she formed an alliance with women she'd never met? Women didn't typically care for her as a general rule, which was why she was prone to having male friends.

Delilah examined the lace bra. It wasn't her size but it was close, and she loved it regardless. These wonderful women didn't even know her, yet they thought enough about her to go out of their way and send her a gift—a *sexy* unexpected gift.

Her brow pinched with confusion. "These women are Amish?"

Before Christian answered, she sensed his disapproval. As he leaned close to examine the note, she protectively tightened her grip on the gift, afraid he might take it from her. He read the note and his proximity immediately awakened her awareness of him. His scent drew her in and the sight of his strong hands filled her with visions of him groping her under the pink lace—

His gaze cut to hers, dark intentions clear in his silver stare. "Did you want to meet the females or spend the day in bed, *pintura?*" The side of his mouth kicked up. "You're projecting quite a distracting image."

Cheeks heating, she dropped her gaze and buried the lingerie in the lap of her chemise. "I want to meet the other women."

He studied her, communicating that visiting others wouldn't have been his first choice, then he returned his gaze to the letter. "Two are newly transitioned. Their mates allow them too many liberties. Sister Larissa perhaps spent too much time away from the farm. I should alert the bishop of this."

"Or not."

"Excuse me?"

"Christian, these women reached out to me with a gift. If you get them in trouble, they'll think I had something to do with it and then they'll never accept me."

His gaze lifted, a strange glimmer of hope in his eye. "That's the first time you've spoken as if you intend to stay."

"I just meant that they won't like me if their thoughtful gesture gets them in trouble. Don't be a narc."

"A narc?"

"Yeah, a narc. An informant. No one likes a narc."

"I'm an elder. I have a responsibility to The Council."

She lifted her chin. "I thought you said I was your greatest responsibility."

His gaze sharpened and his voice lowered. "You're playing with me, *pintura.*"

"Am I wrong?"

His jaw twitched. "No, you're not wrong. As my mate, you're my priority."

Her grin was slow and triumphant. "Then don't be a dick and tattle on my friends."

His stare darkened as his brows slammed down. "I don't appreciate that language."

"And I don't appreciate a snitch. So, you hush, and I won't call you a dick. Will you take me to meet them?"

He drew in a long breath. Their delicate truce seemed reliant on an unspoken give-and-take, a tit-for-tat agreement. Every advance was followed by a concession, sort of like chess. "You'll have to dress appropriately."

She lifted her hand, the hot pink lace dangling from her finger. "In this?"

He cleared his throat. "I was referring to the bonnet."

She gave the fabric a twirl. "So, you don't want to see me in this?"

"Are you offering?"

With a quick twist of her wrist, she gathered the material in her fist. "Nope." Hopping off the bed, she crossed the room and held open the door. "I'd like some privacy."

He hesitated a moment, then set the bonnet on the bed next to the puke-colored dress. "I'll wait for you downstairs."

She swung the door shut.

It truly was amazing how much more...solid she felt since waking. Her energy was bottomless, like she'd had thirteen B-12 shots. Her mind was sharper and her fatigue had completely vanished. Not only was the lethargy gone, she felt stronger than usual...pluckier. She was still adjusting to her heightened senses, which was a little like acclimating to an acid trip, but she was getting used to all the additional noises and distractions.

As she dressed, she noticed a fresh glow to her skin. No signs of acne, no blotchy pigmentations from the sun, and no scars. Her body felt...purified. It was almost as if she could feel her cells regenerating by the second, feel new hair follicles growing, and her nail beds firming.

She opened the door and jumped a step back when she found Christian waiting on the other side. "Jesus, you scared me!"

He growled. "Perhaps we should stay here."

"What? Why?" No way was she staying in the house another minute.

"I've warned you about your language."

She rolled her eyes and brushed by him. "God, loosen up, Christian—"

He caught her by the arm. "I'm very serious,

Delilah. Being Amish is not something I take lightly. Foul language is a deliberate sign of disrespect. If you wish for my respect, you will offer the same and honor me in this by controlling your tongue. It's one thing when you spew profanities at me, it's a completely different matter when you take the Lord's name in vain."

They were so close to getting out of the house and meeting the others, she'd capitulate just about anything at this point. This was her only shot at finding allies who could possibly help her escape. "Fine. I'm sorry. I'll try not to take the Lord's name in vain anymore. Okay? Can we go now?"

He released her but studied her closely with narrowing eyes. "Why so eager?"

"Uh, probably because I've been cooped up in this house for days with no one to talk to."

"I'm here for you to talk to."

"Yeah. Not the same."

He stepped back and averted his gaze but not before she saw him wince. "I see."

She shouldn't feel bad. This was his fault. But guilt soured her stomach anyway. She hadn't meant to belittle his faith. Plus, she needed to play this right so she could get to the women and form an alliance.

"Delilah, they won't help you escape."

His words were but one more cause for concern. She didn't know how he read her intentions because she couldn't read his, but every time he proved to know what she'd been thinking her irritation grew. It was an indescribable violation and she bristled, instinctively wanting to push back.

Mouth tight, she glared at him. "Why?"

"Their first loyalty is to their mates and God."

The problem with conformity was that it looked an awful lot like loyalty. No one saw the force or the stripping away of individualism that occurred first. "You said those women were like me." What was the word he used? *"Transitioned."*

"Yes, but they have accepted their destiny and they are loyal to The Order."

"Dogs are loyal, too, Christian. But if you take too much away from them, neglect them, and trap them, they'll eventually show you a disloyal side and attack those who think they own them. It's in their nature."

"The female's nature is more docile than that of dogs."

She scoffed. "Says the man who thinks all women should be domesticated like pets."

"We honor our female counterparts far more than any other species—especially our called mates."

"I call bullshit."

His hands balled at his side until his knuckles popped. "You're purposefully baiting me. I warned you to watch your tongue."

She hadn't meant to curse, but that wasn't the point. "Warned me..." She rolled her eyes. "Let me *warn you* about women, Christian." She leaned close, pointing her finger near his chest. "We can tolerate a world of pain, far beyond what would make the strongest man buckle. We're patient and know how to bide our time. Like mountains, we seem unmoving, but we're always growing and evolving. Men have suppressed us because they're terrified of how much our little minds can hold. But we remember *everything*, so you men have good reason to fear. *That's* a warning."

"You mistake me for your enemy, *pintura*."

"Well, our relationship status does seem destined to be permanently locked at '*it's complicated*', so let's just agree to disagree."

"Those females love and trust their mates. They've accepted what has been done and cannot be undone."

"That's where you're wrong, Christian. I'll never forget who I was before I met you and neither will those women. You can't take away our memories." She shoved the bonnet over her hair. "Covering our heads doesn't stop us from thinking."

She brushed past him, covered head held high and her nose tipped with the haughty confidence that came with solidarity. Those women were the answers to her prayers. They were all getting out.

Delilah waited at the front door for him to lead the way. His hand coasted over the small of her back as he directed her out of the house. She hated that his touch caused a physical response in her body, hated how much his contact comforted her. How could she enjoy something that also caused her great alarm?

"I wish you wouldn't touch me."

"That will never happen. My body needs to touch yours as much as yours requires the contact."

She walked faster, trying to escape the warmth of his open palm, but he kept pace. *Such an asshole.*

Strolling around the farm created a totally different experience than trying to run away from it. The sights registered, not just visually stimulating her senses but physically stealing her breath.

Beautiful colonial homes and stone walls exploited fine craftsmanship and patience. These were not pre-fab homes like they made today. These were classics.

The shutters were built from strong wood and painted by hand. The railings were spun with impeccable detail, each spindle perfectly aligned with the next. The air was clean. The sky seemed bluer. And the land was so lush and inviting she had the urge to race over the meadows like Julie Andrews in *The Sound of Music*—especially since she was dress-rehearsal ready in her hideous puke green gown and apron.

The openness contrasted greatly with the city life she'd grown up around. The scent of fresh grass and earth tickled her nose in a pleasing way that made her feel more con-nected to nature as if she and the trees were one.

The breeze carried sounds and fragrances she didn't recognize, and the sun teased her skin with a revitalizing tingle.

Her brow pinched as a thought crossed her mind. "Aren't you supposed to burst into flames in daylight?"

"That's a myth, for the most part. I told you, we are not vampire. We're immortal. We are as much a part of God's plan as every other living creature that requires sunlight to thrive."

When he said logical shit like that, she wanted to trip him. She didn't want to see her new situation as enchanting. She wanted a long list of complications so she could blame him and argue how much better her life had been before he showed up.

But at the moment, she just felt abso-fuck-ing-lutely majestic and, for once, didn't feel like having a combative argument when there was so much unmatched beauty surrounding her.

Long, lush fields of amber swayed in the breeze like gentle rolling ripples over a yellow sea. The fresh, rejuvenating air filled her lungs with another powerful urge to run—and she wasn't a runner.

Frowning at this strange urge to play, she considered what might be causing it. It had to be the countryside. That was all.

Her stare followed a long line of trees and she wondered—no, knew—how invigorating it would be to climb one. Her fingers itched to curl around the bark, and she could smell the dark amber sap from a mile away. She could see herself lazing in the shadows of the tall timbers as the sun moved across the sky as if she'd done so a thousand times before.

"It was a dream we shared."

She frowned at him. "What?"

"The trees. We raced through the woods, laughing and playing. When I caught you, we made love beneath a hundred-year-old sycamore, and I held you until the sun faded into the hills."

Her steps slowed and faltered. "That sounds nice."

"You have the memory. We were both there."

Her brow lowered in concentration. "I don't remember anything like that. I also don't re-member inviting you to nose around in my head. So—however you're doing that—please stop."

He noticeably withdrew from her thoughts, but she still sensed him hiding in the far corner of her mind, like a shadow that never moved. It was super annoying but she was getting used to it. They continued in silence.

After hiking up a gradual incline came a view of more houses. They were all dated, lacking the 'connect the dots' strings of wires communities were typically laced up with for technology.

Small mill-wheels pulled through a narrow brook, and she knew that had something to do with energy but really didn't understand the particulars too well. Nor did she care.

She spotted a man working and anxiousness spiked in her belly. She needed allies, people who would see her side of things and choose to help her. She could appeal to their kind Amish ways—

"I do not want you speaking to other males."

"And I don't want you reading my thoughts, so I guess we both lose. Hi—" Before she could call out a full greeting to the man, he caught her arm and drew her into his side.

"We will turn around and go back to the house. Do not push me on this."

She scowled at him with reflexive indignance but then came a flutter of hurt. *Obey or we go home*, he was essentially threatening. She didn't like being bossed around like his subservient little pet.

"My rules are only to protect you, little one. In time, you'll have a better understanding of our culture, and with that understanding will come more freedom."

Of course, he lingered in her mind, but his words weren't in response to her thoughts. They seemed… genuine, as if he recognized his harshness and regretted having to be so firm with her. She said nothing, choosing to wait until she met the other women to ask how they managed this domineering crap.

They walked toward a more communal part of the farm. "That's the bishop's house." Christian pointed to a large white colonial with a long, stone addition stretching off the side. "He's the patriarch of The Order, so to speak."

Her shoulders tensed at the cult-like language.

"We are not a cult. I'll request some texts to help correct your interpretation of our beliefs."

"Great. I love forced indoctrination."

He sent her an unimpressed glare. "You're free to have your own opinions, Delilah. I only mean to educate you on a culture and history you have no prior knowledge of. Once you grasp the basic tenets of our faith, you'll see our rules are for our protection. You'll come to value our seclusion once you fully embrace your immortality. Feeding, for example, is much simpler here than off of the farm."

Her lips firmed. The ticker tape in her head was quickly running out of paper as she mentally listed causes for concern. Her orientation to Amishhood and the secret world of the supernatural was not an easy pill to swallow, and he could have used a bit more tactfulness. When he shoved it all down her throat in one hard dose, it had the same bitter aftertaste as brainwashing.

"I speak plainly because I do not want lies between us, little one. Would you prefer that I disguise my truth with flowery words bedecked with complicated phrases that require sifting and deciphering?"

"I'd prefer if you stayed the hell out of my head. But yes, a little sensitivity would be nice. I mean, would it kill you to lube the hole."

"Lube the hole?"

She rolled her eyes. "You have a habit of

cramming too much in at once. I get it that this is happening whether I want it to happen or not, but you could be a little more delicate in your delivery. It's bad enough that I don't have a choice in the matter, and that I'm wearing this stupid, fucking bonnet."

"When you underscore your point with profanity you only harden my resistance to compromise."

"Well, if you want me to choose my words carefully, you could at least be a little considerate of my feelings and soften your words too. Don't think of it as compromise, think of it as mutual respect."

"You're saying we could both benefit from a little temperance?"

"Sure." If that was the biblical term for it, why not.

He digested her words over the next several steps. "While we are in the open, I only keep a pulse on your thoughts to stay connected. My intention isn't to be intrusive."

"Well, it is. I appreciate you sharing your rationale, but I still don't like having you in there twenty-four-seven. It's also more hypocrisy, because I can't tell what you're thinking, so you clearly have the upper hand."

There is no upper hand. We are one. Equals. And I believe my endless thoughts of your beauty and my intrigue would grow tiresome—

She gasped. "How did you do that?"

"A little push. Try to follow the thread back on your own now that I've opened the door."

She frowned and concentrated. Data suddenly bombarded her regarding everything from livestock to mileage. Then she recognized his real thoughts beneath that subconscious mumbo jumbo. But his mind didn't speak in words. She gleaned visions, of herself, of them, of his emotions. It overwhelmed her and she instantly withdrew.

"Oh my Go—sh."

"You'll grow used to it." He glanced at her, a slight smile curving his mouth. "Shall we agree that I'll work on my communication skills if you promise to work on your language?"

Was that a compromise?

Yes, pintura, it was. His words flitted through her mind like a gentle touch, stealing her breath once more.

"Holy—" Before she could finish the profanity Christian cleared his throat. "—cow."

He chuckled. "Very good, *pintura.*"

He caught her hand and stopped walking. Her initial reaction to pull away vanished as he tightened his grip, not because he held her with strength, but because part of her instinctively deferred to his guidance.

"I'm sorry if I've not been sensitive to your needs. Don't mistake my clumsy handling as any sort of detached indifference. You're always my greatest concern, Delilah."

"So you've said." His brow tightened, and she realized he was trying to express himself, so she eased off the sarcasm. "Sorry. Go ahead."

"I'm a solution-oriented male, and I'm used

to finding resolutions in a concise manner, involving as little emotional trappings as possible. I'm used to only thinking for myself. I'll try to adjust my way of thinking, taking your way into consideration as well. You can see now how differently our minds work."

She nodded, not at all eager to revisit the black-and-white landscape of his conscience.

A strange, heart-wrenching sound of distress screeched in the distance and her spine stiffened, all of her attention jerked to the startling noise.

She stopped walking and Christian glanced at her with concern, immediately filtering through her thoughts.

"Shh!" she said, as if that would help her concentrate. He was in her head, but not making a sound. The faint chirp simpered again and she had to strain to hear it. Her senses pinpointed the location and she pivoted, bolting in the direction of the pained cry.

"Delilah!"

She ignored Christian's call, her focus devoted to the faint wail of distress that pulled her deeper into the wooded tree line and away from their intended path. He shouted for her again, but she kept moving. The cries became easier to follow once under the shade of the tall cypresses.

Her feet moved swiftly over the layer of fallen pine needles, shots of emerald, evergreen, and piercing shards of sunlit blue blurred at her periphery. Her heart raced as she zeroed in on the weak cry, and nothing else registered as she moved faster than she had ever moved in her life.

Delilah wait for—

The snap of their severed mental connection came after a swift, subconscious command she hadn't realized she could order. Her body shifted into fight or flight and she put all her focus on the pained cry howling from the woods.

The hollow of her mind where Christian's presence had been, flooded with new information that guided her toward the wounded creature. She hunted the sound, her heart racing as if she could sense the creature's pain and fear, somehow processing it as her own.

When another cry shrieked, there was a fatal ring to the pained chirp. "No!" She doubled her speed. Christian's desperate call for her to stop was as lost as the wind through the trees.

She stilled, turning left, then right. Her head quirked to the side, eyes closed, ear tilted toward the canopy above as she listened, but the pained cry had stopped. She sniffed the air, her brain cataloging and sorting a thousand sources in the span of a second. Her senses fanned out into the woods, blanketing the forest floor in search of the tiny creature. When she caught the slight murmur of its fluttering heart, she bolted, not stopping until she located the injured fledgling.

Crashing to her knees, careless of the brush

that created little cushion for her landing, she leaned over the broken bird. Her shoulders rounded as she gently scooped the delicate critter into her palms.

"It's okay. I've got you." She cradled its fragile wings in her open hands as she mumbled words of compassion to soothe the animal. Its tiny heart beat so fast within its small breast, she did not wish to frighten it more. "I won't hurt you."

The tiny, green warbler lay on its side, eyes wide, beak open as it tried to sing one last song. "No," she gasped, rocking her body to soothe the poor, dying creature.

Cushioned by the bed of needles and detritus, she stared into the bird's beady, black eyes as they bulged with panic. "Be calm. I have you," she whispered, drawing the wounded bird close to her heart and protectively warming it. It must have fallen from the nest.

The underbrush crunched, and her attention snapped to the trees, protectively using her body to shelter the tiny bird from whatever approached. Christian stood at a distance, watching her with a peculiar look.

Her tear-filled gaze lifted to his. "I think it's dying."

Christian nodded silently.

She turned her helpless gaze back to the nestling. "We have to help it."

Its feathered belly puffed as it quickly breathed, panicked in those last moments of life. Its beak opened on a silent cry, too weak to go on. Life escaped its tiny feathered body, and there was nothing she could do to prevent such an inevitable end.

A broken sob fled her throat as a tear rolled down her cheek. Its little heart stopped and the life vanished from its black eyes. She held the unresponsive feathered body to her heart and wept, the loss deeply personal, far beyond her usual love for animals.

Christian lowered to the ground and gently pulled her to him. She needed his comfort in that moment. "It is life, *pintura*."

"He was only a baby," she cried, pressing her face into his neck.

Christian gently ran his hand over her back. "It's in God's hands."

"It was just an innocent fledgling."

"Birds are fragile creatures—"

"No." She shouldered out of his hold, no longer finding his touch comforting. "I don't want to live in a world where baby birds die and vampires live forever. How is that fair?"

His startled expression unnerved her. She sensed his judgment and his desire to *enlighten* her, but she was sick of his version of reality. Why was she here? What good was this new existence if she would only outlive everything else? She couldn't bear the thought of surviving while every beautiful thing around her eventually died.

"Delilah, there's a natural order we all must follow. God's plan—"

"No!" She shoved him back. "I don't want to hear any more about God's plan."

"The bird fell from the trees. It probably felt very little pain—"

"Stop!" With her free hand, she tried to cover her ears, but it was no use. He was in her mind, pushing his cold logic at her while nothing about her new circumstances was logical. "Just let me be sad about this. You're always trying to—" Her breath hitched. Like a tiny pebble falling into a well a hundred miles away, she felt the slightest ripple of motion and opened her palm.

"Delilah, we must accept—"

"Shh! Do you hear it?"

She gasped again, her fingers coasting over the warbler's breast as the tiny wing twitched.

Christian stilled. His denial clattered through her open mind like a church bell cut from its belfry.

It was dead. He had sensed its last breath.

The rapid tapping of its little heart abruptly beat to life, and Delilah laughed breathlessly. "He's alive!"

The flat, beady eyes reanimated with life. Her fingers coasted over the broken wing, and the bird righted itself. More euphoric laughter bubbled out of her as it fluttered its little body upright and perched in her palm.

Christian's unblinking stare watched the bird as he whispered, "What have you done, *pintura*? Did you give it blood?"

"What?" She frowned up at him. "Gross. No."

Ignoring him, she laughed and kissed the smooth gray head of the warbler then raised her arms high, and the bird miraculously flew from her grip, swooping low under the trees and then shifting, building up speed and zeal as it disappeared into the forest.

"Did you see that?"

When she turned back to Christian, he wore a blank look of shock. "You toy with the laws of nature."

She scowled at him, finally seeing some value in this vampire stuff only to have him shit on her parade. "That bird is alive. Why can't you be happy about that?"

"What did you do?"

"I didn't do anything. You saw me."

"The bird was dead, Delilah."

"Maybe not."

He shook his head in awe. "It was. I felt it die."

She'd felt it too, but that also didn't make sense. Standing, she brushed the pine needles from her skirt. "Well, it's not dead anymore."

"Death is a part of life, *pintura*. We cannot interrupt such things. The warbler was not meant to live."

"Why do you care? It was just a baby."

"How did you bring it back to life?"

She shrugged. "I don't know. I just…wanted it to live. Maybe it's a vampire thing. I mean, I was sort of unimpressed with your species so far, but that was badass. Can we save other stuff?"

He blinked at her. "*Unimpressed?*"

"Well, yeah. You can't fly. You can't turn into a bat—"

"Why would anyone want to turn into a bat?"

"Well, maybe not a bat, but a wolf would be cool, or a bear, or—*Oh!*—a dinosaur! That would be awesome."

He shook his head. "The laws of nature must be respected."

"Oh, please. Why am I here? I mean, really, Christian? If it's all part of *God's plan* then why did *God* leave that bird for me to find? You can't pick and choose what fits into your fairytale and what doesn't."

"It's not a tale."

"Well, it's not any reality I know." She hitched a thumb over her shoulder. "That was a fucking tragedy that turned into a fucking miracle. How can you call *us* miraculous, but not that? Why are we better than birds?"

"Because we are," he snapped. "We're the top of the food chain, stronger than any living creature."

She glared up at him, rising on her toes. "Well, might doesn't always equal greatness, you sanctimonious prick!"

"Do not speak to me with such filthy disrespect!"

"You're the one who started yelling at me first!" She didn't back down when he crowded her. "Doesn't your faith claim we're all *God's* creatures?"

"You're purposefully twisting things."

"No, I'm not. Your hypocrisy folds on its own."

"Tell me what you did, Delilah. I must know the truth."

Detecting something more than censure in his tone, she sobered. "Why?" A cold chill passed between them and she sensed his fear. "Am I in trouble?" When he didn't immediately say no, her worry doubled. "Christian?"

"We cannot interfere."

"I didn't. I mean, not really. I thought it was a vampire thing. Super manifestation or something. I swear."

"Immortal," he corrected.

"Whatever. I don't even know what I did. I just wanted it to live. I didn't *do* anything. Why can't we just be happy it flew away and move on?"

He nodded. "You're right. God works in mysterious ways. Perhaps it was just not the warbler's time."

But deep down she knew that bird lived because of her, not his God. And Christian—ever-present in her mind—knew it too.

By the time they reached the house where Christian assumed the women would be, Delilah's feet were dragging. Her steps had been sluggish since leaving the forest, and the appeal of meeting others was now overshadowed by her desire to take a nap.

Christian opened a low picket gate, and they walked along a naturally carved path leading to a colonial house with a wraparound porch. A toddler dressed in plain clothing dragged a whittled wooden horse over the planked porch. The house was new, the sharp scent of sawdust still clinging to the carpentry, and the paint not yet faded by the weather and sun.

"Brother Christian." A beautiful woman with bright eyes smiled and stood from the rocker. "I was hoping you might visit with your new mate."

Delilah tried not to bristle at the terminology, but she felt a little like a golden retriever brought to show and tell.

Christian nodded to the woman in greeting. "Sister Faith, this is Delilah."

Delilah lifted a hand, unsure how their people greeted one another. "Hi." When the woman just stared at her expectantly, she explained, "I'm the…" She couldn't bring herself to say it. "I'm Delilah." There was the whole Amish confusion but then the immortal mess as well. She figured less was more.

"I'm Faith, and this handsome cherub is my great grandson, Cain." The woman smiled, brushing an adoring hand over the young boy's head, his face hidden by the shadow of a small hat. The mind boggled that this woman wasn't a twenty-something human.

Did the babies drink blood as well? Were they born immortal or did they steal the babies and transition them? Delilah had so many questions.

"Cain is Brother Adam's son, named after his father's twin," Christian explained, shooting her a pointed look that assured no babies were stolen. "It's a lovely day to enjoy the weather, Sister Faith. Are your granddaughters nearby?"

How many vampire grandchildren did this chick have?

Immortals… Christian silently reminded, once again intruding into her mind. *There are many long nights on the farm,* pintura, *but they're never boring or lonely for those who are mated. You'll find lots of offspring here.*

Right. Because when there's no television or cell service, what else is there to do?

The little boy ran over to the porch railing and yelled something in a language Delilah didn't understand. Then he hissed, flashing pink gums and two razor sharp fangs, and she sprang back.

"Holy—" Delilah pressed her lips tight before the rest slipped out. That kid's grill was a licensed weapon.

Faith's eyes creased as she silently chuckled. "Everyone's out back enjoying the shade and the breeze."

Churning butter and drinking blood, no doubt. She was in the freaking Twilight Zone.

Christian's mouth formed a tight smile as he gave her what could only be described as a mental hand squeeze. *Try to keep an open mind, pintura.*

I'm on a farm full of Amish vampires. Believe me, my mind's been blown wide fucking open.

Immortals. And mind your tongue.

I'm not going to stop cursing in my own fucking head. Pick your battles, Dracula. She tried to shove him out of her thoughts as she'd done in the forest, but for some reason, she couldn't. Maybe she was too tired.

"I thought the females might enjoy a visit." Christian told Faith.

"I'm sure they would. Everyone's been so curious and eager to meet your beautiful mate."

There was that word again. Delilah tugged at the laces of her bonnet.

Christian took her hand, his voice once again intruding in her mind. *You're fidgeting.*

This bonnet's choking the shit out of me.

Take a breath, little one. Trapping her fiddling hand in his he sent a calming stroke through her mind, but stiffened the moment he detected her exhaustion.

Eyes creasing with concern, he asked, "Do you need to rest, *pintura*? We can visit another time."

It unnerved her to have someone so in tune with her needs. "No." She straightened her shoulders, forcing the fidgeting to cease and hiding away her exhaustion as best she could. There really wasn't anywhere to put her feelings when he was constantly trespassing in her fucking head. "We're already here. I'd like to stay."

He cocked his head and studied her. "You're very tired."

"The walk winded me, that's all. I'm fine, I promise." Recalling that vampires probably didn't get winded, she tried to distract him by pressing a kiss to his cheek. "Really, I'm fine. Can we meet the others?"

He stilled, his eyes narrowing with suspicion. "I'm sure you're eager to thank the females for their thoughtful gift, but there will be plenty of other opportunities to meet them if you're too tired for a visit now."

She held his stare with a challenging one of her own. "I feel good."

He leaned close and whispered in her ear.

"You can't hide from me, *pintura*. Your exhaustion weighs on me as well."

Faith lifted the little boy onto her hip. "The males are in the barn if you'd like to catch up with them, Brother Christian. I can take Delilah to meet the females. Little Cain's due for a nap anyway. I was just about to take him inside."

"Thank you, Faith." He let the debate over her lethargy drop and said, "I will not be far, *pintura*. Call if you need me."

"Soon as I find a phone," she joked, eager to be rid of him.

Call with your mind, pintura. And you'll never be rid of me.

She scrunched her face with the fakest smile she could manage. *Can you sense my eye roll?*

Very much so. Can you sense this?

She stiffened as a wave of ecstasy stole through her. *What the hell was that?*

Behave, and I'll show you later.

Intrigued and slightly violated, she scoffed and followed Faith inside. *Telepathic pervert.*

The little boy fussed as they entered a den that was disturbingly similar to Christian's. "I don't want a nap."

"Hush now." The boy pouted and kicked a leg in defiance, but Faith didn't bend.

Strangely, the moment Christian was gone, Delilah felt oddly incomplete as if part of her body had been stripped bare. It was an awkward and uncomfortable sensation she didn't understand, especially after days of trying to escape his presence.

Voices carried from out back. Everything was much like Christian's home, aside from a few color variations. Plain curtains were drawn aside to let the sunlight in and cast iron wood stoves occupied every room.

"Is this your home?" she asked Faith.

"Oh, no. This is my son's, but he's been ill and staying with us. For now, my grandson is living here with his new mate and my other granddaughter."

She hadn't realized immortals could get sick. "Oh. I hope your son feels better soon."

She smiled graciously. "God is merciful."

Delilah wondered what was wrong with her son. How old was he? Old enough to own a house, she supposed. Did Amish believe in modern medicine? Could immortals benefit from such remedies? Questions were quickly piling up, and she missed having Christian there to ask.

Do you need me, pintura?

He popped back into her mind with the subtlety of a frying pan to the skull. *No. Bug off.*

"The girls are out back." Faith led her through the spacious rooms.

Long beams marked the wall with pegs every few inches where hats and shawls hung. None of the seating matched and there was very little furniture occupying the middle of the rooms. Oil lamps sat on handmade doilies atop what looked like hand-carved furniture.

They exited the house onto another large

porch. Four women turned and smiled, rushing from the chairs where they had been sewing.

"Is this her?" the tallest of the four women asked. She was a startling beauty with a lithe body, and crystalline eyes.

They were all dressed in similar attire making it difficult to differentiate as they swarmed her.

"That's her!" the smallest woman in the group proclaimed. "Come, sit down, Sister Delilah." The small woman took her hand and pulled her to a wooden chair on the lawn. "Oh, you're exhausted. Sit. Sit. Have a rest."

A curvaceous Latina female and a pale woman with bright green eyes followed. The women gathered in a circle of wooden kitchen chairs positioned directly under the shade of an old oak tree. A basket overflowed with material in the center of the circle. A quilt spread out beneath their feet where several primitive baby toys sat forgotten.

"We've been working on your dresses," the tall woman explained, pointing to the basket of fabric.

"Well, *they* have. I'm hopeless with a needle and thread," the green-eyed girl holding a small baby bundled in a crocheted pink blanket, said. "I've just been keeping them company."

They were all so pretty it was hard to decipher their ages.

The smallest of the four giggled. "Anna's mending and cooking skills are quite abysmal."

"Gracie," the taller woman tsked. "Don't be rude."

"Is it rude if it's true?" the smallest girl, Gracie, wondered.

"I'm not offended," the woman with a baby said then smiled up at Faith. "Is Cain ready for a nap?"

"No," little Cain said, swinging his leg from Faith's hip.

"He's protesting, but I think he'll go down if you lay with him." Faith smiled at the boy. "Do you want to lay with Momma for a bit?"

The little boy stopped fussing and rested his head on Faith's shoulder and nodded, his arms reaching for the woman who held the bundled infant.

"I can take Lucy for a while," the dark eyed woman said, and Delilah detected a touch of an accent. She must be one of the transitions.

"Perhaps introductions first." The small woman pointed to herself. "I'm Gracie. This is my sister Larissa." She waved a hand at the tall beauty with silver eyes.

"The bishop's wife?" Delilah asked.

"That's right," Larissa said. "And this is Destiny and Annalise, my sisters by law."

Destiny took the infant from Annalise, adjusting her hold so she could wave. "*Oi.*"

"And I'm Cain's mommy." Annalise took the boy from Faith and harnessed him onto her hip. "As you can see, it's past nap time. I'll be back in a few minutes."

Delilah tried to memorize each face. The

small one was Gracie, the tall one was Larissa. The curvy one was Destiny. And the one with baby Cain was Annalise. "And who is this?" She glanced at the sleeping infant wrapped in pink.

"This is Lucy, Anna and Adam's newest."

She didn't know who Adam was.

"Adam's my brother. He's Anna's mate," Gracie promptly explained.

"Oh."

"Come. Sit." Larissa waved her to a chair. "We've been anxious to meet you."

As soon as they sat, Gracie's face pinched as if she suffered a sudden headache. "Grandmother, I believe they're in need of you back at the house."

"Yes, I was just on my way. It was lovely meeting you, Delilah. I hope we have another chance to visit soon."

Larissa rubbed a soothing hand on Gracie's shoulder but made no comment about whatever just happened. "So, Sister Delilah, how are you liking the farm?"

"I, uh, it's outdoorsy."

The girls laughed. "I heard Christian built you an indoor bathroom," Larissa said and the other girls smiled appreciatively.

Gracie laughed, all signs of a headache now gone. "I'll never forget how difficult Anna was about bathing in cold water when Adam first brought her here."

"There really is nothing like modern plumbing," Larissa agreed. "Once you have it, you can't go back."

"I insisted Cain had to build me a copper-heated tub before I'd marry him."

Delilah frowned, forgetting which women were transitions and which were raised on the farm.

Gracie's hand closed lightly over hers. "It can be overwhelming to learn so many new names and faces at once. The important thing is that we're all friends. Larissa and I were raised right here in this house with our brothers, Adam and Cain. Annalise is mated to Adam and Destiny is Cain's wife."

"Cain and I are living here, for now," Destiny explained. "With Gracie."

"My father is ill, you see. And my mother won't leave his side."

Just then, a clatter erupted from the house and a child screamed. Gracie stood and sighed. "And that would be our youngest brother, Jaden."

Delilah's eyes widened as another loud clamor shook the house. "Is he okay?"

"He's… temperamental. Excuse me."

As soon as Gracie went inside, Destiny leaned forward and whispered. "Terrible twos can get pretty ugly around here."

Larissa laughed. "Why do you think I left Moriah with her father? Just yesterday she pulled the entire table down, ruining supper."

So far, these women were proving to be an incredible form of birth control. "Is Moriah your daughter?" she asked Larissa.

"Yes, and the apple of her father's stubborn eye."

"And a pain in her mother's ass," Destiny joked, making Delilah laugh as well.

All humor disappeared when Gracie returned holding a small boy, no bigger than little Cain, wearing some sort of leather Hannibal Lecter mask on his face. Delilah's eyes widened at the sight. "Why…"

"He bites," Gracie explained, lowering the boy to the quilt with a bottle. "Behave, Jaden, and I'll take you to the woods later."

The boy plugged the bottle into his mouth, the rubber nipple fitting perfectly between the wire slats of his mask. Humanitarian concerns for the child overwhelmed Delilah and she couldn't take her eyes off of him.

Gracie touched her arm. "Don't stare. He doesn't like that."

"Is he okay?"

"He's perfectly fine."

But how could she know for sure? The boy surely couldn't say much at his young age, and whatever words he meant to say would be compromised by the muzzle.

"I'm telepathic."

Delilah's focus snapped from Jaden to Gracie. "Seriously?" She'd thought that was only a mate thing.

Gracie smiled. "It's a gift. I promise you, Jaden is completely content. He's my baby brother. I would never allow anyone or anything to harm him. But he's teething and a danger to others."

"Poor Grandfather. His knuckle still hasn't fully healed."

She was sitting with the fucking Addams family.

Annalise returned and took the sleeping baby Lucy back from Destiny. "Thanks for holding her."

"I don't mind."

Annalise took a seat with the baby. "I know, but your hands are better at sewing than mine, so I'll hold her."

"And we have much to do," Larissa reminded.

The women—aside from Annalise—plucked material from the basket and returned to stitching. Delilah looked in the basket. "Can I do something?" She didn't know the first thing about making clothes.

"You just relax," Gracie said. "It's a skill that develops with time."

Time was something she had plenty of. "Did you always know how to sew?" she asked Destiny, who didn't appear to have the proficiency of Larissa and Gracie, but she was still more capable than Delilah.

"My mom used to be a seamstress, so I learned from watching her. But I'm nowhere near as talented as Larissa and Grace."

She glanced at Annalise and the woman snorted. "I got nothin'."

Her modern slang made Delilah smile. She

hadn't considered that her clothes were hand-made, and now she felt horrible for comparing her gown to a pile of Jell-O shot puke.

Gracie slowed her stitching. "Oh, my." She placed the green fabric back in the basket. "I think I'll work on a black dress for you."

Delilah's eyes widened. Shit. Was she reading her mind?

"Not purposefully. You newer transitions tend to project your thoughts. It's sort of like you're shouting at me. What's a Jell-O shot?"

"Mmm," Destiny and Anna both moaned.

"Remember Jell-O?" Destiny said in a reminiscently fond tone.

Anna laughed. "Remember Vodka?"

Real concern bloomed in Delilah's gut. "You guys don't drink?"

"Good luck finding a high enough proof to impact our nervous system. We burn the effects right off."

"Speak for yourself. I was drunk last night," Destiny bragged, earning an eye roll from Anna.

"She's a half-breed," Gracie explained.

"Rude," Destiny tossed a spool of thread at Gracie. "You're just bitter because the females aren't *allowed* to drink."

"Do the males?"

"Of course," Annalise said with evident snark. "But even they can't get drunk. To feel any sort of intoxication we would need a shit-ton of drugs mixed into a cocktail."

Delilah waited for the other girls to correct

Anna's language, but no one said anything. She smiled, liking these women more and more. "Thank you for the gifts this morning."

Larissa beamed. "It's our pleasure. Gracie will take more precise measurements, and we'll take in these dresses so they fit more comfortably. Eleazar already told us your height."

"Eleazar?"

"My husband, the bishop. I thought you met him."

She did recall a man stopping by the house, but she'd been so determined to ignore Christian at the time and in the midst of her hunger strike, that she didn't recall much detail about the man.

"Can I get you something to eat or drink?" Gracie asked.

"I'll have some water if you have it." She didn't want to bother her for food and have to explain the whole vegetarian thing again, but maybe that was why she was so exhausted.

Gracie went into the house and returned shortly with a glass of water. The girls watched her as she drank it down. When Delilah emptied the glass, she looked back at them in question. "What?"

Larissa gave her sister a stern look. "Gracie, don't."

"You're not feeding."

"Grace!" Larissa appeared completely scandalized by her sister's observation. "Ignore her, Delilah. She didn't mean to intrude in matters that are absolutely no concern of hers." She sent her sister a scathing glance. "Really, Gracie. You know better."

Embarrassed and, now uncomfortable, Delilah bit her lip. "It's... It's okay. It probably seems silly to you."

"Not at all."

"Nope."

"A little."

"You can't starve yourself. Brother Christian will forbid it."

She looked toward Destiny and Annalise who took a more understanding position on the matter, likely because they weren't born immortal like her. "Did you struggle with it?"

"Yup."

"Cain had to put me in a trance to get me to take his blood."

Delilah's eyes went wide. "They can do that?"

The women exchanged knowing glances and Gracie explained, "New transitions need a lot of blood."

"Wait, are you suggesting that Christian gave me his blood without my knowledge?"

"Not at all," Larissa interjected. "Because that would be none of our business."

After that, the girls sealed their lips, but Delilah had a sneaking suspicion they were right. How else could she explain the change in her this morning?

"Isn't this maroon lovely!" Gracie exclaimed. "Not at all like vomit."

Annalise and Destiny exchanged a glance

and Delilah sensed there were certain things they wanted to tell her, but not in front of Larissa and Gracie. Maybe she could ask for more water. Then it occurred to her that Gracie was probably reading her thoughts.

"Correct. Still shouting," Gracie said without looking up from her work as she stitched the hem of a gown.

"So, how are you coping with the Amish thing so far?" Annalise asked, changing the subject.

Feeling useless, she fiddled with her empty glass. "Um, I guess it's a little weird. Sorry. Is that rude of me?"

The girls laughed. "Not at all," Annalise lifted her bonnet to scratch at her copper hair. "It's totally weird. I'm still not used to it, and I've been here for years."

Delilah examined her, searching for signs of longing or regret. "Do you ever miss your old life?"

Anna shrugged. "Sometimes. But it's more like missing pieces. I'm happy I'm here with Adam."

"What was your life like before this?"

"I was a student and a waitress at a bar. Nothing super glamourous."

"You get used to it," Destiny said. "Although sometimes I miss the internet."

"Destiny was on television," Larissa said, her tone full of admiration.

"Really?"

Destiny nodded. "I was a field reporter for

Channel Six. It's just a small local station."

"Cool."

"It brought me to Cain." She grinned then lamented. "I'm sure by now social media's changed so much I wouldn't even know how to use whatever platform's trending."

It was refreshing to hear them speak in modern phrases. "TikTok's all the rage."

"What's TikTok?" Anna asked.

"The dance app? You're kidding?" Destiny laughed. "I never thought that would stick. Kids record videos of silly dance trends and post them from their phones."

"Well, it's not just for dances anymore. People use it for everything. And it's not just for kids. It got really popular during the pandemic."

Gracie frowned. "The what?"

"Another plague," Larissa explained inaccurately.

Anna rolled her eyes. "Sickness is a tricky thing to explain here. I read about it, but it never hit us." She shrugged. "Immunity is just one of the perks of being immortal."

"I miss dancing." Larissa sighed.

No alcohol or music. No television or social media. How would Delilah ever survive such a lifestyle? Not that she wanted to.

"It's not as difficult as you might think, being here," Anna said as if sensing her concern. "Adam lets me have a record player."

"Really?" Delilah was certain that wasn't allowed. "Like a wind-up one?"

Anna nodded. "Whenever he goes to town,

he buys me records from the old consignment shop. I love the Beatles. That's how Lucy got her name, *Lucy in the Sky with Diamonds*. It was either that or Elenore Rigby." She laughed.

"Or Penny Lane," Delilah joked, feeling closest to Anna.

"Lovely Rita!" Destiny chimed in and the warm sense of belonging expanded.

"Well," Gracie interrupted their fun, sounding slightly left out. "As interesting as music is, I'm sure there are other things we can discuss. Like what you think of your new mate, Delilah. Is he kind to you?"

"He's…"

The women leaned in expectantly. She was torn between telling them what they apparently wanted to hear—that Christian had claimed her and she was now living some sort of cosmic destiny with her destined mate—or the truth.

"He's…"

A strange, protective instinct came over her, making her words difficult to share. She shouldn't care what anyone thought of a man who abducted her and forced her to dress up like an extra in *The Handmaid's Tale*. But she couldn't bring herself to speak negatively about him to people who might unfairly judge him without all the facts.

What were the facts? Why was she cutting him slack? She'd waited all this time to get here and beg the women for help so she could escape and go back to her life, but now she didn't want to betray Christian.

She couldn't fathom where such loyalty stemmed from. He deserved nothing but her wrath. This was her chance to ask for help. She should be pleading with these women and telling them every horrid thing he did to her. So why wasn't she?

"Actually, we're still getting to know one another." She frowned, unsure where that load of horse shit came from.

"Adam kidnapped Anna."

"Grace! Honestly, what has gotten into you today?"

"What? It's true. And look how happy you are now."

"It wasn't our proudest moment," Anna told Delilah then turned back to Grace. "Thanks a lot."

Gracie shrugged. "She's not being honest with us. Maybe if she knew your story, she wouldn't feel so self-conscious about her own."

Delilah really needed to learn how to guard her thoughts.

"That's her choice, Gracie. She'll share when she's ready." Anna rolled her eyes and returned her attention to Delilah. "Is there anything we can do to help?"

She looked at each woman, unsure who she could trust and who she couldn't. "Um...I... How do you block your thoughts?"

Anna sighed. "I got Gracie out of my head by picturing her brother naked. I'm not sure that will work with Brother Christian."

Gracie snickered. "It doesn't. She already

pictured him several times. At least you got lucky in *that* department."

Mortified, Delilah blinked at the girl. "You saw Christian…*naked?*"

"Only when you showed me."

"I wasn't showing you."

"But you were."

Larissa leaned forward and patted Delilah's knee through her gown. "She doesn't mean it. It's actually quite a burden for her."

Gracie nodded. "Mortals are the worst. Their thoughts are like standing next to a blaring siren." There was no malice or accusation in her tone, just regretful acceptance.

Delilah supposed that sort of intrusive noise might drive a person crazy. "Sorry?"

"It's okay. I feel like I'm getting to know the real you."

Self-conscious and unsure what sort of first impression her unguarded thoughts gave, Delilah shrank a little in her seat. "I didn't realize I was blasting my thoughts."

"In time, you'll learn better self-control," Destiny said. "We've all gone through it."

"And I've suffered each and every one of your filthy minds, thank you very much," Gracie added with a touch of sarcasm and a dash of horror. "It's nice to meet a female who *isn't* picturing one of my brothers naked all hours of the day."

Delilah hadn't realized she'd pictured Christian naked at all, but apparently, she wasn't fully aware of her deepest thoughts. "Are you married?"

"I'm still waiting for my calling. I won't marry unless he's my true mate."

"They aren't the same? Mating and marriage are two different things?" She didn't mean to sound stupid, but she'd assumed they were synonymous by the way so many of them interchanged the two.

"Mates are chosen by God. It is our greatest sacrament," Larissa explained.

Destiny rolled her eyes. "Not all mates find a perfect love though. Marriage is a choice. Cain and I are married."

"Not all marriages are by choice," Larissa argued.

Annalise sighed as if to cut the tension. "There are good marriages and bad marriages, just like there are all over the world. And some partners are just assholes, whether they're called by God or driven by some other force. It's possible to have a mate and not love him the way one might love a husband, but there is always a holy link that cannot be broken."

"I thought mates had to protect each other."

"They should," Anna said. "But different mates share different connections. And because the privacy of mates is so protected here, there's still a lot we don't understand."

Destiny leaned forward, cupping her hand over the side of her mouth as she whispered, "And some of the elders have been around since God was a boy. So, if you think it's hard to pass laws with the crypt keepers in congress, prepare yourself for a new level of old-school."

"Careful, Destiny," Larissa warned. "Christian's on The Elder's Council."

"Don't worry if your guy's older than dirt," Destiny joked. "The males here put Charlie Chaplin to shame. I'm sure he's already proven his virility a hundred times over."

The girls giggled all except for Gracie.

A hundred times? Delilah thought, a pinch of inadequacy coming out of nowhere. *More like twice with a chaser of panic and regret.*

"The bonding is sacred," Gracie said, her voice taking on a reverent tone. "The connection to a called mate is formed at creation and fortified during the blood exchange. Most mates cannot live a full life without their other half."

Destiny stopped laughing. "But neither is better than the other. It's not a competition."

Gracie pursed her lips as if she disagreed, but before she could comment, a masculine voice called from inside the house.

"Hello? Anyone home?"

A man appeared in the shadow of the back door and Gracie scowled. Delilah instantly recognized him as Christian's half-brother, Dane, but she didn't recognize the man holding a small child beside him.

"Momma!" the little girl squealed and the man lowered her to the ground. She looked like a doll in her little bonnet and black Amish gown as she ran to Larissa.

"Moriah, How did you end up with your uncle?" Larissa frowned at the man who had been carrying her daughter. "Cain, did Eleazar—"

He held up his hands. "*I* volunteered to take her. The bishop had to deal with an issue in the cells."

Gracie's eyes lit with concern. "Cybil?"

A strange look passed between the siblings and Cain nodded.

"Has there been any news regarding Juniper," Annalise asked.

He gave her a stern look. "Didn't ask. Don't care."

Destiny cleared her throat. "Cain, this is Delilah, Christian's new mate."

Rather than acknowledge her presence, he lowered his head to kiss his wife's lips, lingering and whispering something in a foreign language against her mouth. It sounded… Portuguese. Destiny's caramel cheeks deepened to a dusky shade of rose. Whatever Cain whispered must have been dirty.

Delilah swallowed back the sense of envy constricting her throat, curious what that sort of love and adoration would feel like, having never been kissed like that a day in her life. Not only were the two obviously in love but there was also a protectiveness in the way they touched one another, a coherency of need and respect, sort of like the way the ocean meets the sand, again and again, one forming around the other.

Only when they pulled away did Delilah get

a full look at the man. Talk about an Amish cover model. It occurred to her then that none of the men wore beards, and she wondered if that was an immortal thing or something to do with their sect.

"We were playing with the clouds with Uncle Cain," the little girl exclaimed then hugged Jaden with unguarded affection. "Can Jaden play?"

The little boy looked up at his young relatives, his silver eyes flashing above the disturbing mask. There had to be a better solution to teething. She supposed impetuous toddlers with fangs might complicate things. Forget about nursing.

"Hello, Grace," Dane said with pointed directness.

Grace said nothing, obviously hearing his greeting but choosing to ignore him as she busied herself with the sewing.

Delilah sensed Cain staring at her and turned, but he immediately averted his eyes—deliberately snubbing her. He didn't initially strike her as impolite, but the way he ignored her certainly felt rude. He seemed perfectly friendly with the other women.

Dane had no issue addressing her. "Does Christian know you're here?"

Her hackles rose at the implication that she might not be *permitted* to sit with the other women in their sewing circle. Apparently, Christian's brother was also a dick. It made sense why Gracie would ignore him.

Gracie snickered.

"Careful, Dane, you know how temperamental Christian can be," Cain warned. "New mates are extremely territorial. Don't speak to her in his absence."

Delilah scowled at the men. Did he actually just speak about her as if she weren't sitting right there? "I can talk to whoever I want."

Cain ignored her, but chuckled, his gaze saved only for the others. "This should be interesting." Then he swatted his wife's ass and said something to Destiny in that same foreign language that made her blush.

Destiny tidied up her materials and thread and put them back in the basket. "I better go. You know how he gets." She didn't appear put out as she scampered after her husband. "We'll see you guys at supper. Anna, we're eating at your house, right?"

A loud crack of thunder boomed and they all jumped. Cain yelled from the back gate, "Destiny, your husband has needs! *Anda logo, vamos!*"

"Calm yourself," Destiny snapped then turned back to Annalise.

"Yes. Gracie's cooking."

"Oh, good."

"Hey," Anna whined, scrunching her nose. "That soup I made last week wasn't too bad."

Gracie's eyes widened in obvious disagreement.

"The hogs wouldn't even eat it," Dane said.

"You would know better than the rest of us

what pigs like," Gracie commented under her breath.

Ouch. There was no missing the tension between those two.

Destiny rolled her eyes. "I gotta go before we all end up in a storm. Nice meeting you, Delilah. Let's hang out again soon." She hiked her skirts and ran off to her husband. When she reached him, Cain picked her up and tossed her over his shoulder, planting a hand firmly on her rounded ass before toting her away.

"Ignore them," Grace said, shaking her head. "Cain's a pervert."

"He's not a pervert. They're in love." Anna smiled at the adorable couple.

"Some people like to show affection," Dane said snidely.

Gracie's glare snapped to him. "And some are just whores."

"She's not a whore." Dane said, initiating a chilling silence among the circle.

Finally, Gracie tossed down her sewing and stood. "I wasn't speaking about *her*, you fool. Excuse me."

The moment Gracie disappeared into the house, Anna stood. "You walked into that one, Dane." She laid Lucy in a wicker Moses basket and gathered up the baby items in her apron.

Larissa scooped up Jaden. "I don't think I've ever heard a man referred to as a whore. What do you do all day, alone in that barn of yours?"

"It's her own fault for nosing around in my

head. I don't even know why I come here anymore."

"I do." Annalise chuckled.

Delilah was lost. Was there something between Gracie and Dane?

Dane glared at the house then rolled his eyes. "Whatever. I'm going to visit my sister before supper. I can take Moriah back to the house for you, Larissa."

"Thanks Dane."

Delilah tried to keep up. Dane had a sister? Did that mean that she was also Christian's sister?

Delilah wasn't sure what was going on, but everyone started packing up so it seemed a good time to call for Christian. She wasn't sure how one called from their mind. It wasn't like there was a send button or number to dial, so she just thought his name. *Christian?*

Pintura?

Relief flooded her at the familiar sense of his nearness, then she frowned, not wanting such weird things to feel so regular or reassuring. She needed to hold onto a sane sense of normalcy.

Did you need me?

She refused to say or even think that she needed him. *Um...I'm ready to go.*

I'll be right there.

Dane walked Moriah through the gate and Larissa waited with her, still holding the masked little boy. "Is Christian on his way?"

"I think so." The child watched her curiously

but the muzzle was so off-putting Delilah had a hard time interacting. "You don't have to wait with me."

Larissa smiled. "I don't mind." Holding her baby brother on her hip, she swayed like a woman who was used to caring for children.

The three little ones—Jaden, Little Cain, and Moriah—were all around the same age, but each was uniquely different. Moriah seemed the most independent and strong-willed. Little Cain fit neatly into Delilah's stereotypical definition of toddlers—if toddlers had fangs. But there was something distinctly off about Jaden.

A darkness hid in the boy's eyes. His intelligence wasn't lacking though. Delilah imagined he had much to say when the muzzle came off. Was he cruel with his words? Hurtful? Maybe he was simply teething, but that didn't necessarily lead to viciousness. What could the child have done to deserve to wear such a mask?

The sky darkened into a rosy fuchsia as the sun set behind the trees. "I think it's wonderful that you chose to save Brother Christian," Larissa commented as they waited.

"Save him?"

"Yes, from going unanswered."

Delilah frowned. "You lost me."

"When a male is called, he must find his mate. If he doesn't, he can die."

A cold chill ran through Delilah's blood. Her concern for her captor irritating her once more. "I didn't have a choice in the matter."

"It's a beautiful sunset tonight," Larissa

looked out over the horizon, letting the conversation drop.

Delilah caught her arm, drawing the attention of both her and Jaden. The boy growled and Larissa combed a loving hand through his hair.

"I have no one here to talk to about this stuff," she whispered, her eyes pleading for an ally.

Larissa met her stare then looked away. "You can talk to your mate."

"He only tells me what he wants me to know."

"I cannot discuss this with you." She self-consciously glanced over her shoulder. "It's a private matter between mates. It is against our laws to involve one's self in such personal considerations."

Infuriated by such archaic subservience to a suffocating patriarchy, she snapped, "He's *not* my mate. He's my captor. I don't love him. I have a life I need to return to. You have to help me, Larissa. You're married to the patriarch."

"And as the bishop's wife, I must set an example."

"Of what? Oppression and obedience?"

Larissa's eyes flashed silver and she jerked her arm out of Delilah's hold. "Brother Christian is a good and honorable male. How dare you presume to know my situation and summarize my life so blithely as if my existence is merely a pitiful result of male choices. I've lived through more than you can imagine, and I chose to be here. My husband protects and values me above all things. I am not oppressed and I don't simply obey like a mindless hound. I love and honor him because he loves and honors me." Her gaze lifted. "Your mate is here."

Delilah turned and her heart plummeted into the pit of her stomach, chills racing over her shoulders and down her arms. Christian scowled from the gate. He'd heard everything, as did Dane who was standing by his side with Moriah.

She hadn't meant to offend the woman. She should have never mentioned anything to her. Destiny and Anna were the women to talk to.

Angry that Larissa somehow sounded like a hero while Delilah was gaslit as a criminal, she glared at her. "You set me up."

"No. I helped you. You just don't realize it yet." She crossed the path and walked off with Dane and the children.

Frozen, Delilah met Christian's stare. A tremor of uncertainty rolled through her like building thunder. Had she gone too far? He was her captor. He was holding her against her will. She wanted to go home.

Her gaze followed Dane's shrinking form. Why would no one help her?

"Delilah." Her name snapped through the air like the crack of a whip, commanding her focus away from the other man.

Christian's entire body flared with pent-up rage as he breathed deeply, his shoulders rising as he watched her with that mercurial stare. He was terrifying, but she would not be bullied. Whatever he intended to do to her.

Her eyes narrowed on him. *Bring it.*

"Come. It's time we returned home."

But that wasn't her home. She was tired of letting others decide her fate. This was her fucking life and her fucking decision.

"I'm leaving." Yanking up her skirts she marched past him, heart jackhammering in her chest, her brain a maze of indecision as she tried to figure out her next step.

He followed, but she didn't look back. She had no idea where she was going, but if she walked far enough, she'd eventually hit signs of modern civilization.

"I see I made a mistake, trusting you on your own."

She ignored him, too furious with her adaptation into captivity to unlock her jaw and form actual words. Was this how it worked with the animals? She thought of wild bears, roaming the mountains and living freely, then suddenly trapped and confined, taken to some horrific zoo where they were forced to live within a glass cage, on display for all to watch and judge.

Larissa judged her. Mostly because Delilah had made unfair assumptions about her as well. Either way, it didn't feel good to be judged so openly when so many circumstances were out of her control.

Her eyes narrowed. This was all Christian and his stupid God's fault.

His frustration boiled at her back as if he

were actually targeting the emotion at her, burning her flesh with his irritation and aiming the blame of each complication directly at her skull. A crippling migraine formed between her eyes, throbbing so painfully she was amazed she could still walk.

So much for love and affection. As far as mating went, Destiny was right. Marriage was better. At least then people had a choice.

But who in their right mind would actually choose to live in this repressed version of the American colonies? She was over this Hester Prynne bullshit. She wanted to go back to her own fucking modern way of life and get the hell away from this primitive oppression under tyrannical male law.

If Christian wanted her, the real her, he should be glad for her defiance. He was trying to erase her.

"I am not trying to erase you," he snapped, keeping step at her side.

If he could read her thoughts what was the point in talking? *Get the fuck out of my head, Nosferatu.*

In her peripheral, she saw several other Amish people—vampires—whatever the hell they called them—working in the distance. Most of them were men.

She walked without pause for over twenty minutes, steaming inside and hoping to burn off some of her rage.

Her headache drilled into her temples and exhaustion consumed her. She stumbled and

Christian held out a hand to steady her, but she jerked out of reach. "Don't touch me."

"I thought we were past this."

Bone tired, she didn't have the strength to fight with him. Shouldn't she have superhuman strength or something? Maybe she was allergic to immortality because it wasn't agreeing with her. Or maybe she'd stepped into some sort of vampire kryptonite, as every step seemed to sap away her strength.

Coming up on a lone, flat rock at the corner of a harvested field, she paused to catch her breath. Her body needed a rest and she nearly collapsed the moment her knees stopped pumping. Bunching up her skirt, she lowered her body to sit on the flat stone buried by time.

"What are you doing?" He glared down at her impatiently.

Her bones screamed as if someone were hammering them apart. "What's it look like? I'm sitting." Her fingers trembled as she yanked off her bonnet. Lying back on the cool rock, her arm draped weakly into the grass.

"Your hair must stay covered—"

"Fuck the fuck off, Christian!" She moaned as the pain in her head doubled. "Damn it."

He rushed to her side, realizing something was wrong. "Are you ill?" He sat behind her, touching his fingers to her forehead and throat. "You're burning up. How long has your head ached like this? You're completely exhausted. Why didn't you tell me?"

Too weak to battle him, she simply moaned and leaned into his support.

"You purposely hid your lethargy from me, Delilah."

How could she have done that when she didn't know how? Her tired gaze fell on a dandelion, snapped at the base of its stem. Her fingers gently rolled over the toppled flower, and the weed suddenly pulled upright, as if on an invisible thread. The stem mended itself back together and its yellow petals brightened.

She smiled weakly. *Awesome.*

The thrill was quickly shadowed by a wave of cramping. Doubling over, she moaned.

"Delilah!" Christian's concern chiseled into her like a sharp pick and the last of her strength went toward soothing his worry.

"I'm okay…"

"You're not. You must sleep now."

Sleep sounded perfect. The world tilted and her head lolled as blissful oblivion swallowed her like the tide.

CHAPTER 13

Dane sat on the cool concrete of the Safe House cellar floor, as Council Hall quieted and the bishop and his family settled in for their evening meal above. The hushed sounds overhead played like a symphony of ordinary life.

A piece of silverware scraped along a plate. Larissa softly tittered as Eleazar complimented her cooking. The chatter of their daughter filled the background followed by the occasional outburst of affectionate laughter.

He envied their happiness, wondering if he'd ever find a kind of ordinary joy similar to theirs. But there was nothing ordinary about these folks, and after two years without his sister to talk to or a sense of home, he wouldn't call that kind of contentment anything short of extraordinary.

The downfall of being a half-breed was his

dependency on blood. He'd become reliant on his heightened senses, and his appetite for the stuff sometimes felt more like an addiction—something he relied on to keep up with the others, even though he'd never be their equal.

He'd become a slave to his nature, one of the reasons he invited Magdalene back into his bed as frequently as he did. After two years of feeding, he'd developed a keener sense of hearing, which helped him stay informed. Unfortunately, it also led to overhearing many things he wished he didn't know.

Ignorance was no longer an option when he overheard the whispered opinions about his and Cybil's presence on the farm. Nor was laziness.

Cybil was the only family—true family—he had left. And while the Hartzlers kindly included him in their supper plans, he would never fully belong at their table. But here, in this cold basement staring into his sister's dark cell, he was at home.

The Order's ongoing debate to find the most merciful path to end his deranged sister's life had become his second enemy, the first being the monster lurking in the last cell—Isaiah Hartzler. Every day, Dane strategized ways to keep his sister alive and see Isaiah destroyed. Discussions were endless among The Elder's Council. He supposed when a species lived forever, there was really no reason to rush to a decision.

Dane wasn't here because of his faith or a

desire to live a more simplistic life. He didn't give a shit about agriculture, and he certainly didn't scorn technology the way the others did. He was here for justice. He would stay on the farm as long as it took to see retribution delivered.

It was their fault Cybil was the way she was, their neglected duty that allowed Isaiah to slaughter hundreds of women including his mother, and their enigmatic existence that wrecked whatever illusion of family he once had.

Discovering the existence of immortals complicated everything. Learning he shared their superior bloodlines was a curse because he would never be accepted as one of them, and his life would never feel normal again.

He didn't fully belong here or in the human world. But there was no going back. No return to any sense of fullness. He'd always be half of what he once was. Living a half-life compared to the wholesome one he'd lost. That was the inescapable truth about being a half-breed, half as good, half as powerful, half normal, everything was now half.

They would never fully accept him. Just as racism and xenophobia existed in the outside world, it existed here. Their prejudice toward the human race was only kept in check by their Amish values, but beneath their polite show of acceptance lived a deep-seated disregard for the lesser creatures, and he would always be seen as less.

He came here to get his mind off of Gracie, an impossible task. The nerve of her calling him a whore. Compared to the others, his interactions with the females on the farm were practically nonexistent, save his encounters with Maggie.

Maggie was a distraction, but the longer their association carried on the less enchanted with her sweetness and beauty he became. Gracie remained in the forefront of his mind. He dared not measure the space she occupied in his heart, for there was no recourse there for them.

She made it perfectly clear she would never accept him in any sort of romantic way because she couldn't accept his mortal blood, not when she'd spent her life saving herself for her one true mate.

When he'd learned of his birth father and discovered he shared Christian Schrock's immortal genes, he had hoped Gracie might change her mind, but she hadn't. It had been quite the opposite. The discovery of his partial immortality angered her. Why?

In his mind, his bloodlines made the impossible more plausible. But to Gracie it was a taunt. One step closer to something they would never have. Like a hand reaching through a cage for a prize it would never touch, a temptation that would always be there, existing and forever out of reach.

That was her own stubborn fault. There was no law that said they couldn't find some sort of happiness together. She was the one so dead set on waiting for her calling. That could be a thousand years away. A thousand years he didn't have.

Half-breeds did not live as long as full-bred immortals. They could not be called either, and that lack of divination lost him a lifetime of respect. Many of the immortals on the farm viewed him with contempt, as if he suffered a genetic mutation. They viewed his mortal blood as an infection that tarnished the immaculate flawlessness of what they considered an otherwise perfect race.

Even the bonded mates, like Annalise, were accepted once the transition was complete. Destiny was not bonded, and therefore a half-breed like him, but she didn't seem to mind the label because she had Cain. Cain was the only one who didn't make him feel like a pariah. The others...they would never accept him.

He didn't want to care what they thought. He decided to reject them long before they rejected him. But Grace was different. The Hartzlers were different. They loved him as much as any foster family could love an orphan, but they all knew, compared to their eternal existence, his time here was temporary for more reasons than one.

Gracie didn't believe he was defective, but she did see him as forbidden. And then, once he'd started seeing Maggie, it didn't matter what was in his blood. Gracie despised him for finding comfort in the arms of another female, as if he owed her loyalty when she'd shown him none.

She'd made it more than clear that she wanted nothing to do with him in any sort of romantic sense. But she also wanted no one else to get close to him. It was selfish of her, and he was growing tired of her bitchy commentary and dirty looks.

He hated the prophetic importance The Order placed on callings. He didn't believe the link was any stronger than that of a couple in love. Yet, Gracie had decided long before his arrival on the farm that she would save herself for the one God ordained the other half of her soul.

A shadow moved at the far end of the hall by the door to the stairs. The witch was walking again, which meant that her feet had healed. He wasn't sure what they gave her to make the burns clear up so fast, but when he passed her cell tonight, she'd been sleeping and he caught a glimpse of uninjured pink toes, marked only from the dirt of her cell.

Picking up a chipped stone, he flicked it into the shadows. Part of him wanted to check on her, but Cain had made such a fuss about the witch he figured it was best to leave it alone. He had enough problems of his own to worry about anyway.

Dane had told the bishop about the bruising on her legs and made it clear that he didn't approve of her living conditions. That was more than anyone else had done for her.

While The Council viewed the witch's un-defined sentence as merciful because it per-mitted her to live, it was a ruthless condemnation with no end in sight. He wouldn't be surprised if she eventually became a bondslave—one more layer of cruelty they'd twist and call lenient. But there was no clemency here. Immortals served themselves above all else, and that witch had tried to kill the son of an elder. There was no saving her.

Anger rolled through him in a slow boiling rage as Juniper and many others—including himself—helplessly suffered the hypocrisy of such a pious order. There was no greater power on the farm than that of The Council, and as long as they could wrap their logic up in a bib-lical bow, they felt justified to discipline lesser sinners as they saw fit.

He shamefully took comfort in knowing he wasn't the only victim of their unfair laws . There were a few other ostracized half-breeds on the farm that would never fully fit in.

The women also faced challenges. The dis-crepancies between males and females here were disgraceful, but the females had been op-pressed and sheltered for so long, indoctrinated to fear the outside world, that they actually felt safe and protected by such heavy-handed con-trol. If only they knew the freedoms they could have elsewhere. But no one had it as bad as the witch.

His gaze, once again, returned to the end of the hall. She was quiet, due to her bondage, but he knew she was awake. The shadow of her frame fell past the bars of her cell and stretched toward the torch on the wall.

Could she see him? Was she still blindfolded? He couldn't see her from his angle but sensed she had a better view. Whether she was able to see him or not, he sensed her attention on him.

Acidic emotions soured his stomach. Indigestion had become a familiar and expected part of his day. Like clockwork, he never made it past sunset without suffering the burn of resentment, the sting of loneliness, and the scorching frustration of his powerless position.

There was no cure for that kind of burn. It would only relent if he left this place, but even then, regret would sizzle inside of him.

There was no leaving. He was here. His sister was here. His enemy was here. Gracie was here.

"Pray," Adam had advised him when he once told him about the anxiety keeping him up at night.

Dane scoffed. Their god was not any god he wanted help from. If their god was purely a good god, his sister would not be deranged and in a cell. His mother would not have been ripped to shreds by a vampire and slaughtered right before his eyes.

Breathing deeply, he let his rage settle, deliberately trying to recalibrate his line of thinking so he didn't spiral into a tailspin and burn a stress-hole through his stomach. If not for his minor immortal healing, he'd probably have a belly full of ulcers by now.

Shutting his eyes, he tipped his head back against the stone wall and continued to breathe, intentionally filling his lungs and letting the air out slowly. He was safe. Cybil was safe.

Gracie was safe. The children were safe. Larissa was safe. He did not dare to think about Jonas, the male who had disrupted their world and led them here. He kept his mind only on those he loved.

Ezekiel and Faith. Annalise and Adam. Cain and Destiny. Adriel—and even her shithead son, Christian. They were all safe.

His mind strayed to Christian's tattooed mate and he snickered. "Good luck working that out," he muttered, pulverizing a piece of gravel into dust as he pinched it between his fingers.

He hoped Delilah made Christian's life a living hell, at least for a little while. Eventually, she'd accept this place as her home, just like they all did, even when everything inside screamed they didn't belong here.

When Dane had been told of his lineage, Christian had been present. It was a surprise to both of them. But Dane would never forget the look of disdain in the eyes of his self-righteous half-brother.

"Prick." He picked up another broken piece of stone and tossed it into a pile of gravel.

They were not brothers and they never would be. Christian was a dick, and he deserved everything his almighty god had sent him.

Maggie taught Dane everything she knew about their hybrid kind. She opened her vein to him along with a world of pleasure, and he was grateful for the softness she provided during such a bleak and confusing time.

Their ongoing friendship proved a convenience and solace to both of them. He hadn't meant to hurt Grace, but what was he supposed to do? Wait out his entire life as a virgin until she ran off into the sunset with her full-bred, flawless mate? Fuck that.

Gracie's day would eventually come, and he hoped to be long gone by then. If not for Cybil, he would have left this place long ago. There was nothing here for him anymore. At least Maggie appreciated the little comfort he could offer. No one, aside from Grace, faulted him for having natural urges.

Picturing the way Gracie's dark wavy hair sometimes escaped her kapp had him shifting his weight and adjusting himself. Perhaps he needed to visit Maggie tonight after all.

As a healthy, twenty-year-old man, why wouldn't he bed a willing and attractive female? Maggie offered him blood and her body. There was nothing wrong with them finding comfort in each other. They weren't hurting anyone. Not really.

Fury built and his jaw locked. Eventually, Gracie would willingly give herself over to a perfect stranger, mind, body, and soul. What right did she have to judge him?

Females—regardless of the species—were willful creatures, and Gracie was no different. The foolish girl had been sold a fairytale, and she planned to live her life according to tradition. She planned to be a pure and compliant wife to her true mate, no matter what it cost her. No matter how long she had to wait for destiny to intercede.

Dane's fists clenched. He definitely needed to visit Maggie tonight. Only Maggie's body and warm touch could subdue his anger when it flared like this.

His thoughts were interrupted by the subtle shift in the cell before him. Cybil, his younger sister, once so gentle and kind, now an unhinged transition sick with bloodlust, slept on a pallet in the corner of her cell.

Sentenced to a nocturnal circadian rhythm, she typically woke this time of night, and Dane had become versed at sensing the shift in energy that preceded her stirring. The hair on his arms lifted and he sat straighter, prepared for anything.

He didn't understand how or why the atmosphere tightened or even what changes took place, but he could always sense the shift in her vibration just before she woke. The air throughout the cellar warmed, and dark tension pulled tight like the burning strings of a devil's fiddle. Humidity rose as the vile scent of male desire replaced the dank earthy scent that usually filled the space.

Chains rattled and dragged as blood red eyes flashed in the shadows. Isaiah. A low, territorial growl purred from the cell next to his sister's.

He glared back. "Go to hell."

Chains dragged over the dirt floor as the bastard moved closer to the connecting wall. Closer to Cybil's cell.

"Get away from her."

A wet snarl clapped through the air as Isaiah's jaw snapped with the speed of a viper and the force of a shark.

"Fuck you," Dane snarled.

Cybil was too wild to move. Two years ago, the elders added chains to Isaiah's cell after he gnawed the arm off the bishop's right-hand man. So there was no chance of relocating either of them as easily as they'd moved the witch. But Dane would be damned if the fucker that killed his mother was also going to deprive him of his only time with his sister.

And he didn't care what everyone else said. That girl in there was still his flesh and blood. Still his little sister.

But the sweet child Cybil had once been was gone. He'd forgotten her voice and the dulcet tone of her laughter. Now, she only growled like a rabid animal, trapped in captivity, dangerous, emotionless, hungry, and driven by her baser instincts.

Her body was no longer that of a child's.

Her mind now tortured and deranged. But she was blameless in the horrific outcome of what she had become.

Dane was not.

He had demanded that Cain try to help her and the ramifications were his to bear. She had become this way because of them. Dane wanted to save her when she could not be saved, and now the fading memories that remained had been rewritten by a future that terrified him.

What would happen to her if he gave up his vigil? If he left, who else would watch over her? Only he and Cain truly cared about her safety, but Cain had his own life to live.

The elders allowed her survival and care as a courtesy. Many claimed a quick death would be the most merciful choice. But, once again, Dane selfishly begged to keep her alive.

Perhaps the drawn-out captivity was cruel. There seemed no end in sight, but he sensed an end coming for her, creeping closer and closer, like an unavoidable dawn that would change everything in its wake.

An omen.

Prophets whispered of great biblical ends. Since learning that immortals and vampires existed, a bleak hopelessness surrounded him.

Cybil was in danger, and he had no way of protecting her on his own. As long as she remained in this godforsaken cell under the predatory stare of those glowing red eyes, that danger grew. Every day, she looked more and more like a woman and every night those menacing eyes watched her change, as if waiting for some Ecclesiastical signal.

A time to live, a time to die. A time to plant, a time to reap. Those menacing eyes watched her the way the farmers watched the land, eager to harvest the moment ripened fruit naturally fell from the vine.

Every night he questioned the strength of the cell walls and the chains that held Isaiah. Dane knew if he ever broke free and went after her, he would risk his own life to protect his sister.

A low purr poured from the shadows and he closed his eyes. Cybil was growing into a young woman. She now had hair where there had been none. Curves where her flat body had once been smooth. He sensed Isaiah's awareness of her and desperately wished there was a way to take her somewhere else, somewhere safe and far away from here.

The beast often watched the wall with predatory lust. Dane pictured killing him a thousand times over for the filthy way he stared, for retribution of that and other crimes Dane would never forgive, for the value of his mother's life and all the other women he massacred in the woods.

But The Council had ordered that Isaiah remain alive, his survival following the decree that no harm come to Cybil. Dane hated that her trial had set a precedent that somehow protected the life of the animal that killed their mother.

A sharp growl enunciated the burst of energy that traveled through the cellar in a wave. The atomic shift lifted the hair on the back of his neck. Cybil's eyes opened in an abrupt flash of awareness.

Her head dispassionately turned and blood-red orbs, much like Isaiah's eyes, zeroed in on Dane. She hissed and sprang onto all fours, the tattered remains of her clothing hardly hiding her body as she growled at him.

He sighed. "Cybil, it's me." His presence was becoming less and less sought after everywhere he went.

His masculine voice was met by a vicious growl from the other cell. Isaiah hated when Dane talked to her, so he tried to say as much as possible whenever she was awake, but he didn't believe his sister understood any of it.

With a snide smirk, he taunted Isaiah by calling her name. "Cybil…"

Chains rattled as a blood-thirsty growl ripped through the room. The wet snap of Isaiah's fangs caused Dane to flinch, but he was safe. The reinforced steel bars and chains assured he couldn't break free.

Even if Isaiah did escape, the heavily drugged diet of vegetation and rodent blood the elders fed him left him weak and feeble. However, as a half-mortal, Dane would never be a match for a starved full-bred immortal more than three centuries old. But he'd take his chances if it meant taunting the fucker.

"Did you sleep well, Cybil?"

She straightened and stared at him, hardly registering his voice amongst all the howling and rattling next door, no longer recognizing Dane as anything more than an intruder to her solitude.

A long stick leaned against the stone wall. He used it to nudge a pewter goblet of blood through the bars of her cell. In a flash, she snatched the offering off the ground and guzzled it down. Crimson trickles flooded her chin as she drank thirstily.

She threw the empty cup back at him, angered that there was no more. It hit the wall beside his head with a crash, sending a dusting of mortar flurrying over his shoulder.

While she was given better blood than Isaiah, the elders ordered that she only be fed the minimal requirement. Otherwise, she would grow too strong and need chains as well.

Isaiah had consumed decades of human blood. According to the elders, even after his two years in captivity, the effects would remain in his system for years to come.

Human blood was forbidden for consumption by The Order. The only exception being when an immortal drank from the vein of a called human mate or in extreme times of a life-or-death emergency. The law was not abided by immortals everywhere, but specific to The Order. The Amish preferred everything in moderation, except simplicity, of course.

According to the elders, the adrenaline in mortal blood was too potent for general consumption, especially when fear came into play. It caused bloodlust and addiction among their kind, which was how so many females had died at the hands of Isaiah—including his mother.

Cybil's chin and pale lips were stained crimson to match her eyes. She bared her fangs, as she rushed the bars, growling for more blood. Her wild mass of gold hair formed a halo around her youthful face.

A purr rumbled, low like thunder, from the cell to her right, and Cybil's head turned sharply. She lurched toward the separating wall, her motions abrupt and jerky.

Dane often wondered if she realized Isaiah was the beast that killed their mother.

She pressed her face against the stone wall and purred, red eyes closing, small white fangs showing behind her stained, parted lips. Dane's spine stiffened as Isaiah moved, his chains rattling and dragging over the dirt floor.

"Hey!" he called, but the bastard ignored him. From the dark shadows of his cell, he crept closer to the bars, leaning into the exact spot on the wall opposite Cybil.

The vibrations coming from his sister's throat grew louder as she moved her face, much like a cat nuzzles when wanting to be fed. Dane frowned. He'd never seen her do such a thing.

Rising from the floor, he grabbed a torch from the wall and moved closer to the bars. "Cybil."

She paid him no mind as she rubbed her

face on the wall and purred. Dust crumbled and then he saw it.

"Son of a bitch." He angled the torch, trying to cast more light into her cell. Anyone could miss it if they didn't know where to look, but Dane now saw it clear as day—a missing stone.

"Cybil, get away from there!"

She ignored him, too besotted by the wall to even hiss or growl at him. She just closed her eyes and purred, as did Isaiah.

"Hey!" Dane snapped, banging the stick against the bars. "Stay away from her!"

The missing stone in the wall was small, leaving an opening no larger than a fist, but it was enough for Cybil to fit her small hand through. Luckily, she wasn't doing that.

Then Isaiah lifted a hand and the metal cuff on his arm raised the chain. Bones cracked and popped, as his filthy hand deformed into a misshapen claw. The fucker was literally breaking his own hand.

He should call for help, but who would hear him? "Fuck!"

Shoving the torch back into the hook on the wall, he paced and panicked. Isaiah could easily slide out of the manacle with his hand broken the way it was, but he wasn't trying to escape. He just stood there, slouched against the wall breathing heavily while Cybil purred. Then he raised his broken hand.

"Hey!"

He reached into the hole, fitting his hand

through the crumbling stone, and touched Cybil.

"Get your fucking hand off of her!"

His sister dragged her cheek over his filthy, deformed knuckle and purred, her claws extended, scraping at the stone wall while Isaiah touched her.

"Cybil, stop!"

Her snarled hair wound around the dirt-crusted knuckles as their purrs amplified. Dane bolted toward the door then doubled back, afraid to leave her and unsure what to do. Although caged and chained, they were both immeasurably stronger than him.

"Don't you fucking touch her!"

Their indifference to his rage overwhelmed him with panic. He was powerless to stop the piece of shit from stroking her face.

"Help!" His only hope was that the bishop would hear him.

Without the help of an elder immortal, Dane couldn't safely enter his sister's cell. She would attack him as ruthlessly as she attacked the cup of blood he'd offered.

Snatching the pewter goblet off the ground he threw it through the bars. It hit the stone wall and clattered to the dirt floor. Cybil bared her fangs and hissed, but Isaiah's finger was there, teasing over her lips as he turned his wrist toward her mouth.

Dane stared in horror. They had done this before. It was obvious by the way she seemed aware of his expectation and glad to accept his offering.

"Cybil, no!"

Her jaw swiftly unhinged and her sharp teeth sank into Isaiah's flesh. The masculine grunt that came from the shadows sickened him.

"Stop!" Dane screamed, frantic and unsure how to stop them. *"Eleazar! Somebody!"*

He stared in horror as his little sister moaned and fed. Her body gyrated as she greedily pulled from Isaiah's vein. Dane didn't want to watch but couldn't look away.

"Fuck! Stop it, Cybil! You don't want to do this." His voice broke as the repulsive display continued on.

The disgusting slurping caused Dane to cover his ears in horror. Their labored breathing filled the quiet basement.

"Cybil! Cybil, stop!" Nothing could break her focus as she fed from him.

He didn't understand. Isaiah was starved, fed blood only twice a month with the arrival of each new moon. Why would he offer her his blood when he was already so weak?

The masculine moans took on a carnal cadence and the chains shifted. Dane couldn't see his red eyes anymore but he made out the curve of his body in the shadows, rocking slowly against the wall.

"I said stop!" Dane screamed.

Desperate to break them apart, he reached for the heavy stick and lobbed it through the bars like a javelin, gasping as it soared directly for his sister's face. Isaiah's broken hand twisted with inhuman speed, ripping his flesh from Cybil's bloodied teeth and catching the stick with startling accuracy, protecting Cybil.

A deep, angry growl snapped through the air as he fisted the offensive object and squeezed. His battered, swollen hand dripped with blood as the thick shaft snapped in two and fell to the ground.

No way. No way could he be that strong. He'd been in isolation for two years living off rationed blood. How could he have possibly kept up his strength?

The broken hand gently caressed Cybil's unharmed face then disappeared. Chains rattled, then Isaiah lunged at the steel bars and bared his fangs, hissing viciously!

Dane staggered back, tripping into the wall. The bars shook and he was certain Isaiah wanted to kill him! Plaster loosened from the joints as chains rattled wildly and Isaiah roared. It was then that Dane understood. A meager cell could not detain an immortal of his strength. Something else kept him there, and he had a sickening suspicion he knew what it was.

Cybil jumped and snarled, excited by Isaiah's fury. Only then did Dane hear the muffled moan from the cell on the other end of the hall. Juniper.

Eyes wide, he looked back at his sister. "I'm sorry. I have to go get help."

She hissed at him with bloody fangs. Heart

pounding, he ran as fast as his feet could carry him toward the door to the Safe House above.

Isaiah roared and Cybil screeched excitedly. Juniper let out a muffled scream, unsure what was happening. He'd been in such a rush to find help he'd almost missed the moment he ran past the witch's cell, the moment the torches on the walls all blazed several feet high and touched the ceiling, setting the whole corridor aglow.

He'd almost missed it in his panic as he raced to find the bishop and get help, but in the back of his mind, he knew exactly what he saw.

Only one thing could make the flames of the torches flare and spark like that. And it didn't require free hands, or sight, or even speech. It only required one simple thing. Magic.

CHAPTER 14

A sense of revitalization awoke within Delilah and her mind roused. Comfortably lost between a dream and reality, she moaned softly as her mouth worked. Pleasant. Hot. Satisfying.

No, wait...

Her eyelids snapped open and she screamed, only to choke on whatever was in her mouth. Oh, fuck, she knew what it was. Blood. He was feeding her his fucking blood!

The thick, sticky fluid coated her tongue and she gagged, dry heaving over the side of the bed as every muscle in her body locked.

"You're going to make yourself sick!"

She angrily pointed a finger at him and spit on the floor. Tears blurred her eyes as she tried to breathe, not wanting to focus on the metallic taste drowning her senses.

"You," she wheezed. "How could you?" She

gagged again and wiped her mouth on the back of her arm. The trail of pink saliva turned her stomach even more.

"This is ridiculous. You needed to feed."

The copper taste of death was everywhere, in her sinuses, down her throat, filling her belly like bile on a rocking ship.

"You're purposefully making a dramatic—"

His words cut off when her shoulders tensed and she covered her mouth with a heave. Too late. She vomited the crimson contents of her stomach all over the floor.

Her lungs labored, yet she couldn't draw in one useful gasp of breath. She vomited again. The sight was even worse than the horrific sound, but nothing beat the ungodly smell.

Her body convulsed with shivers once her belly was painfully hollow again, and she fell back onto the bed, panting and sweating. How had this become her life?

He came to her side, and she weakly swatted his touch away. "Don't."

"Enough!" he snapped, catching her flailing arm and dabbing her face with a cool cloth. "I will not be pushed away when you're ill and in need."

She was in need of normalcy. Her eyes struggled to stay open as nausea swam through her in waves. "How could you do that?" The violation of trust was unfathomable. But for trust to be betrayed it would first have to exist, and that was impossible.

"*Pintura, d*o you have any idea how malnourished an immortal has to be to suffer the sort of weakness you suffered last night? You needed nourishment."

She hissed at him, a completely animalistic response, but she didn't care.

"You've been digesting my blood for days—"

"I knew it! The other women said as much! You had no right to feed me your blood!"

"*I had every right!* You. Are. My. Mate."

Her hands covered her ears. "My name is Delilah Starling!"

He caught her arms in an unbreakable grip and put his face close to hers. "Yes, and Delilah Starling is mine—just as I am hers. Do you have any idea how terrified I was last night when you fainted? *Fainted,* Delilah. That is not something immortals do. You deliberately hid your needs from me, and look at what it cost you. Fevered and in pain. *Why* would you put yourself through that?"

"I don't want to be a fucking immortal! This is your fault!"

"Then it's my fault!" he shouted. "Blame me for a thousand years if you must, but I will not sit idly by and watch you starve yourself to near death."

Her jaw trembled as her eyes narrowed on him. Too weak to shout. "Maybe you won't have to. Maybe one day I'll succeed and die."

He stilled. "That's not funny."

She wasn't trying to be funny. "You sentenced me to an eternity of drinking blood. Ask me if I want to live like that." She paused, and he said nothing. "Right. Because you never ask, do you? You just decide and take." A jagged breath slipped down her throat and a sob exploded in her chest. "You deserve to lose me."

This time he didn't comfort her. He could only hold her stare for a moment before looking away in shame.

She hated it here. She hated him for bringing her here. His only hope was eternity, because that was how long it would take to change her opinion of this awful place and him.

He stood and crossed the room. At the pitcher on the dresser, he filled a glass of water and walked it back to her. "Here. It will wash away the taste."

She sat up and took the water, drinking down every last drop. He studied her with pained concern, and she hated that behind his stubborn façade she sensed compassion in him. She pushed the glass onto the nightstand. "I don't feel bad for you."

"I don't want you to."

"Good." She stared so long at the wall that her vision blurred. The creeping sense of guilt tightened her muscles and her stomach pinched, but she refused to take pity on him.

Every time she covertly glanced his way, a strong need to comfort *him* took hold. This was about her. She was the victim here! She needed to feel numb. The futility of her situation was unbearable. Drinking blood…

He literally robbed her of her last shred of hope.

"Delilah?"

Her eyes closed. *Leave me alone...*

The weight of his body left the bed, and she shut her eyes as his steps retreated. A moment later, he returned with rags and a bucket of water. She refused to feel guilty that he was cleaning up her mess. This was his mess. He'd done this.

Finally, the door quietly clicked shut and she was alone, but not. He might have left the room, but she still sensed him in her mind.

CHRISTIAN STARED out the window at the fading sun. It had been six days. Six days since he brought her here. Six days of opposition. Six days of quarreling. Six days of progress followed by mishaps and failure. *He* was failing, not just himself, but her. If he couldn't take care of her, what good was he? She was his sole duty and purpose.

His head lowered as he sent a silent prayer to God asking for guidance. Never, in all his years, had he expected anything this difficult. He was starting to wonder if he should let her go.

Her hunger wasn't abating. Since emptying her stomach, the pains came more frequently, so immense the vicarious waves even caused him to tremble at times. Her emotions were a mix of confusion and rage, but he also sensed her concern and guilt.

The tension in his neck radiated down his spine. They couldn't go on like this. Failing was an unacceptable outcome, yet failure seemed the only thing he could successfully do where Delilah was concerned.

The sound of someone approaching his home caught his ear and his shoulders stiffened, his attention darting to his mate upstairs. He sniffed the air, identifying the intruder as male.

Delilah, someone's approaching the house. Stay put.

She didn't respond, but he sensed her weak attempt to push him out of her head, so he knew she heard his command. Without proper nourishment and training, she wouldn't be able to manage such control.

The male continued to approach, now trespassing on his private property. With a growl, he left the window to confront the issue outside but paused to glance up at the second floor leading to the bedroom.

Exiting the house, he slammed the front door with more force than necessary, scenting Dane from several hundred feet away. He also scented the boy's anger. Christian bristled for a fight, glad to have a target for his pent-up rage.

His half-bred half-brother locked his eyes on him, glaring from a hundred yards away. Christian hardened his scowl, his hands balling into fists. "This isn't a good time."

"When are you coming back to The Council?" Dane barked, not at all what Christian anticipated hearing.

"Why would that be any concern of yours?"

"You have a duty to The Order!"

His nostrils flared at his castigating tone. "You did not just march onto my property and make demands at me as if you have any sort of authority here."

He reminded himself the boy was half mortal, and Christian could likely end him with a single blow. While he didn't care for the half-breed, his mother seemed to have a soft spot for the orphan, so it was best not to kill him.

Dane flung his hands out as if he had nothing to lose. "Turns out, I fucking did. I'm sick of acting like your bullshit isn't affecting other people. Shit's getting out of hand, and you've been MIA for weeks!"

Racing off the porch Christian caught him by the front of the shirt, yanking him up to his toes. "Not one more word."

"Or what?"

Christian took in his disheveled attire and haphazard hair. Dark circles shadowed his eyes. "What's happened to you?"

"If you ever showed up for your job, you'd know—"

He abruptly released his grip with a shove and Dane stumbled back, falling to the ground. "I don't need the theatrics."

His jaw locked and he panted. "He touched her!"

"Who?"

"Isaiah!"

Christian frowned. "Who did he touch?"

"My fucking sister! She fed from him!"

"Isaiah is out of his cell?"

"No, there's a hole in the wall separating their cells. He broke his hand to reach her, but by the looks of it, this wasn't the first time."

If Isaiah, an elder *feeish* vampire of great strength, was receiving blood from that abomination that was once Dane's mortal sister, this could be catastrophic. "You've reported this?"

"Days ago. The elders can't reach a decision. He needs to die."

"Agreed."

As soon as the word left his mouth, Dane stammered. "I…" Pent-up emotion contorted his face and tears flooded his tired eyes. "Thank you."

It was the first time Christian saw him with any sort of empathy. As a bastard, he knew what it was to be an outcast in this place. He took pity on the boy. "You do realize she's not your sister anymore."

His sorrow instantly transformed to fury and he shoved to his feet. "She'll always be my sister."

"Dane…" It was the first time he used his name and it felt…odd. "When a transition takes place outside of God's command, there will always be consequences."

"She's my blood. She could also be yours. Doesn't that mean anything to you?"

"Her blood is diseased. We'll never know

her true lineage. Look at the secrets your parents kept from you. She might not even be—"

"She's my sister," he snapped. "I'll never see her as anything less."

He shook his head. There was no recourse aside from letting her go. In Christian's opinion, none of those misfits belonged in those cells, and they should all be destroyed, the witch included.

"You're living in a world of ideals. It's time you faced the reality. Brother Cain broke the laws of nature when he interfered. He broke the laws of God."

"Then why is she still alive? If your all-powerful God wanted her dead, she'd be dead. She's meant to be here."

"He's your God too." His thoughts strayed to his mate. More than once she called herself a captive. Was he being merciful where Delilah was concerned? Or was she just another victim in a cell? He believed in God's greater plan, but his faith had been shaken over the last few days.

Out of comforting words, he simply said, "God works in mysterious ways."

Dane's face pinched as he turned his glare to the distant trees blocking the view of the Safe House. "I would rather see her put down than let that monster sink his teeth into her again," he rasped.

Taken aback by his confession, Christian frowned. "But you love her." He could feel the boy's affection for the girl as much as he could read it in his mind.

"Exactly. I love her, and it's my responsibility to protect her. I want Isaiah dead. If that brings her survival back into question, so be it. I can't stand by and let him do that to her again."

He picked through the boy's chaotic memories, seeing how much he thought this through and how resolute he was in his belief that Isaiah deserved to die.

Isaiah was once Christian's dear friend. It pained him to lose him again, and his return to the farm had been a lot for the elders to process. Old wounds reopened and difficult decisions rested on their shoulders once more.

"His crimes are beyond comprehension, I know. But like your sister, the Isaiah who existed decades ago is lost. Gone, I'm afraid. I've mourned him for nearly a hundred years, and yet my grief remains. And those that have died, I grieve them the same. For immortals, death is sometimes more agonizing because we hold onto the relentless pain of loss for eternity."

"You said you wanted Isaiah to die."

"No, I said he needs to die. None of this is what anyone wants. You must understand, he was once our friend. Isaiah was an elder on The Council. He was with us when we founded The Order. Just as your heart tells you to protect your sister, our instincts push us to protect him."

"My sister was innocent. What Isaiah did..." His words choked him. "My mom... Those other women..."

Again, Christian found himself taking pity on the boy. "It's incomprehensible."

"If The Council doesn't kill him, I will."

He stiffened. "Do not act hastily. Even contained, Isaiah has great strength. Not only that, acting without The Council's consent will carry consequences."

"I don't care."

"You should care," Christian snapped. "*This* is your life now. We've offered you protection and sanctuary when you had none. If you wish to stay here, you will obey The Council's decree."

"Then do something! I'm trying to play by the rules. The Council won't listen to me because they don't respect me. You're one of them —an elder." He swallowed and glanced away before meeting his stare again. "As your half-brother, I'm asking this one favor of you. Please help me."

The laws that protected Isaiah were the same laws that protected the girl. The rules kept them in a functional society. Disregarding the laws would lead to anarchy. They'd also get the boy killed.

Glancing up at the bedroom window, he saw the curtain flutter and a shadow drift back from the glass. He considered what Dane was willing to sacrifice for the sister he so deeply loved. Would a true mate suffer the same if it meant seeing to his partner's happiness? Could he lose Delilah? Could he put her happiness before his own and let her go? Was that what real love was? He hadn't expected it to hurt so much, and he wasn't ready to answer such questions.

Or perhaps he already had his answer but wasn't ready to face the truth.

A wall came down. He couldn't make these decisions right now when his personal life was in shambles. He wasn't in the right state of mind to champion his old friend's death or consider what might happen to the deranged girl. His focus was needed here.

"I can't help you. I told The Council where I stand on the matter. That hasn't changed. There's nothing more I can do."

"You can demand that they listen! You can tell them—"

"You've already reported the issue. The decision is up to them. They know where I stand."

"But they aren't listening! She's a teenager! She's innocent! Coming from you, it will be different. I'm nothing to them! You have their respect and their ear, you just have to use your position, and you can make all of this go away."

"Did you not hear me?" Christian snapped, growing tired and wanting to get back to his mate. "The grief never goes away. The laws protecting Isaiah are the same laws protecting your sister. A death sentence for one will likely end her life as well. If you love her, truly love her, that can't be what you want."

"Like you said, it's not what I want. It's what needs to happen. But it's never going to happen at the pace The Council's moving."

"These things take time."

"She doesn't have time! He touched her. Fed her. There is a literal hole connecting their cells. If he could break his hand to feed her through a hole, don't you think he can get out of his restraints? You're all fools if you think you actually have any control over keeping him there. He's biding his time for something bigger. I can feel it. He's using her as part of a bigger plan."

"That doesn't justify a revolt. The laws are the laws."

"Then change the laws! You're a fucking elder, for Christ's sake! What if he's conditioning her to trust him only to drain her of blood in the end. If he gets his strength back, we're all fucked."

"Watch your tongue!"

"Or what? You'll say a few Bible verses and put me in a cell? Great, we'll call it a family fucking reunion. Be sure to bring a dish to the potluck, you useless fuck." The boy turned his back on him and marched furiously toward the tree line.

Christian growled. "Your sister is *vampire* now. There's no innocence left in her." His frustration lashed out with such force the cruel words burned his throat. "There's no mending a mind as broken as hers. Do not come back here again asking for help on a matter that cannot be fixed. I have more important uses for my time." He pivoted toward the house before he lost his temper and did something regrettable.

"How's your mate?"

Christian's spine stiffened, and his steps faltered. "She is none of your concern."

He scoffed. "Oh, I think by now everyone's concerned. They're all whispering about you, you know."

He spun and lunged off the porch, grabbing the boy by the shirt. "Do not think yourself above our laws of privacy, half-breed. Mention my mate again, and you'll find yourself without a home and no way to ever see your demented sister again. I'll see to it."

Any man with a shred of common sense would have been terrified, but the half-breed only sneered. "She hates you." He snickered.

Christian's pulse throbbed as his grip tightened, a low, threatening growl spilling out of him as he snarled, "So help me God, you say one more word about her, and I will feed your sister to Isaiah myself." Disgusted, he threw the boy to the ground.

"She'll run again."

Christian continued walking, but the boy continued to taunt him.

"This time, I'll be sure to help her escape."

Fangs fully extended he caught him by the throat and slammed him into the dirt. "Hear me now. You even look her way and I'll carve your eyes out of your skull. She's mine. Understand? *Mine.*"

Dane sputtered for breath until Christian finally let him go.

Rising to his full height, Christian straightened his clothing and returned to the porch, ripping the front door clean off the hinges and slamming the dilapidated wood shut. It clattered to the ground.

He planned to speak to Eleazar about this.

CHAPTER 15

The house rattled as the door slammed. Delilah jumped back from the window and hurried to the bed. Christian's heavy foot-falls marked his approach and matched the pounding in her chest. The door flung open and she threw her body back, pretending she was asleep.

"I'm aware you're awake. If you can be bru-tally honest with me about our future, why on earth would you pretend to sleep over such foolish nonsense?"

She opened her eyes but didn't answer. He loomed in the doorway, not entering, not com-pletely meeting her stare. His palpable dark mood siphoned the oxygen out of the room.

"Good. Quiet is preferable at the moment. You're my mate, and it's time you understood the full scope of what that means. I expect you downstairs in five minutes."

The door shut behind him with a conclusive snap.

Well...

Her mind reeled over everything she'd just overheard. Dane said he would help her leave the next time she tried to escape.

Dane also hurt Christian and, for that, she didn't like him. But that made no sense. She had no reason to feel protective about Christian. She didn't like him either.

Maybe she disliked Dane because he didn't help her before and then he spoke to her in that condescending way that implied she was someone else's property. He wasn't trustworthy then, so why should she trust him now?

Tangled up with the urge to comfort her captor when she should be running for her life, she paced. The desire to escape overwhelmed her, but so did the ache in her heart, an ache that was not of her own pain.

Rubbing a hand over her chest, she wondered how she could feel such empathy for someone she hated. She physically felt his stress like a tightening web chilling her heart.

This was stupid. Christian wasn't there. She could finally run. All she had to do was get up and go. Her mind reviewed the layout of the farm and she tried to think of the fastest route. How far was civilization? If she moved quickly...

He would be faster. Damn it.

But Dane would help her. Good old, untrustworthy Dane.

Dane. Christian's half-brother. Dane, the guy who hurt Christian's feelings. *Gah!* She was being ridiculous. None of this mattered. She hated Christian.

But again, he was in pain. She could feel it. Like, really feel it, as if his emotions were opening her chest. Empathy consumed her heart, indecision twisted her gut, until her mind instinctively reached for his.

An impenetrable wall slammed down between them, and she jerked back and stiffened.

Oh no he didn't.

Shocked he would actually shut her out, she stomped to the door. He wasn't waiting in the hall, hovering like he usually did. She scoped out the other rooms, wondering if he was spying from one of the doorways, but the other bedrooms were empty.

Without their mental link, she relied on her other senses to find him. Shutting her eyes, she breathed in and found his comforting scent.

Comforting? No, she meant familiar.

Creeping down the stairs, trying not to make a sound, she held her breath as the last step creaked under her weight. Pausing, she held her breath and glanced toward the open parlor, craning her neck to see the kitchen.

Christian braced his hands on the counter, his shoulders hunched and his back tense as his head dropped low. Her brow pinched. She couldn't connect with him mentally, but the force and intensity of his pain nearly toppled her.

A soft breeze teased the loose hair at her shoulders and her head turned. The front door was open, hanging cockeyed off the hinges. She didn't even have to touch it. She could slip right through the narrow crack. Two seconds and she could be gone.

She took a step, only to pause and look back at the kitchen. A strange tethering knot tugged at her gut, urging her to go to him as much as the temptation of freedom pushed at her back. Her brow pinched, and she looked at the front door once more. Jaw locked, she swallowed back a frustrated growl.

"Shit," she hissed, her hand sliding down the banister as she rounded the staircase, softly padding toward the kitchen.

"Good, we can begin," he said without turning the moment she entered the kitchen.

She gently placed her hand on his back and he tensed, glancing over his shoulder in question. They held each other's stare for a pregnant moment.

She didn't like being shut out any more than she liked being trapped in. "Are you okay?"

His eyes closed and his brow creased with worry. Mouth tight, he shook his head. "I'm losing you."

"You haven't lost me yet." She didn't understand why she reassured him or said such things. It was a lie. She was gone the moment she had the chance…

But she had the chance now. The door was wide open. What was she doing?

He didn't deserve her compassion, but she couldn't leave him like this. Sometimes, people just needed a moment without fear or pressure. A moment to catch their breath. Maybe they both did. This week had taken a toll on both of them, and her nerves were rubbed raw.

"Do you need a hug?" The moment the words left her mouth she felt dumb for saying them, but then he turned and pulled her into his arms, hugging her tightly as he pressed his face into her shoulder.

Her breath hitched at the instant comfort. The physical contact soothed her as much as it did him, and she immediately felt his tension ease, but it didn't fully abate. His relief unwound the knots in her stomach and she could breathe easier. They both could.

"I'm sorry Dane said those things to you."

"We were both out of line."

She didn't fully understand what she'd overheard, but she gathered enough to know they discussed a sensitive subject. "Is Cybil your sister?"

"No."

"Who is she?"

"A tragedy no one will remember a hundred years from now."

The chilling finality of his words reminded her of his cold resoluteness. She drew back to look at him. "Could you change that?" She didn't know who Cybil was, but she knew Dane was his half-brother, and Cybil was important to him. "For Dane's sake."

He released her and paced the kitchen, his fingers raking through his hair and leaving it standing on end. "I don't want his name spoken in my house."

"But…he's your brother. Siblings fight."

"He's nothing to me."

"Christian—"

He held up a silencing hand. "The discussion is over. We have more important matters to address."

His rejection stung and she bristled. He not only declared the topic off limits, he'd once again proved she was not his equal. Whatever he wanted from her, it wasn't any sort of relationship she cared to entertain.

Hurt and bitter he'd shut her down so quickly after she gave him a hug and tried to be nice, she snapped, "Like what? How you take your coffee in the morning?"

"For starters, yes."

"God, you're unbelievable. There's no middle ground with you, is there? It's either your way or nothing."

"And why shouldn't it be my way?" he practically snarled. "This is my home, my life. I've waited centuries, lived through plagues and wars, and watched thousands die from foolish mistakes that could have been avoided with a little prudence and sense. I've been around long enough to know the right way from the wrong way. I don't ask for much in this world, but I expect to have what's mine because I damn well earned it!"

She took a step back, startled to hear him raise his voice at her in such a way. "And that's how you see me. *Yours?*"

"You *are* mine."

She scoffed, baffled as to how she could have possibly felt bad for him a minute ago. Shaking her head she laughed, finally understanding.

"As long as Christian gets what he wants, everything is fine, is that right? Fuck everyone else. We're all just little tragedies no one will remember a hundred years from now." Her eyes burned as her vision blurred. She pointed a finger toward the broken front door. "That man—your *brother*—asked you for help, and you couldn't be bothered. You preach all this bullshit about faith and God, but you only help others when there's no imposition to yourself, right?"

"I won't apologize for taking—"

"I'm not finished." A tear tripped from her lashes and fell to the floor. Her arm lowered as did her voice. "You'll never understand love, because you refuse to put anyone else's needs before your own."

"I put *your* needs before mine all the time."

"No, you don't—"

"*Don't I?*" he shouted. "I could have had you a hundred times by now. I could have used compulsion to bend you to my will—"

"Don't act like you haven't! It was your blood choking me when I woke up today!"

"Pardon me for not letting you starve."

"Are my values getting in your way? Funny, yours are indisputable, but mine are just tedious little interferences. You're bigger, stronger, and will always be more powerful than me. That's what you said, right? Opposition is futile. Just like my submission, you plan to bend my morals so they fit neatly into your perfect world. Fuck it if you break me in the process. I'm just one more thing you own."

"You're not a toy to me! I would never take you for granted."

"But I'm also not a person to you. I'll always be second because no one could possibly be equal. No one can feel pain as deeply as you feel or know the depth of your longing. We're all just background pieces to this profound masterpiece you call life where you're the only important person whose feelings really matter. Well, I think your life sucks! I mean, really, are you even happy?" She scoffed, shaking her head at how incredibly blind and one-sided he could be. "You're not so perfect. Maybe God sent me here to teach you *that!*"

His jaw twitched as he held her stare, and the energy between them pulsed as his jaw clenched and he seethed. "I will not let you go."

Her head was literally throbbing. "That's what you took away from all that? Were you even listening?"

"Yes, I listened. What does it matter if I'm happy? You're my mate—"

"Don't use words you don't understand!" she screamed. "I don't care about your traditions. A

mate is a partner, a friend. It's not a subordinate. Not an opponent. And not a fucking possession!"

Eyes sharp, he stared at her with uncontainable frustration. His nostrils flared with every panted breath, and his shoulders pulsed with building fury. It beat at her, pulsing and building like invisible steam that took up every inch of space and put pressure on everything as it desperately sought an outlet. If he didn't get it out—

A roar exploded from him, rattling the windows and hurting her ears as he flipped the kitchen table on end, knocking two chairs down in the process.

She jumped back. "What the hell are you doing?"

"I'm angry!"

"At the table?"

"At the world!" He growled and kicked another chair. The wood smashed into the wall and splintered into kindling. "This wasn't supposed to be this difficult. Love is supposed to feel good."

"Love?" She laughed nervously. "Christian, just because you planted your flag on me doesn't mean you laid claim to my heart. How could I love you when you refuse to even listen to what I want?"

"Listen?" He scoffed. "I have listened. I know what you want. You want to go home. It's all you've talked of since coming here. All you've thought about. I can't give you that."

"I didn't *come* here. You kidnapped me."

He waved away her words. "Details."

"Details matter! Pebbles can change the course of a river and carve canyons over time. You dismiss everything as insignificant if it's not important to you, but what about how other people feel? You won't even compromise."

"I've tried. I took you to meet the other females and you betrayed me."

"I did not."

"I heard you speaking to Larissa. I read your intentions with Sister Annalise and Sister Destiny. You were planning to leave."

"That surprised you? It can't be a betrayal if you knew it was coming. You've been in my head since I got here. You knew what I was planning to do when I met them."

"It still disappointed me! I showed you kindness by taking you to meet them and it changed nothing—"

"*I. Am. A. Prisoner!*" she yelled. "I'm not a bird you can cage. Even if I live forever, you'll kill my soul if you try to keep me in captivity. Do you want that?"

"No!"

"Then there has to be another way."

"I don't know of any other way. I only know that losing you will destroy me. The mere thought causes me unbearable agony." He rubbed his chest. "I...I don't want to lose you, Delilah, but I also don't want to be the root of your unhappiness. I want you to choose to stay, to choose me over everything else."

That was an incredibly tall order and one she didn't expect to ever meet. "Maybe set a smaller goal."

"Why? Why should I compromise when *that* is the only thing I want."

"But it's not the *only* thing you want. There are bonnets and blood and God knows what else!" She pinched the bridge of her nose. "And, like I've been trying to explain, a relationship involves two people. You have to consider the other person. I want things too. Happy couples —" *God, was she really using those words?* "Couples compromise."

He turned away and glared out the window. They both needed to catch their breath and let their tempers cool.

After a few minutes, she said, "At this rate, we're going to be at each other's throats forever. This isn't getting us anywhere. We're both miserable. If we keep on fighting like this… Well, it's the definition of insanity, is what it is."

"What other choice do we have? One of us will always be miserable if the other one gets their way."

"Not if we compromise."

"You're willing to negotiate? Peacefully and honestly?"

Was she? She should have walked out the door.

No, reasoning with him was safer. If she could get him to see her point of view, she might be able to win his compassion. It was clear he had no intention of letting her go, so she would only get out of there if she somehow changed his mind. If she could actually get him to love her, he would put her happiness above all else, including himself. It was the only way she could see him allowing her to leave.

She exhaled, seeing no other option. "I'll try negotiating."

He eyed her suspiciously. "I'll expect you to keep your word."

"What is love without trust?" How she didn't roll her eyes was a miracle.

"All right."

She couldn't believe she was actually doing this. Her body ached and she needed to rest. "Can we sit?"

He righted the table and pulled out a chair, eyeing her with great concern. She sensed him fighting the urge to nag about what she *needed*, but he held back. Smart man. If they were actually going to negotiate, she was going to use every bargaining chip at her disposal. From here on, no concession would be free.

The moment she was off her feet her breath shook with relief. She looked up at him. "Okay, what's your first condition? Think carefully, Christian, because I'm not agreeing to wash your feet or cut the heads off of chickens for your dinner."

"Intercourse."

He answered faster than anticipated, catching her off guard with his request. She really expected him to push the blood issue.

When it came to males, the species really didn't matter, they were all focused on one thing.

"Like, right now?"

"Whenever I desire it."

Her brows lifted. How often could immortals do it? They had to have higher stamina than humans.

The idea wasn't completely appalling. She didn't want to examine her attraction to him too closely because any woman with a shred of dignity wouldn't go for this. But the truth was, despite everything he'd done, she still found him incredibly attractive.

This was about survival. She had to take shame and judgment out of the equation. If she did that, it wasn't a bad deal. She just didn't want to turn into some used-up concubine. There had to be balance.

"*Whenever* sets a pretty wide-open expectation."

He met her stare and repeated slowly, "*Whenever* I desire it."

Despite the hostility between them, she liked knowing he craved her to such a degree. It was...empowering. She also liked the direct way he made his intentions clear. He was firm, and, in the sex department, that didn't bother her.

She tried not to get distracted as her thighs clamped tighter and her hands balled into fists on her lap. When he looked at her with that unbending, silver stare she understood just how alpha he could be.

Christian liked control and despised when things were left open. She liked a forward lover and being taken aggressively—but not kidnapped. She had to draw the line somewhere.

This was a big request, one that would earn her a pretty big ask in return. She could definitely use this to her benefit. After all, it was only sex. She enjoyed his body, and he made her come whenever they fooled around in the past. It wasn't like she'd suffer through the act—at least she hoped she wouldn't. It could also be a great outlet and distraction, especially while trapped on an Amish farm.

He reclined and watched her, propping an elbow over the back of his chair, no doubt enjoying the pros and cons running through her head. She wanted specifics.

"How, exactly, would this work?"

"It's simple. You give yourself to me. Whenever. I. Desire," he repeated, emphasizing each word so she felt the implication at her core. "Take the thinking out of it, *pintura*. I'll see to your satisfaction. Your pleasure will always come before mine."

She fidgeted. What woman would complain about that? "So, like, if we're just sitting around and all of a sudden you want to…"

"The moment I want it, you'll know."

"How?"

"I'll be buried inside of you."

Her body clenched and her heart skipped a beat. "Oh." She swallowed. "Right."

The need for important details lost importance as his plan took shape in her head. "What if we're not home."

"Anywhere."

She sucked in a sharp breath as he flooded her mind with images of their bodies entwined in a mess of sweat slicked limbs. On a bed. Against a wall. A tree. The grass. The hardwood floor. A window sill. The bath. A lake.

Her throat was suddenly bone dry. "You've really thought about this."

"Fervently."

Her breath caught as more images came to her. Christian in bed—touching himself. Christian under a stream of cool water, muscles taught, bringing himself to completion. Christian throwing his head back as he came. A shiver chased up her spine.

His nostrils flared as he tipped his head back and closed his eyes, breathing deeply. "You're aroused."

Her gaze dropped to the table. "Well, what do you expect? You just played a highlight reel of raunchy porn in my head."

"And you liked it."

She did. Not only that, she wanted everything he'd shown her.

Unclenching her fists, she flattened her palms on the surface of the table. "So, this table…"

"I'd make a feast of you."

"Right." She swallowed, picturing him pushing her skirt to her waist and spreading her wide.

A wave of pleasure teased through her and she swayed forward, gasping. "What the...? How did you just do that?" It was as if his tongue literally just licked into her, just as she pictured.

The side of his mouth quirked. "The bond between mates has a magnificent link. You'll find, in terms of intercourse and intimacy, my pleasure will only amplify your own. And vice versa."

"But I *physically* felt you."

"What did you feel, *pintura?*"

Was he screwing with her? "I felt...your tongue."

"Where?"

He was definitely screwing with her. Her breath hitched as he did it again. *"How are you doing that?"*

"I'm not sure I know what you're asking."

Another wave of pleasure and her lips parted. He was going to knock her out of the chair if he kept going. Another lick. Her eyes rolled back and she shivered.

"Okay, okay!" The sensation abated but not before he gave her clit a little mental flick. She exhaled jaggedly, trying to compose herself. "That's a neat trick."

"It is."

She suddenly felt like she was getting hustled. He was playing it super cool, like he had an ace up his sleeve. But now she wanted the sex, so she couldn't tell him no. "Fine, we can have sex, but no biting."

The side of his mouth kicked up and a full grin took over his face. She had the slightest instinct she'd just been swindled and signed off on something more than simple intercourse. "I'll refrain unless you make a request."

"I'm pretty sure I can contain myself." Sex was one thing. But biting…no thanks. "And just to be clear, this isn't some archaic husbandly right to my body. I own this body. Me. And if I change my mind, all bets are off."

"You won't change your mind."

God, when he looked at her like that… It wasn't fair for a man to be so beautiful. His dark lashes, full lips, and carved cheekbones, women would kill for such features, and he somehow pulled them off with chiseled masculinity.

It was getting warm. She prepared to shift closer to the window but paused when her body cooled. "Did you just lower my core temperature?"

"No, you did."

"I did?" She hadn't meant to.

"Just as our hearts know how to beat and our lungs know how to breathe without our brains sending a command, your body will know how to regulate such things. It's your turn, *pintura.* What do you want from me?"

He'd gotten her all hot and bothered with the sex talk—clearly a distraction tactic meant to throw her off her game. She needed to get her head out of the gutter and focus.

Her brain quickly prioritized her desires in

terms of probability. If she asked to leave the farm, he'd say no. They already circled that ride a hundred times. She needed to start smaller. "I want to leave the house whenever I wish."

"No."

"What do you mean, *no?* You didn't even think about it. And I just gave you sex!"

"You haven't given me anything, *yet*. Regardless, you're a mated female and a new transition. You need an escort."

"You mean a chaperone."

"If you want to call it that."

She rolled her eyes. "Fine. You escort me, but I control my own schedule. I'm a people person. I can't stay cooped up in this house all the time."

"I can accommodate your request within reason. But you must stay on the farm."

"A bigger birdcage," she muttered. "Fine. Whatever. Agreed."

"And you will not speak to other males outside of my presence."

"That sounds like another condition."

"Trust that I'm self-aware enough to know my limits, Delilah. You don't want to trigger my possessive side."

"I'm pretty sure I've seen—"

"You've seen nothing compared to what I might do if I suspected another male of trying to take you from me. Trust me. Some beasts are best left to hibernate as long as possible."

"How evolved of you."

"In many things I'm reserved. Where you're

concerned, let's just say I'll stop at nothing to protect what's mine."

She expected him to fill her mind with another wave of images that showed how far he would go, but he did the opposite, putting up a wall between them, censoring sides of himself he did not wish her to see. And that made her more nervous. "You can't hurt anyone, Christian."

"I'll do whatever I have to do."

"But…" She believed him, and her pacifist nature ensured he'd get his way. "I don't like being told who I can and can't speak to."

"You asked to venture outside of the house. That comes with rules. You can either accept my conditions or take the prospect off the table."

She was definitely being hustled. "Fine. But I don't like you very much right now."

She flinched when a feather-light caress ghosted over her throat, tickling. Her hand rushed to her neck and the playful sensation stopped. "That's not normal."

"Neither are we."

She drew in a long breath. "Fine. I accept your condition."

"Good. Now for my next negotiation."

"Oh, boy." She couldn't imagine what he might request next. She waved her fingers egging him on. "Let's hear it."

"No more swearing. That goes for in your head or spoken aloud."

She gaped at him. "That's how I talk."

"Practice self-control."

"That's impossible." She groaned. "I have none."

He chuckled. "Then I'll assist you. There are ways to reinforce positive behavior just as there are deterrents to keep us from repeating bad habits."

She shifted in her seat, cocking her head curiously. "Such as?"

He splayed his fingers wide and flattened his palm on the table. "Would you like a demonstration?"

"What do you mean?"

"Stand up, bend your body over the table, and I'll show you."

She drew back, comprehending his meaning as he sent a wave of sensation rolling over her ass and flexed his hand. "I'll pass." She couldn't decide if he was playfully suggesting a little slap and tickle or pushing more of his heavy-handed patriarchal bullshit.

"Are you sure? Demonstrations can be quite motivating."

"I'm all set."

"Are you rejecting my terms?"

"I'll do my best with the no-swearing thing, but I can't make any promises." *This was going to be fucking impossible.*

"Then I'll make one. I promise to give you a little grace and time, but there will be consequences, *pintura.* Your language can be atrocious, and a little self-control never hurt anyone."

Self-control might not hurt, but spanking did. "You don't discipline a partner."

"Not a well-behaved one."

She scoffed. Suddenly he had jokes. "Christian, I'm not going to let you spank me."

"Keep your language clean and it won't be an issue."

She gaped at him. He was really serious. "This isn't the middle ages."

"I'm aware."

"Are you?"

He drew in a calm breath. "Delilah, 'discipline yields the peaceable fruit of righteousness.'"

"Christian," she said dryly. "Don't quote scripture at me."

"I want this," he said point blank, showing no inclination to budge or bend.

An exasperated breath huffed out of her. Tempted to see how far he'd go if she broke his rules, she considered letting an F-bomb drop, but what if he really was serious and it hurt? *Forget* that.

It was already starting to work.

Was it really her language or was her language just a vehicle to get him off on some Amish discipline kink? He said he could never truly hurt her, so it was a bit of a catch twenty-two.

"Fine. I'll try not to swear."

"Good. I'm pleased with how our negotiations are going."

She supposed he would be, being that he got

sex and spankings with a side of no talking to boys or cursing. How had he managed all of that while she only got chaperoned field trips around the farm? It was time to go for the jugular. "My turn. I want to visit my shop."

"No."

"Do you know another word? What the hel—eck? Why not?"

"It's too dangerous."

"Why?"

"Because you're different now. Your body has needs. The more you starve yourself, the less self-control you'll have. You could injure someone unintentionally. And you still haven't learned the basics of compulsion. It's too great of a risk to you and to others. It's my duty to protect you, so the answer is no."

"You could go with me."

"Of course, I would. But it's still out of the question."

"You're not negotiating with me. You have all these conditions and demands, but you won't compromise if it's something you don't want. How is that fair?"

He hesitated then suggested, "I'll reconsider in two weeks. If I feel you still aren't ready, then my answer will remain no."

"And what criteria qualifies me as ready?"

"Trust, for one. Right now, I don't trust you."

"At least we have that in common," she grumbled. "I still feel like you're getting more out of this deal than I am."

"You asked for no biting. I agreed. You asked

for freedom on the farm. I granted your request within reason."

"But you added conditions. I didn't limit you when you asked for fucking—shit! Sorry. Screwing. Can I say screwing?"

He sighed. "The preferred phrase is intimacy."

She rolled her eyes. Like anyone called it that. What was next, her flowering vagina and her heaving bosom? Dear God, she was rotting away in a bad romance. Lady Gaga could write a lyrical masterpiece on this one.

"Ask me for something realistic, *pintura*, and I'll be more than happy to grant you it."

She couldn't think of anything he wouldn't instantly shoot down. Then it came to her. "No more feeding me without my consent."

His head lifted, all playfulness replaced by serious concern. "Will you feed on your own?"

"I'll eat."

"Feeding is different from eating. Blood serves a different purpose than food."

"Has a vampire ever starved from not drinking blood?"

"Immortal. And it can become very painful. The body begins to atrophy over time. Flesh rots and bone crumbles—"

"All right, all right. I get the picture." She felt sick just picturing that. "I don't want you doing that bedazzle thing on me again. I want you to respect my choices and trust that I know my body best."

"Fine, on one condition."

"Of course, you have a condition."

"When you decide you've had enough pain and you need to feed, it will be from my vein alone. Your lips will never touch another living thing."

"Not a problem."

"I believe we've negotiated enough for one night." He stood and held out a hand. "I'd like to put our agreement into practice."

Her stomach bottomed out as several emotions stirred. Worry. Anticipation. Lust. Frustration. Stress. The need to abate said stress.

Visions of what might happen upstairs filled her head. She agreed to this. He was going to touch her. Put his hands on her body. Kiss her. Push inside of her. And she agreed to let him. As much and as often as he wanted.

As understanding dawned and she truly understood how much he could actually demand of her now, the scent of his arousal filled the kitchen. She looked up at him with big eyes. "Now?"

"Now." He waited for her to take his hand.

She agreed. They negotiated. She wasn't repulsed or regretting her choice, but there was no mistaking the fear coursing through her veins. This was going to change things.

Her hand slowly lifted. Her heart pounding like a battle drum. He watched her with dark hunger, as if set to devour her. She swallowed tightly and closed her eyes, putting her hand in his.

CHAPTER 16

There was no such thing as a quickie on an Amish farm. Christian insisted on drawing her a bath, which turned out to be a thirty-minute process of heating kettles and transporting water. She adapted her regency theory to a more gothic pace, one where bicycles were considered too modern and shampoo came in oddly shaped blocks of soap.

He'd bathed her before, but at that time she'd been in shock. Now, she was fully alert and prepared for what came next, even if it took a decade for them to get to that step.

"What are the rules on visiting a Walgreens?" She was pretty sure he just washed her hair in tree ash and rendered fats.

"What is a Walgreens?"

"It's a store. Well, a pharmacy. They sell makeup and birthday cards and hair products. You can also get pictures developed there while you wait for your prescription to be filled, but who does that anymore? You guys totally missed that era, I guess."

He gently poured a pitcher of warm water over her hair and down her back. "You mean an apothecary?"

"Yeah. The old pillory, good for blood-letting and medicinal herbs. There's usually one located on every corner, somewhere between the hatter and the blacksmith."

"You're mocking me."

"A little."

They formed a delicate truce since their fight in the kitchen. Arguing allowed them both to get some frustrations off their chests, and the negotiations made each of them feel heard and acknowledged.

She was doing okay with the no-cursing rule, for the most part, but it had only been an hour. She'd assumed they'd come upstairs and get right to the fuc—*intimacy*, but Christian insisted on seeing to her *needs* first. According to him, she had a lot of needs.

"If there's something you need from town, I'll send for it."

Of course, he would, because she wasn't allowed off the farm. "Isn't that against the rules?"

"There are always exceptions."

Interesting. "I'll make a list."

"Head back."

She tipped her head and warm water cascaded over her hair and shoulders. No one had ever washed her hair outside of a hair salon. She supposed her mother did when she was young, but she had no memory of that. It was nice.

Christian's hands were strong but gentle, and he took great care to work out any tangles, massaging and stroking her long strands with his strong hands. Considering the guys she knew, this kind of stuff never happened. And she couldn't call it torture. On the contrary, he had her eyes rolling back in pleasure.

She relaxed and sighed. "That feels nice."

"Your hair will grow faster now. It's already thicker and healthier than it was a few days ago. A female's hair is her glory, *pintura*, and I find yours to be a radiant beauty I hadn't considered admiring so reverently. I believe it looks best coiled around my hands." He gave her hair a firm tug that tipped her head back, and water trickled from the damp strands.

"Mmm, well, you just keep doing what you're doing, and you'll get no objection from me."

He massaged her scalp a while longer and her body thoroughly relaxed. Finally, he poured water over her shoulders and hair one last time then set the pitcher aside and gathered a plush bath sheet, holding it open for her.

Self-conscious, she bit her lip, a bit of her tranquility fading as she anticipated what would come next.

"No need to be shy with me, *pintura*. I've already seen every inch of you."

Her belly tightened. They'd never taken things slow until now. Feeling exposed and nervous in ways she hadn't before, she wished he would just get on with it. At this pace she was going to overthink and worry herself to death, shattering any chance of actually enjoying the act.

Slowly, she rose from the tub and water sloshed off her body. He took her hand and helped her step onto the floor, gathering her into the bath sheet that had been warmed by the fire. The unexpected warmth was another pleasure she hadn't anticipated.

"Oh." She moaned, luxuriating in the warmth.

His lips pressed to her back. "You see, you have no cause for fear around me."

He dragged his lips slowly over the slope of her shoulder, and she sucked in a breath. She was awkwardly skittish and on edge. His hand drifted between the fabric and her stomach, rising slowly to cup her breast as he kissed and nibbled up her neck.

The possessive way he held her spoke of a confidence she couldn't match. Why was she suddenly shy?

"I should put on a gown."

As soon as she took a step, his touch firmed, holding her in place and pushing her body into his. "No need."

His hard length pressed into her back, the weight a heavy implication of the things he planned to do to her. She fisted the towel at her chest. Why was this so intensely difficult? She'd had sex plenty of times before, but this felt different.

He kept touching her softly. Quietly. Reverently. It felt almost…ceremonious.

She wasn't used to such slow seduction. Slipping out of his arms, she moved to the bed.

"Where are you running to?"

The walls closed in on her. She only had so many places to hide. The corner on the other side of the bed seemed safest. "I was shutting out the lights."

He waited as she examined the old oil lamp. Twisting the floral screw on the side, she dimmed the light until the glowing flame extinguished, blanketing the room in inky black shadows. Her eyes immediately adapted to the dark, snuffing out any hope of distance or privacy.

Damn vampire night vision.

That's one, pintura.

Startled by the reminder that he was always hiding in the back of her mind, she frowned. "One what?"

"Profanity."

Crap.

He chuckled. "There are better uses for a filthy mouth."

A vision of her on her knees filled her mind. Her scalp tingled, a feather-light tug pulled as if his hands fisted in her hair. He was somehow touching her despite being on the other side of the room separated by the bed.

She scoffed. "And what about your dirty mind?"

"I think you like it."

Well, he definitely got points for creativity. Her mouth pinched around a smile. He was flirting with her.

He had a way of keeping her off balance. He could go from intense and threatening to playful and seductive at the literal drop of a hat.

Her heart pounded as he removed his shirt. All of those hard, chiseled muscles covering his chest and carving his abs in beautiful relief begged to be touched. He crossed the room, and she took a step back.

"We haven't had a chance to take our time with each other, *pintura*. I've been looking forward to this."

"This?"

"Having you, exactly as I want you, as many times as I want."

She preferred spontaneous. Too much thinking scared her orgasms into hiding.

He toed off his boots and chuckled. "Have I told you what a skilled hunter I am? When I seek something, I find it and claim it."

He truly reminded her of a predator now. And she was his cornered prey. As he rounded the bed her body turned, mirroring his position so he was never at her back.

"It's fine to feel shy, *little one*, but your pleasure can't hide from me. I'll drive it out of you one way or another."

His determination and devotion was another difference between him and the guys she'd known in the past. Men typically didn't care about anything beyond their own release. She wasn't used to that sort of attention.

A low growl filled the room and his eyes flashed. "Mind on me, Delilah."

She didn't know how to shut off such memories when her brain naturally drew comparisons. She tried to focus on the present as he pursued her with slow, calculated shifts, never truly walking but closing in on her all the same.

The back of her knees hit the bed, and she toppled to the mattress. He was there, taking up the space, filling her view as he towered over her with that hungry gaze that promised to devour her. She was trapped.

"Exactly how I like you."

His weight pressed into the bedding as he lowered his mouth to hers, teasing rather than kissing. The moment she leaned up to meet him, he pulled back, toying with her.

"Look at you," he said as if speaking to himself, then she realized he was showing her everything he saw. A mirror image of her body filled her mind clear as day, yet she still watched him through her own vision, her mind somehow able to hold multiple views at once.

When she saw herself through his eyes, she felt all of his admiration. His esteem overwhelmed her in a way that chased away any self-doubt or insecurities she experienced in the past whenever she'd pick herself apart in front of a mirror.

It felt *good* to see herself in such an appreciative way for a change. Light and refreshing. Safe, cherished, and maybe even a little addicting, because she didn't just see through his eyes, she comprehended how he processed and cataloged every detail.

She didn't want the deluge of positive sensations to end. Just one glimpse of what he saw repaired years of damage to her self-esteem, bathing her heart in gentle compassion.

"Wow," she breathed. "You're doing incredible things for my confidence."

His hands framed her waist and dragged slowly down her sides, then back up again, lifting her breasts. "And why shouldn't you feel confident? You're flawless."

She wasn't, but through his eyes she was. It was a paradox that massaged the self-conscious mind and eradicated the urge or need to criticize her appearance. Her insecurities disappeared the longer she saw herself from his point of view.

They said humans only used ten percent of their brains. She was coming to suspect that wasn't the case for immortals. Layers of awareness unfurled within her imagination. Sensory details multiplied until she lost track of the improvements.

Every time he pushed their mental link, her brain seemed to undergo a software update, perceiving new colors she couldn't name and seeing the world around her in such vivid contrast to before, that she cognitively gobbled up all the delicious details. It was sensory overload, but not in a bad way.

He was a drug. An organic form of ecstasy that awakened every nerve and overdosed her brain in pleasure hormones. She could literally feel her happiness rising as he looked at her. And when he touched her... She felt him in every single cell of her body and the ethereal matter that made up her aura, until nothing but pure euphoria rushed through her entire being.

His finger brushed delicately over the wing of her collarbone. "Soft." He caught her knee, quickly tugging her legs apart. "Docile." His thumb traced her lower lip, gently pulling her mouth open and dipping inside. "Pliant."

Without exerting force, she bit his thumb and he chuckled.

"But never without fire." He pulled his finger away and grazed the press of her pierced nipple through the damp towel. "I think your vivacious spirit arouses me even more than your body."

She was definitely a vibe and should probably be grateful he was one of the few people who appreciated her fiery energy and volatile temperament. Most people found her intensity draining.

"Your intensity matches my own," he said, fully present in her thoughts. "I enjoy your beautiful mind as much as I enjoy your body." He tugged open the towel, exposing her naked breasts and bare sex, then nudged her shoulder so she fell flat on her back.

"*My* beautiful *pintura.*"

A jagged breath passed her lips when he caught the underside of her knees and dragged her to the edge of the bed, spreading her thighs wide. Warm lips pressed to the sharp curve of her hip and she gasped. His tongue traced the jutting curve of her hip lower until he was at eye level with her sex.

She shut her eyes, alarmingly exposed. This was more intimacy than she knew how to process.

The press of his kiss to her clit drew a sharp gasp from her lips. "Breathe, little one. There's nothing obscene or shameful about the closeness between mates. It's as intimate a bond as two creatures can share. Let me show you."

His tongue trailed over her sensitive flesh with provocative intention, slowly opening her with shallow dips of his gently probing fingers and tongue. Heat gathered at her core and a soft moan built in her throat. He kept his exploring touch delicate, which only put her more on edge.

Stoking, kissing, petting, delicately thrusting, he awakened all of her. A fire built in her core and spread through her veins, and her body began to purr—literally purr.

"See how nicely your body responds to my touch?"

An ache formed deep inside of her, begging to be filled. She arched as the pleasure intensified. He knew exactly what she felt, and his complete devotion to her pleasure made every heightening sensation inescapable.

He pulled her closer, burying his face between her thighs and lifting her bottom off the bed. He greedily tasted every hidden crevice, savoring each pleading moan that escaped her throat. He devoured not only her body but her mind as he feasted, his own hungry growls matching her needy mews.

"Christian..." The first tremors of her release fluttered through her body, and his mouth closed over the piercing of her swollen, sensitized flesh.

Long fingers pressed into her, sliding deep and teasing out her pleasure. Her head fell back as he hit that secret spot. A kaleidoscope of light burst behind her eyes. Her fangs punched through her gums, as her claws ripped into the bedding.

"Christian," she cried out as her muscles locked in sweet release.

He continued to devour her, thrusting his fingers faster as his wicked mouth tormented every over-sensitized nerve. Her mind spun as one climax tumbled into the next. Somewhere in the midst of her delirium, he'd removed the rest of his clothes.

Tremors rushed through her bones as she shivered. He adjusted her on the bed, the heat of his naked body burning hot as his skin pressed into hers. Chills raced over her flesh as aftershocks continued to push whimpers from her throat. She didn't have time to come down from her release before he filled her in one hard thrust.

The weight of his body articulated his possession with an unmistakable claim. She could hear the deep male satisfaction growling through his mind as he drew back and thrust again, filling her with an almost boastful exhibition of dominance.

She reflexively moaned with each forceful lunge. Harder. Rougher. He buried her in the bed with heavy purpose, his thick cock stretching her body wider every time he stabbed deeper. But there was no pain. As if her body was designed for his, he fit into her like a missing puzzle piece.

Her legs wrapped around his hips as he caught her wrist in an unbreakable grip, pinning it to the bed as he lunged again. The masculine rumbles of satisfaction left her slick and hungry for more. She knew his pleasure as well as she knew her own.

"I can feel what you feel."

"Yes," he agreed, cupping her breast and kissing her flesh. "Feel how your body grips mine. We were made for this."

His fingers wrapped in her hair, urged her head back, exposing her neck and he growled. His desire to sink his teeth into her flesh struck like the need to breathe. The exerted effort he expended as he consciously denied himself the pleasure of biting her was a palpable force suffered by both of them.

As if trapped at the bottom of a body of water, starved for air, her lungs burned with frustration. The uncontainable fire spread throughout her body, demanding he sink his teeth into her.

Consumed by such a distraught and all-encompassing panic, she wondered how he resisted the instinct to feed, but then she remembered it was up to her. No biting unless she asked.

His worry became her own as she felt the crush of responsibility and indecision. She wanted to tell him to do it but knew she wasn't thinking clearly.

"We have to switch positions!" she blurted, desperately trying to outwit her natural reflexes and his.

Rolling him to his back, she changed their position and got on top. She rode him hard, literally trying to outrun his desire to possess all of her. His eyes closed in tortured ecstasy, and his mouth opened, exposing razor sharp fangs.

Dear God, he was sexy.

The moment the thought crossed her mind, his eyes flashed open. Was he seeing himself through her eyes the way she saw through his? Yes. The answer came to her the moment she wondered, his mind opening to show her a double view that matched her own.

The view from her mind's eye ricocheted off his, creating an infinite echo that reflected in her conscience like a kaleidoscope of mirrors. Her sixth chakra went on sensory overload, and she bent down and licked at his lips, letting her tongue graze the sharp tip of his fangs.

He caught her hair in his fist and growled. "You're teasing me, Delilah."

She was definitely playing with fire. "A little." He was an irresistible flame, and she was the dumb little moth willing to burn.

"Careful, little one. You might get exactly what you wish."

What did she wish? Even she couldn't sift through the hurricane of her mind. Riding his cock faster, she leaned down and smiled at him. "I like fucking you like this."

He thrust his hips, showing her how hard her teasing made him. "You have a mouth made for sin."

She sucked in a breath and moaned. "How shameful."

"Indeed." His finger traced over her mouth, pulling her lips apart. He cupped her jaw possessively, sliding his hand down to her throat until his long fingers cuffed her there. "Show me how wicked it is."

Her motions slowed as she met his stare. His unmistakable desire became her own. Like a slave to his needs, more than happy to serve him when his pleasure became her own, she shifted off him and scooted back.

"Is this how you want me?"

He groaned as she kneeled between his parted thighs. "Delilah, my love, I want you so many ways it would be impossible to pick just one position."

Her chest warmed and she scooted closer, stroking his engorged cock with both hands. His flesh glistened with her arousal, the scent of sex mingling in the air. She licked the thick vein climbing up his shaft, and his cock reached for her mouth like a flower seeking the sun.

His nostrils flared and he growled when she licked him again, this time encircling the smooth tip with her teasing tongue. His fists tightened at his sides.

His stare never left her, nor did the vision of her on her knees pleasuring him once he'd purposefully planted it into her mind. She was watching him watching her, while also watching herself through his eyes, taking it all in and reveling in every reverberating ripple of pleasure.

When she sucked his cock into her mouth his hips bucked, and his hand pressed at the nape of her neck, urging her lower. The thick tip hit the back of her throat and she moaned.

"That's it, *pintura*." He let out a string of foreign words. Without knowing what he said, she knew his words were profane.

"*Lutsche.*" His fist knotted in her hair, dragging her mouth up and down his shaft, leaving the skin slick and wet. "*Haerzhafdich.*" He held her to him, her throat full and her lips smashed against his pelvis. When it was impossible to take him any deeper, he purred. "*Yetz schlucke.*"

Her shoulders bunched reflexively and her eyes watered. She had no knowledge of the language he spoke, until the English translation rolled through his mind. *Suck. Nice and hard. Now swallow.*

She followed his every command, feeling his incredible pleasure as if it were her own, all the while taking him deeper than she'd ever dreamed. When he let her up, she gasped for breath and looked at him through watery eyes.

"Beautiful."

As he dragged his finger over her mouth, she noticed how swollen her lips were. Seeing herself through his eyes, she gasped at the sight of her fangs. "Did I hurt you?"

"My pain comes only from wanting more of you." He lovingly tucked a strand of hair behind her ear. "Don't stop."

Lowering her head, she took him in her mouth again, sucking him with long, deep strokes until he was panting her name and thrusting hard. When he was ready, she sensed it. His release built within both of them, so potent and intense concentration became impossible.

He threw her to her back and slammed into her, stabbing deep and burying his face in her hair as he climaxed inside of her. The briefest thought about children and birth control crossed her mind, but it was chased away by too many delicious sensations.

Their bodies trembled in unrefined bliss as her pleasure gave way to his and his returned to hers. It was an incredible cycle she'd never experienced before, one she didn't wish to end.

When their bodies finally collapsed, she

panted in a state of stunned euphoria and weakly gave him a thumbs up. "Intimacy for the win."

He chuckled, lacing his fingers with hers as their heads rested side by side. "It will only get better with time."

"Better than that?"

He met her stare and smiled. "Better than anything you could possibly imagine."

She let that sink in then frowned. "How do you know?"

Possessive jealousy slithered through her. Had he been with someone else? Had another mate? It should have angered her, but instead it broke her heart.

"Easy, little one. I only know what we are taught. There's no one else."

Her relief was instantaneous.

He kissed her temple. "But I'm glad to see I'm not the only territorial one."

One would have to be emotionally invested to feel possessive. She had no claim to him. Didn't want one.

He chuckled again and lifted her hand, pressing a kiss to the back of her knuckles where their fingers entwined. "I'm yours, *pintura*. There's no shame in that. I'll be there whenever you have need."

Her stomach growled and she blushed. All humor disappeared from his easy expression.

"You're hungry."

She was. There was no point in denying it.

"I can't eat another peanut butter and jelly sandwich."

"I'm not sure you'll like the other options."

If he meant blood, he was right. "Do you have eggs?"

"Will you eat eggs?"

She was too hungry to be difficult. "On occasion I do."

"I can visit the coop."

She winced. "You're going to take them from actual hens, aren't you?"

"That's where eggs typically come from."

"I prefer the ones that come from cartons in the grocery store."

"Ah, yes, because those only come from mother cartons."

"Exactly."

"What if I put them in a bowl?"

She was being ridiculous, but if she overthought the source, she'd lose her appetite. Her stomach growled again, this time louder than before. "That'll work."

Christian went to visit the coop while she nosed around his kitchen, pulling supplies from his pantry. Nothing was labeled in the familiar fashion she recognized. Flour and sugar were stored in sacks and seasonings were kept in unmarked jars she had to sniff to identify. By the time she had the ingredients for French toast gathered, he was back with the eggs.

She frowned at the sad collection. "Did the mothers fuss?"

"No. We collect their eggs daily, so they

don't have a chance to get attached and broody."

She still felt guilty. "Maybe we should just eat sandwiches."

He picked up an egg and cracked it in the large bowl she'd set out. "Now, it would be a shame to waste such a sacrifice."

She bit her lip. "We need four more."

"Shut your eyes."

She covered her eyes until the next three eggs were cracked, appreciating his willingness to do the dirty work. She was a total hypocrite, but he was polite enough not to say so.

"Do you have bread?"

He went to the Hoosier cupboard on the wall and pulled open a drawer with metal sides, removing a linen sack. "It's a few days old."

Pulling back the linen flap, she revealed an untouched loaf. "Did you make this?"

"A friend makes it for me."

She took a step back, without touching it. She saw the friend in his mind. She was a beautiful young woman, one he held in high esteem. That was the second time she caught herself getting angry at the thought of him having any sort of intimacy with someone else, but she couldn't help it.

"It's only bread, Delilah."

She'd remember that next time he got jealous over something silly. She took the loaf and grabbed a knife.

It never occurred to her how spoiled she was until she learned what a whopping pain in the butt slicing bread could be. Her slices were plump and crushed from trying to gently hold the loaf while sliding the blade of the knife. She had crumbs everywhere. "This is a fucking disaster."

"That's three, *pintura.*"

"Three?"

"Profanities."

"Are you counting to a certain number or just doing an impression of Count von Count?"

"Who?"

"He's a vampire puppet."

He drew back, appearing appalled such a thing would exist. "This is something for children?"

"Yeah. He counts, thus his name—The Count." For emphasis, she did an impression. "One, ah-ah-ah. Two, ah-ah-ah…" Realizing he wasn't getting it, she grumbled. "My Transylvanian accent isn't the best."

"It's not very life-like. I don't understand the connection between vampires and arithmetic."

"Well, you know, we try not to scare the children. Don't want to desensitize them too soon. Biting and blood-sucking are a little too PG13 for the little ones." Her mind instantly jumped to Jaden. "Speaking of which, when I visited the Hartzler's, their baby brother wore a leather mask. They said he was teething, but isn't that a bit extreme?"

He carried the eggshells to the rubbish bin. "I'm sure it's just a case of colic."

"Is that normal?"

He leaned into the wall, crossing his arms over his chest and smiled as he studied her.

"Why are you looking at me like that?"

He shook his head, still grinning. "I enjoy this, chatting with you. It's nice not to bicker for a change."

She met his grin with a tentative one of her own. "It is nice."

"To answer your question, I was the last baby in the Schrock line. That was a long time ago. In terms of child-rearing, normal is a fad."

She considered how old he actually was as she whisked together the ingredients. "You're really robbing the cradle with me."

"I've always been a fan of veal."

"Gross." She dipped the bread into the batter and carefully laid each slice onto the skillet. "How hungry are you?"

His hands went to her hips, startling her. Sometimes he moved with such agility she didn't hear him approach. He pressed a kiss to the curve of her neck. "Well, I just ate, so…"

She looked up at him from over her shoulder, recalling how good he looked and felt between her thighs. "Where do they mention *that* in the Bible?"

"Genesis," he said all too quickly. "*Every moving thing that lives shall be food for you.*" His hand slid between her thighs. "*You* are food for my soul."

Her bare legs gave him easy access under the long shirt she stole from his drawer. His hand slipped easily between her folds and he cupped her suggestively. She sucked in a sharp breath and stilled when his finger sank inside.

"And you're just my taste."

She squirmed, but he held her back to his front, splaying his fingers over her chest as his other hand did wicked things to her body below. Clutching the bowl of batter to her stomach, she moaned softly, her feet stepping out to give him more access.

He penetrated her slowly, dragging his long finger in and out as he gently nibbled at her ear and whispered, "I could eat again."

It was stunning how quickly her body responded to him. "And I'm the one with a filthy mouth?"

He withdrew his touch and took the bowl out of her arms then lifted the skillet, taking it off the flame and closing the burner. He pulled her away from the stove. "Come with me."

She followed him to the table, laughing when he lifted her off her feet and perched her on top. "What about the French toast?"

"I have a craving for something else." He pulled her to the edge of the table and she dropped back to lean on her elbows. He dipped his head only to pause at the last second. "It pleases me very much to see you keeping your word."

It wasn't like she hadn't benefited from his conditions, but that didn't need stating, so she simply nodded. "And you'll keep yours, right? Two weeks."

He held her stare for a pregnant moment,

his thoughts moving too quickly for her to track. "Open your legs."

Taken aback that he would skirt her question with a command like that, she frowned at him. "Christian?" She needed to hear him say it.

"Yes, Delilah. In two weeks, if you show me you're ready, I'll take you to your shop," he all but snapped, pivoting to pace the kitchen.

He didn't want her to go, that much was clear. The playful mood they shared minutes ago disappeared, and she regretted messing up that fragile balance.

He faced the wall, but she sensed his scowl. "Christian, I'm sorry." He wouldn't face her, and his mind was blocked. "Please look at me."

His shoulders lifted with a deep sigh and he turned to face her. Not knowing what else to do, she spread her legs apart like he asked. His frown deepened and he turned away.

"Another time."

Her breath caught, his rejection cutting sharp and deep. "Asshole. That's four."

He pivoted quickly, furious that she would deliberately break their bargain. "Do you think this is funny?"

She scrambled to her feet. "No, Christian, I don't think anything about this is funny. I'm, sitting there, completely exposed, and you reject me. Yeah, I'm laughing my fucking ass off."

"That's five."

"Why don't we just make it six and forget the whole fucking agreement since you don't seem willing to meet your end of the bargain."

"I gave you my word, and I said I would keep it! What else do you need from me?" he shouted.

She drew back, her eyes stinging and her chest tight. "I don't know," she admitted quietly, unsure how he was hurting her feelings like this. Or why. "I guess a little kindness."

He dragged a hand through his dark hair and his face pinched with tension. "You're right. I'm sorry. That was cruel of me. All of it." Regret flashed in his eyes as he continued to pace the kitchen. "It was foolish of me to think that intimacy could change your mind. I just thought..." He shook his head. "I don't know what I thought."

She sat up. "Christian, I liked what we did. Having those moments with you... It doesn't make this easier on me. Well, it does and it doesn't." He had to understand that sleeping together would only complicate matters. "The things we can do together, I've never experienced anything like that with anyone else."

His scowl returned. "For me, there is no one else."

"No, that's not what I mean. I'm saying it's not norm—wait." She replayed his words, this time hearing what he actually said. "When you say there's no one else, you mean right now, like, you're single? Same as me. Right?"

"Yes. And also that there has never been anyone before you."

She cocked her head, sure she was misunderstanding him. "Since when? How long?"

"Since… ever."

"No. You're lying."

"I don't lie."

"But you're, like, *really* old."

"I was eight when we traveled here. I watched heart stricken elders lose loved ones. Three hundred years later and their grief is still palpable to me. Nothing ever seemed worth that pain."

"How is that possible? You've *never* had sex with someone?"

"You."

Ohhhhh, boy. "What did you do all these years? How did you…?"

He grimaced. "I'm perfectly capable of seeing to my own needs. Prayer also helped."

This put the *Forty Year Old Virgin* to shame. "Oh, Christian."

"It's nothing to be ashamed of. And it's no longer an issue."

"I'm not trying to shame you."

"Well, I don't need your pity either."

She didn't pity him. She did have the strangest urge to comfort him, though. Crossing the kitchen, she put her arms around him and hugged him tightly. "I'm sorry it took so long for you to find me. I was busy being…" She couldn't even say she was busy being born. She hadn't existed. Her parents hadn't existed or her great, great grandparents. She laughed. "If reincarnation's real, maybe I was busy being a beetle or a wild bird."

He cupped her chin and smiled. "I'm afraid,"

he admitted softly. "I'm afraid of losing you in two weeks or whenever we take that journey. I'm not sure I'm enough to convince you to stay here."

He spoke as if she had a choice. Was he implying that he'd eventually give her one? "Let's not think about that right now. I still don't have any survival skills, so for all we know that trip could be months away. I told you I won't run. And I have no desire to go anywhere until I feel safe and know I'm not a danger to anyone else."

Tipping his head down he kissed her softly. "I'll always see to your safety. No matter what the future holds."

She smiled and leaned her ear against his chest, taking comfort in the steady beat of his heart. His hand rubbed soft circles over her back. Realizing how relaxed she was in his arms, she let go of him and took a step back. It was best not to get too invested in that sort of comfort.

Clearing her throat, she awkwardly said, "I don't know how to turn the stove back on."

He stood and pulled a lever on the side of the porcelain oven. "The wood's still burning. And the thermostat's adjusted here, on the side. You just have to let the air in."

"Right. Mine has a nob."

He gave her space while she grilled the French toast. A lot had happened today, and they both needed time to process.

Christian was a paradox. He was so stern and resolute, but also fragile and incredibly sensitive. She sensed the good in him, but experienced his faults firsthand, so it was hard to call him a good guy. But maybe he wasn't as terrible as she originally thought.

When the bread was crisped to a perfect golden brown, she carried the plates to the table. When they sat, Christian lowered his head and Delilah stilled, fork in hand. He'd never done this during the other times they ate, and she didn't know what to do as he bowed his head in silence, so she stayed perfectly still and waited.

He didn't move for nearly thirty seconds, but when he lifted his head, he smiled. "Thank you for preparing this lovely meal, Delilah."

She no longer felt the need to poke fun at his faith because he stopped trying to push it on her. His gratitude was sincere and kind, and she could pay him a kindness in return by respecting his beliefs just as he was coming to respect hers. "You're welcome. I hope you like it."

"I'm sure I will."

Well, weren't they just the happy couple living off in Northern Bumblefuck on the farm.

"I'm not sure what that word was, but I'm certain it was profane. Seven." He took a bite. "This is delicious."

"How high do you plan to count?"

"I'll stop counting when we hit a number that would make it difficult for you to sit."

She gaped at him. The son of a bitch was really planning to spank her.

"Eight. Your meal's getting cold."

CHAPTER 17

The sky was pitch black when they made their way upstairs, putting on a great show without the intrusion of city lights or vehicles. Stars glowed like planets and everything appeared bigger and closer.

"Did you see that?"

Christian approached the window. "What was it?

"A bird just whizzed by."

"Bats."

She smiled up at him. "Are you sure it wasn't a shape-shifting vampire?"

He chuckled. "I told you, we don't do that."

Her gaze returned to the sky. "Are there other things out there that do?"

The starlit fields cocooned them in miles of privacy and the world felt a million miles away —a thought that equally comforted her and disturbed her. Her breath hitched as a comet arced overhead.

He loosened the tie and the curtain fell shut. "Myths always have a source. Time exaggerates the truth, but there's usually some hidden at the root."

"So, like, werewolves… are they real?"

He pulled back the quilt. "Come to bed."

Things had changed since that morning, and the animosity between them faded. She willingly, without force or manipulation, climbed into bed.

Christian pulled her close and she let herself have this moment of comfort without guilt or pressure. But the longer she lay there, the more her mind stirred.

So much silence. No horns or sirens or music bumping. Just silence. It could have been peaceful if her mind wasn't set on sabotaging the moment with ongoing inner turmoil.

The big client she landed right before meeting Christian would have come to collect the work she owed him by now. He was probably pissed and thinking she skipped town with his money. Technically she had, but not intentionally.

CHRISTIAN'S ARM draped over her waist. She closed her eyes, trying not to obsess over things outside of her control. She would get that guy his money. As soon as she got to a phone, she'd set up a meeting and return his deposit—minus her rent.

She winced. How was that going to work? She'd have no choice but to complete the art, since she'd already spent a large chunk of his deposit. And why wouldn't she want that? Doing the work would make her more money.

Christian's fingers moved slowly over her body, softly caressing her while slowing her heart rate and breathing. Truth be told, she liked having a man's arms around her. The novel experience made her feel safe and protected. Of course, Christian was the one she needed protection from, so it wasn't very sound logic, but it was still gratifying.

Would he let her stay long enough to finish the job when they visited her shop? Their agreement was a visit, but visits could be of various lengths. Maybe they could stay at her place for a while—she frowned—because what captive doesn't want to play host to their captor?

Stressed, she closed her eyes and rolled to her back. Lacing her fingers in Christian's, she lifted his hand to her lips without thinking and breathed in his familiar, calming scent.

Realizing what she was doing, her eyes opened. The duality of the situation wasn't lost on her. She was developing feelings for him.

You have Stockholm's.

The truth was there, an always present, intrusive thought that taunted her since the moment she accepted his negotiation terms that morning. The problem with Stockholm syndrome, she was coming to find out, was that she really didn't care if she was developing feelings for him or not. He made her feel good when so many other circumstances felt bad. Of course, those circumstances were his doing, so she was pretty much losing her mind.

Christian was a comfort as much as he was a complication. *Stockholm's.* She inwardly groaned. *All right! Fine! So what?* Neutrality was easier than being at each other's throats constantly.

Their peaceful truce should have made it easier to sleep, but it severely complicated matters, and little worries like emotional attachment, desire, forgiveness, acceptance, and resentment kept her up. None of those worries were actually small, but thinking of them as such made her panic easier to manage.

Two weeks. She could return home in two weeks. In the coming days, she'd learn the ins and outs of this immortal stuff and then she could branch off on her own and get back to her life.

The thought should have motivated her, but it only made her anxious. What about Christian? She couldn't explain the dread that overcame her at the mere thought of separating from him, possibly saying goodbye forever. Did it have to be forever?

Would they still see each other if she left? He could visit on occasion—like a booty call. No rules or strings. That way they could each have the life they wanted without sacrificing too much.

Yes, something casual and sporadic sounded perfect. Perfectly awful.

She shifted and punched the pillow, trying to find a more comfortable position. Without the distraction of sound, her mind continued to wander. Thoughts of work and the life she abandoned intruded, but it was mostly her concerns about Christian that kept her awake.

How could she be this tired and unable to sleep? She didn't think it was normal for immortals to feel this lethargic. Or maybe it was. She was still trying to sort the facts from fiction and figure out how this whole super-human species thing worked.

The longer she lay in silence the more pronounced the hollow ache inside of her became. Her stomach was full, but her body still wasn't satisfied. She knew what it needed, but she wasn't willing to go there. She shifted again, dislodging the blankets and upsetting the whole bed.

"Delilah."

"Sorry." She huffed. "I can't sleep."

"Would you like me to help you?"

"No." She didn't like when he did that glamour thing to her because it took away her control. Shouldn't she be able to do things like that to herself? What good was this new body if she couldn't control it? "Is it normal to feel this weak?"

He pulled her body back to him, once again

holding her tightly in his arms. "No." He didn't go into detail because there was no need.

They both knew she needed blood, but he'd promised to let her decide when she would feed. The thought still repulsed her enough that any sense of appetite disappeared. It was more like a hankering.

It made Delilah think of one of her clients who got pregnant and said she started craving dirt. Actual dirt. Turned out, eating dirt was a symptom of a nutrient deficiency and that was her body's way of obtaining the minerals the baby needed.

But why did it have to be blood? Dirt she could eat.

She must have exhausted herself because she bolted out of sleep, startled awake by something. A sharp knock had her jackknifing out of bed. She scanned the room with bleary eyes.

"Christian?" He was gone. Sunlight spilled into the room, leaking past every crack in the closed curtains.

Downstairs, pintura.

When the knocking sounded again, she frowned, touching his side of the bed and finding it cool. What time was it?

"Good morning, Sister Abigail." Christian's voice carried from downstairs, and Delilah's attention jerked to the door. Who the hell was Sister Abigail? And why was she visiting Christian at the butt crack of dawn?

"Good morning, Brother Christian. My father sent me to deliver the notes from the meeting you missed. He assumed you'd want them."

"Thank you."

"I also have some fresh bread for you."

This was the bread source. Recalling how pretty the woman was from Christian's memories, Delilah scrambled out of bed.

"That's very kind of you. You look well."

"I am well, indeed, thank you."

Delilah rifled through the drawers. Shirt, shirt, shirt, shirt. She was fresh out of dresses.

Snapping the drawer shut, she shoved her legs into a pair of Christian's pants, hiking them all the way past her boobs so she wouldn't trip. She rushed out of the room to see the woman Christian thought looked so well.

"I hope it's not too forward of me to say congratulations on your *goddeslieb*."

"Not at all."

The woman's voice softened and Delilah detected an edge of disappointment. "I'm happy for you. You've waited a long time for your *pare* to come."

"Your time will come as well, Abby."

Now it was Abby?

A burst of reassurance hit Delilah, but rather than comfort her it annoyed her, like a light spritzing rain that ruined hair with frizz. She imagined gathering up all his reassurance and flinging it back at him on a medieval catapult.

"You'll be busier now," sweet little Abby said.

"I'll always make time for your visits."

Visits? Delilah's claws dug into the wood of the banister.

"I hope so. Well, I had better be returning home before Abraham loses patience."

"Stop by again soon."

"I will. Enjoy the bread."

The door, now repaired, shut. Before fully facing her, Christian greeted her. "Good morning, *pintura.*" When his gaze found her on the landing, he chuckled. "What are you wearing?"

"How often does she visit you?"

"Sister Abigail? *Wechentlich.*"

"English please."

"Weekly."

"Why so often?"

"We play cards together to pass the time, and she brings me bread on occasion. Is there an issue?"

She wasn't allowed to talk to other men but he was hosting game night with Abigail? "She single?"

"Yes."

I don't like it. She couldn't block the thought before Christian overheard it.

He smiled. "Abigail is a friend. Nothing more, *pintura.*" He lifted a basket from the bench in the hall. "Sister Larissa dropped this off for you. It's your dresses and a few other items."

Larissa was there? "What time do you people get up?"

He glanced at the clock by the door. "It's nearly noon."

"Oh." It had been a draining week, and she had a restless night.

He carried the basket to her. "These should fit you better than my pants."

Once back in the bedroom, she sifted through the gowns, paying each item much more respect than she initially had shown days ago. Now that she saw the work that went into making them, she felt spoiled by such generosity. "How can I thank them for all of this?"

"They're happy to help. No thanks is necessary."

"I can't accept all this without doing something to show my gratitude."

He studied her for a long moment. "That's very thoughtful of you. I'm sure a simple thank you will suffice."

"In person?"

"We can pay them a visit."

She fanned out a gown, admiring the fine work. "So, this Abby chick, why didn't you introduce me?"

"You sound jealous."

"You mean curious."

"Of course." He chuckled. "I like the blue one. And Sister Abigail is a friend—to both of us. Her father is an elder on The Council. He lost his mate on the journey over and never recovered. He's very protective of his daughter. She's rarely permitted out of his sight, but he trusts her to come here on occasion because he knows me to be an honorable male."

"Sounds…creepy. How old is she?"

"About my age."

She scoffed, shaking the wrinkles out of the blue dress. "Why doesn't she tell her dad to fuck off?" Her head snapped up and she froze. "Sorry. It was a slip."

He sighed and crossed the room, taking the dress out of her hands and walking her to the dresser. "Because that's not how it works here. Daughters heed their father's rules and do as they're told. This includes respecting elders and following the rules. Abigail is a good daughter who obeys her elders." He turned her to face the dresser. "Place your hands there."

"But she's an adult now."

"He's still her father. Until she has a mate or a husband, his rules are final." He tugged the pants loose and they fell to her ankles.

"What are you—*Ouch!* Christian!" She spun to face him. "Are you nuts?"

"That's one. You have nine more."

"It was eight last night!"

"You let one slip while thinking of Abby."

"Stop calling her Abby!"

"Hands on the dresser, *pintura*."

She backed up, protectively pressing her burning backside into the wooden drawers. "No."

"You agreed to this."

"I agreed to try. I kept my word. I tried. You can't expect me to break a lifetime of bad habits in one day."

"And I told you there would be consequences." He turned her shoulders, guiding her hands back to the surface of the dresser. "We'll see to this and be done with it."

His hand came down again and her body stiffened. "What the—heck?" She spun and scowled at him, rubbing her sore…keister.

"Seems to be working already."

She clenched her teeth. "Hit me again, and I'll hit you back."

"That's not how this works."

She backed away from him, careless of her nudity. "You're Amish. Aren't you supposed to be a pacifist?"

"We are pacifists, but we also believe in discipline. You're not finished."

"Oh, yes, I am." Keeping her back to the wall, she circled away from him, using the copper bathtub to secure a safe distance.

"This is for your own good, *pintura*. The ache will remind you to mind your tongue."

"Why do I need that when I have you reminding me every minute of the day. I already have one pain in the ass. I don't need another."

"That's another one."

"Christian, you're out of your mind if you think I'm going to let you hit me."

"You'll feel at rest once it's done." He circled the tub and she mirrored his steps, never letting him get close enough to reach her.

She snatched the basket of dresses off the bed and threw it at him. "Stop following me!"

"Stop trying to outrun the consequences of your actions. It's best to face these things head-on. You entrusted me to show you our ways. This is our way."

"I was talking about the immortal stuff, and you know it. I draw the line at Amish thrashings."

"Domestic discipline is a common practice and nothing to fear. In many cases it can bring a couple closer to each other and God."

"Says the one with the sore palm." She side-stepped the pile of dresses on the floor and backed up a step. "No!" He reached and almost caught her.

"Think of it as me helping you. Self-control is a virtue. You must tame your tongue."

"That's not what you said last night when my mouth was wrapped around your cock."

His nostrils flared. "That's another."

"They're just words, Christian." She circled the tub, a little dizzy and fatigued from the chase.

"If they were just words, there would be no strength behind them. You use your words as weapons, Delilah. You've tried to hurt me and others. Don't pretend they have no power."

A cramp pinched at her side. "Okay. Okay." Holding up her hands, she kept moving on account of his endless pursuit. She knew he could catch her if he exerted the slightest effort, but that wasn't what he wanted. This was about her submission.

He wasn't going to let her out of this room until she willingly took her medicine. He wanted her to stand still and submit to his will, like a good little Amish wife.

She couldn't do it. Well, she could, but she had to find the nerve. No one willingly volunteered to get spanked. At least not in this capacity.

"So, how does this work?" she asked, winded from circling the room. "You swat my butt a few times and we move on? What about you? Who spanks you?"

"I'm the head of the house."

She dropped her chin and stared at him. "You're kidding, right? You own a home so you're somehow infallible? You hear how stupid that sounds, right?"

"Discipline comes with governance. It is my duty to rule my home as I see fit."

"Not if you want me in your home."

"Delilah, you made a promise to me. You'll keep it if you expect me to hold up my end of the bargain."

She paused and stared at him. He was really serious. She either let him spank her or their truce was over. "No. I'm leaving." She turned to the open door and it slammed shut.

"You're nude."

She spun and glared at him. "Well, I tried to get dressed and you hit me. I thought we were going to be honest with each other. Isn't that what we agreed?"

"I am being honest. This is how I believe my house should be run."

"You mean me. You keep saying house, but

I'm pretty sure you're talking about governing me."

"Fine. Your foul language is a monstrosity that must be corrected if you wish to socialize with the others."

"I told you I'd try."

"You need to try harder."

"Spanking me is not going to make me curse any less. If anything, it'll probably make me curse more."

"This is the way it has to be."

She laughed without humor. "Why don't you just admit you get off on it?"

He frowned. "I take no pleasure—"

"Bullshit." She gasped dramatically and covered her mouth. "Oopsy, I slipped again."

"I'm not amused."

She smirked. "Oh, I think you are. As a matter of fact—" She cocked her head. "—I think the thought of me bent over your lap as you slap my rosy ass amuses you very much. Oops, there goes another one. Slippery little fuckers. Hard yet?"

He lunged, but she anticipated his move and leapt to the other side of the room, laughing when his hands closed around thin air. "Nice try."

"Don't toy with me."

"Or what? You'll spank me? Sort of seems like a nothing to lose situation. I think I'll take my chances." When he sprang again, she moved too slow and he caught her. "*Ah!*"

He dragged her down to the bed, pinning

her beneath him so her stomach and face pressed into the mattress. "Still laughing?"

Humor slipped out between her squeals. The whole thing struck her as hilarious because never in a million years had she pictured herself in such a situation. What else could she do but laugh? Then his hand came down and she sobered.

"You fucker!" It really stung. He wasn't taking it easy on her. However, the sting vanished fairly quickly due to her rapid healing abilities, but it still hurt like a son of a bitch.

"I'll continue tallying if you continue speaking and thinking filth."

Catching her breath, she seethed beneath him and thought of a strategy. She knew what this was. It was no different than playing king of the mountain. He wanted to assert his dominance and feel powerful. Then he'd probably fuck her.

"That's another." He pinned her arms behind her back, he leaned down and whispered. "I think you get a thrill from indecency."

"No, I think that's you." She struggled, but his grip only tightened. She wasn't afraid because she believed him incapable of truly hurting her. This wasn't about pain. It was about control. "You know, if you want to spank me for the kink you could just ask, Christian. I'd probably say yes."

He frowned. "A male does not need his mate's permission to govern as he sees fit."

"Oh, yes, how silly of me. You're right, force is much better." His grip loosened.

"What are you suggesting?"

She turned her face so her other cheek pressed against the bed, finding the position incredibly uncomfortable. "How about you ask nicely, and I'll agree to lay over your lap for ten juicy ones? Then you can fuck me, and afterward we can go for a walk so I can thank the Hartzlers for my dresses."

She sensed his skepticism. "Why this sudden submission?"

"Tomato, *tow-mah-tow*. You say submission, I say compromise." Besides, she was too tired to keep fighting him. "At least be honest with me and admit part of you likes it. That makes it much more acceptable than this whole *this is going to hurt me more than it's going to hurt you* nonsense. You could try explaining to me how it makes you feel and we can discuss it."

He released her arms and the blood immediately flowed back to her hands. "Are you mocking me?"

"No. I'm dead serious. Let's talk about it."

He climbed off of her and she sat up, pulling the sheet over her body for a bit of modesty. "Tell me how you want it to work."

"I want you to clean up your language."

"Check. Still working on it. But let's talk about the kink."

"It's not a kink."

"I don't think you understand the meaning of kink." She mentally reached for his mind.

"Do you like the thought of me lying over your lap?" She didn't need his answer. "You do. Good. We're getting somewhere. And you want me to get into that position willingly, correct?"

"Submission is a great sign of respect."

"So, yes again. Now we're getting somewhere." If she broke down the process into bite sized pieces, she could actually find the idea palatable. He got off on her submission and respect. "I'm not going to let you demean me in the process."

"I would never."

"Good. And keep in mind, *I'm* allowing this. If I *choose* to submit to you in this, it's only this. I can stop at any time if it gets to be too much. I'm not giving you absolute authority."

"I'm your mate."

"Again, not synonymous with authority. Do you agree to my terms or not?"

It was clear he didn't agree with her philosophies for total equality, but he was learning how to compromise. "Yes. I want your absolute submission in this."

She met his stare and sensed the thought of such an act aroused him greatly. Dropping the sheet, she crawled to him. "You have it."

His nostrils flared as his pupils darkened. "Lie down."

He shifted to the edge of the bed and she stood, folding her body over his lap so her hands and feet touched the floor. "Like this?"

His hand softly caressed the curve of her ass. "Yes."

Blood rushed to her head as she waited, but he didn't do more than lightly caress her. "Did you change your mind?"

"Quiet."

She shut her mouth, unsure what was taking so long. The scent of his arousal filled the room, but he seemed to be having some sort of moral dilemma.

"Would it help if I told you my pussy's wet?" She flinched when his palm slammed down on her ass with astounding accuracy. "Jesus!" Another slap and her shoulders tensed. She grunted. Maybe this wasn't such a good idea.

Her searing flesh burned as if a hundred bees stung her. He soothed the sore area with his palm, rubbing softly only to scrape over the sensitive skin with his nails.

"Ah!" When she reflexively squirmed, he pressed a stilling hand on her back and wedged his fingers between her thighs, pressing into her wet slit. She went completely still.

"You like this," he said, withdrawing his fingers only to smack her again. "Why?"

She flinched and tensed then groaned, not necessarily enjoying the pain but finding something about the process satisfying. "Maybe it has something to do with the fact that your cock's stabbing me in the stomach. *Ah!*"

Three hard swats rained over her reddened flesh. "You're purposefully baiting me."

"Am I?"

She spread her legs only to have him slap her pussy. "This isn't for your pleasure, Delilah."

"I'm sorry?" She wiggled her ass and he slapped it again. Hard.

Her breath labored, and she swallowed and tried to regain her composure. She was aroused, but her eyes were also tearing. "I'm sorry," she said, chastised and sincere. "I'll stop."

Closing her eyes, she centered her mind and loosened her muscles. It hurt less if she didn't tense. Several more slaps came down, each one adding to the building burn in her backside. Tears reflexively flowed from her eyes, and her breath caught every single time he slammed his palm down on her tenderized skin, but she didn't ask him to stop.

In a way, he was right. The longer it went on, the more at rest she felt. When the spanking finally concluded, a literal noise filled her head. Her pliant body gelled together in such a fragile way she was afraid to move.

Christian's heavy breathing clocked the silence like a metronome. The scent of his arousal thickened the air. He scored his nails over her sore flesh, and she twitched, sucking in a shaky breath. But she didn't curse.

Instead, she swallowed tightly and shocked them both as she said, "Thank you."

"Come here." The air tightened and he pulled her fully onto his lap, arranging her legs so she straddled him.

Her face naturally tucked into his neck as she hugged him tightly and let out a stammering breath. He massaged the sore muscles of her arms and legs, whispering soft words of praise.

"That was a stunning show of submission, *pintura.* You've pleased me greatly."

She nuzzled deeper, needing his comfort and wanting his arms around her. He'd softened her in ways she hadn't thought possible. Dormant parts of her psyche had opened in the process and her thoughts were no longer clouded.

She felt…purified. Clean and innocent. Blameless. But also delicate and in need of his sheltering strength.

The fear of judgement disappeared. She could say anything to him in that moment, certain he would protect and cherish her no matter what. How could she feel all of that after he spanked her?

She didn't understand, but she trusted his guidance, and even craved it. "Christian?"

"Yes, little one?"

She dragged her nose along the underside of his jaw, rubbing her face to his like a kitten craves attention. His scent intoxicated her as his strong arms held her tight.

Catching the lobe of his ear between her lips, she tugged softly and whispered, "I want you."

He stilled for a split second and then he was kissing her. Spreading her tenderized body out beneath him, opening his pants to thrust into her.

Her body accepted him without resistance,

and she wreathed her arms around his neck, her fingers sifting through his hair as he took her mouth with long drugging kisses. She gasped when he lunged forward, filling her to the hilt.

His pleasure melded with hers and she arched into him. "Yes, more." Her fingers raked and knotted in his hair, pulling his lips back to hers.

Her breasts crushed against the wall of his muscled chest as he kissed her harder, deeper, giving her all he could to show how desperately he wanted to please her. The intensity of his strokes increased. With every hard thrust, he stretched her body a little more, folding her legs back until she was completely open to him.

"I want to feel your skin against mine."

Drawing back, he removed his shirt and tossed it aside. Slowing his strokes, he watched his cock sliding in and out of her. He shared the view, sending the erotic vision to the forefront of her mind. He reached between her legs and stroked a thumb over the piercing of her clit, and she sucked in a breath.

His eyes flashed as their gaze connected. "You're doing it again. Look at how pliant your body has become to my touch." He dragged the back of his fingers affectionately down her cheek and she preened, leaning into the caress.

He drew back and shoved into her. A moan pelted past her lips, propelled out of her by his forceful strokes. He liked subjugating her, displaying his dominance without opposition. He craved her surrender, and it was easy to submit to him this way, especially when it enflamed his darkest pleasure and she experienced his satisfaction through their shared mental link.

She opened her body more, stretching her legs as far back as her muscles allowed so he could take his pleasure, all the while giving it right back to her.

His speed doubled and his strokes turned almost punishing, but he wasn't trying to discipline her. He only wanted to possess her. All of her. More than anyone else ever had.

"I love when you soften for me," he growled, dragging a hand through her hair only to curl his fingers around her throat. "You were perfect, *pintura.* Your submission honors me."

Maybe that was why she liked it. She liked pleasing him.

The friction of the bed on her raw flesh reminded her of his dominance, and her sex clenched. He drove into her, leaning down until her body folded beneath his weight. She was completely at his mercy.

No one had ever expressed such an all-encompassing desire for her. Despite the roughness of his touch, adoration radiated from him. His possession was complete, holding not only her body but her heart and soul. She was safe in his arms and didn't have to worry or fear. He would always protect her.

Moved by the realization of her trust, she offered him another display of relinquished control and raised her arms over her head, lifting her chin to fully expose her under his grip. It was an unmistakable show of vulnerability and trust.

He growled with deep satisfaction and thrust harder. His hand moved to her hair and knotted in the strands, holding her head still and dropping his mouth to her exposed neck. Teeth scraped as his mouth closed over her shoulder, his fangs pressing into her but not breaking the skin.

An agonizing ache knifed through her as his desire for her blood slammed into her. He beat it back with incredible force of will, but she didn't have his self-discipline and she cried out in disappointment, wanting his teeth to sink into her. The mere thought reawakened the hollow throb she'd been fighting for days.

Her body needed it. The sharp, relentless craving crawled through her like poison seeking a host.

He drew back, cupping her jaw and forcing her to meet his stare. "Delilah, do you have need?"

Sweat broke over her body, and she ground her teeth, refusing to let her jaw open. "I'm fine."

"You're not. I can feel your pain."

This wasn't about her. He was the one who originally wanted to bite her. Her body just got confused. She rocked her hips forward, urging him to keep going, but he pulled back.

She gasped at the sudden emptiness when he pulled out of her. "Christian!" Her body unfolded and she weakly sat up, wincing when her raw cheeks pressed into the bed.

"You're too weak."

He only gave her the truth but it stung like inadequacy. "So that's it? We're done?"

"You need to feed."

"That's my choice—"

He held up a silencing hand, refusing to meet her stare. "I didn't say I would force the subject. I'm merely saying we should refrain until you're feeling stronger."

And how exactly was that going to happen as long as she didn't feed? He was forcing the subject, just not directly. "So now you're withholding sex? You just negotiated for it yesterday!"

"I will not put my needs before yours."

She scoffed. "What about my needs? What if I need sex?"

"You need nutrition more."

"This is ridiculous." Gathering up the sheet, she scooted off the bed, wincing again when the blankets scraped against her flesh. "Do whatever you want. I'm taking a bath."

"Delilah…"

She dashed away a tear, unsure why she was crying.

"You're emotional because you're not feeding properly."

"I'm emotional because I'm on a farm without modern plumbing. How do I empty this thing."

He stood and fastened his pants. Bending at

the backside of the tub, he turned a spigot she hadn't noticed. "I built piping into the floor before you arrived. It empties into the gardens below."

"Oh." That was thoughtful. She didn't know how to act when he told her stuff like that. In a way, he was only confessing to a premeditated crime. But in another way, it was sweet of him to put so much thought into her comfort. "Thanks."

He sighed and she understood he wasn't happy about her ongoing hunger strike, but he kept his word not to pressure her. "I'll heat some water."

"Christian." He glanced back at her from the door, and she wondered why she called his name. She didn't want him to be upset with her. Crossing the room, she stood before him and lifted to her toes, pressing a soft kiss to the underside of his jaw.

He blinked at her in confusion. "Sometimes, I think God sent you to challenge me."

God didn't send her here. "I'm here because you took me, Christian. That's why this is a challenge."

"Would you have willingly come if I'd asked?"

She considered how she convinced herself to submit to a spanking through her own volition. Would she have done the same if he'd simply reasoned with her about coming here and becoming his mate? Was there a limit to her agreeableness? If he had been honest, could he have convinced her to give up her human life and come live on an Amish farm?

She looked him in the eye and gave him the truth. "No."

Although he didn't move, she felt every muscle of his body tighten. Without another word, he turned away from her and left the room.

CHAPTER 18

She was a sorcerous. Somehow, his mate had used her mind and body to turn him completely around. It wasn't a compulsion. He would have recognized any sense of forced obligation. This was different. This was a longing, coming from his heart.

She gave him something he needed—a sign of submission—and he was prepared to give her anything in return, which was how he came to trudge his way back to Cain Hartzler's door holding a dish of strawberries.

He'd agreed to take Delilah to visit the Hartzler females so she could express her gratitude. How that evolved into dinner he still didn't understand. The females used phrases like *have to* as if they had no choice in the matter.

"You and Christian have to *come for dinner!"*

"We have to *get the guys together!"*

"You have to *taste Destiny's cooking!"*

He didn't care about the other female's kitchen skills, nor did he have an inkling to eat at her table for hours of forced socializing with the youngest Hartzler males.

"Can we go?" Delilah had quietly pulled him aside during their visit to ask his permission.

It made him proud that she deferred to him, but it wasn't enough for him to agree. "I don't think so. That's not something I want to do."

He only realized how happy the offer made her when the joy in her eyes disappeared. Hardening her jaw, she scowled and asked, "Did I want to do any of this?"

He quickly understood that he had no choice in the matter. Her cooperation implied his. He was obligated to go. But he also truly wanted to make her happy.

"Fine. We can have supper with your friends."

Christian could tolerate many unfavorable circumstances, but socializing with immortals two and a half centuries his minor wasn't a sacrifice he was eager to make. His time was valuable and could be put to much better use.

Irritated to have to make such a concession, he almost changed his mind. Then he saw how happy she was to tell her new friends that she could go, and he realized he'd walk through fire for her.

"He said we can go!" she had squealed, her smile once again radiant and in place.

He'd sit through endless annoying dinner parties if it brought her that much joy, he realized, wondering if that was how she'd managed to submit to him earlier that afternoon. He found it difficult to name a torture he wouldn't endure when her happiness was on the line.

His reluctance to socialize had him twitching, and he was already anxious for the night to end.

They approached the door, and she frowned at him. "What's wrong?"

"Nothing is the matter."

"Then why are you making that face?"

"This is just my face."

"No, it's not. You're grimacing."

He relaxed his muscles and moved his brows. "Better?"

She frowned. "You should smile more. You have a nice smile."

His steps slowed and she walked ahead. The corner of his mouth curved. His smiles were for her and her alone.

His mood could have been better if he'd had her several more times, but she still hadn't fed, and he didn't want to make her any weaker than she already was.

It was only a matter of time before nature took over and she gave in to her needs. When they were in bed, her struggle with the hunger gnawed at him. Not only did she need to feed, she wanted him to take her vein. She couldn't fathom how he could resist such an overbearing urge, but life had taught him great self-possession and reinforced his unbreakable will.

It wasn't easy. While she bathed, he had to visit the stables to feed. She was making him ravenous, but nothing involving his mate was simple.

He hoped his concession to have supper with her friends would encourage more cooperation on her end. Every hour she grew weaker and weaker. He knew her hunger was causing her pain, because he was in her mind witnessing every twinge and ache.

Her stubbornness was so infuriating he had to turn off his empathy on occasion. He wasn't used to such willful opposition.

She crushed him when she so blithely admitted she would have never agreed to willingly go with him. He should have appreciated her honesty because that's all that was, but he didn't want to hear such a painful truth. He wanted her to change her mind and accept that this was where she belonged.

He'd been willing to give her everything he had to offer and she still rejected him. He was beginning to wonder if her acceptance would ever come. How many dinners would he have to sit through only to have her reject him again and again?

It had been some time since they lay together, several hours since his body experienced the explosive euphoria that accompanied their intimacy, and his logic no longer struck him as sound.

"Remind me again why we're doing this?"

She shifted the dish of whipped sweet cream she carried. "Because we're having date night."

"Date night," he grumbled under his breath.

"A courtship is between two individuals. There should be no need to involve others."

"It's normal, Christian. I need normal."

"We're standing at a door holding berries and whipped cream. Nothing about this feels normal to me."

She growled then leaned forward and knocked. "We're making friends."

"I don't see how this will strengthen our bond—"

The door opened. "You made it!" Sister Destiny squealed and pulled Delilah into a hug. "What's this?"

"Just something for dessert. Nothing fancy."

"It looks delicious. Come in, come in!"

Delilah was dragged into the house, and he was left standing in the moonlit shadows of the porch holding a bowl full of fruit. More shrill squeals peeled from inside. Nothing about this decision felt *normal.* But he liked when Delilah referred to them as a couple. That was progress.

The dwelling had a smell—not an unpleasant odor, but a scent he didn't recognize. Cinnamon, coriander, nutmeg, and the scent of young, territorial immortal males teased his nose the moment he crossed the threshold.

It was common for newly mated males to mark their mates with their scent. The females of the house all reeked like their partners. He supposed his scent clung to Delilah strongest of all, a thought that thrilled him and had his gaze seeking his mate and his body hardening. One glance in her direction and he wanted her every which way he could have her.

"Christian, welcome to our home." Cain approached, far too at ease in his composure for Christian's liking. Even if they were in the male's private home, one should address guests with more composure and formalities. "What do you have here?" He lifted the glass lid from the dish. "Strawberries. Perfect. You can set them on the side table."

He walked away before telling Christian *which* side table. Christian scanned the room, finding their furniture overly crowded with useless items. He didn't see the sense in so much clutter, nor did he see a space for the strawberries.

"Christian." Delilah reappeared while voices chattered from the other room.

She was a vision. Rushing to his side like the ocean dutifully returns to the shore. His tension lowered with each step. His beautiful mate was an oasis in the heat of a brutal desert.

Lowering her voice, she took the bowl of berries from him and whispered, "You're just standing there. You promised not to be weird."

"I'm not—"

"Everyone's in the dining room." She set the strawberries on a long sideboard and pulled him toward the chatter.

A female laugh cut through the noise, uncontained and riotous, speaking of subjects that weren't appropriate for mixed company. Perhaps these females weren't the best influences for his mate.

The Elder's Council encouraged refined, docile behavior from the females of The Order. Delilah should be influenced by tradition. While these females might be devoted to their partners, their adherence to Amish life looked blatantly different than his interpretation.

"Good evening, Brother Christian." Adam Hartzler greeted him the moment Delilah dragged him to the long table.

Christian preferred this male's calm and conventional attitude over his twin's un-orthodox nonchalance. "Good to see you, Brother Adam."

He frowned, distracted by the females lazing around the table, cackling and gossiping rather than preparing the meal. Was this not a dinner party?

"They've had some wine."

Christian's attention jerked back to Adam. "You've given them alcohol?"

He lifted his brows and laughed. "More like they took it. Destiny's brother, Vito, visited this afternoon and dropped some off. It's harmless. It takes nearly a case for them to feel tipsy."

Vito Santos was a mortal half-breed who lived off the farm. He was not a part of The Order, and therefore, Christian didn't trust the outsider. But the bishop had bartered a deal with him.

Vito provided frequent shipments of out-side goods to the farm. His immortal bloodlines were weak and diluted by time, so the male was unaware of their species or the fact that he was not a pure-blooded mortal. Secrecy was an unbreakable condition for the man to come and go. It was the only way The Council would grant Destiny such an opportunity to remain connected to her brother. Christian had voted against granting an outsider such access, and still strongly believed the treaty put them in precarious danger.

The females appeared intoxicated and loose. Christian scowled at the bawdy way they lounged around the table, shrieking with laughter and shirking their responsibilities. Having *fun* when there was obvious work to do.

His eyes widened when he spotted a glass of dark wine in Delilah's cup. He crossed the room and bent to speak softly in her ear. "You did not ask—"

"Oh," She smiled and took a quick sip. "Did you want some wine? Destiny's brother brought it."

He frowned at her misunderstanding, his disapproval sidetracked by her cheery smile. The Hartzlers were more responsible for her joy in that moment than him. His cheek twitched. He wanted to make her smile like that.

She leaned up on her toes and whispered, "You're making the grumpy face again. Why don't you have some wine?"

While progressive Amish sects had no prohibition laws, and The Order did not take issue with alcohol consumption on account of immortal blood burning off the effects so quickly, Christian was of a different time. Spirits were best saved for males and used only by females of a more lascivious nature. He didn't approve of his mate partaking in such behavior, yet he seemed incapable of stopping her when she appeared to be having fun.

An outburst of laughter poured from the females and Cain's wife stood. "I have to check on dinner. Anna, you wanna help?"

The informality of her speech sounded too English for his ears. He detected a Portuguese accent but her mannerisms were completely Americanized. His eyes widened when he caught the flash of a bracelet on her wrist.

"Your beauty should not come from outward adornments, such as elaborate hairstyles and the wearing of gold jewelry or fine clothes."

"Which is of great worth in God's sight." Adam once again stepped beside him. "Peter 3: 3-4."

He glanced at the male and back to the females. "Your brother permits much lavishness under his roof."

Cain's wife's gown was not of traditional modest coloring, but a vibrant red he had not seen females of The Order wear before. Assuming this was a formal gathering, he'd come dressed in his vest and jacket, but the females appeared casual and rumpled as if they threw themselves together that morning with little effort or intention.

"I'll help," Delilah volunteered following the females into the kitchen.

The two brothers watched the females go, each one grinning with admiration. Christian did not understand their arrangement, as Adam's bonding had caused several concerns, and Cain's wife was not his true mate. He once more feared regretting allowing such influences around Delilah.

Cain's wife returned a moment later, and Christian looked away. She had removed her *kapp*, a violation of their laws when in the company of others, and dark curly hair fell past her shoulders. It was complete anarchy.

Cheeks rosy from wine, she stumbled into her husband and laughed. "Babe, can you get the big dish down from the hutch for me?"

"Of course." Cain headed toward the den where the china cabinet stood.

Destiny smiled at Christian. "Short girl problems."

He glanced at Cain as he retrieved the dish, finding it inappropriate to address another man's wife while his back was turned.

She took the dish from Cain and carried it into the kitchen where the other females cackled. Destiny returned to the kitchen, speaking to the females before the door fully closed. "So, Christian, he's a little stiff, huh?"

His gaze crossed with the other men. They all heard the comment.

"She's excited," Cain explained. "Usually Gracie does the cooking."

"Or Anna," Adam said.

Cain looked at Christian and silently made a face as if choking. "Tonight, Destiny's making a traditional Portuguese meal like her mother and aunts used to make. She prepared goat, *Cabidela,* a rice soaked in blood, and a side dish of suckling pig marinated in citrus."

He considered Delilah's dietary restrictions. "Excuse me. I need to speak to my mate."

The kitchen was absolute mayhem. Pots of boiling sauces bubbled as empty wine bottles gathered beside an empty sink. Modern amenities that were not sanctioned boasted of an entirely different set of values.

"Delilah."

His mate laughed at something Anna said then turned. "Yeah?"

She looked so happy in that moment, he didn't want to replace her joy with worry. "Nothing."

"*Mio Dios,* I'm drunk!" Sister Destiny fumbled as she gathered dishes for the table.

Sister Annalise snorted into her wine glass. "It's that weak blood of yours. I'm jealous."

"We'll just have to drink faster," Delilah teased, clinking her glass to Sister Annalise's.

Christian frowned. He had allowed her one afternoon visit and supervised the second. How had she formed such camaraderie with these females?

Returning to the den and feeling out of place, he asked Adam, "Is Bishop King attending?"

"I'm afraid not. Larissa offered to take the children, so they're at home."

He wondered how the bishop managed such reformist in-laws. He flinched when a sharp clacking sound stole through the air, accompanied by a rapid drumming beat. The noise blared from the kitchen as the women hollered.

"Here they go," Cain grinned. "You might want to cover your ears, Christian."

Cover his ears? The noise, which was some sort of pounding music got louder and then all three women barked in unison, *"Ob-la-di, ob-la-da, life goes on, brah! La-la oh their life goes on!"*

His shock was complete when he heard his mate's voice collide with the others, as if this was something she'd heard a hundred times before.

"Anna loves The Beatles," Adam said as if that explained anything.

"You allow her music?"

"The machine has to be wound, so I see no real harm in it."

Christian peered into the kitchen where the women bounced in a circle, smiling and laughing as if best of friends. He glanced back at the two brothers and scowled. This would not be a reciprocal arrangement. They would not be hosting such heathens at their hearth anytime soon.

The door opened and the youngest Hartzler sister, Grace, appeared. Her focus went directly to the women bouncing about in the kitchen. Another round of squealed greetings was abruptly followed by uproarious laugher erupting from the females.

"So, Chris," Cain said, slapping a hand on his back. "How goes the mating? Tired yet?"

"Christian," he corrected. The front door opened again and Christian stilled.

His half-brother's stare hardened the moment he saw him. "What the hell are you doing here?"

The Hartzlers had brought Dane and his sister to the farm, complicated residuals from Jonas Hartzler's calling. He supposed the boy's entry created a sort of bond with the family, but he was not their family. He was Christian's. And, even then, he was not.

Rather than answer the boy, he turned to Cain. "Will there be any other guests?" He had reached his limit and wanted to leave.

The door shut behind Dane. His narrow glare followed Christian as he entered the house.

He supposed that was kind of the Hartzlers to include the boy, but that didn't mean Christian had forgotten his threat. If he saw the half-breed so much as look at his mate, there would be consequences.

The rumpus in the kitchen quieted and then the females sang in a much softer, harmonized tone. A story of lonely people.

Ignoring the males, he drifted to the kitchen door and curiously watched. The females laced their arms forming a huddle and swayed in a circle. Together, they howled, *"Ah, look at all the lonely people!"*

Delilah sang with the familiarity one might know a hymn by heart. *"Eleanor Rigby, died in a church and was buried along with her name."*

"Nobody came," Sister Anna sang.

"Father McKenzie..."

He turned back to the den, pleased they at least chose a song that vaguely mentioned faith.

His displeasure at having to attend the dinner party was curbed by his mate's light-hearted joy. The uncomfortable visit could only last a few hours, but it would pass like an eternity. After the females finished their uproarious performance, dinner was served.

Delilah sat beside him, staring at the flavorful spread of prepared meats. Her expression remained tranquil, but her thoughts had shifted to utter panic.

Christian reached under the table and closed a supportive hand over her thigh. *You're not breathing, pintura.*

It's a Portuguese slaughter. Even the rice is soaked in blood.

"Dig in," Sister Destiny said.

Delilah reached for her glass of water and guzzled it down.

"Delilah," Sister Grace spoke softly from across the table. "Perhaps you'd like to start with some bread."

Christian reached for the basket she held. "Thank you, Sister Grace. You're very kind."

The female nodded, and he recalled she had a gift for telepathy.

She's reading you, pintura.

Shit—

His hand returned to her thigh. "Take some bread."

His mate took two rolls and picked at the dough. No one seemed to notice that she wasn't eating the main course. But when the dishes were passed around the table, he felt obligated to place a small serving of each on Delilah's plate.

Just move it around with your fork.

She lifted her fork but only stared at the sliced meat and soaked rice.

"This is delicious, Destiny," Sister Annalise praised.

"Very good," Brother Adam agreed.

"Do you like it, Christian?" Sister Destiny asked. Her husband should correct her for not addressing him correctly.

"It smells very flavorful. Thank you." It seemed to escape everyone's notice that there had not been a prayer. "Shall we say grace?"

The scraping of forks over china silenced. Sister Grace was the first to bow her head. Adam looked to Cain being that he was the head of the house.

"Right," Cain said, bowing his head. The others silently followed, but Christian did not feel the usual unification he experienced at service. There was disquiet in the hearts of these immortals.

"Amen," Cain announced, and everyone, save Delilah, continued to eat.

By the end of the meal his mate had a napkin full of meat and a belly full of bread and water. He'd found Sister Grace the most abiding of the group, until she started bickering with Dane. Christian couldn't imagine why they would invite the boy if the two could not tolerate each other.

They like each other.

He frowned as Delilah's thought swept through his mind. *They haven't stopped bickering since we sat down. They despise each other.*

That's how they flirt. Trust me. She likes him and he likes her. But Gracie is saving herself for her mate. Oh! Maybe Dane's her mate.

That would be impossible. He's a half-breed.

A chair scraped and Sister Grace abruptly stood. "I think I'll clear the dishes."

Delilah's guilt flooded him. *Do you think she overheard us.*

Christian couldn't form the concern Delilah felt for such petty drama. He only wanted to leave.

"Really, Christian?" Delilah said, standing and going after Sister Grace.

Brother Cain snickered. "Gotta love a modern woman. She's a feisty one."

"I'll ask you not to speak of my mate."

"Right."

The females cleared the table and lingered in the kitchen. He wished Delilah would return so he didn't feel such pressure to make idle conversation with the males. They were much younger than him and he did not know their interests.

"I have a wagon that needs mending," he told Adam.

"Of course. Bring it by tomorrow and I'll take a look."

The tedious task of crosstalk drained him. Why did Delilah insist they do this? He'd barely spoken to her all night. She could have simply asked to visit with the females again. He'd gladly put any trust issues aside if it meant avoiding such awkwardness in the future.

Leaning back in his chair, he glanced into the kitchen. The females gathered around the desserts and spoke in a huddle. They were always forming circles as if conjuring.

"So, how's it going with you and Christian?" Sister Annalise asked, nibbling on the crust of the freshly baked pie.

Christian's shoulders tensed. Another violation of their laws—gossip and a blatant disregard for the privacy of family law.

Sister Grace slapped her fingers away. "Wait until everyone takes a slice before you chew off the crust like a little mouse."

"I can't help it. The crust is my favorite part."

"Well, no one wants it after your fingers have been all over it."

"Hush, Grace. Delilah was about to spill some tea." Sister Annalise went back to picking at the crust.

"It's…not as bad as I thought it would be," Delilah admitted.

"I'm sure the sex helps," Sister Destiny teased and Christian frowned. These females were grossly indecent.

"That's pretty much the only time we get along," Delilah said and his scowl deepened.

She should not discuss such private matters with others, but his curiosity prevented him from correcting her.

Sister Annalise worked her way around the entire pie. "He doesn't say much."

"He's quiet," Delilah agreed. "And I guess you could say today was actually pretty nice. He took me around the farm to see all the animals. I named them."

He smirked, recalling her peculiar but adorable need to name each creature. She had looked into the eyes of each animal, scratching their ears and speaking to them as if they might understand. He'd asked if they spoke back, wondering if she possessed some sort of discipline for communing with the wild, but she only laughed at such a question, claiming she just liked to be friendly.

How silly to name a cow Marmaduke, he thought, smothering a chuckle.

"Can I see your tattoo?" Sister Annalise asked.

"Sure." Delilah held out her arm, drawing back her sleeve.

"You have so many." Sister Grace admired the colorful ink. "Does it hurt?"

"Only in the beginning. Then it just feels like regular skin." Delilah frowned. "Some of them need touching up." She lifted her skirts and Christian's eyes bulged. "I have more on my legs."

The females crouched and tittered with interest. "Oh, look at this one!" Sister Grace exclaimed. "How clever!"

"I like the butterfly."

"What's this one?"

"Oh," Delilah blushed. "That's a drawing my friend made one night on a napkin. I thought it was cool so I turned it into a tattoo."

He'd seen enough. Rising from the table, he went to the kitchen before his mate's knees were on display. "Delilah."

She looked up with a smile. "Yeah?"

Cover yourself.

She dropped her skirt, and her smile fell.

Sister Grace also frowned. "Did you need something, Brother Christian?"

Only to keep his mate's modesty intact.

Delilah's fist rested on her hip. "Why don't you go play with the other boys?"

"I'm three centuries old, Delilah. I do not *play.*"

"Well, go discuss plows or whatever interests you guys. Be a good guest. Us girls are talking." Then she sent a mental poke. *And you just embarrassed me.*

Shunned, he backed out of the kitchen and came face to face with Dane. The boy scowled at him and pushed past him into the kitchen, intentionally knocking his shoulder into Christian's.

He spun, prepared to snatch the boy up by the scruff of his neck, only to hesitate when his gaze collided with Delilah's.

Don't you dare.

Christian scowled. *He shoved me.*

Get over it.

Grumbling under his breath, he returned to the den.

It never occurred to him how shy he was until God had paired him with an exuberant extrovert. By the end of the night, he would be exhausted from tedious conversations and abiding social niceties he did not see as necessary.

It occurred to him, save the bishop, he really didn't have many friends. And in all honesty, Eleazar was his mother's friend before his. Until meeting Delilah, his life was a lonesome rotation of work, prayer, and quiet reading. On occasion, he'd play a game, but even then, it was usually solitaire, save the occasions Sister Abigail visited .

Delilah's laughter cut through the house, and he felt the strongest compulsion to go to her. He needed the evening to end. He wanted the tedious mingling to stop, desperately longing to return to his quiet home. He desired his mate in his arms without the competition of others stealing her attention from him.

Her stare lifted and found his, her smile suspended until her brow pinched with concern. *Christian, are you all right?*

He smiled, in awe of her beauty and taking great relief from her concern. He decided he could tolerate her friends a few more hours. *Perfect, pintura. Everything is perfect.*

The soft curve of her mouth set something afire in him. He would stay as long as she wanted, but when they returned home, he needed to have her.

Worry for her increasing lethargy returned. Maybe he was approaching this incorrectly. She seemed most tempted to feed when they were intimate, so perhaps intercourse was the key.

When the females carried out the dessert, a rich *Portuguese* cake, Delilah's strawberries and cream, and Sister Grace's crustless pie, servings were dished out to each of the males.

"Oh, I forgot coffee," Sister Destiny turned back to the kitchen. "Cain, can you give me a hand?"

The male jumped to his feet to do his wife's bidding. Nothing about their dynamic struck Christian as traditional. As soon as the couple disappeared into the kitchen, they fell into an intimate embrace, overestimating their privacy and making no attempt for discretion.

"You're drunk," Brother Cain growled, his observation lacking any disapproval.

His wife giggled. "Perks of being a half-breed."

This was becoming a sort of infestation, Christian thought, turning his glare back on

Dane who was scowling at Sister Grace who happily talked with Brother Adam and his wife. He had no interest in their conversation.

Like the moon pulls the tide, his attention returned to Delilah. She watched the kitchen door, observing more than Christian could see from his vantage. A look of deep longing filled her eyes. He gently pressed into her mind to identify what made her appear so forlorn. Through her thoughts, he could see what she saw and feel the emotions the vision stirred.

The married couple in the kitchen shared a personal moment as they waited for the coffee to brew. Cain hoisted his wife onto the counter and fit himself between her knees. The female's arms wreathed his neck as he kissed her. Delilah's heart filled with wistful envy at the sight of such affection, and Christian wondered if he had shown her enough tenderness.

He silently vowed to be more affectionate with his mate, as she seemed to value and long for such things. He'd been so determined to show her domesticity, intimacy, and the sensual joys of feeding that he'd overlooked the simple pleasures of touch and praise.

He closed his hand around hers where it rested on her lap, and she turned and blushed, realizing he saw her watching the other couple. A shy smile curved her lips when his hand tightened around hers and a pleasant warmth spread in his chest.

He wanted to whisper something to her the

way Brother Cain whispered to his wife, but he didn't know what to say.

Leaning into his side, she gazed back at the kitchen and whispered, "They're so in love."

Love, that's what it was. The couple was not mated, but they shared a bond so strong they often moved as one. Each anticipated the other's next move and happily offered to help. It was a partnership, very fitting to his mate's definition of one. Their rhythm, cooperation, and verve moved in perfect harmony.

"It's beautiful," he agreed, not knowing what it was to share such a connection as theirs.

She looked back to the kitchen and continued to watch, her mind acknowledging his presence in her thoughts and welcoming him to observe with her. When Brother Cain's fangs flashed before he bit into his wife's throat, Delilah stiffened and gasped.

Christian squeezed her hand, reminding her that others were present. Delilah's pulse increased when the other woman quietly moaned and quivered, running her fingers through her husband's hair, her face a picture of absolute ecstasy.

It was a good image for his mate to see. So much passion and intimacy stemmed from sharing one's vein. Not only did the receiver enjoy the sensation, the giver also took great pleasure from the act. There truly wasn't anything more satisfying than meeting a mate's needs.

The scent of Delilah's arousal met his nose,

triggering his own. "We should say goodnight, *pintura.*"

"But the coffee…"

He didn't want to embarrass her, but the others would soon become aware of the pheromones her body was secreting.

She read his mind and her eyes widened. "Oh. We should go."

They made their goodbyes in a hurry, Delilah's rushed mannerisms drawing some concern. The brothers jested with him, re-calling how pressing some matters became when they first found their mates. Christian despised feeling so exposed and resented the tedious social niceties that delayed him from taking his mate home to his bed.

"Yes, thank you for supper. Goodnight." He quickly steered Delilah out the door, grateful that the socializing had concluded.

Taking her hand, he walked swiftly towards home. The scent of her body crawled into him, and his hardened response made each stride a trial.

"Christian, slow down."

"Your wicked thoughts tell me you don't want slow." He glanced back as she skipped after him, trying to match his longer steps.

Her arousal competed with the strong scent of honeysuckle in the air and he slowed his pace. "Or is that what you prefer?" It always surprised him when he naturally set aside his pressing desires to see to her needs first. She had become his greatest priority and it was shockingly simple to put her needs before his own. "Did you want to take things slow?"

She looked up at him, the moonlight highlighting her face in a blue glow. "I want what they have." Her mind flashed with images of the couple. Hands gripping possessively. Mouths whispering filthy secrets. Teeth biting. Lips parting. Breath panting.

He rushed forward, only to pause when he sensed how frail she was after hardly eating supper. "Perhaps we should get you home fir—"

Her lips pressed to his, silencing his concerns as his mind overflowed with dark images of everything she wanted from him. Hunger was the last of her concerns.

Lifting her off the ground, he pulled her legs around him and pressed her into the nearby wall of a barn. His hands pushed up her skirts as she kissed him passionately, her mind continuously filling his with erotic visions.

"I can give you that and more." Loosening the front of his pants, he gripped his thick cock. "Our bond is deeper than theirs. You will see."

She gasped when the fabric of her underclothes tore. He shoved into her and growled, claiming her body like a male possessed. Gripping his shoulders, she locked her legs around his back, and cried out.

Moonlight hit her exposed throat, the narrow column drawing his attention as his fangs punched through his gums. Grunting, he looked down at her breast, but the urge to sink his teeth into her flesh only doubled.

Harder, he bucked his hips, pulling her slight body down on his as he tried to slake his thirst, but nothing would stop the relentless craving for her blood.

"Do it," she gasped, tipping back her head.

His stare shot to her throat with rapt attention on her fluttering pulse. "What?"

"I want you to. Just do it."

He was beyond thinking. Drawing back, he snapped forward with perfect accuracy, piercing her delicate flesh and plunging his teeth into her artery. The rich, decadent essence flowed over his tongue and down his throat as his hips snapped forward, driving into her with possessive force, his scent marking her skin.

He'd forgotten how unique her blood was, unlike any other source. She was made for him, and as his mate, nothing would ever taste better than drinking directly from her vein.

She spiraled into a release when his ecstasy became her own. Her sex fluttered and clamped down on his hard length, gripping him like an iron fist. His seed rushed forward, spurting deep inside her womb in an explosive finish.

The force of passion had him arching back, his mouth opening on a guttural growl as her delicious life force worked through his body. Muscles twitching, he leaned his weight into her, not wanting the euphoric sensations to end. Every aftershock of her climax became his own and he shivered, licking delicately to close the puncture at her neck.

She sagged against him, sated, panting and smiling. He gently kissed her eyelids, then her nose, then her mouth. "You honor me."

She hummed softly, still not opening her eyes. "I think you're going to have to carry me home after that."

"My pleasure." But as he withdrew from her heat and righted her clothes, she stumbled. "Careful." He caught her in his arms, lifting her to his chest, and waited for the dizzy spell to pass. "I shouldn't have done what I did. You're still very weak."

Her eyes barely opened when she looked up at him, a warm burst of affection coming from her heart and warming his chest as she touched his cheek. "I'm glad you did."

She sighed, her lashes lowering once more. Then her knees softened and she sank into his hold. His arms tightened, his panic surging. "Delilah?"

Her head lulled and her body went limp in his arms. He needed to get her home right away.

CHAPTER 19

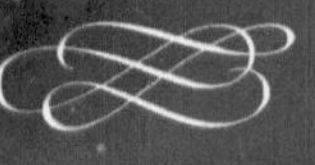

*D*inner with the Hartzlers left Delilah more confused than ever. After seeing how much the other women loved their partners and life on the farm, she worried she might be missing an opportunity. She and Christian had been getting along great, but could their progress negated the fact that he abducted her? Her resolve was crumbling.

The longer she stayed with him the more torn she became. He was opening up new worlds and showing her things she'd never imagined. What if she was wrong to want to leave?

Their bond got stronger every day, and as her hunger strike waged on, the weakness consumed her. She found herself frequently daydreaming about him, recalling the passionate way he took her and how incredible those moments of intimacy were.

Even when he drank from her... She loved it. There was something spectacular about having a man possess her so completely. He looked at her as if she were the air he breathed. What sane woman would walk away from that?

She'd been suffering such intense cravings she knew she'd have to do the unthinkable soon and take his blood. On some subconscious level she wanted to, but then she pictured the actual act and couldn't stomach the thought. She recalled how passionately Cain and Destiny took care of each other's needs. She didn't want to admit how erotic she found it when Christian bit into her, but the truth was there. Part of her liked the idea of feeding—maybe even craved it.

What's happening to me?

Hunger for ordinary food didn't compare to the intense way her body ached for blood. The cravings were so strong and painful it reminded her of the way women described pregnancy.

The moment the thought crossed her mind she stilled. "Oh shit." She rushed downstairs, only partially dressed. "Christian?"

He was out front and came to the front door immediately. "What's the matter?"

"Can I get pregnant? I mean, could I be?"

He cocked his head and crossed the foyer, flattening his hand over her belly. "You could, but you're not." His touch disappeared.

"What the hell was that?"

"Language, *pintura.*"

"Right. But, uh, you touched my stomach."

"To check if you were with child. You're not."

"Shouldn't we be a little more thorough? Pee on a stick or do that old-fashioned thing with a rabbit? Unless the old-fashioned way means the rabbit dies. In that case, I'd prefer to pee on the stick."

"We don't need a rabbit or a stick, *pintura.* You're not pregnant."

Then how did he explain the cravings?

"You're having cravings because you're not feeding properly. I warned you this would happen."

"You said I'd get stiff and old. You mentioned nothing about cravings. And what about condoms? We should probably talk about protection."

"We don't need birth control. When God decides we're ready—"

"*Errrrrt!*" She made a sound like breaks squealing on the road. "Let me stop you right there. *I* decide when I'm ready. *Me.* And I'm not. So we need to start using something."

"Mortal methods will not work for us. My seed was created for your body."

"Made for me or not, I don't want a baby."

"Ever?"

"Definitely not right now." And who was to say she'd ever want to have children with him.

He stepped back. "I see."

"Christian…" She hadn't meant to insult him, but it was impossible to filter her private thoughts.

"I can read your body. I'll know when you're most fertile and take the necessary preventative precautions."

"Please don't be offended. Becoming a mother is a huge decision." She considered her own mother and how unprepared she'd been to raise a child. "I'm just not ready to be a mom. That should imply nothing about my feelings for you or the sort of father you might be."

He caressed her cheek and tucked a hair behind her ear. "I know. Just as you should know, I'll only want children if we have several. I never want our kids to be alone."

She unintentionally recoiled at his use of *our.* "Can you teach me how to read my body so I know when I'm fertile?"

He frowned. "You're my mate. It's instinct. I can scent the hormones in your pheromones when your body is fertile."

That didn't give her any sense of security. "I think I need a little more science than your sense of smell and Jedi mind tricks for my own piece of mind."

He placed his hands over her arms and looked into her eyes. "There is no science. Only nature. Trust me on this."

"Trust you? Christian, I'm saying I don't want to get pregnant, and your response is that you've got it all handled."

"I do have it handled."

He was asking for a lot of trust and control over her body. "There's no other way?"

"I'm afraid science has never been our

species' strong suit."

Because the more records they kept the higher the risk. She understood the need for secrecy and why they were limited by any chance of exposure.

She had no choice but to trust him. "I don't want to get pregnant, Christian. Tell me you understand my wishes."

"I understand."

"Promise me you'll take precautions."

"I can't."

Not expecting him to deny her, she gaped at him. "Why not?"

"Because the only precaution is abstinence. When an immortal female is fertile, she has needs. As your mate—"

"You must meet my needs. I get it. But consider this permission to ignore my needs in that instance."

"I couldn't if I tried. Your craving for my seed will be too strong. You'll be in agony without the proper care."

"You're making it sound like I'll be an animal in heat."

"We are animals. And it's very similar to what smaller creatures experience, but much more intense."

"Well, this is just great." She scoffed and paced into the den. "I have no control over anything." Dropping into the chair where Christian liked to sit and read, she scowled. "There has to be another option. What about condoms or an IUD?"

"Your body is more of a medical marvel than mortal science could ever comprehend. Those methods won't work for immortals."

"So, it's just sex or nothing."

"I'd prefer it wasn't nothing."

"This is bullshit."

"That's two."

She scowled. "I'm not in the mood." With a huff, she left the den and marched up the stairs.

After witnessing the happiness of the other females, Delilah was more inspired to conform. She was coming to like her new clothes and tried thinking of subtle embellishments she could make to add a touch of originality. Maybe Gracie could teach her how to sew, and Delilah could eventually add little embroidered details to the cuffs.

She carefully braided her hair and pinned it in place, centering the thin white bonnet on top. Stepping back, she studied her reflection. "Holy...buttermilk." Her closest friends wouldn't recognize her in this getup.

When she returned downstairs, Christian was once again in the yard. He was always working on something around the house. She puttered around the kitchen, looking for anything to keep herself busy. He had a beautiful garden out back, so she helped herself to the crop.

Fat carrots and cucumber as long as her arm, tomatoes bigger than her fist. The harvest was more than she could hold in her apron. As she walked back to the house, Christian spotted her. Although he stood several yards away, she sensed his surprise at finding her in the gardens and then scented his desire mingling with the fresh earthy air.

He approached the small gate. "That's quite a harvest."

"I was going to make a salad. Did you plant all of that?"

He nodded and stepped into her path. She held the corners of her apron out, the material sagging under the weight of so much food. Bending forward, he pinched her chin and kissed her. "You look beautiful."

The compliment burrowed deep in her heart and she smiled. "Thanks. I wasn't sure if I should wear this bonnet or the black one—"

"White is proper for mated females. You look perfect."

No one had ever used words like perfect to describe her, but Christian spoke and thought that word a lot. "I tried."

"It shows." He glanced down at her harvest. "Is this for supper?"

"Yes. There's plenty if you want some."

His eyes darkened. "I want you."

"Oh." Her cheeks warmed as her smile pinched tight. "Now?"

He nodded, leading her into the house. When she reached the kitchen, he unloaded the produce from her apron, setting it on the table then took her hand, towing her into the den.

"Here." He sat in his chair and loosened his pants. "I want you on my lap."

Her body instantly responded to his request and she bit her lip, glancing at the windows to make sure no one would be able to see in. "Okay." Sliding off her undergarments, she kicked them aside and gathered her skirt at her knees.

He helped her climb onto his lap, fitting her legs outside of his as he gripped his shaft, stroking slowly. "Lift up."

She did as he asked, bunching her skirt at her waist and leaning forward. The engorged tip of his thick cock glided through her arousal and she gasped as he pressed her down.

"You're in control, *pintura.*"

She looked up at him, surprised he would say such a thing. "What do you want me to do?"

"I want you to take your pleasure."

A shy smile crossed her lips as she rocked slowly. "Like this?"

"However you want."

He typically took the lead so she wasn't sure what to do. Gathering her skirt, she reached between her legs and rubbed her fingers over her clit , riding him slowly and moaning softly as she tried to find a rhythm that worked. He studied her, his chest expanding with each heavy breath and his pleasure rolling into her in waves. But it wasn't enough.

She leaned forward and kissed him softly, dragging her nose over his skin as she kissed her way to his ear. His labored breathing teased the fine hairs slipping past her bonnet and she shivered.

"I want you to do it," she whispered, presenting him with the side of her throat.

He growled. "You need your strength."

She slid her body up and down, taking him slowly. "I need *you*." Her hands crawled over his broad shoulders as she looked into his eyes. "Please. Just a little? I like when you do it."

He caught the back of her neck and her breath hitched. In one aggressive pull, he yanked her to his mouth and she gasped when his teeth bit into her. It wasn't painful. On the contrary, the sensation of him drinking from her vein felt more intimate than his lips around her clit.

She sucked in another breath as her sex clamped tight. It was all connected in one euphoric sexual act. The harder he pulled the faster she rode him, her needy cries matching his masculine groans of satisfaction.

"Yes! Please!" She gasped, riding him faster.

His grip tightened on the back of her neck as she came in a flash of white light and ecstasy. Her body went lax in his arms as he licked over the puncture. His cock remained buried inside of her as she cuddled into his chest and sighed. "Thank you."

His arms closed around her, simply holding her close. The familiar beat of his heart filled her ears and she rested, safely in her mate's hold.

"I love you, Delilah."

Her lashes lifted and she sat back to look at him. "What?"

His blank stare couldn't hide his vulnerability. "I said…I love you."

Those three words were not taken lightly. Even her mother hadn't said such things to her. And while she believed her grandparents had loved her, they never expressed it in words.

"Christian…I don't know what to say."

His gaze cut away. "Then don't say anything." He was disappointed.

Her lips pinched, but not quite as sharply as her heart. She wanted to tell him that she cared about him. Compared to a few days ago, that was a huge improvement. "I—"

"Delilah, please. Let's not trivialize it. I think silence is best."

She shut her mouth, respecting his wishes, but her heart ached. Everything inside of her wanted to say something, but he only wanted to hear those three words.

Pressing a kiss to his cheek, she slipped off his lap and lowered her gaze. "I'm sorry."

His hard stare turned further away as he glared toward the front windows, ignoring her. She couldn't leave him like that, not after the beautiful moment they just shared. Didn't he realize how confusing all of this was for her? Didn't he see?

Apparently not.

Worrying her lip, she lowered her body to the floor, kneeling between his thighs. She folded her hands and mentally reached for his mind, but hit a wall.

Shocked he would shut her out, her breath

caught. "Christian, please."

He met her stare but said nothing. She could feel his regret. He disliked showing vulnerability, and there was nothing more vulnerable than love.

What if he took back his beautiful words? She couldn't bear the thought, but she also couldn't lie. She needed more time. "Can we talk about it?"

"What else do you want me to say, Delilah?"

The pain in his voice gutted her. He opened himself up to her, bared his heart, and she did nothing. Now his mind was closed to her and she felt chillingly alone.

He had to understand that just because she moved at a slower pace it didn't mean she felt nothing for him. "I'm here. Yours." She picked up his hand and touched it to her cheek.

He caressed her face, prepared to speak only to change his mind and turn away again. It hurt to reach out and not be met halfway.

Even if their situation was temporary, it was very real to her. She felt things for him she couldn't explain, things she'd never felt for anyone before.

"I'm sorry I hurt you." Leaning forward, she rested her head on his lap. "Please don't be upset with me."

His hand opened as if to comfort her, but then his fingers balled into a fist and he pulled his touch away. "I know."

He was afraid. Afraid of opening himself up to others, afraid of being hurt, afraid of being abandoned. These were not unique fears. She too worried about similar things, knowing firsthand how terrible rejection could feel when one's heart was on the line.

Their burgeoning trust was still so fragile. It took courage on both their parts to navigate so many uncertain emotions. He'd bravely shared his feelings and not gotten the response he'd wanted. But that didn't mean he made a mistake.

She needed to courageously bare herself to him in return, to remind him that she was also fragile and scared, but willing to trust him not to hurt her.

"We don't have to talk," she whispered, closing her hands around his shaft. She slowly stroked his length, keeping her eyes on him as she kissed the tip.

"Delilah, you don't—"

"I want to. Just let me do this for you."

He softly stroked the backs of his fingers down her cheek then gave a nod.

Nuzzling his flesh, she spread kisses over him. His body thickened and he stretched out his legs, leaning back and setting his arms aside, making himself comfortable. Unlike the time she'd done this to him before, this time he avoided directing her.

He had no intention of touching her and made that clear, which was fine. This was not about him, but about her. She wanted to show him that she hadn't intentionally hurt him. That it was safe to share his vulnerable side with her. She could only express that by baring herself to him.

She wanted to show him that she could be brave too, even when it scared her. She appreciated his patience when she needed extra time. She needed him to know how much she cared without labeling her feelings with words she didn't fully understand.

She was on her knees for him. Pleading for so many things she lacked the courage to say. Baring herself in an act of contrition so that he might fully understand how much she was willing to surrender, how deeply she cared for him.

Taking him into her mouth, she sucked him slowly, each time deepening her strokes until the swollen tip of his cock pressed to the back of her throat. She held herself there, much like he'd shown her to do before.

It wasn't enough. She felt his extreme arousal, scented it in the air, but she also felt his lingering uncertainty. Lifting her palms from his knees, she stretched out her arms, placing the backs of her hands on the arms of his chair, wrist side up. It was meant to show no resistance. A sign of capitulation that expressed just how much she trusted him.

Her focus returned to pleasuring him as his hands closed over her wrists, pressing them firmly into the cushioned arms of the chair. Gradually, his insecurities started to wane. His hips lifted, nudging her to continue, and his mind slowly opened to her again.

She felt everything in that moment. The stretch in her muscles as he held down her arms. The hard floor beneath her knees. The throb of his veins over her tongue. The restriction of air when he pressed into her throat. The weight of his stare as he watched her service him. And his pleasure at seeing her perform such a show of supplication.

"Such a selfless display." His grip tightened on her wrists, squeezing then loosening as she sucked him. "On your knees, beseeching my approval." He lifted his hips, thrusting slowly to meet her efforts. "What is it you want from me, *pintura*? You're pleading for something."

At that, she lifted her head and looked up at him, her lips swollen and her arms still open and bound by his grip. There was one thing she needed to ensure her return home.

"Trust."

His stare held hers for a long moment, then he stiffly nodded, not denying the implication that his trust had been shaken. For any of this to work, they both needed to rely on each other and understand neither of them took pleasure in hurting the other, but sometimes, even the best relationships faced moments of pain. "Finish."

She continued to pleasure him and he took his time climaxing. When he finally came, he released her arms and gripped her shoulders tightly, his body tensing and his muscles jerking.

Only then did she realize that he'd blocked

her from sharing his pleasure, but the moment he removed the block his release triggered her own. Her throat worked and her eyes teared as they finished together.

"Now look at me."

Shaken by the intensity of what they just shared, she drew in an unsteady breath before lifting her gaze. Eyelashes damp, she looked up at him with parted lips, her arms lowering so her hands folded in her lap as she kneeled before him.

"That was a beautiful declaration of your trust, *pintura*." He traced a smear of his release away with the pad of his thumb, pressing it into her mouth. She sucked the salty drop away and demurred at such praise, especially shy and delicate in that moment.

He shook his head in awe. "You're so strong-willed, yet you yield so flawlessly when we're intimate."

She didn't understand why she behaved in such a way. It wasn't just that her submission pleased Christian. She liked the way his dominance made her feel. Safe. Cherished. And now loved.

"Say something."

He told her not to speak and she'd listened. In that moment, silence had been exactly what they needed. But now, she owed him something more. He was ready to hear the truth. "No one's ever said those words to me before."

"What about your parents?"

"No. My mom...she died from a drug over-dose when I was young."

"And your father?"

She shied away from any thoughts of the man who raised her. "I only had a step-dad. He's in jail. My grandparents raised me."

"Surely they loved you."

A lump formed in her throat. "I guess. They never wanted the responsibility of raising another child, but they took care of me when I had no one else. I lived with them until I was eighteen." She thought about the boxes they started collecting when she turned seventeen as if they were counting down the days until she could go out on her own. "I suppose that's more love than other kids get."

He frowned and reached for her, pulling her onto his lap, pressing a kiss to her temple as he held her close. "I understand now."

She hated the uncensored accuracy her mind applied when recalling those painful years. It had been too much fear and unbending rejection. Too much time feeling like an un-wanted burden to her family.

She sniffled and dashed away a tear. "I just wanted you to know. I've never said those words to anyone."

"I understand. You don't need to say them. Just know that I love you, and nothing will change that."

She hugged him tightly unsure if her per-sonal experiences with love would ever allow to trust something so unlikely. "Thank you."

CHAPTER 20

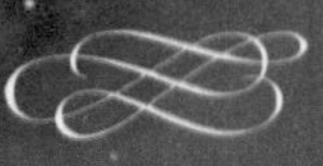

The mood in the house remained somber until nightfall. She set the table and prepared a beautiful salad with butter leaf lettuce from the garden, nuts, and shaved carrots.

Christian roasted the carcass of some small bird over the fire, the scent of roasted herbs drawing out her hunger until she resented her fresh little salad.

There was nothing wrong with her dinner. It just wasn't as mouthwatering as chicken. Chicken was wrong. Chicken was very, very wrong. She shoved a carrot into her mouth and chewed miserably.

She didn't like feeling so exposed, but that afternoon had emotionally wrung her dry. She had the urge to poke at him, simply to get herself out of this melancholy schlump. She didn't like to think about her upbringing. So much of that time in her life had been littered with criticism, the kind that slowly whittled away a person's self-esteem.

Her grandparents' constant disapproval of everything—from her style to her friends—left her feeling like a steady source of disappointment. They frequently threatened to send her to reform school and warned she was following in her mother's footsteps even when she wasn't.

Once, her grandmother even cut off her hair because Delilah had died it purple without permission. They believed her mother died because her upbringing lacked discipline. In an attempt not to repeat the same mistakes, her teenage years had been overly oppressive, which only caused her to rebel more.

Remembering such hard times put her in a bitter temper. "You better eat that whole bird. It sacrificed its life for you."

Christian eyed her curiously. There was no mystery to her mood. He was in her head.

A mess of unwanted thoughts kicked around in her memories. Arguments. Disapproving looks. Bewilderment. Memories of being evicted three days after her eighteenth birthday. Having no choice but to beg them for money when she couldn't pay her bills. Seeing the lights on and the glow of the television when they wouldn't answer the door. Funerals.

Some memories were better left compartmentalized and permanently packed away.

"The bird had a long life."

She glared at his plate, wondering what the

grease on his fingers would taste like. "And now it's dead."

He stilled at her harsh tone. "What's gotten into you?"

"Nothing." She picked at her salad.

"You're irritable because you're neglecting your needs." He pulled a strip of succulent meat from the bone.

She had the urge to attack him and rip that chicken leg right out of his mouth. The scent of the crisp skin and dripping juices literally had her drooling. "That better not be Andrew."

Christian stilled. "Who?"

"Andrew. Or Bert. Oh, it's not Lilly, is it?" She covered her face and groaned.

"I told you not to name the stock. They're not pets."

She pushed her salad away, depressed about whatever bird he ate and pissed because he wasn't sharing. No. She didn't want to eat meat. She was better than that. She needed a distraction.

Sex was their go to diversion, but she was hungry for something else. Glaring at the roast, she tried to distract herself from the barbaric fantasy playing in her head, the one where she slaked her relentless hunger on that poor bird and sucked every bone clean.

Think of Andrew. Poor Andrew. Innocent, delicious, plump little Andrew. Her stomach growled.

She looked at the salad, but the green lettuce and ripe veggies held no appeal. She looked at Christian with hungry eyes, watching the way his full lips glistened as he bit into that bird. Her gaze moved a little lower to the hard edge of his jaw and the delicious way his Adam's apple moved when he swallowed.

She was working on several physiological theories at the moment, Stockholm syndrome quickly becoming the least concerning. Sure, Christian kidnapped her, bit her, killed her, turned her, dictated to her, fucked her, spanked her, dominated her, and yet, she found herself less and less willing to leave him—actually dreading it at times.

And now she was salivating over him like a Pavlovian dog. The mere sight of Christian turned her inside out. She wanted him, but not just sexually. She wanted his blood.

She was starving, and the cravings were making her insane. Food simply wasn't cutting it anymore, and while she blamed him for that excruciating inconvenience, every time she thought to yell at him, she was distracted by her desire to bite him—seriously bite him. Sink her teeth into his flesh, puncture his vein, and drink like a possessed cannibal.

Disgusted—and turned on—she glared at him. She ought to rip that savory—juicy—dripping—plump—delicious—chicken right out of his beautiful mouth.

Her chair scraped back and she stood. "I'm taking a bath."

"Call if you need a hand." He sent a vision of his hand dipping under water to stroke between her legs. She rushed up the stairs, needing to get as far away from him as quickly as possible.

It was the blood. She knew it was the blood.

This relentless, ever-present hunger crawled through every cell of her body demanding to be fed. Never in her life had she wanted something this badly. Her need for sustenance was literally consuming her every thought.

Maybe meat would subdue the cravings. That wasn't as bad as drinking blood, right? Or was it? If she ate meat, an animal had to die. But if she drank the blood, there would be no going back. She'd be one of them.

Pacing the floor, she considered her options. What if the animal was already dead? There had to be some beef lying around the farm waiting to be eaten. She could just ask Christian to cook her up a steak. A nice rare steak.

Rare, or raw?

"No!" She shook her head and continued pacing. He was right. She should have never named the animals.

Becoming vegetarian when she was a teenager had been easy compared to this. This wasn't a usual hunger, it was bone-deep and insatiable.

Her body instinctively recognized Christian as a food source. Her voracious thirst tied her unquenchable need to his body in more ways than she could handle. She wanted him inside of her in every possible way. Mind, cock, tongue, fangs, blood, all of it. She needed him. Desperately.

Delilah, do you have need?"

No! She snapped, still unsure how to boot him out of her head. But even that gentle presence brought a swift sense of relief.

Maybe if she just ate some meat, she'd feel better. Digesting protein was less repulsive than drinking blood. There were plenty of animals on the farm. But she couldn't do that, not to poor Bessie. But maybe a pig. Pigs were known to bite. She might not even need to do the killing. Christian would hunt one down if she asked him to. Not that there was much of a hunt, being that the pigs were living their best pig life chilling over in the pens.

"Oh, God, poor Wilbur and Forrest." She doubled over and held her stomach as she waited for the kettle of water to warm.

She couldn't do it. But if she could, how would she do it? Bacon? Pork chops? Ribs? No, she wanted him fresh squeezed.

The door opened and she jumped to her feet. "I wasn't doing anything!"

Christian stilled and raised a pail. "I brought you more water."

She shook off her *Silence of the Lambs* thoughts—*Ooh, lamb!*—and dropped back into the chair.

A wave of lightheadedness tingled through her. She blinked, her vision going wonky for a moment as she swayed, falling forward. "Christian?"

He poured the heated water from the kettle into the tub. "One more should do—*Delilah!*"

He caught her before she hit the ground. "Delilah, look at me."

His image wavered as woozy sensations pulled at her equilibrium. "I don't feel so good." Her limbs went numb and her neck went limp.

Through a dark haze, she heard him call her name. Over and over again, until his worry consumed her. She called back, weakly, but he couldn't hear her.

Christian...

"Delilah, open your eyes. I command you to look at me."

The impulse to abide his wish rode her every nerve but she lacked the strength. Cool fingers touched her face, lifting her eyelids and measuring her pulse.

"Please do not hate me for this, *pintura.*"

He lifted her limp body and carried her away. *No...Don't leave me. Christian...*

Seconds passed like eons when his touch disappeared. Her worst demons taunted her. He left her. That was it. She was too much and he was taking his love away. Her stomach cramped painfully. She wanted the pain to end.

The bed dipped and she was once again cocooned in his reassuring warmth. She shivered as he pulled her to his lap and lifted her.

"You've left me no other choice, little one."

Her ear pressed to the solid wall of his chest. The familiar, steady beat of his heart comforted her through the darkness. *Thump-thump. Thump-thump. Thump-thump.*

The first scent of blood awakened something inside of her, but she was still too weak to open her eyes. Her jaw slackened, her fangs punching through her gums when he smeared the blood over her lips. She struck like a viper, sinking her fangs into his flesh and latching onto his vein with greedy need.

He grunted, and those first few spurts of his warm, life-giving blood returned her strength. It trickled down her throat, and her hands curled around his arm, holding him to her mouth as she drank heavily.

"Take what you need, little one. I am yours."

She drank like a babe. The involuntary response to the source of food as natural as a baby's instinct to nurse.

Her lightheadedness subsided. The internal disquiet that had been punishing her for days uncoiled and repaired. The tension in her shoulders disappeared with the ache in her head, and a delightful euphoria took hold.

Gentle fingers stroked through her hair. *Christian.*

She'd recognize his touch anywhere. She welcomed it, and leaned into it because she loved when he touched her.

"That's it," he whispered, his voice no longer sounding miles away. "Take as much as you need."

She gorged herself, moaning deeply as she accepted his blood into her body without inhibition. The longer she sipped the more aware she became. Her hips shifted, seeking purchase and her claws dug into the muscled flesh of his arm.

The scent of his desire crept into her, feeding her own. She wanted him. Needed him in every sense of the word.

Overwhelmed by gratitude for his offering, her chest tightened. This was what she needed. He knew she would, yet he refused to pester her about feeding once he gave her his word. He left the choice to her and tolerated her nagging hunger pains for days.

His perseverance proved his commitment to the truth—to her. He truly did want trust between them, because even now, as her cloudy mind awoke and her body repaired, she recognized that she was not under any form of compulsion.

Her lips dragged over his shredded skin and she opened her eyes only to gasp at his torn flesh. She'd been so starved, she'd ravaged him. Blood seeped and gathered at the raw wound As she looked up at him, her eyes brimming with regret. "I hurt you."

"No, *pintura.* There was no pain."

The gnawed pulp of his flesh was irritated and raw. He kept his wrist exposed to her, an ongoing offering to take more. She licked her lips, sensing his encouragement but sure she'd had enough.

"Take a little more. You're still rather weak. It will make you strong."

Looking up at him with uncertainty, she pulled his wrist back to her mouth and slowly opened her lips. She no longer needed to bite, and regretted tearing into him so brutally.

He watched her drink her fill. "Good, *pintura*. That's very good." The fingers of his free hand caressed her hair and shoulders.

Her gluttonous moans took on a carnal tone as his aged blood pumped through her veins.

He tasted rich and potent. As her strength returned, she softly purred.

"Ah," he grunted as she finally let go.

"Did that hurt?"

He shook his head. "Quite the opposite."

She blushed and instinctively licked over his torn flesh, cleaning away any mess and closing the wound. When his arm pulled away, the skin was unflawed. Perfectly unbroken, she wondered how such a thing could be possible. And how did she know to do that?

"It's called innate intelligence," he said, reading her mind and trailing his fingers through her hair as she rested in his arms. "Your body knows what it needs and it will make those unconscious choices for you."

She supposed it was like choosing to breathe. Feeding was an involuntary act. She'd tried to control the primal instinct, but the dogmatic impulse would always be stronger than her will.

Christian breathed out a jagged breath. "Never again, Delilah. I forbid it."

He wasn't flaunting his authority. She'd truly scared him when she passed out.

She realized now how futile her resistance

had been and agreed, "Never again." She couldn't go back to the shaky, malnourished, lethargic weakling she'd been. "I'm sorry I scared you."

"Shh," he gently caressed her cheek. "We've moved on. All is forgiven." His smile was fragile, too delicate to reach his eyes.

She lifted her hands, admiring the healthy pink glow of her skin. Her plump veins darkened and her flesh no longer clung to the bone.

"It is God's design."

She didn't need to assign miracles to a supreme being to believe they existed. He called it God, she called it nature, either way, her body just proved how seamlessly it could self-correct by design.

"I didn't believe it would be like this."

"What do you mean?"

Resting in the safety of his arms, she luxuriated in the overwhelming sense of completeness they shared. "Gratifying. It's…undeniable." For the first time since meeting him, she accepted what she'd become. "You truly did change me."

"This was always who you were meant to be, Delilah."

He was far from infallible. On the contrary, he was absolute, with far too many outdated views. She initially thought his claim about receiving a divine calling to find her was a lie, a misguided belief only a cult could justify. But now she wondered if it was true.

"You know, you're always saying I'm yours,

that God chose me for you. That I somehow saved you."

"He did. Without you I would have been lost."

"Did he?" She wondered. "Because you don't seem like anyone who needed to be saved, Christian. And I'm beginning to think you got it backwards."

"How so?"

"Maybe your God sent you to save *me*."

He pulled her into a tight hug. "I'll always save you, *pintura*. You have my heart and my protection, for all of eternity."

She kissed him softly, her body fitting perfectly against his as they lay as one. Yin and yang. She was more content than she'd been in days—weeks even. Until she noticed something strange about her skin.

"What is it?" Christian sat up and looked at her arm where the vibrant indigo lotus had paled to a pallid cornflower blue.

"My tattoos are fading."

He examined her arm. There was no denying it. Just as her saliva had healed his skin, his blood was regenerating hers. She'd been turning her piercings daily since she noticed these changes, afraid that those might heal as well.

"I'm being erased."

"No, my love. You're still here."

He didn't understand. Her tattoos were a part of her. They represented the identity she chose, not the crap she'd inherited. "Will they all disappear?" Would *she* disappear?

"I don't have these answers for you."

What was happening to her? Would the person she was a week ago recognize who she was today? *No.* The resounding answer came with little concern for her feelings, knocking the breath from her lungs.

She looked at her finger. The ladybug, her first tattoo and the oldest, was practically gone. "How do I stop it?"

"Delilah, all transitions must eventually let go of their mortal self. We can't move forward until we accept that we can never go back."

Was that it then? Would life truly never go back to the way things used to be?

CHAPTER 21

Her back slammed into the wall, rattling the dresser and all of its contents. Delilah snapped her jaw, but Christian was faster, as usual.

His teeth clamped down, piercing her flesh at the curve of her shoulder as his hand cupped her sex possessively. *Mine.*

His claim ran through her like heroin, drawing out a long shiver as she preened and those first delicious pulls from her vein forced her to soften. "I'm not going."

His fingers hooked into her, possessively driving her passion higher until she was arching and moaning in completion. "You are."

Her hand curled around his length, tugging and working him to that precarious edge. Then, when he was least expecting it, she sprang.

They crashed onto the floor in a frenzy of jaw-snapping snarls. She clawed and tumbled with him, rolling across the hardwood until she landed him on his back, laughing when she got him to submit.

"My turn." She lunged, sinking her teeth into the flesh over his heart.

Christian grunted as his body went still for those first few pulls and then he was holding her to him, rocking his hips against her body, as he growled and took back control. "Yes. That's it, *pintura*. More."

She drank heavily as she gripped and stroked him—teased him—marked him, all the while never letting him regain the upper hand.

The moment she paused, dislodging her fangs to take a breath, he propelled forward and once again had her on her back, his hard length driving into her as he pinned her body to the floor, arms spread overhead, suspended by his unbreakable grip. "There can only be one alpha, little one."

She moaned and took every dominating thrust as their pleasure blended as one. She could keep fighting him, but why bother? She lived for this part when he finally took her the way he wanted—hard, greedily, and without apology.

They came in an explosive release of ricocheted euphoria. Only when he marked her in every possible way—scent, sweat, seed, bite— did his grip on her arms loosen.

His weight blanketed her as he leaned down and caught his breath. It had been like this ever since her *come to Jesus* moment about the blood.

She was immortal. She needed blood. How had she ever assumed it could have been any other way? Some battles just couldn't be won.

But others could. "I don't understand why I have to go to service."

He pushed up from the floor in a stunning show of carved muscles roped with thick sinew. "Every member of The Order attends." He held out a hand to help her off the floor.

Technically, she wasn't a member. There had been no swearing in. She had no letterman jacket or lanyard. She was more like a visitor. A sponsoree. "Can't you tell them I'm an atheist?"

"You're not an atheist, Delilah."

"Don't tell me what I am—"

"A poor choice of words." He held up his hands before an argument began. "But an atheist believes in nothing. You believe in something."

She did. She now believed that they were meant to find each other, but that was beside the point. "I believe that no one should try to indoctrinate others into a religion. That, my dear,"—she poked his nose—"is how cults start."

"No one is indoctrinating you. I'm asking you to attend service—"

"Asking?" They both knew she didn't have a choice. She shook the wrinkles out of a dress.

"Fine. I'm ordering you to attend because I have a responsibility to be there and I don't feel safe leaving you alone for hours while the entire Order is otherwise occupied."

"Stop pushing your worry at me." There was

no guilt like that of an immortal bond once that mental link was forged. It was bad enough she had her own emotions to contend with. Now she had his as well.

His refusal to let her stay home had nothing to do with trust. He literally feared something bad might happen to her in his absence.

"Christian, I'll be fine."

"No. If you don't go, I'll have no choice but to stay home as well."

"Good. Then it's settled."

"Delilah."

Running out of negotiation tactics, she flounced her arms and whined, "I don't wanna go! It's going to be boring and in a different language."

He crossed the room, capturing her arms at her side and pressing a kiss to her head. "It's only a few hours. I've already missed one service. I can't miss another."

She narrowed her eyes suspiciously. "Missed one service in..."

"Three centuries," he mumbled.

"Ha! I think you're entitled to miss a few. Don't you guys accumulate vacation days?"

"Worship is important. You'll enjoy it. The other females will be there and after service, we have a large meal."

The thought of seeing her friends did make the idea more enticing. "Like a party?"

"Sure."

"Fine. I'll go, but only to support you. Your faith is not mine."

He cupped her ass possessively, drawing her front to his. "Thank you."

"You're welcome," she grumbled. "What does one wear to worship around here?"

They'd been careful with each other lately. Concessions were negotiated and appreciated. He took more care with his words and often showed his appreciation in small displays of affection or praise, which she liked.

Since coming to terms with feeding, she stopped fighting her impulses so hard, choosing instead to reflect and ask questions as they occurred.

Rummaging through the selection of dresses, she frowned at the options. "How come Destiny can wear red?"

"That color's not sanctioned. The Council will speak to Cain about it."

She lowered the deep blue dress she held out and looked at him. "Because of you?"

"I'll inform them, yes. I have a response—"

"Christian, you can't."

"I'm an elder. It's my duty."

"I don't care. They're our friends. If you tell on them, they won't invite us over anymore."

That would kill two birds with one stone, he thought and she scoffed.

"They're not birds, they're friendships. And you're not killing them! I need friends, Christian."

"You have me."

"You're different. Look," she sighed. "You might be an introvert, but I like having a social life. I need this. Please don't make things weird."

"I don't see why your friendships should be affected by my adherence to The Order's laws. The females understand what's expected of them."

"Destiny's different."

"That is clear. But it does not excuse her from our laws. When an immortal chooses to live here, they in turn accept the rules and responsibilities that exist within such a society. It's a small cost for the protection we receive in return. Straying from the rules puts everyone at risk of exposure. Conformity allows us to hide in plain sight. Trust me, *pintura*, you do not want to go back to a time when our kind had to lurk in the shadows and sleep far away from civilization. Here we are at least alive and living."

She pouted. "I don't want her to be mad at me."

"How could she be? You're blameless. Females cannot interfere with Council Law."

"Ew. You have no idea how gross that just sounded."

"I don't make the rules."

She dropped her chin. "You *literally* do." Rolling her eyes, she got back to her point. "Look, you're mine, so I have to answer for your actions. If you report her, she'll know any backlash came from you because you were the only elder at that dinner. Then she'll call me out, and I'll have to explain that you didn't mean to be a dick but it's your duty. Don't put me in that position."

"That's five." He lifted her chin. "And she should know that you have no say over such things."

"But I—"

He silenced her with a soul-spinning kiss.

"Um," she said dazedly, unsure what she'd been saying a moment ago. "What was that for?"

"You called me yours."

"Oh. Well, you are, right?"

He grinned and kissed her again. "Irrevocably."

"Then please try not to be a dick to my friends."

"Six. And I'll do my best."

She sucked in a breath, shocked he actually conceded. "Really? You won't tell on her?"

"Not this time. But a good friend would remind her that a female's clothing is an expression of faith." He poured water from the pitcher into a bowl and washed his face like he did every morning.

"Yeah, I'll jump right on that." Sorting through her clothing options, she considered a bright blue gown she hadn't worn yet. "This color's pretty."

Christian glanced over his shoulder and stilled.

She looked down at the blue dress then back at him. "What? Why are you looking at me like that?"

He swallowed, his Adam's apple making a slow glide under the damp skin of his throat. "That's your wedding dress."

She looked at the plain gown again. "It is?"

He nodded. "Amish believe blue is symbolic of life's most important moments. When a female gives her life to her husband, she wears a blue gown. The gown is only worn again when she gives her life to her maker."

"You mean when I die? That's sort of creepy."

"Not all Amish traditions apply to us immortals."

"Right. Because we don't die."

"No race is without tragedy." He crossed the room and closed his hand over hers. "Your safety is everything to me, *pintura*."

Such familiar statements filled her with a sense of security. "I know." He released her hand and returned to the dresser. "Um, out of pure curiosity, how do you kill a vampire?"

He stilled as he pulled on his shirt. "Are you researching for future endeavors, *pintura?*"

"No, I just figure it's something I should know. I mean, can I die if someone shoots me with a silver bullet or if I accidentally stab myself with a wooden stake?"

Barn raisings could be treacherous—all those splinters flying around willy-nilly.

He chuckled. "First, you're immortal. Being vampire means something very different. Second, those things would hurt, but they would not end an immortal life."

"Are you saying I could throw myself in front of a train and live to brag about it?"

"Delilah," he said with censure in his voice. "Immortality is many things, unfortunately, it is not without pain. I suggest you stay away from all moving locomotives and other uncomfortable endeavors."

"Like worship?"

"Very funny."

She selected a purple dress and spread it on the bed then sorted through the underclothes, smirking when she found a few lacy options built for speed more than any sort of comfort.

"So, how does it happen? I should know, right? Not just in case I meet *Nosferatu* walking alone at night, but so that I can protect myself."

"You won't be alone. I'll protect you."

"Why won't you tell me?" Despite their recent accord, there was still the matter of her abandoned life and shop. Now that she fed, she was stronger and in more control of her impulses. She was pretty certain she would get her wish and get to go back to her shop in a few days.

"Very well." He sighed and came to sit beside her on the bed. "Immortality does not promise eternity. There are risks. True, we have rapid healing abilities and can withstand much more than mere mortals, but some injuries are impossible to survive."

"Like starvation?" She could never put herself through that kind of suffering again.

"Our bodies can atrophy without proper

nutrition. When immortals are without a proper food source, our bodies cannot heal as quickly. When a body fails to repair itself, decay naturally occurs."

"Decay but not death."

"The mind will die long before the other organs stop working. If an immortal is trapped without food long enough, their life will essentially be lost."

That sounded horrific, sort of like living in a conscious coma. "But how would an immortal get trapped?"

"There are hunters, *pintura*. Legend is not simply imagined. It all traces back to a thread of truth. Historically, we have been stalked, chased out of villages, slaughtered, tortured—it is why so many of us chose to escape. The Order protects us and allows us to live in the open."

Her imagination drew a descriptive image of an old village bursting with chaos. Flames exploded from stone dwellings as people screamed in pain and horror. The disturbing vision was not of her own imagination, and she understood he was showing her an actual memory.

Her hand went protectively to her throat. "You lived through that?"

"I was only a boy, but the memory has not left me. Things were different then, we lived without laws or discretion. Much has changed since then. But we remain a superior race with cunning strength, loyal to our nature. Mortals are wise not to trust us when they're our primary food source."

The thought of Christian feeding from anyone else's vein angered her. "You said we don't do that."

"*We* don't. The Council has outlawed many of the barbaric practices once accepted by our kind. But immortals not associated with The Order live a lawless life."

"So how do the hunters do it?"

"Same as one bates a fish. They lure us into traps."

"With blood?"

He nodded. "Mortals were sacrificed for the cause. Tempting traps were set to distract us. They seduced our sinful nature, enticing our gluttonous hunger. Our lust. They despised our pride. As soon as we displayed a hint of our vicious nature, they had proof and we were destroyed. "

She thought about the things that distracted her now—the sound of his pulse, the scent of his body, the desire to feel him inside of her. They were completely unguarded when they fed. "How did you and the others escape?"

"Never underestimate the depravity of a predator cornered."

She took his hand, offering comfort. "It sounds horrific."

"It was a chaotic and lawless time I do not wish to return to."

After centuries of living as Amish, he wouldn't easily adapt to the modern world.

That meant, if she left, she would likely leave on her own.

"That wouldn't happen," he said, reading her thoughts. "I would never let you face this life or that sort of danger alone."

She wondered how far their telepathic link reached. If they were separated by hundreds of miles and the noise of modern civilization, would he still be able to read her thoughts and communicate with her?

"One mile between us is insufferable, *pintura.* I could never abide hundreds."

If she left, he would follow. That brought her comfort. "You still haven't told me how immortals die." He had a responsibility to her. She needed to know how to protect herself in case there was ever danger and he wasn't around.

"Very well. A stake to the heart will do no more than wound an immortal. It can be a debilitating injury that slows our body's ability to heal, but once the stake is removed the threat is gone. A little blood and the damaged cells repair. However, if staked to the point of crucifixion, we become unable to remove the threat and our bodies begin to decompose."

"But we wouldn't die."

"No, but there would be great suffering, and we would be incredibly vulnerable to torture. Some fates are worse than death."

She couldn't imagine being suspended in endless agony.

"There are some still trapped and suffering from those times."

"From three hundred years ago?" Her stomach spoiled at the thought.

"And longer, I'm afraid. It's best to leave them be. The mind has a breaking point. Once broken, the thoughts only poison the soul."

She took a shuddered breath. It was a chilling thought.

"You must remember, little one, not all immortals are as peaceful as the ones you will find here. Some still believe they have a right to take whatever is available. They feed, rape, and kill as they see fit."

"Can they make more immortals?"

"Only a true called mate can transition a mortal—safely, that is. If a transition occurs without the blood of a destined mate and the bond is not completed, the mind is lost. Something *otherworldly* results, a vile abomination that has not been sanctioned by God."

"You've seen this?"

He nodded. "It's what happened to Dane's sister. There's no hope for her soul. It would be merciful to put her down."

"How do you do it—mercifully, I mean?"

He once again hesitated and studied her. As an immortal, she had a right to know what could kill her. "Decapitation is best, in terms of mercy. It's fast, but not always easy. *Feeish* immortals do not surrender easily."

"Feeish?"

"Possessed. They are without humanity, a slave to their animal nature. *Vampire.*"

"Can that happen to anyone?"

"You're safe, little one. The bond protects our souls. You see, the soul is here." He pointed to his chest. "It's where our memories live. Our limbs will regenerate, but life ceases when the mind separates from the heart. As a precaution —in terms of ending an immortal life—those parts should always be burned. There can be no resurrection beyond dust."

"What happens if we're burned?"

"It's very unpleasant and can be fatal. And in rare cases, infected blood can make us very ill. Plagues are not something we take lightly."

The blood rushed from her face.

He pulled her into a hug and pressed his lips to her hair. "God willing, this is nothing you or I will have to worry about. We can enjoy a long and peaceful life here. The Order keeps us safe."

It really was a clever cover, one that outsiders would never suspect or violate. They could stay on the farm, protected by the Amish boundaries. That meant living forever. She couldn't wrap her brain around such an endless length of time.

What would they see? How many terrible atrocities would they survive? She now understood why they didn't maintain friendships with mortals. They would all eventually die.

Her mind went to Destiny and Dane. "How long can half-breeds live?"

"We aren't sure. We know they can die, which is why they're so rare, but we have no records of any passing. We don't know what age they reach or what degree of injury they can sustain without permanent damage. They do consume blood, however, so there is a higher rate of recovery. And when that blood's immortal, they will inherently acquire superior strength."

"So Destiny's stronger because she drinks Cain's blood?" That was somewhat of a relief.

He cupped her cheek lovingly. "Yes, your friend is safe, *pintura*. You need not worry."

She smiled, glad for the reassurance. "What about Dane?"

"He has his own source."

"An immortal?" She sat up. "Is it Gracie?"

"No. And gossip is the wood that fuels disputes. It's best not to discuss such things."

She didn't want to add to her friend's stress by any means, but without television or internet this was the only drama available. She needed to know who was feeding Dane.

"Is he dating someone?"

"Intimacy isn't a requirement to feed. Immortals can survive on animal blood alone."

No way was Dane drinking goat blood. There was a reason Gracie was always short with him. "You have to tell me who it is! I need to know!"

"Delilah."

"Christian, please! You can spank me for being nosy. Just tell me who's giving him blood."

He studied her for a long moment. "Her name is Magdalene. She's another half-breed living on the farm."

"Aha, I knew it was a woman!"

He caught her in an unbreakable grip, his fingers digging suggestively into the soft flesh of her ass. "You have a penchant for godless chatter, I see."

She leaned into him. "The sexual tension between Dane and Gracie could choke a horse. I think they should bang it out. "

"Careful what you wish for, *pintura*. I've witnessed happy marriages get torn to shreds when one immortal is suddenly called to their true mate. There's nothing in this world stronger than that calling. It's a need that will not be denied. God willing, Sister Grace will eventually be called, and where would that leave Dane?"

She thought of something alarming. "Larissa said you guys could die if you don't find your mate. She said that's why you needed me."

He smiled. "I also *wanted* you. Remember, predators are made to hunt. It was a thrill to find and claim you. But yes, it's very dangerous for an immortal to ignore God's call."

"Why?"

"We become *feeish* and more susceptible. Without completing the bond, we develop sensitivity to the sun, vertigo, insatiable hunger, bloodlust. We crave the blood of our mate and only her blood will do. It is an incessant sort of madness that does not yield until the bond is complete."

"So, if you hadn't found me…?"

"I would have been consumed by a homicidal rage. Crazed. I would have ripped open countless throats in a fit of madness as I searched for your blood."

She couldn't picture him ever acting so violently. "But you're a pacifist."

"Before all else, I'm your mate. The unanswered are usually destroyed. Without their mate's blood to complete the bond, there can be no redemption. The soul is lost."

She didn't want to imagine what would have become of Christian if he hadn't found her. She hated that he'd permanently altered her life—essentially killed her and brought her back—but she couldn't fault his decision. "You really had no choice but to claim me."

"It's our greatest instinct."

Now that she understood, she might one day forgive him for transitioning her without permission. Thinking back to that first night, she recalled how their bodies came together in an explosive, carnal joining. It had been perfect, until he gripped her with animalistic need and forced his blood down her throat.

She shivered, remembering that horrific moment of unrivaled fear. "What would have happened if I'd shot you down at the bar?"

Closing his hand around hers, he whispered, "I wish it had not been so terrifying for you."

She dropped her gaze, still haunted by the memory. "First times are never what we hope."

"I know it's difficult to fathom, but I was doing my best to protect you."

Because he would have taken her eventually, with or without her agreement.

His hand squeezed hers. "I can only be grateful it did not come to that."

She shuddered. With everything he just explained, she could only imagine how vicious an immortal would get when pushed to the limits. After the episode the other day, she understood how overpowering the need for blood could become. And now, since having a chance to process her own experiences, she was convinced the link between mates was real. "You would have hunted me."

"And stopped at nothing to claim what's mine."

"How do you do it?" She was learning to track him from one room of the house to the next, but finding a stranger in the world would be like searching for a needle in a haystack.

"The dreams helped."

"Dreams?"

He cocked his head. "Yes. Don't you remember?"

"I hardly ever dream."

"Every calling starts that way. Perhaps your memories have merely been misplaced. Shut your eyes. I'll help you find them."

Her eyes closed and she felt him push into her mind, stronger than the usual gentle presence he assumed. Flashes of images turned in her mind's eye, some familiar, others only teasing a discomforting sense of déjà vu. When an image of them lounging together on the grass came to mind, she gasped.

The vision was so real. They lay under the shade of an ancient tree. She could smell his familiar scent and feel his love for her as she leaned into him and laughed affectionately. They were so happy.

"Is this a prophecy?"

"We have an eternity to make it so."

She might have questioned the authenticity of such an image if she hadn't recognized them as lost visions of her own. "Can you show me another one?"

He showed her several more and she watched in awe, slightly jealous that he had this knowledge all along.

"I would have been more prepared if I'd recognized you."

"Perhaps on some level, you did."

She looked at him so differently than she had a week ago. Her mind simply couldn't go back to hating him now that she was coming to trust him. "Will you teach me?"

"What would you like to learn?"

"All of it. I want to know everything you know. I want your strength and confidence and skill."

Leaning forward, he pressed a soft kiss to her lips. "It will be my honor to teach you everything you wish to know. But first...we must attend service."

She groaned and threw herself back on the

bed. "Why can't we just stay here? I'll give you your six."

He paused, but then quickly stood. "It's seven, and as tempting as that offer is, I must decline. We can settle that score after worship."

"Great." Nothing inside of her wanted to sit through a long, boring, German sermon.

"Keep in mind that others will be able to overhear your thoughts, little one."

Her eyes widened. "You really need to teach me how to guard my mind."

He stood, bending only to kiss her head. "Today will provide many opportunities for you to practice that skill. Get dressed."

CHAPTER 22

"*H*ey, how come you guys don't wear beards?"

Christian found it encouraging that Delilah was now showing more interest in their culture, so he didn't mind answering her numerous questions. "Beards are not a defining factor in living a pure life."

She eyed his jaw. "But I never see you shave."

"Mortals have a greater need for body hair as it helps with thermoregulation. We regulate our own body temperature. We have hair follicles where we need them, eyelashes, eyebrows, and the hair on our head to protect us from debris." Adjusting her *kapp*, he said, "We must go or we'll be late."

Grateful she agreed to attend service, he took the stairs with an optimistic bounce to his step. She had started braiding her hair and dressing like the other females. Such small but positive signs of conformity brought him much hope, as did her curiosity.

Exiting the house, he staggered to the porch steps as a rooster tripped him, fluffing its wings underfoot and clucking at him. It puffed its chest at Christian and rudely pecked at his boot.

"What are you doing up here? Get." He toed the bird out of the way, recalling this one's name was Beavis or Stanley or some such nonsense. "Go on. You shouldn't be here."

Its little eyes bulged as it stared up at him, crowing loudly as if it had as much right to be there as anyone else. Then Christian noticed the three kittens lounging on the wood planks of the step. The animals never strayed this far from the barn.

The front door opened and Delilah stilled. "Gonzo, what are you doing here?" She spoke to the rooster as if it could answer. She crouched on the step and pet the kittens.

"Did you give them cream?"

"No. Should I?"

"It will only encourage them. They usually don't stray this far from the barn."

"What the!" She jumped up as a small rodent scurried over the step and bolted back down to the shrubs. "Was that a mouse?"

"Chipmunk."

"Aw! Alvin." She called the tiny creature, but it ignored her, confirming she could not commune or control the animals.

He clapped his hands so they would scurry off. "Go on, before I put you in a pot."

She scowled at him as she nuzzled a small gray kitten. "Not funny."

He pulled the tiny ball of fuzz out of her arms and set it back on the step. "We must ready the horses."

"Dwight and Michael?"

"I suppose." He couldn't keep all the animal names straight.

She took his hand and skipped down the porch steps. "Can I drive the carriage?"

"No."

"You didn't even consider it."

"I know."

When they reached the barn, he readied the buggy and quickly checked the horses' hooves. Delilah curiously explored the interior.

"Hey, there's electric in this jalopy." She examined the metal clutch sticking out of the floor.

"Modern law requires us to use battery-operated lights for night travel. The English aren't very respectful when it comes to sharing the roads and the lights offer protection. Shall we?"

She smiled and her enthusiasm to take a common carriage ride amused him.

He plucked up the worn leather reins. "Hold on."

The carriage jostled and she swayed into his side. "Whoa." She gripped his arm. "Don't you guys believe in seat belts?"

He glanced at her and chuckled, directing

the horses toward the back road.

"Right." She chuckled. "Immortal."

The steady clip-clop of horse hooves sped up as they got on their way. Fresh air mingled with her scent, creating a nice breeze as they picked up speed. Several horse-drawn vehicles traveled ahead, all moving in the same direction toward the Safe House.

They pulled behind a long line of carriages parked on the grass. "The bishop's house is the church?"

"Every house is a house of God." He secured the carriage and helped her down.

"Good day, *Bredder* Christian," Elder Thaddeus Christner called.

"Good day to you."

The first few months after a mating were a delicate time for couples and greatly respected by the members, especially in cases of new transitions. Brother Thaddeus did not greet or acknowledge Delilah's presence, as the elder understood Christian would make a proper introduction when he was ready for other members of The Order to address her.

"Who was that dude?"

"Elder Thaddeus Christner. He's the maternal grandfather of your Hartzler friends. Sister Abilene is his daughter."

"It's crazy how none of you guys look older than thirty."

They walked toward the old colonial, following a dawdling line of females who watched them pass.

"Everyone's staring at us."

He took Delilah's hand. "They're curious and anxious to meet you, that's all." A tremor of insecurity rippled from her. "You'll be fine, *pintura*. I'll be by your side for most of the day."

"Most?"

"During service, I'm required to sit up front with the elders."

"What?" She stopped walking. "You're leaving me?"

He urged her to keep moving. "We'll be in the same room."

Another wave of insecurity passed, this one spiced with a touch of irritation. He supposed her separation anxiety was a positive sign that their bond was solidifying.

The main room of the house flooded with natural light. Hats covered every free surface as bodies crammed together in long rows of benches, making the air warm and stuffy. He led her to the right where only females sat.

"This is where you will sit."

She looked out at the sea of bonnets and hesitated. *I can't believe you're abandoning me.*

I'll be right over there. He pointed toward the front of the room, but she only scowled. *Go on. Be brave.*

She took a seat on the bench and squirmed, her thoughts cataloging every detail as she mentally complained about the lack of cushions on the backless pews.

He thought to remind her she was projecting her musings but did not wish to add to her stress. Bending to kiss her cheek, he whispered, "I have to meet with the elders in the back. I'll return soon. I'll be sitting right over there, in the front."

She caught his sleeve. "What if they expect me to do something?"

"No one expects you to do anything but listen quietly. The service will be said in mostly High German."

"Sounds thrilling," she grumbled, and he hid a smile, coming to enjoy her dry wit.

He glanced at the surrounding females. *The female to your right is Magdalene.*

She instantly turned with interest. *Dane's Magdalene?*

He nodded. "Sister Magdalene, this is my mate, Delilah."

The young girl smiled. "How lovely. You can call me Maggie."

He stepped away just as Delilah said, "Hi. I have no idea what I'm doing here."

Magdalene was a personable female who would put her at ease.

After briefly meeting with the elders in the back, Christian returned to the main room. The Order opened with a hymn, and Delilah's wide-eyed stare looked from side to side. His mouth pressed tight, hiding a smile. Her thoughts were shooting off like fireflies.

This is what you guys call singing? They sound like the oh-Eee-oh monkey soldiers in the Wizard of Oz.

I do not understand that reference, pintura, but try to quiet your mind and be respectful.

She frowned as some of the females dabbed their eyes with handkerchiefs, the high German hymn carrying much emotion for many of the parishioners.

Opening the book of scriptures, he stood and delivered a reading. When he finished, a traveling creek rolled through the room as everyone kneeled. Delilah did a double take and then moved to her knees. Silence followed.

What are they doing?

Praying.

She watched the others curiously. *Don't you guys believe in cushions? This floor's killing my knees.*

Try to focus, pintura.

On what? Nothing's happening.

Just be still.

She mentally scoffed. *I have the attention span of a fly and the energy of a bunny. I don't know how to be still.*

Try.

SHE SHIFTED her weight from side to side, her thoughts overly dramatic as she decided she wouldn't last long in any sort of torture situation.

Dear God, just tell me what information you want and it's yours! I need to sit!

Several heads turned toward her and Christian's neck heated.

Fuck. They can hear me?

He had warned her. *I'm afraid so, pintura. And that's eight.*

She looked down at her folded hands, attempting to blank her mind. *Who's on first, What's on second, I Don't know's on third. Well, who's on first? Yes. That's the fellow's name. Who. The guy on first. Who.*

Christian frowned, as did many of those overhearing her unguarded thoughts. She seemed to be having some sort of mental fit in an attempt to occupy her mind. When everyone returned to the benches, she rubbed her knees. The bishop stood to deliver the sermon.

She could only maintain silence for small increments before her inner monologue ran wild again.

She silently hummed, her thoughts projecting over the bishop's words. *Beer-neer-neer, neer, neer, neer, neer, neer, neernt... Beer-neer-neer, neer, neer, neer, neer, neer, neernt... So, no one told you life was going to be this way. Bop-bop-bop-bop! Your job's a joke, you're broke, you're love life's D.O.Ayyyyy...*

Eleazar paused from speaking the sermon and cleared his throat. Several of the females hid giggles.

It's like you're always stuck in second gear, when it hasn't been your day, your week, your month, or even your year...

The males turned to scowl at such disruptive behavior and the laughter stopped, many of the females blanked their minds and straightened in their seat, but Delilah continued to silently sing, her eyes scanning the rafters and moldings, completely oblivious to the others' scrutiny.

Delilah.

Her head snapped forward, and she flushed, realizing everyone was waiting for her to quiet her thoughts. She lowered her gaze, repentantly, and the bishop continued with the sermon.

For the next hour she improved her self-control but left much to be desired in terms of silence. He would have to teach her ways to more effectively guard her thoughts before the next service.

After three grueling hours of standing, kneeling, and sitting in mostly silence, the service finally concluded. He usually didn't find service so tedious, but experiencing it from Delilah's point of view altered his perspective.

He crossed the room to rejoin her as she stood and rubbed her backside. Several of the other females grinned and greeted one another.

The moment he came to her side, she gripped his sleeve and whispered, "You guys do this every week?"

He chuckled. "No, only every other."

She blew out a breath and twisted her spine. "It must be nice up there on the chairs."

She was being dramatic. Immortals might experience slight bouts of discomfort, but rarely did their bodies ache the way she implied. He put his hand on her lower back and steered her toward the doors. "Come, let us break our fast and join the others outside."

Several tables and chairs dappled the lawn as females carried covered dishes. He was proud to introduce Delilah to the others and eager for her to meet the elders, but she had other plans.

"Oh, there's Destiny and Cain. Can we sit with them?"

Reluctant to join them, he hesitated. "The elders typically…" His words drifted off when he sensed her disappointment. "Of course." He led her to the table with her friends.

The females welcomed her with warm smiles while the males looked surprised to see him approach. Fortunately, the eldest Hartzler sister was mated to the bishop, so Eleazar joined them as well.

"I see your mate's adjusting," the bishop commented, noting how the females chatted easily.

It made sense she would feel a stronger connection to those who were from the outside world like her. "She's adapting."

Eleazar nodded. "She appears much improved from the last time I saw her." He observed the females, his focus directed mostly to Delilah. "She has much to learn about discipline and self-control. We don't want her running off."

It was a level of censure he wasn't used to from his friend. "Your concern's unwarranted. I have everything under control."

"Do you? My mate told me she asked for—"

"I know what she asked," Christian snapped. "I was there. I'm managing the situation."

"Very well."

The bishop moved to sit closer to his wife, and Delilah turned, frowning when her gaze caught Christian's. She scooted closer, slightly leaning in to whisper, "Are you okay?"

"Perfectly fine."

"Sister Adriel, join us," Sister Larissa pointed to an open space on the bench across from the bishop.

His mother glanced at him and hesitated. "I wouldn't want to intrude."

He rolled his eyes. "Mother, do sit down. You're a terrible martyr."

She lifted her chin, sniffed, and lowered herself into the seat across from Eleazar. Dane followed, sitting beside her and causing a slight ripple in the energy around the table. Sister Grace shifted to the end of the bench.

"Oh, there's the girl who sat next to me at service," Delilah said as she waved. "Do you guys know Maggie?" Delilah called the female over. "Maggie, do you want to sit with us?"

Dane's head snapped up and Sister Grace scowled. "I'd love to. Is there room?"

"I'll move." Sister Grace stood, taking her plate with her.

"Gracie," Dane called, but the female ignored him, as she quickly walked toward the house. "Excuse me," he said, leaving the table and plate to follow Sister Grace.

Sister Magdalene stared after him.

DANE FOLLOWED Gracie toward the Safe House. "Gracie, slow down!"

"Leave me alone." She sped up and dashed into the bishop's private home, an area he wasn't comfortable entering without an invitation.

"Gracie?" he called, not finding her in the den.

The house was silent, all the guests now outside enjoying the picnic. Dane quietly moved through the common rooms, uncomfortable with the sense that he was trespassing. He was used to visiting the Safe House to see his sister, but he rarely entered the bishop's home unless summoned.

A floorboard creaked and he stilled. Following the sound to the kitchen, he found Gracie staring out the back window, with her arms braced on the dough trough.

"You shouldn't be in here," he said from the doorway of the kitchen.

"This is my sister's home. I have every right to stand in her kitchen."

She was clearly upset. "What are you doing, Gracie?"

Locking her jaw, she glared at the wall, purposely not looking at him. "I didn't want you to follow me."

"Then why did you run off like that?"

"Because when someone runs off, Dane, it usually means they no longer want to be around others."

He approached her slowly and touched her back. She flinched, her shoulder drawing up to her ears as every muscle in her body seemed to tense. "I'm sorry. I didn't invite her to sit with us."

"I know." She sniffed, her hard stare forbidding any show of emotion.

"Delilah didn't know any better. You can't be mad at her."

"I'm not." A tear tumbled down her cheek and she batted it away. "I'm mad at myself."

"Hey." He turned her to face him. "You're crying."

Unable to deny the proof of her tears, she glared at the ceiling. "It has nothing to do with anything. I was touched by the service."

"No you weren't."

She scowled at him through bleary eyes. "I was. The bishop spoke beautifully of his testimony to God. It moved me."

He studied her, knowing she was lying to him, but her thoughts had been blocked to him for so long he wasn't entirely sure. His gut said her tears were about something else. "All you have to do is say the word, Gracie, and I'll stop seeing her. You know I'd rather be—"

"How you pass your time is no concern to me, Dane Foster."

He gritted his teeth. "Why can't you just admit you're jealous?"

She scoffed. "Of Magdalene? Hardly."

Frustrated by her lies, he gripped her arms and she sucked in a breath. "God knows you're lying. So does everyone else."

"Take your hands off me," she said slowly.

He looked into her crystalline stare, searching for any sign of hope that she still cared about him. It had been so long since she treated him like a friend. He couldn't accept that her cold disregard was an honest telling of how she truly felt. "I know you care about me."

"You know nothing."

His grip on her arms tightened. "Liar," he whispered.

She finally met his stare and the truth was there in her eyes. Another tear fell and he dashed it away. Leaning closer, he brushed his lips over hers.

Her breath hitched and she drew back. "Don't," she whispered, the quiet plea at odds with her obvious curiosity.

He debated letting her go, but she didn't move. There was no struggle or opposition in her stance, only longing. His hands slid around her waist and he stepped closer, pressing his front to hers.

"Enough lying, Gracie." He tipped his head, his mouth slowly descending to hers. A small whimper escaped her throat as he touched down, softly tracing his tongue over the seam of her lips, silently begging for entry.

His tongue teased over hers and his body

rejoiced. His hands glided to her neck, until he was cupping her face.

She pressed her palm to his chest. "No."

"Yes." He leaned in again and hissed, jerking back. Razor sharp pain ripped through his arm. He examined his sleeve as crimson bled through the fabric. She'd cut him. She fucking cut him. "What the hell, Grace?"

Trembling, she stared up at him, her brow hard and her jaw locked. Her claws had lengthened and his skin burned where she'd sliced him. "Get out of here," she hissed.

He gaped at her. "You ruined my shirt."

"Go!"

He winced. "Gracie—"

"Do you hear me?" The venom in her voice cut deeper than her claws. "I want you to leave."

"Why are you being like this?"

"*I said go!*"

A wave of energy slammed into him, shoving him into the wall. He bolted forward and glared at her. "You're out of line—"

"*You* are out of line. How dare you touch me with such familiarity? I'm not yours. I'll never be yours. God knows where your mouth has been!"

Furious, he seethed and blasted her with every image he could muster of his mouth on Magdalene. "I'm tired of you holding this against me. Yes, I kiss her. I kiss her *everywhere,* Grace. Do you know why? Because she's not frigid and she doesn't play games! She likes my hands on her! She likes touching me. And I like being inside of her!"

"*Get out!*" she screamed, shoving him with the force of twenty men.

He staggered back, stunned this was what had become of their friendship but tired of trying to fix what was so obviously irreparable. Meeting her glare, he sneered, "Enjoy your long, cold wait for a call that might never come."

"*Leave!*" she shouted, shattering the glass in the windows on the back wall.

ADRIEL JOINED them for the ride home from service. Delilah enjoyed Christian's mother, though Christian was quieter than usual when she was around.

As he steered the horse, she and Adriel spoke about various things having to do mostly with food and Delilah's 'odd' diet. Adriel was helping her think of recipes that didn't require meat.

"I suppose you could have biscuits, but any gravy would lack flavor without the sausage. Do you eat pork?"

"No. No pig."

"Delilah doesn't eat anything with a face, Mother," Christian commented, his attention focused on the road as he gripped the reins.

The countryside was untouched by modern

civilization. In the distance she could see smog clouds and hear motor vehicles rushing down the highways, but they were far removed from such things. The trip to service today had shown her the outskirts of the farm and gave her a better understanding of just how large the land was.

He pulled the carriage onto a paved road and she lifted her face, enjoying the breeze as they picked up speed. An engine purred in the distance, the hum getting louder as they crossed a covered bridge. She spotted the car in the distance, speeding toward them on the narrow road.

The engine got louder and then she saw it, ripping around the bend. The carriage jostled and Delilah almost slid off the bench.

Adriel caught her sleeve and steadied her as the car sped by.

Christian glanced back, his eyes lit with concern. "Are you all right? Foolish English drivers do not like to share the road. I apologize. The car spooked the horse."

Delilah nodded, shaken but fine. Despite being fairly invincible, her brain still viewed danger like a mortal.

"She's fine, Christian."

Suddenly, another car whizzed by. The horse jerked again, but this time she was prepared and remained seated. A loud crash followed and Delilah cried out, grabbing her temples as a sharp pain knifed through her head.

"Delilah?" both Christian and his mother said at once.

Adriel touched her arm and hissed, pulling back her fingers as if scorched by the contact. "Christian, she's burning hot."

She was going to be sick. So much pain. Oh, God … "What was happening?"

The carriage abruptly veered off the road and she lunged forward when it stopped. Christian was there. "Look at me, *pintura*. Tell me what hurts."

"Everything," she moaned, holding her ribs.

"Christian, what is this? Has this happened before?" Adriel asked frantically.

"Mother, please—"

Delilah gasped, sucking in a hard breath and searching the back window. She couldn't see it, but she could hear it. Faint, tiny, agonizing. The pain became second to her sudden need to go to the source. "Let me out."

She sprang to her feet, pushing past Christian and jumping onto the pavement.

"Delilah, wait—"

She bolted towards the puny screams. The world whooshed by in a smear of green and blue. When she crested a slight hill, the vehicles came into view.

Black smoke billowed from the one T-boned against a tree while the other car's wheels spun, the car completely flipped. Where was the baby?

Loping down the hill at a neck-breaking speed, she zeroed in on the damage. A horn blared steadily over the hissing of the engines, but nothing was louder than the fading heartbeat of the screaming child.

Delilah slammed into the flipped car and closed her eyes to focus her senses, taking a quick read of the situation. The driver of the T-boned car was hurt, but not mortally injured. There were two of them. They were young and both male.

Her head snapped back to the van. The crying stopped, the baby's heartbeat fading quickly.

"Delilah!" Christian yelled.

Her mind cut off all distractions as she shot into action. She yanked the door of the van open, the sound of metal scraping metal alerted the driver—a female.

"My baby. Please help my baby!"

Her body hung suspended from the seat, her forehead bloody. The scent of human blood cut through Delilah's urgent haze and she hissed, her fangs flashing.

More squawking wails screamed from the car seat. The baby looked about ten months old. His car seat faced the rear, but the airbags had pushed it out of place. The horn continued to blare.

She fumbled with the buckles, unable to free the baby.

"Come on," she growled, panicking when the crying stopped, its little heartbeat hardly more than a murmur. "Unlock!"

Recalling that she had claws, she sliced

through the belt and cradled the infant to her chest. He wasn't' breathing.

"Is he okay? Oh, God! Please help him!"

Delilah's heart raced as she carefully maneuvered the baby out of the van. The blaring horn numbed her skull like the needle of a tattoo numbs the skin. She rushed the baby to the grass and lay his still body down.

"Come on, little guy. Breathe." She loosened his tiny clothes.

"Delilah!"

Her fingers pressed over his chest and she detected the faintest beat of a heart. A shuddered breath pulled through her nostrils and Delilah wiped her eyes.

"Oh, God, Ethan." The mom screamed over the blaring horn. "My Ethan. Is he okay? Oh, God. Help him. Please help him," the mother frantically cried.

"Quiet," Delilah snapped and the woman immediately silenced. The child was dying. She needed to think.

Tilting her head, she petted the soft side of his little cherub face. "No pain," she whispered. "No pain."

Lifting her palm to her lips, she bit into the plump curve of her thumb.

Pintura, no! You cannot!

She slammed down an impenetrable wall on her thoughts, blocking Christian's intrusion into her mind. She became wholly focused on little Ethan. With absolute tenderness, she scooped the child off the grass and cradled his limp little body in her arms.

She brought her palm to his pale lips, her curled fingers soothing his soft brow. "Drink, baby."

His precious mouth was turning blue. She dabbed a drop of blood over his tongue. The child's mouth latched on and he pulled from her. Instinct drove her actions and sweet relief broke out of her in a sob when his heart beat back to life.

The more he pulled from her blood the stronger his suckling became. Translucent little eyelids pinkened and fluttered and he was looking up at Delilah with those precious baby blues.

She laughed through her tears. "There's a big, strong boy. There you go."

"Delilah, drop it!"

She jumped at the snap of Christian's voice, her hand ripping from the baby's mouth and tucking behind her back.

He stood by the door of the van, his fury radiating like a heatwave. Ethan's mother who silently screamed her fear, and suddenly Delilah could hear the woman's thoughts. *Please don't hurt him. Please. Please! Why, God? Why? Help my baby!*

She saw what the woman saw. The blood. The fangs. The claws.

She wasn't going to hurt the little guy. She just saved his life.

"Put the mortal back, *pintura*," Christian ordered, ice in his tone.

Adriel stood stiffly observing the situation from several feet away.

Delilah kept her eyes on Christian as she pressed a kiss onto Ethan's soft head. "You're okay now."

"Delilah, now!"

Ethan's mother whimpered as she approached the car. "He's okay. You can talk to him."

A sob bellowed out of the mother. "Help me down so I can hold him."

She set the baby down where there wasn't shattered glass—

"That's enough, Delilah. Go back to the carriage. Now."

"Wait!" the woman screamed. "You can't just leave me like this!"

She glanced from the woman to the baby. Christian closed a firm hand on her shoulder. "Now."

"We have to get her down."

"No. You need to do as I say." Sirens wailed in the distance. "I'll handle the rest."

She didn't want to leave until she knew everyone was safe. "Don't hurt them—"

"Get in the carriage." His tone turned threatening. "Now. My mother will take you home. Do not speak to anyone about this. Do you understand?"

"I just—"

"Do you understand?" he snapped and she jumped back, quickly nodding.

CHAPTER 23

When they arrived at the house the yard was flooded with animals. Cows had come from the field, and kittens and barn cats lolled in puddles of sunshine on the porch. A goat ate at the shrubs. Squirrels raced over the gutters and two fat gophers sat up like prairie dog gargoyles guarding the gardens.

"What in the world…?" Adriel whispered.

Baby geese waddled after their mother and Delilah gaped, certain this wasn't normal.

It had something to do with her. She just knew it.

A cow eyed her with big brown eyes as she walked past. It stunk, and its tail swatted at flies as its mouth chewed a hefty swallow of grass. She ran her hand over its back and recognized the flower-like splotch of brown on her back.

"Hey, Cher, what are you doing all the way over here?"

Cher batted her long lashes and continued to chew. Something told Delilah to look under the cow's belly.

"Delilah, we have to go inside and wait for Christian."

"Hold on." She ducked low and sucked in a breath at the sight of the cow's udder. It was red and irritated, maybe even infected.

"He won't be happy if you disobey him again."

She frowned. "I have to do something first." She turned her attention back to Cher and spoke softly. "Does your booby hurt?"

Delilah knew absolutely nothing about livestock and had never touched a cow before, but she saw the issue and thought there would be no harm in trying something. Squatting down, she gently cupped the teat in her hand.

The cow bleated and shifted her weight.

Shutting her eyes, Delilah focused on the pain. Cher stilled as she poured her energy into the sore utter, imagining it coming out of her in a white, healing light.

As the burning sense of irritation faded, Delilah swayed. She released the swollen udder and dropped to her knees, lowering her head to the cool grass.

"Delilah?" Adriel approached cautiously.

"Mmhm," she moaned, dizzy and weak with fatigue.

Christian's mother examined the cow. "You healed her."

She caught her breath and looked up at the

woman, smiling weakly. "I don't know how this stuff works."

She smiled. "You have a gift."

The idea that she might possess a unique skill pleased her very much. "I have to help the others."

"But Christian—"

"They're in pain."

Adriel glanced in the direction of the accident. They were too far to see the damage, but the scent of smoke tinged the air, and Delilah sensed Christian was preoccupied. The blaring horn had stopped but the sirens still wailed.

Adriel looked back at Delilah and gave her apron a tug. "How can I help?"

They started with the geese. The goslings were fine, but the mother goose was terribly dehydrated and suffering from a stomach disease. As soon as Delilah put her hands on its body, she felt the issue and was able to pull the infection out.

Next came the goat. The poor thing had an aching tooth. Bastard tried to eat Delilah's apron, but she helped him anyway. The one barn cat was pregnant and due soon. There wasn't anything Delilah could do for her. And some of the other animals just seemed to be hanging around.

By the time she checked on each one, she was exhausted, barely able to remain standing. She plopped into a rocker on the porch and huffed.

"How did you know to do that?" Adriel

asked quietly. The woman had been so silent watching her.

Delilah weakly lifted a shoulder. "I don't know. I just … can." Her gaze went to the horizon. Clouds drifted overhead, darkening the fields below. Shouldn't Christian be back by now?

"It is like a sixth sense to you. Even our healer needs the use of tonics and tools, but you're able to heal with only your mind and hands."

Heat crept up Delilah's neck. "You guys can't do that?"

Adriel tried to hide her amusement. "Guys?"

"It's an expression."

"Oh. No, child, what you have is a very unusual talent. Christian needs to tell the elders."

Her expression fell. "Why?"

"In case they have need for such skills. All disciplines are recorded in the big book."

"Do immortals get sick?"

"Rarely. But our animals do." She looked into the distance where the sky had darkened. "We do feel pain, however, and it would be nice to never feel such things again if possible."

"I don't know the extent of my skills." She had very little self-control at the moment. She thought about the accident, recalling how she'd heard the woman's thoughts. "I'm still trying to figure this whole immortal thing out."

"Just something to think about."

At that moment, all she could think about was

Christian. Why wasn't he back yet? What was taking so long? Needing a distraction, she said, "So service was a literal pain in the ass today."

Adriel's focus snapped to her and she laughed. "The sermons can be quite long when Eleazar speaks. You're lucky it wasn't Abraham's turn. He can be quite pious."

"Abraham?"

"My brother-in-law. He was married to my sister who passed some time ago. His poor daughter Abigail has to listen to him all day long."

"Wait a minute. Abigail's your niece?"

Adriel nodded. "Yes, have you met her?"

"That makes her Christian's *cousin?*"

"Yes. Is there something wrong?"

"That jerk. He knew I was jealous, and he didn't tell me they were related."

"I'm sorry?"

"It's nothing." As soon as Christian returned, she was going to call him out on his bullshit. He purposely deceived her.

"I know my son can be exacting at times. He might lose his temper on occasion, but he has a good heart."

"Oh, I know. I've seen him—"

"Seen me what?" Christian stood at the edge of the porch frowning as he watched the goat nibbling the hedges.

"Uh, we were just talking about how much of a pain in the butt you are."

He lifted his gaze. Lines of stress bracketed

his eyes. "Mother, I need to be alone with my mate. Thank you for seeing her home."

Adriel stood and touched her hand. "I'm not far if you need a friend."

"Thank you."

He watched his mother leave the property and then she was gone, moving too fast for either of them to track. He turned back to Delilah and scowled. "Get in the house."

Her spine stiffened. "I'm sorry. You must have me confused with a St. Bernard. Did you just give me an order?"

"I need to speak to you privately." He pointed toward the door. "Inside."

She scoffed. "Well, I don't know if I feel like going inside. Are you going to put me in a crate?"

He pressed his lips together. "We need to discuss your actions today. I'm in no mood for games. Move."

"Move?" She practically choked on the word. "Why are you talking to me like that?"

"Because you disobeyed me," he snapped. "You deliberately ignored every order I gave when you carelessly helped those people. You put yourself and The Order at risk. There are consequences for such crimes. Can you grasp that? Do you understand the situation *you* put us in? I'm your mate, but I'm also an elder. I have a duty to uphold our laws, and the last thing I need is another disobedient female with my name."

"Well, lucky for you, I don't have your name."

"You're still my mate. Your behavior reflects on both of us."

"My behavior?"

"You had no right to touch that mortal child!"

"He would have died, Christian!"

"Then he would have died. Mortals are fragile by design. We cannot interfere with God's plan."

"This isn't about God. This is about an innocent baby that almost lost its life today, but didn't. That child is alive because of me."

"There were witnesses!" he roared. "They saw you! Don't you see? Our blood could save all of them, but the minute they realize that, our entire race would be endangered. They are not our allies. They're greedy. They would capture us and bleed us dry if it ensured their own advancement. Is that what you want? For them to hunt us, tear us from our homes, rip our families apart? Do you have any idea how dangerous your actions were today?" He threw two phones onto the porch and she flinched.

Weak from healing so many animals and losing blood, she bent to pick them up. Her first thought should have been her salvation. It was the first time she held a phone in more than a week. She could call someone to come get her. But instead, she thought about The Order.

"They took video?"

"Yes."

"Did you erase it?"

"I don't know how."

Her hands shook as she activated the devices. The unfamiliar settings were different from her own, so she had to search for the camera app. Once she found it, she located the video.

"Holy shit!" The voice of the man recording said. "Look at her fucking eyes! What the fuck…"

"Dude, she's got fangs!"

Delilah winced as the camera zoomed in. She looked horrifying. She knew she was saving the baby, but it looked much worse on video.

She deleted the clip and made sure the recently deleted folder was empty. "It's gone."

"It's a phone, Delilah. How do we know they didn't send it to others?"

Her heart dropped. Fingers shaking, she opened up the text messages and checked for recent threads. "There's nothing in texts." She checked the email. That was also clean. Her stomach pinched when she slid through the apps and saw how many social media platforms there were. "This is going to take a minute."

She dropped into the rocking chair, her body shaking with tension and her vision blurring. He was right. Her actions put them all at risk. She hadn't considered how quickly a video like that could go viral.

Her shame grew when she considered the unwritten rule about not photographing the

Amish. The Order had done everything in their power to ensure the safety of hundreds of immortals trying to live peacefully, and she'd put them all in jeopardy within one week.

As she worked her way through each social media app, searching for any traces of uploaded footage, a tear dripped onto the screen. She deserved to feel terrible. She deserved Christian's fury and more.

"It's clean," she said, handing him back the phone only to have him give her the other one. This one had a video of her running, her speed alarming, and probably what caused them to video her in the first place while they waited for the EMTs.

By the time she scrubbed both phones it had started to rain. She had questions but sensed Christian's reluctance to speak any more about the victims of the accident.

Had he erased their memories? Was the baby going to be okay? What if she gave him too much blood? What if they ran blood tests at the hospital and found traces of her blood in little Ethan's labs?

Sick with worry, she couldn't bring herself to meet Christian's eyes. "I'm sorry."

"Are you?"

"Yes." Twin tears fell and she wiped her eyes. "I'm new at all of this. I was just acting out of instinct. I only wanted to help."

"You have a very big heart, *pintura*. I know you meant no harm."

She pushed away more tears. "How do you

do it? How do stand by while innocent people die, knowing you could help?"

"We must protect our own."

Even knowing everything he just explained and regretting that she put The Order in danger, she couldn't fully regret her actions. If put in the same situation again, she might take the same risks. "What will they do to me?"

"The punishment for exposure is one hundred lashings per witness."

His words knocked the wind out of her. They were going to whip her?

"No one will touch you, Delilah. I won't allow it."

"But…you said—"

"I'll take your punishment. You're my responsibility."

"Christian, no—"

"You don't have a say in this." The wind picked up and rain pelted the wood planks under the awning. "You need to feed. It's time to go inside."

The house was dark, and he made no attempt to light the candles. They each washed and changed into fresh clothes, because Christian said they needed to return to the Safe House right away to speak to the bishop about what happened.

"Why do we have to tell anyone?" she asked, fearful of what other consequences might come.

"Because we do not bear false witness. Deceit leads to darkness. We live in the light and speak the truth, even when we are afraid of what will come."

She fixed her braids and met him downstairs. Her body wavered as she approached the stairs. He hadn't fed her while they were in the bedroom, and she worried he'd forgotten about her, until she found him in the kitchen, emptying his vein over a tall glass.

"What are you doing?"

"You need to feed."

She stared at the glass. "Why are you—"

"This is what I'm offering. I suggest you drink it." He licked the slice on his wrist shut and turned his back on her.

His disappointment slayed her. A lump formed in her throat, and her hand trembled as she lifted the glass. Her fangs extended at the first whiff of his blood, only to clank against the glass. She struggled to swallow it all down with her throat so tight, but she managed.

When she set the empty glass on the table, he turned and faced her again. "It's raining, so we'll take the carriage."

He walked out of the kitchen without touching her. She bowed her head and swallowed back the urge to cry.

Voluntarily walking out the front door was one of the most difficult steps she'd ever taken in her life. Last week this house was a cage. But today it was her sanctuary, and she didn't want to leave.

Wind whipped through the trees as rain pelted the carriage. Christian waited under an umbrella, leaving her to take that first step on her own.

Drawing in a galvanizing breath, she trudged into the mud and quickly climbed into the carriage. He followed, closing the umbrella and taking up the reins. His hand briefly touched her knee but then quickly disappeared.

The rattle of rain hitting the flat roof of the carriage muffled all other sound. The roads were slick and dark. Taper candles filled every window of the bishop's house, making it shine brighter than all the rest.

"Wait here," Christian said as he parked the carriage and walked the horse into the shelter of the stables. When he returned, she was shivering with fear. He held out his hand to her. "I'll do the talking."

Her hand slipped into his and he squeezed her fingers with added reassurance. Larissa opened the door, her daughter Moriah perched on her hip. "Brother Christian."

"Good evening, Sister Larissa. We need to speak to the bishop."

She glanced at Delilah and flinched, no doubt reading her mind and seeing her crimes first hand. No wonder they had to tell the truth. She was a liability in every sense of the word.

"Of course. Come in."

The inside of the house looked completely different than it had at service that morning. The benches had all been removed and ordinary furniture filled the den. They stood in silence while Larissa went to get her husband.

She was grateful Christian didn't let go of her hand.

"Christian," the bishop greeted without directly addressing her. "What brings you—"

That quickly he understood. Delilah bowed her head in shame, and Christian's hand tightened around hers.

"Let's go into my office."

They followed the bishop to a small room off of a long wing annexed to the back of the house. Braided rugs and doilies didn't adorn any of the furniture in this area. The benches were plain, and biblical verses written in German rotunda hung on every wall.

"What is this place?"

This is the Safe House. It's where The Council conducts all its business.

He hadn't answered out loud so she sensed he wanted her to hold all questions and comments until the end. When they entered the bishop's office, he waved them toward two chairs facing the large desk.

"Please."

She sat beside Christian, adrift and terrified the moment he let go of her hand. A gaping fireplace dominated one wall, but not a speck of ash filled the hearth. A small stain from a steady drip formed a puddle as water slowly trickled from the flue.

"How many mortal witnesses?" the bishop asked, cutting right to business.

"Four"

Her gaze cut to Christian's, prepared to object but he sent her a mental command to keep quiet. He couldn't mean to count the baby.

"That's four hundred lashes." It was clear that the bishop did not relish, but great authority came with great responsibility. As the lead magistrate, he was obligated to uphold their laws and discipline his flock as necessary.

"I will be her proxy."

"I assumed as much." The bishop looked at her for a long moment. "Do you understand the consequences of your actions? Has Christian explained this to you?"

Her jaw trembled.

"You have my permission to answer the bishop," Christian said.

Her voice wasn't easy to find. "I...didn't mean..."

Just answer his question, pintura. No excuses.

"Yes, I understand."

The bishop nodded gravely and turned to Christian. "Tomorrow, you will attend council. Brother Abraham will perform the flogging. Your mate will also attend and watch in silence."

"Eleazar—"

"My decision's final, Christian. This is not a minor offense."

Her desperate gaze sought Christian's. This was barbaric. She couldn't do it. It didn't matter that his skin would heal. Christian hadn't done anything wrong. These were her crimes. "Wait."

Both men looked at her expectantly. "I don't

want Christian to do this. It was my fault. I should be the one to face the consequences."

"Absolutely not," Christian objected. "The decision's been made."

"No. I have a say—"

"You have no say in this, Delilah. As your mate, I'm deciding for you."

"I can't watch them whip you, Christian."

"You can. We'll get through this together." He turned his stare back to the bishop. "Before we leave, I'd like to take her downstairs."

What's downstairs? She wondered, sending her thought directly to Christian. When he ignored her, she asked again. *What's downstairs?*

"Be careful. They're all awake. You can let yourself out when you're finished."

"Thank you, Bishop King."

She glanced up at Christian when he stood and held out a hand to her. "What's downstairs?"

"Something you need to see."

CHAPTER 24

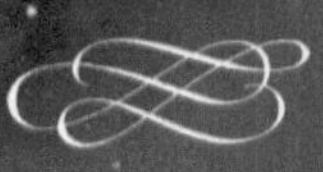

hristian led Delilah to the cellar doors and paused. The necessary distance this evening required of him was gutting him. Everything inside of him wanted to take her in his arms and reassure her that everything would be okay. But what she'd done today was not a minor crime, and she needed to understand the gravity of her choices.

He didn't trust himself to touch her beyond holding her hand, which was why he'd forbidden himself to let her drink from his vein tonight. He'd also blocked her from his thoughts so he could rein in his temper and find his bearings.

"I don't want to go in there," she said, backing away from the doors.

He placed a staying hand on her lower back. "You need to see what happens when we give our blood to mortals outside of God's divination."

She shook her head. "I don't want to see that, Christian. I trust you, and I know what I did was wrong. Why do I have to see anything else?"

He took both her hands in his and sent a wave of calm to her. "Delilah, my love, you must be brave. Had the child died today, had he taken his last breath before you gave him your blood, you would have saved his life but destroyed all traces of innocence."

"What do you mean?"

"Dane's sister is down there. Two years ago, she had an accident and was gored by a bull. In a foolish attempt to save her, Cain Hartzler fed her his blood, but it was too late. Her heart stopped on impact, and she was already gone. You see, there's a window when mortals can be brought back to life, but it's a very different life when this happens. Their soul is lost."

Her brow pinched and she took a step forward. "Can we please just go home? I don't like it here. I don't want to see what's down there."

"You must. It's the only way you'll fully understand." He unlocked the door and led her down the dark corridor.

Moans echoed in the distance, followed by a pattern of inarticulate screeches. The scent of damp earth greeted them as they took the stairs lower. A torch was lit when they entered the long corridor, and he stilled. "Dane's here."

He expected to find the half-breed by Cybil's cell, but instead, he was seated on the floor across from the witch. Christian frowned at seeing him in such a place.

Dane scrambled to his feet the moment he saw them. "What are you doing here?"

"I should ask you the same." Christian glanced dispassionately at the plebe, and Delilah staggered back. He read her misunderstanding. She assumed this witch, in her bondage and blindfold, was Dane's sister. "This is one of the bishop's guests."

She looked up at him in shock. *Why is she bound like that?*

He silently gave her the short version. *She's a witch who tried to burn an elder's firstborn alive. He's been ill and under her spell for two years. When she decides to cooperate and reverse the curse, we'll set her free.*

Dane took in Delilah's discomfort and frowned. "Are you okay?"

Christian growled. "Do not speak to my mate." Giving the troublesome boy no more of his time, he steered Delilah down the long corridor toward the rattling chains and snarls.

"Stay to my left," he instructed, keeping a firm hand on her arm.

A shrill scream rent the air as Cybil flung her body against the bars of her cell. Delilah jumped back, and a low growl purred from the shadowed prison at the end.

Christian directed Delilah to face the cell from a safe distance. "Look at what happens when our blood is misused."

The deranged girl screamed with blood-curdling hysteria. Her shift was filthy and shredded to her stomach. When she climbed the bars, she exposed herself and hissed.

Chains rattled from Isaiah's cell, diverting his mate's horrified appraisal. He caught Delilah's chin. "Not there. That cell isn't for your eyes. This is what I want you to see." He pointed her attention back to the rabid girl.

A threatening roar shook the bars when Christian stared at the deranged female. Isaiah threw himself into the wall separating the cells.

The hole Dane had described was evident and worrisome, something Christian would address with The Council. They couldn't leave such an opening. It wasn't safe.

Another roar. Isaiah's filthy hands closed around the bars, heavy iron cuffs bolted tightly to his wrists. Delilah sucked in a sharp breath and backed into the wall.

Isaiah snarled and snapped his jaws, aggravated by their presence.

"What is he?"

She should know the truth. "He's *vampire.*"

"Why is he here, in this cell?" Her eyes were wide, taking in the tattered remains of what was once his friend. The longer they stared the more overwrought the two prisoners became.

"His name is Isaiah Hartzler."

"Hartzler as in Destiny, Anna, Gracie, Cain, and Adam?"

"Yes, and Larissa, who is now mated to our

bishop. Isaiah was their uncle, an honored elder amongst The Order, and my close friend."

She looked up at him, empathy pouring from her wide eyes. "What happened to him?"

"His calling went *unanswered*. He failed to find his mate and never completed the bonding. He went mad."

Deep compassion radiated from her as she stared into the shadows at Isaiah's blood red eyes. *"Feeish?"*

Cybil screeched madly, drawing his attention. "Very good, *pintura*. Your pronunciation is improving."

Isaiah lunged forward, snarling with a predator's growl. Delilah gripped Christian's arm, and he pulled her protectively into his side.

It wasn't easy seeing this reality and recalling the honorable male his friend had once been. It was a good reminder why his work with The Council could not rest. They had a responsibility to their race and a debt to the mortal community.

"After Isaiah lost control," he explained, "his rampage killed and brutalized many innocent females—Dane's mother being one of them."

"Is there no cure?"

Christian shook his head regretfully. "Only feeding from his true called mate could stem such bloodlust. I'm afraid his soul is lost."

Her attention diverted to the hysterical creature climbing the walls of the next cell. "And *this* is Dane's sister?"

"What's left of her." He glanced to the end of the hall where Dane made no secret of watching them. Christian took pity on the boy and wondered what measures he could take to help the situation, within reason. "The Order is studying the genetic abnormalities that occur when a mortal is unjustly transitioned. Isaiah has conjured quite the fall out."

"What do you mean?"

"He was missing for decades. In that time, he unjustly transitioned many mortal women. They're still out there."

"Transitions like her." He followed her stare to Cybil's cell, and Isaiah snarled.

"Yes. They're beyond hope. Violent and soulless. The Order is hunting what remains of the *others.*"

Delilah looked into Isaiah's cell, and Cybil screeched, commanding their attention. His mate frowned and blindly took his hand. "Can we go now?"

He hesitated, alarmed by how territorial the possessed immortal was of the neighboring space. He recalled what Dane had said. "Give me a moment."

Taking a step toward the female's cell, Christian tested his theory. Isaiah went ballistic, snarling and clamoring about the dark cell, roaring with unmistakable fury. It seemed Isaiah had formed an alpha attachment to the child.

The territorial scent of a possessive male seeped into the dank corridor with pungent warning. Christian had assumed Isaiah would be worked up over Delilah's presence, but the immortal seemed more distressed at the sight of him, mostly when he encroached on Cybil's space.

"Christian," Delilah snapped. "I want to go."

He stepped back and nodded, a cacophony of shrieking erupting as they left the two wild abominations to their own devices. They walked the long corridor in silence, Delilah's grip tightening on his hand with each screeching howl that followed.

Dane scowled as they passed. "What did you do?"

Ignoring his half-brother, he held tight to Delilah's hand and led her through the door. They had more important issues to address than Dane's preoccupation with what rotted in those cells.

As soon as they made it outside, she asked, "Why didn't you answer Dane?"

The bitter memory of his half-brother's threats still burned. "I have nothing to say to him."

He helped Delilah into the carriage, and they rode home in silence. The rain continued to fall, the slick roads requiring his full attention.

When they reached the house, he dropped her off at the door. "I have to tend to the horses. I'll be back shortly."

She went directly into the house.

The rain had finally stopped when he left

the stables, but the ground was saturated. He toed off his boots and sensed Delilah upstairs. Taking the steps slowly, he braced for a fight. But when he entered the bedroom, all was calm.

The furniture was tidy, and she lay curled on her side, her soft whimper drawing his immediate concern. "Delilah?"

She sniffed.

He stripped out of his wet clothes. "You're upset."

Another sniffle.

He sat on the edge of the bed, but when he reached for her, she recoiled. "Delilah," he said more firmly. "It's been a long day. Say what's on your mind and let's be done with it."

Her shoulders shook as she released a jagged breath. He pressed into her mind, only to find her blocked to him. His head cocked in surprise, unsure when she learned to do that.

"We can't fix anything if we don't communicate. Those are your words, are they not?"

"Some things can't be fixed, Christian."

Losing patience, he reached for her and pried her away from the edge of the mattress, forcing her to roll on her back and look at him. "What has you so upset?"

"Everything!" She gasped, choking on a sob. "They're going to whip you. There's a little girl in a cell. And a *witch!* Is that even a thing? And you didn't let me speak when we were in front of the bishop, knowing I had something to say."

"Because I knew what you planned to say.

You will not put yourself on the line like that. Not for me. It's my duty to protect you. Leave well enough alone."

"But this is my fault! I can't bear the thought of them hurting you! I'll never be able to sit through that! I'd rather be the one getting hit."

"Hush." He pulled her onto his lap and rubbed a soothing hand down her back, urging her close. "If anyone ever laid a cruel hand on you, I'd fall into a murderous rage, and then we'd really be in a mess. By the end of the day tomorrow, this will all be over and we can put it behind us. You have to be brave. I need you to be brave for me."

She buried her face in his neck and sucked in another sob. "Why did you make me feed like that earlier?"

He sighed. "Because I needed to keep my wits. We couldn't afford to be distracted. I wanted us both clearheaded when we faced the bishop."

"I don't like that guy."

He chuckled. "Eleazar isn't a bad male. He has a difficult job and does it well, with honor and impartiality. Tonight wasn't easy for him. Try not to think too cruelly of him for only doing his duty."

She scooted back and looked up at him through reddened eyes. "We can leave. I know you love it here, Christian, but we can run away together. We can make our own laws and live however we want."

He tucked a strand of hair behind her ear

and smiled into her tear-streaked face. "No, little one. This is the safest place for us."

"But I don't want them to whip you." She covered her mouth and whimpered. "Four hundred lashes is too much."

"I would take a thousand lashes every day if it meant keeping you safely by my side. Four hundred is nothing, my love. Your tears are injuring me far worse than a whip ever could."

She sprang forward, wreathing her arms around his neck and hugging him in a chokehold. "I didn't understand. I mean, I heard you. I heard Larissa. You all kept saying that terrible things would have happened if you didn't find me, but... Until I saw Isaiah tonight, I didn't truly understand what you meant."

His arms closed gently around her back, and he kissed her temple. "It's all right, *pintura*."

She leaned back. "But I still don't trust your bishop."

"You must understand something about our bishop. He was a friend to my mother and like a father to me in many ways. As the only male of the Schrock line, a large responsibility rested on my shoulders from a young age. Eleazar taught me how to manage such encumbering duties. He demanded I get the same respect as every other elder on the bench, despite my young age and misbegotten start. He punished anyone who dared to call me a bastard."

She nuzzled closer. "That doesn't give him the right to force you into this."

"There is no force, my love. I surrender willingly so that we may stay here and live a long life under the protection of The Order."

"Protected maybe, but not free."

"Every society must have rules." He pressed a kiss to her nose and then another to her lips. "Come now, no more sadness today."

She leaned forward, pressing her face to his. "I'll never be able to sleep."

"Let me help you relax." He lowered her back to the bed, stripping away her shift and spreading a trail of kisses to her breasts. She stretched her body out beneath him in beautiful surrender as he dragged his lips lower.

When she willingly opened her legs, his tongue teased the small piercing at her apex, and she moaned, her sensual cries music to his ears. Tasting her there was akin to sipping from the fountain of youth. He could drink her sweet honey forever and never have his fill. He licked and teased, bringing her slowly to climax as her pleasure rolled into his. He savored her sweet release down to the last drop.

When he was ready for her, she accepted him into her body. He pressed deep until their pelvises kissed.

"Taste yourself on my lips," he whispered, kissing her slowly.

Her tongue stole into his mouth, and he moaned as her fingers raked deliciously through his hair. He thrust into her, driving his cock deeper with every stroke and claiming her body.

Pressing her arms into the bedding over her

head, he looked into her eyes, sensing how the day's events had strengthened their bond.

It was his belief that God strengthened them with challenges so that they had a better chance of survival. Just as a chrysalis must struggle to break free of the cocoon, the effort was necessary. His mate was going through a beautiful transformation, a chrysalis on her way to becoming a radiant butterfly.

"Tell me who you belong to, *pintura*."

"I'm yours," she rasped, gasping and arching as he rocked into her.

"That's right, my love. You're mine. All mine. Forever."

She cried out as another wave of pleasure crossed that euphoric precipice. Her sex fluttered, gripping his cock as it stroked into her. Deeper. Faster. He couldn't get enough of her.

"Christian, let me touch you."

He released her arms and her fingers forked through his hair, pulling his mouth to hers in a passionate kiss. His hips snapped forward as his body throbbed. His scent seeped from his pores, marking her. Tomorrow, there would be no mistaking who she belonged to.

The bed rocked as he possessively drilled into her. Soft cries punctuated every forward motion as his mind repeated his relentless claim. *Mine. All mine.*

"I'll never let you go, *pintura*. I want to spend all of eternity just—like—this." Throwing his head back he growled, spilling his seed deep in her body where it belonged.

Her tight sex clamped his throbbing cock, milking every last drop. Her cries turned frantic as his release spiraled into hers,

"Yes, yes! Ah, Christian, don't stop." Her voice broke on a moan of ecstasy. "I love when you touch me like this."

"I love *you*."

She sighed in soft contentment, her brow pinching as she studied him for a curious moment. "I love you too."

Her words shot through him. His intellect battled with his carnal nature to process what she'd just said. He cupped her face and looked into her eyes. "You love me?"

A tear rolled from her lashes and she nodded. "Please just..."

"What?" He'd give her anything she wanted. "Tell me."

"Just...promise you won't give up on me."

Stunned she could even think that a possibility, he hugged her to him. "I could never. You're my Delilah. My beautiful *pintura*. My soul." He kissed her softly. "Do you remember what I told you about the soul?"

She nodded and pressed her hand to his heart. "It's right here."

"That's right. You're my heart and my soul, Delilah." He closed his hand over hers, pressing it into his chest. "An immortal's lost without a soul. I would die if I ever lost you."

CHAPTER 25

"Sister Delilah, they're ready for you." She stiffened at the strange title then stood. Christian had kissed her goodbye nearly an hour ago and left her in the bishop's office to wait. She looked at the man with his sleeve pinned to the shoulder and wondered what happened to his arm.

"Come with me."

She didn't speak to the man and appreciated that he made no attempt to touch her. Walking closely, he escorted her down the long hall to the room where The Council meetings were held.

At the far end of the corridor, she spotted Adriel and Dane waiting on a bench and her breath caught. Their familiar faces brought a level of unexpected relief. "You came—"

"No talking."

She had been reminded by Christian several

times that she must obey the rules while in the Safe House. Females were not permitted into Council Hall unless subpoenaed. Her required presence came with an order of silence, which she must abide at all times or they would take her voice away.

Adriel caught her hand and squeezed, sending her a wave of reassurance. Delilah squeezed back, knowing this would be brutal for her as well.

"No touching."

Their hands pulled apart, and Dane met her stare, something cold and hard in his eyes, but his animosity wasn't intended for her. His concern for her well-being last night forged a strange, unspoken alliance between them. She felt oddly aligned with him when only days ago she assumed he was her enemy.

The double doors opened, and benches creaked as a hundred immortal men turned to look at her. It didn't matter that they were all in the prime of their lives and gorgeous. Their meek Amish appearance wouldn't soften her guard. These men were all lethal immortals, and their power stole the air right from her lungs.

"To the front," the guard said, leading her down the narrow aisle.

Her gaze found Cain and Adam in the pews. Cain slightly nodded, his eyes somber and his mouth tight.

Council Hall was similar to an ordinary court room. A male clerk sat in the left corner and a justice bench stretched across the front, the eyes of several grave men—including Christian—watching her every move. She assumed that was the Elder's Council.

When her gaze met Christian's, she allowed herself to blink. Her eyes burned from staring so long, and if she'd had the ability to make tears in that moment, she would have cried.

Breathe, pintura.

His soft command filled her mind, traveling straight to her lungs as air whooshed into her.

It will all be over soon.

His love surrounded her, and she returned the comfort by sending him a burst of her own. *I love you.*

"Sit." David pointed to the simple wooden chair placed in the center of the floor.

She lowered into the seat, her back to the men in the audience and her eyes locked on Christian. David then moved to the marshal's seat on the far right and waited. The silence stretched for several agonizing seconds until the bishop rose.

"We call Brother Christian Schrock to the floor."

Christian stood and walked from the bench. When he reached the floor, he faced the elders and the bishop said, "Christian Schrock, you are being sentenced, by proxy, for the crimes of your mate, Sister Delilah Starling, who has violated The Order's holy laws by exposing our species in the presence of four mortals. For this crime, you will receive one hundred lashings for each mortal witness. What say you?"

Christian stood stoically before the bench and lifted his chin. "I accept my sentence."

"Kneel."

He glanced at Delilah. *I love you. Be brave.*

Her body tensed the moment he severed their mental link and dropped to his knees. *Christian? Christian!* She hadn't expected him to remove that connection, which she'd come to rely on in times of worry. Her eyes blinked rapidly as fear sizzled through every nerve.

"Brother Abraham," the bishop called and another elder stood, this one holding a long leather whip that coiled around his fist.

This was Christian's uncle, Abigail's father, yet he looked as young and fiercely beautiful as the rest of them. The golden tan of his skin complimented his wheat-blond hair. But when he spoke in that thick Germanic accent, his sharp blue eyes remained flat and lifeless, his voice shooting a chill up Delilah's spine.

"Nephew," he greeted Christian, as the whip unraveled from his fist to drag along the floor. "Remove your shirt."

He carried himself with an almost Aryan arrogance that chilled her to the bone. His flawless, athletically toned body was underscored by a lethal air that needed no explanation. No wonder Abigail was so obedient and meek. Her father was terrifying.

"Let us begin."

Delilah swallowed as Christian stripped off

his jacket, vest, and shirt folding them neatly and setting them aside.

Abraham loosened his wrists, wagging the whip back and forth, finding the proper hold. Christian, although kneeling on the hard floor, kept his spine straight and his head bowed. Delilah's hands wrung nervously in her lap.

The first strike came fast. She hadn't been ready, and she gasped as the leather struck down, leaving an angry stripe across Christian's flawless skin. The deep red lash darkened, but the flesh remained intact.

"One," the entire gallery of immortals counted aloud and the whip came down again.

Delilah tensed, her mind instinctively reaching for Christian's, only to hit a wall.

"Two."

Abraham moved quickly, making the ordeal difficult to witness and process at the same time. The males at her back counted off each stroke in monotone observance of their brother's debt, marking each sentencing slash as payment for her crime.

"Nine." Her shoulders tensed. The terrible snap of leather biting into Christian's flesh took on a wet percussion as his body began to sweat.

"Ten." The first trickle of blood appeared, his skin breaking open under the aggravated welts. Every lash after this would do more damage than the last.

For the next ten, she closed her eyes, flinching at every snap and whisk as the leather moved heedlessly through the air. When she opened her eyes again, the breath in her lungs clattered past her lips.

Christian's back was a mosaic of welts and blisters. The angry red markings embossed his flesh, stretching his skin like an overworked canvas as the leather strap came down again and again.

"Thirty-two."

Her vision blurred as the blood on Christian's back diluted with sweat, running over his torn flesh in rivers of red. Each little tributary raced with gravity, soaking the fabric of his pants. The bulk of his shoulders trembled and twitched, but he never made a sound.

Every gutting swipe of that long leather tail caused her muscles to tense another degree, until her entire body coiled into one impenetrable knot. The whistle and crack as the whip cut through the air and her mate's skin embedded a trauma deep in her soul that she feared would scar her for life.

"Fifty." They were only halfway through the first one hundred and his back was already pummeled and torn in a way that made every motion excruciating.

She watched his spine soften and the sinew of his arms tremble whenever the whip stopped. The air pressing into each wound during every brief pause seemed as intolerable as the actual strikes ravaging his flesh. It was too much. Any mortal would have screamed for mercy by now, but Christian hardly cowered.

Abraham brought the whip down again, the

flogging no longer lashing as precisely as it began. Blood saturated the leather tip and dripped from Christian's clothing, speckling and streaking the floor. Delilah's jaw trembled as the thrashing went on, the seventy-ninth lash forcing a grunt from Christian.

She jolted forward. "No—"

"Silence," the one-armed immortal ordered from the marshal's seat.

A tear spilled down her cheek as the elders looked at her with cold disregard. Christian's tattered flesh pulsed with each labored breath, his blood seeping onto the floor.

"You will keep quiet, Sister Delilah," the bishop ordered. "Or there will be consequences."

Her jaw quivered as she silently nodded, tears now falling unchecked from her eyes.

Abraham stretched his arms, shaking out his tired muscles as he tightened the grip of his dominant hand around the whip.

Delilah had to cover her mouth to keep from crying out when the whip struck again.

"Eighty."

When they finally reached one hundred, Christian's body had curled forward to bear the pain more than to escape it. Every lash tightened his tense muscles until his body naturally closed up like a fist. Besides that, he hardly moved or made a sound.

"Brother Christian, would you like some water?" the bishop asked, and Delilah held her breath as only silence answered.

Finally, Christian's head tipped in a partial nod, declining the offer. "Continue," he rasped, his voice seeming to work around a fist at his throat.

"We will begin again at one. Three hundred lashings to go," Abraham announced, giving no other warning as the whip whistled through the air and cut into Christian's skin.

By two hundred the floor was drenched in blood. Christian kneeled in the dark puddle, his white-knuckled fists freckled in red spatters as he seethed under the pain.

Delilah's chest physically ached as she struggled to look at what they'd done to him. His back was scored, an open wound of blood and pulp that likely burned with every breath, no matter if he inhaled, exhaled, or forbid himself to breathe.

Tears soaked her face and gown. Her fangs and claws extended a hundred lashings ago. Her body existed in a knot of tension as she forced herself to remain still.

"Do you have need for water, Brother Christian?"

She held her breath, waiting for him to answer. How would he survive this? They were only halfway through. She couldn't bear any more. The ruthless torture had gone on long enough.

Staggering to her feet, the chair scraped as she swallowed back a sob. "He needs blood."

"Sit down," an elder on the bench snapped.

The one-armed immortal stepped down

from the marshal's seat, prepared to intervene. If anyone touched her, she was certain Christian would lose his shit.

"Please," she begged, her tearful gaze falling on the bishop. "Let me give him blood."

"You will sit in silence as you've been ordered to do, Sister Delilah," the bishop ordered with little inflection in his voice.

She glared at the man who called himself Christian's friend. "You're killing him."

A low, masculine chuckle rippled through the gallery, and her body quaked at their cold mockery. It didn't matter that he was immortal, there was no justification for this level of cruelty.

Her eyes narrowed on every brutal face staring at her from the elder's bench. "You should all be—" Her words suddenly cut off and her hand snapped to her mouth . She tried to speak, but no sound came out.

"You were warned that silence would be enforced," the elder beside the bishop said. "Now sit down."

They were barbaric and brutal. Looking the bishop in his cold, dark eyes, she lifted her chin and raised her wrist, holding his ruthless stare as she bit open her wrist. The moment the scent of her blood hit the air, Christian's head snapped up from his shoulders and several of the males shifted on the benches at her back.

She took a step forward toward Christian and jerked to a stop, her blood trickling freely down her arm as her body froze under an imposed paralysis.

"You overestimate your autonomy here, Sister Delilah." The stern elder beside the bishop narrowed his eyes. "You're here by order of The Elder Council to be disciplined for your actions. Look at what your disobedience has wrought."

Despite her refusal, her head physically turned to face Christian as they made her look at him.

"This is the consequence of your careless actions. You will sit quietly and watch without one more interruption or you will be silenced and restrained. Do you understand?"

Under the enforced palsy of the elder's command, she was completely powerless. Her body shook as they dominated her will.

A low growl rumbled from Christian, but he did not move from his position on the floor. She had no link to his thoughts, but she was certain his fury was for the bishop and his colleagues, not her.

Unsure if they could hear her, she projected her thoughts forward. *You're evil.*

Your antics only prolong his suffering. If you love him and want this over, sit down and let us be done with it.

She recoiled at the strange intrusion of the bishop's voice in her head, and the paralysis lifted as she staggered back to her chair. She was powerless here. They were too old, and their authority too absolute.

Dropping into the seat, she convulsed in a steady tremble, frozen in shocked outrage as the flogging continued. Every lashing contracted her muscles with finite totality and her body weakened, but the beating never ended.

Her posture dissolved until she sat like a body of broken bones. Tears fell unchecked from her eyes as she blocked out their voices, the taunting counts no longer making sense to her shattered thoughts as the endless torture went on.

Somewhere in the midst of their cruelty, her empathetic link overdosed. In desperate self-preservation, she shut off her senses, unable to hear any more of their savagery.

Her ears numbed to the dull sound of the whip cutting into Christian's raw, bloodied flesh, the scent of his blood permeating the room, the sight of his cowering shoulders as he shuddered to breathe and remain upright. Staring ahead at the horrific mess, her vision blurred and her head lulled. It was simply too much and her mind couldn't bear it.

"Delilah."

She jerked at the strange sensation of a hand on her shoulder. In a haze, her bleary gaze lifted to find Cain looking down at her, brow pinched and deep grooves of concern bracketing his eyes.

"It's over."

Jolted out of the woozy fog, she clambered to Christian's side and let out a horrified sob. He lay in a puddle of his own blood, his face pinched with pain and his eyes squeezed shut. She fell to her knees, afraid to touch him and cause him more discomfort.

"What have they done to you?" she cried, unable to make sense of such horrific cruelty.

He didn't acknowledge her presence. His fist and jaw clenched so tightly he seemed locked in agony.

"Christian," she whispered, tracing a finger over his brow.

His nostrils flared as he sucked in a breath.

She reopened her wrist, aligning the gash with his mouth, carefully trying not to aggravate his injuries. "Take what you need, my love. Drink."

His lips hardly parted as he pressed his mouth to her flesh. A sob broke from her chest as she wept for what they had done to him. Those monsters had weakened him to this unrecognizable state. It was criminal.

"Please," she begged. "I need you to heal."

An agonized grunt worked from his throat as he shifted slightly, his lips firming around her wrist as he latched onto her vein. She sucked in a shuddering breath as he slowly began to pull.

An announcement was made, and the room slowly emptied. She paid the others no mind as she delicately stroked her fingers through Christian's damp, sticky hair.

"That's it," she encouraged quietly.

His pulls strengthened, then a burst of white-hot pain seared through her body and she screamed. Her limbs shook violently as his mental block came down and she experienced a brief glimpse of the extent of his pain.

Her body couldn't hold it. The enormity of his agony shot through her in a fusillade of sting that lit up every nerve in her body and stole her strength.

"Help her!" A rush of commotion filled the back of the room as Adriel yelled for assistance.

"Get back! You're not permitted beyond the doors," someone shouted.

"Remove Sister Adriel at once," another male voice commanded.

"Eleazar!" Adriel's voice spiked as a commotion ensued at the back of the hall. "Do not let this stand. He's my son."

The shared pain knocked the wind from Delilah's lungs, and she collapsed to the floor, the cool molasses of Christian's spilled blood drenching her sleeve and gown as she looked into his eyes.

Keep drinking.

His arm weakly lifted and he cupped her cheek. She blinked, her eyes heavy as his injuries drained much of her strength, and his thirst depleted the rest.

His mouth unfastened from her wrist, and he caught her hand weakly in his, pressing a soft kiss to her palm. "No more."

Tears spilled from her eyes. "You need more, Christian."

His lashes lowered. The sheer effort to

breathe seemed to sap the little strength he had regained. "No. I've taken enough."

"Christian." She panicked when she felt him pulling back from her mind. "Don't you leave me again. You have to keep feeding."

He weakly smiled. *"Pintura."*

The gash on her wrist started to close. She lifted a claw.

"Wait." A shadow fell over them and she looked up, her body tensing at the sight of the bishop. "Let me help."

She hissed, shooting to her knees to protectively block his broken body from further damage. "Don't touch him!"

Christian's hand brushed weakly over her knee. "Eleazar…is a friend…*pintura.*"

Her jaw quivered with uncertainty as she looked at Christian's desperate face, so wrought with pain, and back to the bishop.

"I only mean to help him. My blood's aged and powerful. I offer it freely to him so that he may recover quickly."

A jagged breath ripped through her as she nodded and scooted back, desperate to see her mate healed. "Fix him."

She covered her mouth, trying in vain to silence her whimpered cries. The bishop kneeled beside her mate and opened his wrist, pressing it to Christian's lips. "Drink, my friend."

Christian grunted and snatched the bishop's offered arm, sinking his fangs deep and drawing heavily from the vein. The bishop grunted and braced as Christian gorged himself. Only then did Delilah understand how much he'd been holding back, always trying to put her needs first and keep her safe.

She watched the bishop shut his eyes as the feeding exerted him. She wondered if he too had felt the intense empathy she'd suffered during the flogging. The others had vacated the room, and they were now alone, just the three of them.

Christian grunted as he greedily took from the bishop. The elder's veins bulged in his neck and arm as his healing blood flowed to her mate, his skin paling as his strength drained.

She couldn't understand why he would show such compassion after ordering such barbaric abuse. Then she followed his downcast gaze and found the explanation.

"You love him."

Eleazar's dark eyes flashed to her. "I love all of them. They're my flock, and I, their shepherd."

She realized then that his job went beyond boring sermons and judicial duty. He loved them like a parent loves a child. He was their leader, a father, and when his children suffered, he suffered with them. This ancient immortal loved her mate like a son, reminding her that Christian reciprocated such affection, assigning the bishop as close a role to father as any bastard could ascribe.

"I'm relieved to see that you've forgiven him."

Stunned that he would comment on her

mistreatment of Christian, she narrowed her stare. "You'll never do anything like this to him again."

Not because she'd learned her lesson about discretion, but because she would never survive watching her mate punished like this twice. They would leave before she ever allowed anything like this to happen to him again.

The bishop read her thoughts. "Everyone is here by choice."

Prepared to dispute his claim, because she saw what was in the cells below, she scowled, then considered what he was actually suggesting. Would she have been able to leave? She hadn't been permitted to interfere with the flogging, but nothing had stopped her from walking out the door.

She recalled the moment Christian asked her to wait in the bishop's office.

"Try to be brave, pintura. *I'll need your strength today."* He hadn't ordered her to stay or even instructed her to wait. He only requested she do her best.

"The door's right there," Eleazar said, and she followed his stare. "Save Christian's objections, you'll meet no resistance from us, little one."

Little one. That was what Christian sometimes called her. He'd said it was a term that marked her innocence in this new world, not one that implied anything about her age or maturity.

Her jaw hardened and she straightened her

spine, lowering her hands to her lap and drawing back her shoulders. "I won't leave him."

The bishop glanced down at his ravaged back. "In this condition?"

In that moment, she understood the full extent of their bond. "Ever." The truth resonated in her, burrowing deep in a way that reformed so much of the inner turmoil that had tied her in fiery knots.

She looked down at her mate, lying in a puddle of his own blood as he drank from the bishop's vein. Pride and affection overflowed her heart as she watched the life slowly return to his silver eyes.

Her mouth curved with deep-seated conceit as she smiled down at him. Forgetting the bishop's presence, she looked into Christian's watchful stare and smiled softly. "I'm not going anywhere." His eyes closed with relief as she brushed a comforting hand over his hair. "You're mine."

CHAPTER 26

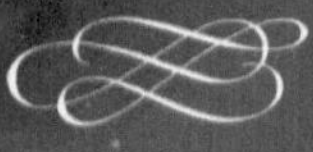

*C*hristian's back remained ravaged for days. However, it wasn't the strain or the lingering ache that accompanied every motion that he despised, but the concern that followed him in his mate's stare.

"Delilah, I'm fine."

She dropped her gaze to the counter. The distance between them had stretched to the point that they both suffered the strain. "Your mother sent over a jar of ointment."

"I'll apply it later."

She tsked. "You can't apply it on your own. Why won't you let me help you?"

The truth was he didn't like her to see him in such a feeble state. Although the brunt of the pain had eased and he only suffered a minor twinge here and there where his broken skin had hardened, he still had a long journey of recovering mentally from such an ordeal.

He'd made sure to block Delilah from his thoughts during the flogging, ensuring that she not suffer any overlap of pain. But he had not completely severed their link, and once the whipping began, he'd been too distracted to do anything outside of bearing down and breathing through the horrific ordeal.

Through the entire four hundred lashes he suffered not only the excruciating bite of leather tearing open his skin, flaying his flesh off the muscle in chunks, but the maddening stab of his mate's agony as she was forced to watch such a harrowing display. Her heartbreak and pity debilitated him. It was an unendurable misery he simply couldn't abide.

Since the flogging, whenever she looked at him with concern, his stress heightened with the need to soothe her worries. He'd decided to swallow any discomfort and complete the process of healing on his own.

"I must run an errand. I'll be back within the hour. Do you need anything?"

Flour coated the front of her apron when she faced him. She'd been attempting to follow a recipe Sister Grace had offered for shoofly pie. "Where are you going?"

"I need to take something to my mother's."

She frowned. "She was just here."

He reached for the basket of produce and grabbed a fist full of root vegetables Delilah collected from the garden. "Carrots. The rabbits have been stealing hers."

She scowled at him. "You're a terrible liar."

Rather than dispute the truth, he pressed a kiss to her cheek. "I'll return soon."

Guilt rode him all the way to his mother's house. She was expecting him, despite appearing displeased when she opened the door. "Come in."

He followed her to the kitchen.

"This isn't right, Christian. You're being deceitful to your mate."

"This is best for everyone. Delilah's suffered enough. Everything will revert to normal once my strength returns."

"You're newly mated. I find it hard to imagine you've experienced *normal* yet." She placed the mason jar of blood on the table. "Here."

He unscrewed the lid and guzzled down the potent blend. The glass was still warm from the contents. Her aged blood took immediate effect on his aching nerves. "Thank you."

"I need a favor."

Anxious to return to his mate, he moved toward the back door. "What do you need?"

"I want one of your hunting rifles."

Of all the favors he expected his mother to ask, that was not one he anticipated. "Are you going hunting?"

"*Der schrim.*"

"For protection from what?"

She met his stare and he understood she wasn't going to justify her actions. "How much more blood will you need?" She was bartering.

"Have you asked the bishop's permission?"

Weapons were not permitted in the hands of females, and males were only allowed to use firearms for hunting, but immortals had little need for such things.

"Eleazar doesn't understand. He actually suggested I find a husband if I feel unsafe."

"Not a terrible idea," he muttered. "Mother, you know the laws."

She snatched the empty jar from the table. "I want a gun, Christian. Bring one with you tonight when you come to feed again."

Truthfully, his mother was such a hard-headed female he wasn't sure a husband could rein her in after so many centuries of being on her own. He pulled the carrots from his pocket. "These are from Delilah."

When he returned home, his mate's attempt at the homemade pie was cooling on the windowsill. He smirked at the lopsided crust and concave surface.

"It doesn't look like Gracie's."

He turned to find Delilah watching him from the door. "I'm sure it's delicious."

"Did your mother appreciate the carrots?"

"She did." He crossed the room, holding her stare. "What do you have planned for the rest of the day?"

She'd been settling in and exploring the house, which filled him with immeasurable pride. Each day he found little touches that never existed before. Jars of fresh-cut flowers. Cloth draped over furnishings. And dishes set out on display.

Holding his stare, she pulled the strings of her *kapp* loose, exposing her hair and revealing her throat. "You must be hungry." She tipped back her head and looked up at him, challenge in her astute stare. "Drink."

He frowned, not used to her initiating such things. "Delilah…"

She pulled the pins from her apron and let the garment fall to the floor. "You haven't fed in days and you're still not fully healed, so I don't understand why you won't accept what I'm freely willing to offer."

He took a step back. "Delilah—"

"I know you're feeding, Christian." She loosened her gown, stripping down to her underclothes as she stood before him, certain he would not be able to resist her laid bare for him as she was.

Her bare chest lifted as she faced him, the twin piercings stark against the sharp pink tips of her breasts. His mouth watered and he swallowed tightly, hungry to taste her.

"Why won't you take my blood?"

"The other day depleted you."

She shook her head. "You've fed me three times since then, but you've yet to touch me. I feel fine. But still, you hold me at arm's length. Is it my blood? Is it too weak?"

"Your blood is fine, *pintura.*"

"Then why won't you take it?"

Her sorrow gutted him. Taking her in his arms, he pulled her close. "It's me. When we're intimate, our mental link is at its strongest. I don't want my pain to hurt you."

She stood stiffly and shoved him. "*You* are what's hurting me. I thought we were a team."

"We are. This is just a ripple in time. As soon as things iron out and get back to normal— Where are you going?"

She gathered her clothes and marched up the stairs, bare chested and furious. Her middle finger shot into the air. "I'm packing. You obviously don't need me around as you recuperate."

He was on the second floor blocking her path before she could take another step. "Packing for what?"

"It's been more than two weeks, Christian. I have to go home. I need to deal with things at my shop, and I can't do that from here."

This was her home. "What things?"

She flung out her arms and slapped them down at her side. "I have clients, people who paid me for services. I need to either conduct said service or refund their money."

He reeled in his panic. She wasn't talking about permanently leaving. She only wanted to conclude her open-ended business. He would need more blood if he planned to accompany her. "We can leave tonight. You should rest."

Her mouth opened, and he sensed her surprise. "That's...that's it?"

"I made you a promise, and I keep my word. We can leave at nightfall."

Delilah had very little to pack beside a few

snacks. When she learned they would be jour-
neying by foot, she decided to rest. That gave
Christian time to clean a rifle and visit his mother
again. He drank as much as he could stomach of
her ancient blood and left her armed but weak.

When he returned to the house, Delilah was
waiting on the steps, petting several animals
that had come to greet her. "There's something
I want to show you before we go," she said,
rising from the porch steps and leading him
back inside. "Take off your shirt."

He hesitated. "If you want to make decent
time, we should—"

"Do it, Christian." She knew he fed after rejecting her vein, and she was now more upset
with him than before.

He sighed and lowered his suspenders,
watching her as he opened his collar. "It's my
mother's blood," he confessed, stripping off his
shirt.

"I know. I recognize her smell." She drew in
a deep breath as if centering herself. "Turn
around."

"Delilah—"

"I'm not asking, Christian."

He hesitated then slowly turned to face the
wall. Her breath caught, and he used their link
to see what she saw. Maimed flesh had healed
over with thick grooves. The scars would eventually fade and his skin would regenerate like
new, but for now the damage was evident.

She lifted her hand slowly and pressed
down with a feather-light touch. He flinched

at such tenderness, but he didn't sense her pity.

Frowning, he tried to identify the feelings she held in that moment. There was extreme concentration paired with her unbreakable will.

His muscles jerked as a strange sensation traveled over his mangled skin and soothed the nerve damage with a cooling wave. He sucked in a sharp breath when the sore spots started to tingle. "*Abwehre*." He took a step but she caught his arm.

"Stay still."

"What are you doing?"

She returned her focus to his back. "I'm healing you."

Another cool wave rushed over his battered skin, penetrating deep into the nerve and muscle in a way that instantly relieved the inflammation. "Delilah..." He'd never experienced anything so soothing. "How did you learn this?"

She concentrated in silence, too focused to answer. The longer she moved her hands over him the more his pain eased. Not only did his back start to feel better, the inflamed burn under his skin dissipated.

He moaned at such sweet relief and shut his eyes, swaying as the removal of pain literally transformed into pleasure. When she lowered her hands, the ache was gone. He looked through her vision and saw his skin was once more smooth.

He faced her in such awe he didn't know what to say. "You healed me."

"It takes a lot of energy." She swayed and he caught her arm. "I think I need blood."

Gathering her in his arms, he carried her to a kitchen chair. "Take what you need."

She shifted on his lap, blanketing his body with hers, the act of feeding from his vein now a natural practice in her life. Her teeth sank deep, and he stiffened the moment she began to feed.

Dragging his palms down her back, he rocked his hips, stealing whatever friction her body provided in such a position. She moaned softly, the scent of her arousal filling the air as she suckled at his vein.

He wanted to get inside of her, but she needed to regain her strength. It had been days since they were last intimate, and his need in that moment was great.

Rising, she gripped his shoulders and rocked over him as she fed. *Take me, Christian.*

He reached between them, loosening his pants. Her hand followed his, closing around his thick shaft as she dragged her body over his length, drenching his hard cock with her arousal. Her clothes were an annoyance he wanted gone.

She squeezed him tightly in her fist, tugging him to a point of no self-possession. Only raw, carnal need existed between them in that moment. As soon as her mouth lifted from his vein, he was rising from the chair and carrying her to the table.

Her back hit the surface and he shoved her skirt to her hips, growling at the obstacle of her underclothes. "I need you."

"I'm yours."

Jerking her to the edge of the table, he stripped her legs bare and lunged forward, stabbing into her heat with possessive force as she cried out in pleasure, her body accepting him. He slowly withdrew. His cock rested in her opening, not buried the way it had been, but still touching her, taunting her needy sex.

"Christian, please."

He loved when she begged, and he rewarded her, taking her hard, rocking the table and holding her thighs wide as he thrust quickly, demanding she take his full length.

"Yes," she cried, so supple and open to him. So willing and responsive.

She belonged to him. She brought him more pleasure than he'd ever dreamed possible. She healed him. She loved him. She claimed him as her mate. "I love you, Delilah."

"I love you, Christian." She pulled him down, demanding a kiss and he delivered.

The table skidded across the floor with every hard pump of his hips until it slammed into the adjacent wall. She lifted her arms, surrendering to his lust in such a beautiful show of trust and submission. His seed rushed into her as a roar exploded from deep within his chest and her climax echoed his own.

He collapsed forward, panting hard as his body twitched and his cock pulsed inside of her. "You're perfect," he rasped, pressing a kiss to her throat.

She sighed, her fingers dragging slowly down his spine. "How does your back feel?"

"Incredible." He stood, wincing when his body pulled out of hers. That was always the worst part. "How did you learn to do that?"

"I've been practicing with the animals."

"You healed me without blood."

"Your mother said it's a gift."

"My mother knows about this?"

"She watched me help the animals around the farm a few times, but you were there the first time it happened. Remember when I saved the bird in the woods? I've gotten better with it since I started feeding.

Guilt penetrated his pride. She'd discovered a gift and honed her skill without him even realizing. "I've been a bit preoccupied of late."

"It's okay."

"It's not. These firsts for you are important. I don't want to miss them."

She sat up. "You won't, Christian. It's not as if I was hiding this from you. It's just been a terrible week, and we're still figuring things out."

He considered the week before this one. "I haven't given you the welcome I'd hoped, little one. My expectations were so different from the reality. I'm sorry."

"Hey." She scooted off the table and looked up at him. "This is big shit." Her finger pressed over his lips. "And before you lecture me about swearing, maybe take a minute to appreciate that we're both here—together—in love, and taking the necessary steps to move forward."

He nodded. "You're right. This is…big shit."

She laughed. "That just sounds wrong coming from you." Lacing her fingers with his, she hopped off the table and righted her clothes. "Come on. Let's go empty my savings and figure out how I'm going to pay back my clients."

His grip tightened, halting her steps. "Wait. Why wouldn't you be able to pay them back?"

She shrugged. "I'm not what anyone would call financially flush."

He went to the den and rolled back the cover of his desk. "How much do you need?"

She eyed him suspiciously. "Are you serious?"

"Delilah, you're my mate. Whatever you need, I'll provide."

"But you're Amish."

He frowned. "I'm not sure I understand your implication."

"You guys don't have anything."

"We might not fit your English definition of affluence, but we have substantial wealth. Take a look." He handed her his ledger.

She glanced down. "I'm not going to take all your—*holy crap!*" Her eyes bulged. "Whose account is this?"

"Mine."

"Just yours?"

"Yes. Keep in mind I've been building it for generations under a proprietorship. I also have cash hidden throughout the house and about the yard."

She gaped at him. "You're a millionaire. How did you get all of this?"

"I was a cooper during the seventeen hundreds. I owned a market to sell my goods for a short time also."

"What's a cooper?"

"Someone who makes containers." He pointed to the pantry. "I made all of the jars, barrels, and buckets you see around the farm."

She laughed. "I thought you were just a farmer."

"Having a craft helps pass the time during the winters." He thought back to the times when the loneliness had become unbearable and he feared his calling would never come. "But now I have you."

She sprang forward and wreathed her arms around his neck, hugging him tight.

Startled by her response, he slowly closed his arms around her. "What brought this on?"

She sighed and pressed a kiss to his heart. "I'm just really grateful you found me."

A tentative smile teased his lips as his arms closed around her. "So am I, *pintura*. So am I."

When she pulled back, she had tears in her eyes. Dashing them away, she said, "Please don't think I'm some sort of a gold digger. I'm not. It's just that no one has ever offered to help me the way you just did. I feel like all the weight

I've been carrying on my own for the past few years, all the pressure and stress, just disappeared."

"I enjoy helping you."

She laughed. "I believe you. I just don't think you understand how much this actually means to me. It's like the boulder that's been living in my stomach for years just vanished. Thank you for that, Christian."

He dashed away a fallen tear. "Money is never something you'll have to cry over, *pintura*. *That* I can promise."

CHAPTER 27

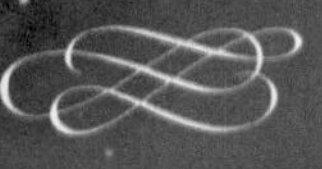

elilah never assumed traveling by foot could be so much fun, but as she leapt from trees and clung to the branches with unfathomable dexterity, her opinion changed. "Who knew I was outdoorsy?"

Christian dropped out of the sky as if from nowhere and landed stealthily beside her.

"Show off."

Unlike mortals, the older an immortal became, the more power and strength they developed.

She hip-checked him playfully. "I'll race you." Before he could answer, she bolted into the woods.

Seconds later he whisked past her.

She cupped her mouth and yelled, "You took the fun right out of it!"

He doubled back, adopting a leisurely pace

at her side and grinned at her. "You were trying to lose me?"

"Like that could ever happen."

He shot her a pointed look. "True."

"Do you guys ever play Manhunt on the farm?"

"Manhunt?"

"It's like Hide and Seek on steroids."

His gaze turned smoldering. "We play with our mates when we are not working."

She caught his drift, but kept walking, not wanting to get sidetracked. They were making good time. It was almost dawn and they had been walking for hours. Christian knew a route that kept them out of view and removed from traffic and civilization. He said they would be there by noon if they kept a decent speed.

"You know, if I were still human, I'd be limping by now. I have so many newfound abilities."

He chuckled. "I didn't realize walking was a skill you struggled to master."

"This isn't walking, Christian. Immortals are, like, ambulatory savants. Did you see how high I was jumping back there?" She laughed. "We would crush it in the Olympics."

"You'll discover there are many gifts we enjoy."

"I want to learn all of them." She glanced over her shoulder. A constant menagerie of small-pawed creatures scurried behind her like a train of blimps in the Macy's parade. "So, what do you think this Snow White power thing I have is all about?"

He lifted a low hung branch for her to duck under. "Perhaps they sense you're no threat because you won't eat them."

She smiled as several rabbits, a few chipmunks, and a bevy of deer trailed her. It was like Walt Disney's wet dream. "I think feeding helps. Your blood's like the best enhancement drug in the world. It's literally modifying my genetics. I feel so much more than I used to feel."

"You're handling the feedings much better now."

She shrugged. "I don't mind it. I sort of ... like it, I guess."

He gave her a knowing look. "You guess?"

He knew she loved it.

His blood was robust, flavorful, and potent, like doing a line of speed laced with X and the finest cut testosterone. It was addicting, but good for her and without any negative side effects. She could have told him all of that, but his ego was big enough, so she simply said, "You're a literal pain in the neck, so I feel justified biting you on occasion."

He took her hand, lacing their fingers together. "Whatever the reason, I'm glad. I enjoy sharing that intimacy with you."

She glanced up at him, her body instantly responding to the meaningful look in his eyes. He sent her a vision of them making love and she nudged him. "None of that or we'll never get there."

"You're right."

Christian was the sort of drop-dead gorgeous reserved for airbrushed photos online. Sometimes it was hard to believe he was real. That got her thinking of other beautiful men. "Is Brad Pitt a vampire?"

"Who?"

"Brad Pitt."

"I do not know this name."

That was a pity. How cool would it be if Christian were friends with someone like Brad? Maybe all the beautiful men were vampires. She thought about Tom Cruise and his role as Lestat. Clever casting? *I think not!* And what about Matt Damon? He was a hottie too.

"Are there vampires in Boston?" That was where Matt was from, right?

Christian frowned. "There are immortals on every continent, in every major city."

"Sounds like a credit card commercial. *They're everywhere you want to be...*" she laughed.

Christian's frown deepened. "Other immortals—especially males—are to be avoided. Their location should be of no concern to you."

"Relax. You're more than enough immortal male for me to handle. I'm all set." She once again admired his muscular physique, finding it hard to concentrate on anything else. Trying to distract her filthy thoughts, she asked him random questions that had piled up in her head over the past two weeks. "Can you teach me some super-human tricks?"

"What would you like to learn?"

She thought about shows like *Bewitched* and *I Dream of Genie*. "Can you teach me how to move objects with my mind?"

He considered her request then stopped walking. "Find something small. A rock or a twig."

She turned and the animals dispersed. Reaching down, she scattered some wet leaves and dirt and dug up a rock that fit nicely in her palm. "Like this?"

"Perfect." He placed it on a large flat boulder a few feet away. "Try to move it."

She looked at the rock and then back at him. "How?"

"You simply…command it with your mind."

She squatted and focused on the small rock. Speckles of moonlight wobbled through the trees as she leaned in, angling her stare at the stone as it sat perfectly still.

Move.

It didn't budge.

Mooooooooooove.

Nothing.

Open sesame. Move? Go-rock-go! Rock, get the steppin'! Mooooooooove!

Nothing happened. She turned to Christian. "Nothing's happening."

"You're being silly. Look at it, and push with your mind."

She stared at the rock again and imagined a

little version of herself pushing the stone with all her might. It didn't even wobble. She huffed and turned back to Christian. "I think it's broken."

"Watch me." He turned his stare to the stone, and it scooted about six inches to the right.

"How did you do that?"

He shrugged. "Exactly as I told you. I simply pushed with my mind."

She scowled at him and then at the stupid rock. Taking a deep breath, she tried to push the damn thing again. It trembled and shifted an inch. She gasped and spun to Christian, who instantly looked away. "*You* did that!"

His guilty expression gave him away.

"Christian! I'm never going to be good at this stuff if you do it for me."

"It's a silly trick, Delilah, and exactly why God gave us hands. You'll eventually learn everything."

They rotated between walking and running, but her favorite was when they jumped in and out of the trees. Whenever they slowed their pace, they talked. Usually about silly questions that crossed her mind, but Christian was always patient and amused by her endless curiosity.

"Can you run faster than a speeding bullet?"

"How am I to know how fast a bullet travels?"

"How about a train?"

"I've never measured my speed. Is it not enough to say we're fast?"

"But *how* fast?"

"Why are you so interested in such things?"

"Why are you so uninterested? Don't you think it's neat?"

He considered her question for a moment. "It is what I always have been. Do you think it is neat that your hair grows or that you can walk on two feet?"

She jumped over a downed log and landed with amazing agility. "Now, I do. I'm like super-dexterous Barbie." She did a cartwheel that ended with a flip. "*Woo-hoo!* Come on, Ken!"

"What is Ken?"

By dawn she was ready to rest. They crossed several state lines, and she wasn't exactly sure how many miles they traveled. "How much longer?"

"We should be there by the time the sun is directly overhead."

"That tells me nothing."

"About five more hours."

Good thing they were built for endurance.

She spent the next mile observing him, taking in every detail from the fullness of his lower lip to the sureness of his steps. Christian was unfairly beautiful and she could admire his lean, muscular body for days.

"Delilah."

"Huh?"

"Your filthy thoughts will only slow us down."

"Why?" She turned, skipping alongside of

him at a silly trot. "Do they make you want to do dirty things to me?"

His nostrils flared and his eyes dilated. Those silver irises bore into her as if marking her with his gaze alone. "Yes." He glanced back at the animals trailing them. "Hunger can be confusing around so many mortals. We should stop for a bit to feed."

By feed, he meant fuck. That was probably wise.

She stopped skipping and knelt, trying to entice the animals close enough so she could pet them. Most of them scurried whenever Christian turned, probably because he was a dangerous predator, but some of the braver ones ventured close to her and curiously sniffed her fingers.

"Look, Christian," she whispered as a small squirrel came right to her extended hand. She wasn't compelling them with any effort of her own—as if she even knew how to do that. She simply existed, and they wanted to come to her.

"I should feed as well," he said

She hoped he would. It had been days since he took her vein, and she missed sharing that intimate act with him. When he remained still, she glanced up at him, but he was looking at the animals.

A cold dread settled in her stomach. "No, Christian. You can't feed from them."

"In order for you to feed I need to replenish my blood. It's how it works."

"You can't. They trust me."

His gaze moved to the larger creatures in the distance, settling on the three doe and a fawn. "I wouldn't hurt them. I make sure they feel nothing, not even fear."

She understood he fed from the animals on the farm, but this seemed more barbaric, namely because she was present for it. The logical part of her mind reminded her this was more humane than shopping for meat at the grocery store. At least when he fed no animals died. Her romantic heart still didn't like the idea.

"Fine." She stood. "But I'm walking. You can catch them yourself."

"Don't go too far."

Shaking her head, she strolled in the direction they had been moving. "Don't choke on a deer tick."

When they finally reached her apartment, it was much later than noon. After Christian fed, he insisted on feeding her and that led to other things, which ended up delaying them for several hours. The novelty of walking had worn off by the time they reached her neighborhood.

The sight of her apartment building restored a sense of self she'd almost forgotten. A pile of bills and weekly sales papers scattered outside of her door reminding her how long she'd been away.

She patted her pockets and looked up at Christian. "Um, I don't have my key."

He looked at the door and held out his palm. The latch clicked and the door popped open.

She gaped at the open door. "See! That's the sort of Harry Potter stuff I should be learning."

Pressing open the door to her home, she anticipated familiar smells but recoiled at the stench of stale air and sour God knows what. The kitchen reeked. A bowl of fruit on the counter had rotted to mush, and tiny fruit flies had claimed it as their utopia.

She carried it to the trash and gagged when she dumped it inside. "Sorry. I didn't have a chance to properly clean before my last kidnapping. In the future, a little notice would give me some time to prepare." She tied up the trash bag and tossed it into the hall. "I'll deal with that later." Opening the fridge, she found nothing that appealed. "I'm gonna order a pizza."

Christian glanced around. He picked up a bottle of nail polish and read the label. "You have so many possessions."

She self-consciously bit her lip. "I'm actually, um, pretty poor—by American standards anyway."

He frowned, taking in the mismatched furniture and the many eclectic decorations that cluttered the space. He cocked his head at her Salvador Dali reproductions. She supposed it was a far cry from the Amish simplicity he was used to.

Taking his hand, she led him to the sofa. "Why don't you relax and watch TV while I shower?" She handed him the remote. "If the pizza guy comes, there's some money in the vase on the counter."

She snatched some clothes off the pile on the coffee table and dashed into the bedroom. The space felt foreign to her as if it belonged to someone else. Christian was right. She had a lot of crap. But none of it really held any true value in her heart.

Hot water, however, she appreciated very much. The moment she turned on the spigot and steam billowed into the air, she laughed. Who knew plumbing could be such a source of joy?

She gasped at the sight of her hair products. "Hello, my loves!" It had been weeks since she washed her hair with more than oils and lard.

Bathing had never felt like such a luxury.

When the water cooled, she was ready to get out. She wiped away the steam on the mirror and frowned at her reflection. Her skin was re-generating faster now that she was feeding reg-ularly. Every day her tattoos faded a bit more. She wondered how long it would take until they were all gone.

Funny, so many people talked about how regrettable tattoos were. The only regret she held was the sense of loss she felt at seeing them disappear.

Not wanting to get in a dreary mood, she dressed in her favorite cozy gear and went to see what Christian was doing. A closed box of pizza rested in front of him on the coffee table.

"Did you eat?"

He shook his head.

She glanced at the dark television. "Are you okay?"

He looked at her and promised, "I'll build you a water heater as soon as we return."

He'd clearly been listening to her thoughts while she bathed. She must have sounded like an absolute fool making such a fuss over such a simple amenity as hot water.

"That's very sweet, Christian, and I'm not going to turn your offer down." She dropped beside him on the sofa. "But don't stress over that stuff. I love you. With or without a self-heating shower." When he met her stare, she mumbled out of the corner of her mouth, "A little more *with* than *without*, but still, I love you either way." She kissed him on the cheek. "Let's eat."

Opening the box, she handed him a slice. Popping the string of cheese that fell into a warm blob onto the paper into her mouth, she hummed, "So good." She missed pizza.

Christian took a small bite. His brows rose as he chewed. "It is good."

"Yeah, this place is better than the one I used to order from."

"What did you say it was?"

She stilled. "Christian, it's pizza. Haven't you ever had pizza before?"

He shook his head and took another bite. "It's *abbeditlich.*"

"Abbeditlich?"

"Appetizing."

"Oh. Right." She finished her slice and

tossed the crust in the box, grabbing another piece. "Will you teach me Pennsylvania Dutch?"

"I'll teach you anything you want to learn." He looked at her abandoned crust. "You don't eat that part?"

She shrugged. "You can, but the cheesy part's better."

He took a bite of his crust, chewed it, then tossed it in the box next to hers.

"Do you want to watch a movie?" She glanced at the television wondering if he had a hard time navigating the remote. "We could watch *Dracula*."

His mouth tightened. "*Dracula* is fiction."

She laughed. "We can critique it. Or we could watch *Witness*. You might like that."

"What is *Witness*?"

"A movie about people hiding from criminals on an Amish farm."

"I wouldn't know. I've never watched a television."

"Ever?"

"No."

"Oh, my gosh! Do you have any idea how much good stuff you've missed? *The Office, Stranger Things, Survivor, Sopranos, Keeping Up With The Kardashians*!" She nestled close to him and got comfortable. "Finally, I get to pop one of your cherries."

Lifting the remote, she turned on the TV and went straight to the menu of streaming channels. Christian sat stiffly as he worked his way around the pizza.

"Christian, you can sit back, you know. It's a sofa, not an electric chair." He looked at how she was sitting and scooted back.

She wanted to give him the full 'English' experience.

"This is what's called reality TV. People apply to be on a show, and they live in a house where cameras follow them around non-stop. There's no privacy and plenty of drama."

"Do they not feel violated?"

She shrugged. "They sign up for it. Watch. This is a good one. Those two fight."

He frowned. "You've watched this before."

"Yeah. These are old episodes."

A catfight broke out on screen and he scowled. "You find this entertaining?"

"Extremely."

She snuggled into his side and reveled in the realness of the moment. She'd never done something so normal with him or been so thrilled to simply *Netflix and chill.*

When the show ended on a cliffhanger, he looked at her expectantly. "Is there more?"

She laughed. "See? You're already addicted."

"I feel less intelligent since sitting here, but now I feel pressured to know what Kourtney is going to do."

"You'll get sucked in for days. There are so many better options." She picked up the remote and flicked through the channels, stopping when she saw a movie on Horror Net. "You might like this."

The credits opened with a quick montage of

a house in the woods. Eerie music played as a woman innocently prepared dinner. Then the scene changed. A deranged serial killer chased a young girl through a graveyard. She screamed and tripped. The killer caught up to her and broke her neck, silencing her screams.

Christian bolted to his feet and hissed, scaring a real scream out of Delilah and a reflexive, *"What the fuck?"*

He looked at the television, but it was back on the woman making supper. "The girl…"

"It's just a movie, Christian." She shut it off. "Mental note, no Horror Net for you."

He lowered to the sofa and retracted his claws. "Perhaps we should sleep. Tomorrow's going to be a long day."

She sensed all of this modern technology was wearing him out. "Okay."

She shut off the television and carried the empty box of pizza to the kitchen. At least he liked that.

A wave of self-consciousness hit her when she led him to her room. Christian had acre upon acre of beautiful countryside to call his own, and she had an eight-by-eight room with a bed and a dresser cramped up against a wall.

She flattened out the worn coverlet and fluffed a pillow that had mascara and hair dye stains on the case. "So, this is my room."

He looked down at the small platform bed. She couldn't imagine what he was thinking and she honestly didn't want to know. As much as she'd begged to come home, now that she was here she was anxious to leave.

This place now felt like a holding spot, a purgatory that occupied her before her life officially found meaning, sort of like a warming station under hot lights in the back of a restaurant. Christian's life was the three-star dining experience on the other side. The real deal.

She glanced up at him, noting the displeased expression on his face and the tight set of his jaw. He hated it. "We can leave first thing in the—"

"Who was he?"

She paused. "Um, what?"

His hard stare hadn't lifted from the bed. "Someone else has been in this room. A male. Who?"

"No one's—"

"Delilah, I smell him."

What looked like judgment a moment ago now revealed itself as heartbreak. She had to think back to the last time she had company. "No one's been in here for months." She'd washed the sheets twenty times since then.

His hands balled into fists at his side. "Then you don't deny it."

"No. Why would I—Oh, Christian, you didn't think..." This was awkward. "You know I wasn't a virgin when we met, right?"

The hard muscle of his jaw ticked. "I just assumed..."

If it was possible, she became more self-conscious. "Maybe we should sleep on the couch—"

"Did you love him?"

She laughed, and his confused stare snapped to her. This wasn't a laughing matter to him, so she sobered. "No, I didn't love him. I told you, I've never loved anyone. You were…" She should have never brought him here. "You're the only person I've ever said those words to."

She didn't think it was possible, but she missed the farm. The farm felt safe. There was no pressure there, and she could unravel all the confusing feelings inside of her at her own pace. Here, she felt pressure. Pressure to answer for her life. Pressure to own her mistakes. Pressure to be a specific version of herself the world expected. But when it was just her and Christian, she only needed to be herself, and he accepted her. *All* of her. For that, she loved him in a way she never loved anyone.

But what if this place showed him things he didn't want to see and his opinion of her lowered? She couldn't handle the thought, didn't want him to think less of her. But this was her life and it hadn't started the day he walked into her world. She had a past and prior boyfriends. She would never be some innocent virgin bride.

Lowering her head, she said, "I don't know what you want me to say."

"Why haven't I found this male in your memories?"

She scoffed. "Because he wasn't memorable.

Sometimes people just have meaningless sex to pass the time and break up the monotony. I'm not going to apologize for dating."

He frowned. "Apologize?"

"Isn't that what you want?" He was making her really self-conscious.

"I'm the one who owes you an apology. If I had found you sooner… If I had been more open in prayer, perhaps… Or possibly—"

"Stop." She wasn't going to break it to him that he would have had to have shown up when she was seventeen if he wanted a virgin. "Let's not do the thing where we feel bad about things in the past we can't change. Tomorrow, this room isn't even going to matter. You and me, that's what matters. Us."

His frown deepened and she sensed this moment was about more than a bed to him. "I want to give you the comforts you love, Delilah. Pizza, television… You have so much here."

"I have nothing here, Christian. All that stuff, it's crap from yard sales and discount stores. None of it holds any real value. *You* are what I value." In that moment it became so clear to her. She knew exactly where she wanted to be. "You're my home."

"It won't bring you sorrow to leave this place?"

She looked around. The connection she'd expected wasn't in this room or the other rooms. As a matter of fact, after the last two weeks, she felt more disconnected than ever from this place. It was like she'd graduated and moved on. None of her old belongings fit her future anymore.

"I think I've outgrown my life here."

She scanned her worthless furniture and the cheap jewelry falling out of the shoebox on the dresser. None of it mattered if she didn't have him. Even her clothes, which had been an outlet of self-expression for her in so many ways, expressing someone she used to be.

Looking down at her arms where her tattoos had faded, she considered why she'd chosen each one. Maybe some were indications of who she was and how she wanted to be seen, how she wanted others to know she was complicated, so she'd feel validated when others misunderstood her. Maybe they made her interesting when deep down she'd been scared and alone and terrified the world would find her too boring to love.

But she wasn't alone anymore. Nor was she scared.

She laced her fingers in his. "You see the real me, Christian. No one has ever gotten as close to me. You've seen how my mind works and overheard my secrets and fears, yet you're still here. It's…incredible. No one has ever accepted me—in all my messy, broken entirety—as completely as you have. I don't have to hide parts of myself away from you, because I know you'll love me regardless of what you find."

Even now, she could feel him present in her mind, sending gentle waves of comfort and support to her as she worked through all of these confusing revelations. He was always present. A quiet support. Available if she should need anything at all.

She lifted an old corset from a partially opened drawer. "All of this… It's all artificial. A distraction so they never look too deeply and see all the things I want to hide." She dropped the corset and held his large hand in two of hers, facing him. "You forced your way past my insecurities and saw all my jagged edges. I can't hide from you, and I don't need to. You love and protect me regardless of my shortcomings because you see what's at the heart of me. You love me for my soul."

He pulled her close and hugged her. "I do love you, *pintura*. Every exquisitely complicated part of you." His head kissed her hair. "I love your softness, your stubborn bullheadedness, the chaotic wonderment that flows from your mind then escapes your unfiltered, filthy mouth. I love every part of you—so much so it frightens me. You're a constant surprise and I'm… I fear I won't be enough for a female as remarkable as you."

"Oh, Christian, you're like the nicest, most patient guy in existence—well, you did kidnap me—but I'm—" *Oh God,* was she actually saying this? "I'm glad you did. I finally feel like I have purpose. Like I'm going to make it. For once, I don't feel like a failure or like I'm letting people down."

He pulled her close and kissed her. "You could never disappoint me, Delilah. We are one.

Our future is whatever we choose to make it —together."

Her arms cinched around his waist and she hugged him tight, her worries drifting away as he encircled her with pure, invigorating acceptance. "And that's why I love you."

"I love you too." He once again kissed the top of her head. "I would like the name and address of the man who—"

"Not a chance." She released him and pulled back the covers. "But if we're making requests, I have one."

He followed her into the bed. "Tell me."

She climbed into bed, instantly finding it less comfortable than his big overstuffed mattress on the farm. "I want modern shower products."

He laughed and lay beside her. "*That* I'm sure I can manage."

She stretched to kiss his cheek. "Thank you, Christian. For everything."

He rolled to his side and studied her. She held his stare, curious of what he was thinking, but preferring to keep some mystery alive. She didn't need to nose around in his thoughts. His presence in hers was enough to reassure her that he was there.

"Would you marry me if I asked?"

She balked. There was mystery and then there was knock-her-over-with-a-feather-shock. "Are you actually asking?"

"Would you say yes if I did?"

She could have told him that wasn't how

guys propose or that he should at least get down on one knee, but she didn't need any of that. Smiling like a smitten school girl who was just asked to the prom by the hottest hottie in school, she cupped his jaw and kissed him. "I think you would be an incredible husband, Christian. Yes, I would say yes if you asked me to marry you."

Satisfied, he rolled to his back and grinned. "Then we will be married as soon as we return to Lancaster."

She laughed. "Thanks for making that life-altering decision for me."

"Is that not what you want? You said—"

"Forget it." She rolled to face the wall. "That actually makes perfect sense. Why start asking for permission now?"

"Delilah—"

"Goodnight, Christian."

Several minutes passed until, finally, he placed a hand on her back and softly asked, "Delilah, will you honor me by sharing vows in front of our friends and being my wife?"

She grinned, hiding her smirk under the blankets as a warm, gooey feeling filled her heart. She left him hanging for a whole minute. "Can I have a vodka luge at the wedding?"

"I don't know what a vodka luge is, but I promise to arrange one if that's what you need."

Flipping over, she kissed him hard on the mouth and laughed with giddy delight. "Then I'll marry you."

He took over the kiss, and she softened beneath him, letting the moment roll over her as she fully processed what this meant for them. Forever. He was asking permission to spend his life by her side. She finally got to choose and she chose to spend an eternity with him.

"You make me very happy, *pintura.*"

She arched beneath him, pulling him back to her lips and whispered, "You make me happy, too."

CHAPTER 28

Christian awoke in an empty bed in an unfamiliar room with the lingering fragrance of his mate and pungent traces of another male. He detected Delilah close by as he fanned out his senses, finding unprecedented comfort in her nearness.

"This afternoon would be fine," she said softly from the other room.

He sprang to his feet, his mind scanning the apartment. He frowned. He didn't sense anyone else in the home. Pulling on his pants, he entered the main room and found Delilah sitting on a chair with a telephone to her ear, but he had destroyed her phone the night they met.

She clicked a pen in her hand and jotted a note on a pad of paper. When she saw him, she smiled. "Yes, I'll be there at four. And, again, I'm so sorry for the inconvenience."

"Perfect." A male voice purred from the receiver. Christian's claws lengthened. "I'll see you then, Ms. Starling."

"Sounds good." She sighed and hung up the phone. "That was my big client. He said he could meet us at four. I feel bad. He wanted a lot of work and would have paid me a lot of money to do it."

Christian remained silent. He didn't like her speaking to other males, but this was why they were here, so she could conclude any open matters and they could begin living their life.

She stood and her appearance stole his breath. The cinched waist of her dress defined every feminine curve and her shoulders were exposed. Her rounded breasts rested pertly above a red patent leather belt that matched her sharp, pointed heels.

She looked so…English. His gaze dropped to the device in her hand. "You found a telephone."

She glanced at the cell. "It's an old one. I needed to call the phone company to get all my contacts back since *someone* stole my last one." She rose on her toes and pressed a kiss to his jaw. "How did you sleep? Was the bed okay?"

He frowned, recalling how he'd struggled to relax with the constant city in motion below. He'd slept later than usual. This place was muddling his senses. "My sleep was adequate."

"Good." She appeared energized as she moved about the home. "I was thinking, could we possibly rent a moving truck to take some of my stuff home? I know it's mostly worthless, but there are a few things I'd like to keep. The rest can go to Good Will or into storage. I haven't figured out what to do with my studio equipment, but it doesn't make much sense to keep it. I mean, who ever heard of a tattoo artist with no tattoos?"

Whenever she brought up her tattoos, sorrow flared from her. He wished there was a way for her to keep her markings, but he had no control over such things. "Whatever you need, I'll take care of it."

She smiled sweetly. "Thank you." She tossed something called Everything But The Bagel Seasoning into a box. "Right now, I need to eat. Do you want to grab some fast food for breakfast and then we can hit the truck rental place?"

He hadn't expected her to be in such a hurry to get back, but he was also eager to return home. The world off the farm reeked of deceit and immoral temptation. He wanted his mate safe and protected, two things he could provide much easier on the farm. "Whatever you need."

While her spirits were high at the moment, he suspected the day would be a difficult one. Sooner or later, she'd recognize the finality of her choice. Seeing her life, her belongings, and the modern amenities she owned filled him with a strange sense of regret and worry. What if she missed those things and he was not an equal replacement for so many luxuries?

She stilled from packing spices into the box. "Why do you look like that?"

"Pardon?" He glanced back at her, wondering if he missed something.

"You just got the saddest look on your face."

He blanked his expression, evicting all worries from his mind. "It's nothing. I was just thinking."

"Of?"

"Nothing." He turned back to the bedroom. "I'll dress and we can see to your needs."

"Christian, wait." She followed him Into the sitting area. "What's going on?"

He hesitated then admitted, "Are you positive you can give all of this up?"

Her eyes moved from side to side, taking in her apartment. She scoffed. "*This*? You do realize I live in squalor, right? Like, here's poor." She flattened her hand so her palm faced the floor and held it in front of her face. "Then here's dirt poor." She lowered her flat palm to her midsection. "And I live about five stories below that."

"Your technology—"

"There are libraries and other ways around that. I mean, I'm not going back to be your hostage. I'm going to be your wife. We can figure that stuff out. I just want to be with you."

Her lack of opposition was a strange and welcome change. He nodded and his worries abated. "You'll be my wife."

"Yeah." She smiled. "And you'll be my husband. Wow. That sounds so weird." She laughed to herself and pecked a kiss on his jaw.

To his ears, it sounded perfect.

CHRISTIAN WATCHED Delilah dress a salad with a packet of sludge that poured from a small pouch. She tore open a clear wrapper with her teeth and revealed an oddly formed fork in the shape of a spoon.

"Are you going to eat?" She tilted her chin toward the hot parcel he held.

He unwrapped the waxy paper and found a greasy sandwich. It looked like a patty of sausage but smelled like a pancake. Sauces and orange cheese seeped from the sides. He sniffed the strange bread that did not smell like anything they baked on the farm. Hesitantly, he took a bite.

Flavor burst in his mouth and he drew back, surprised to discover such a salty-sweet combination inside. "It is good." He chewed, further unwrapping the paper for a larger bite.

"I'm lovin' it," Delilah sang, stabbing her fork into her salad. "Try your shake." She plugged the cups with two fat straws and slid his forward. "I'm shocked the machine was working for once."

Swallowing another bite of greasy meat, sauce, and cheese, he leaned forward and sucked on the straw. The veins behind his eyes pulsed as the chilled contents moved like sludge. "I can't get any into my mouth."

"Keep sucking." She chuckled. "That's what he said."

Christian frowned. "Who?"

"It's from *The Office*."

"What office?"

"It's a sitcom. A television show." She smiled, about to say more, then the excitement in her eyes faded. "Never mind. We're never going to watch it."

He sensed the day was becoming more overwhelming for her as she relinquished more of her modern amenities. "Delilah, tell me."

"I can't. There's too many episodes to explain. Too many seasons." She frowned and looked down at her salad, appearing not to *love it* as much as she had a moment ago. "Too many shows."

He didn't understand her attachment to television. Mortals were mentally invested in the lives of characters in a way he couldn't comprehend. But this was important to her. These memories made her laugh and he didn't want her to lose that joy. "We will watch the shows you love."

"How?"

"We have an eternity ahead of us, *pintura*. We'll visit places with televisions and you can show me all the episodes. And then, we can laugh together at the jokes."

She looked up at him in surprise. "You mean, we could visit hotels or Airbnbs?"

He nodded. "I don't see why we couldn't travel off the farm on occasion."

She smiled and stood, leaning across the table to plant a grateful kiss on his lips. "I love that idea, Christian!"

He grinned, pleased they found yet another compromise. Taking another sip, a burst of sweet, chilled strawberry cream filled his mouth, and his eyes widened. Some things were worth the extra effort.

After lunch they walked to an establishment that rented moving trucks. Delilah had spent the morning packing up her apartment, sorting items into piles she called *keep* and *toss*. Her electrical possessions would not be of any use on the farm, and she had quite a few, so they would be donated.

They entered a small office building located at the front of a large lot that had various-sized vehicles and trailers. The counter was unattended. Delilah rang a small bell, and a woman appeared from the room in the back.

"Can I help you?"

His attention instantly pulled to his mate when she tensed at his side.

"Oh, my God," the woman said, looking at Delilah. "Morticia? Is that you? Holy crap. I thought you ran away or died or something when you dropped out. What happened to you?"

He frowned as a wave of discomfort radiated from his mate. Who was this woman? And why was she upsetting Delilah? He scanned the area for danger, but sensed no immediate threat.

"We are here to rent a vehicle," he said, taking over the situation. Delilah squeezed his hand in an unbreakable grip.

The woman looked up at him and smiled. "Oh. Yes. Of course." She turned her attention to the computer screen. Her lashes fluttered as she twirled her hair around a finger with a claw-like nail painted in bright pink polish. "What size were you looking for?"

"The largest available." He didn't want Delilah to feel limited in any way.

"Let me see what we have on the lot that isn't reserved. This is for today?"

"Yes."

While the woman checked their inventory, he pressed deeper into his mate's memories. Visions of a younger version of the woman at the desk were at the forefront of Delilah's mind. He sensed his mate in her youth as the other female taunted her.

"What's wrong, Morticia? No one wants to go to prom with a freak show?" The girl laughed cruelly, and Christian felt how deeply her words wounded his mate.

Though Delilah was only a young female in the vision, she still had a fire about her. *"Bite me, Meghan."*

Christian's eyes moved to the nameplate on the desk. The woman's name was in fact Meghan.

The memory shifted to another one. This time in Delilah's childhood home. *"Please!"* she begged. *"Everyone else is going."*

A wrinkled female Delilah recognized as a maternal figure named Nanna, looked at her and said, "I don't have fifty dollars for your ticket, Delilah.

Maybe if you didn't dye your hair every color of the rainbow and wear all that black makeup, you could have found a date to treat you. Boys don't want to date girls who look like you."

Shame and sharp heartache bit into him. He sifted through her memories, to her experience with the girl named Meghan.

The memory of the bullying blonde returned. *"It's better this way anyway. Prom's a classy affair. No trash allowed."*

"You're lucky I don't steal your date."

Young Meghan scoffed. "Yeah, right. Joey wouldn't even look twice at you. No hot guy would. Maybe try the burnouts and losers."

Christian saw enough. His eyes narrowed on the woman behind the counter. She was nothing particularly special to look at, and now, knowing that she was unkind as well, he found her grotesque.

He glanced at Delilah, who stood oddly silent at his side. It bothered him that this human could trigger his feisty mate into silence.

"Did I ever tell you about the first time I saw you," he asked softly but kept his words intentionally clear for the other woman to hear. "You were sitting next to that man at the bar. He wanted you. They all did. You were the most beautiful female there."

The clicking of computer keys slowed as Meghan glanced up from her computer and frowned. He kept his stare on Delilah. "I'll never forget how your eyes shined when you looked up at me that first time. I knew, in that moment, my heart was gone."

She looked up at him now, much the same way as she had done then.

"I was enchanted by every part of you." He traced a finger along the line of her jaw, sliding his hand under her hair, his thumb lightly caressing the soft spot where her pulse raced. I've seen many fine things in my life, Delilah, but nothing ever as beautiful as you. You were perfect."

Her cheeks flushed pink and she smiled up at him. The sorrow that emanated from her moments ago was replaced with great pride and gratitude.

"I needed to have you," he confessed, leaning closer but keeping his words clear. "The first time I heard your voice, my body literally burned for you. I thought, if I could just make her love me, if I could just teach her to trust me, I would gladly take care of her every need for the rest of my life." He looked into her eyes, their lips a mere kiss apart. "And now you're going to be my wife."

Tears quivered in her eyes. She didn't look at the other woman. They didn't need to. Jealousy had an unmistakable sour stench, and Meghan was swimming in it.

"I love you," Delilah whispered, and he grinned, closing the distance to kiss her. She drew in a fortifying breath and turned to the woman at the counter. "My name's Delilah, not Morticia. And I didn't run away or die. I moved on, to get away from prissy little bitches like you." She glanced up at the water-marked ceiling and the particle board walls. "But it looks like you're doing great. How about that rental?"

The woman's expression fell as she dropped her gaze. "We were kids. You know how it is in high school—"

"Not really. You and I had different experiences. I just wanted to peacefully get through my day, and you wanted to make sure that didn't happen, all while getting banged by half the varsity team. That must have been exhausting for you."

She scoffed and glanced up at Christian, but Delilah stepped in front of him.

"Don't look at him. Just get us the keys and whatever paperwork we need to sign. Then you can go back to roasting in this box of an office as you finish your shitty burrito in the back to whatever pathetic soap opera you're watching while wishing your life had turned out differently."

He didn't comment on her language because, in this case, such profanity seemed justified and appropriate.

When he pulled out several hundred dollar bills Meghan gaped. "We don't accept cash."

"Cash will be fine," he said, compelling her to take the money. "Find us keys."

As soon as they left the stuffy office, Delilah squeaked and bounced by his side. "Holy crap, that was incredible! Did you see how jealous she was? I could literally smell her envy."

He smiled, glad to see the woman had not upset her for more than a minute or two. "What is prom?"

"It's a dance. Girls wear pretty gowns and get their hair done, and the guys wear tuxedos. It's sort of a rite of passage that comes at the end of senior year."

"You did not attend?"

"No. We were dirt poor and my grandparents couldn't swing it. I dropped out anyway, so it doesn't matter."

But it did matter to her. "We will have prom."

She laughed. "It's sort of a teenage thing. I'm over it. Besides, we're going to have a wedding. That's better. Oh, this is us." She pointed to a large truck in spot 347.

When they reached her studio, there was much to do. Christian stripped the artwork off the walls while Delilah wrapped and boxed her equipment. She said she could visit the local library in Lancaster and sell the items online. The plan filled her with a sense of purpose, and money seemed to motivate her, so he didn't see the harm.

"Christian, can you come here?"

He went to the back room and stilled at the sight of the chair where he first took her. His blood instantly heated as he scented her desire. "What do you need?"

She bit her lip and grinned. "I was thinking,

before I pack all this stuff, we should have a little fun."

He read her thoughts and chuckled. "You want to use that gun on me?"

"It's only a piercing gun. Or..." She lifted a plastic package with several sharp silver needles inside. "You said the sterling silver stuff was a myth, right? How about we pretty up your nipples?"

He thought about the many things he asked of her. "This is something you want?"

"I think it's hot."

That was all she had to say. He removed his shirt and sat back in the chair.

Delilah unpackaged a needle and selected a medium gauge barbell. Once she had everything spread out on a metal tray, she stepped close to the chair. "Ready?"

His gaze never left her face as he nodded. The chair lowered with a low hum as she pressed her foot into a pedal on the floor.

Leaning over the leather arm, she sucked his flat nipple into her mouth. He moaned and arched as she teased the tip into a tight point. Standing back, she admired her work.

"This is going to look so sexy on you." She lifted a small clamp and the long needle.

"You don't use the gun?"

"Not for these guys." She used a pen to mark two dots on his skin then clamped the tip of his nipple and then pulled. "Stay still."

Christian breathed heavily as the needle pressed into his skin. His claws ripped into the arms of the chair when the tip punctured his flesh. Breath hissed through his fangs. She worked quickly, pressing the needle and barbell through the small hole.

She screwed on the ball and admired her work. "That's one."

She dragged a finger down his hard stomach and his muscles twitched. His cock lengthened. Despite the lingering pinch of pain, he liked her attention on him like this.

Leaning over him again, she sucked on his other nipple and repeated the process. When she was finished, he was rock hard, the strong musk of his arousal filling the room and triggering his mate's. She placed the needle on the silver tray and gave his nipple a flick.

Christian's hand shot out and gripped her wrist, yanking her onto his lap. "Now you're mine."

She moaned just as the bell from the front door tinkled.

"That's my client," she whispered, scraping a sharp claw along his chest.

The scent of her arousal filled his head, and he resented the interruption. "Pay him and send him away."

She hopped off his lap and smoothed her dress into place. "I'll be back in a minute."

He caught her hand. "Be quick."

She glanced at the bulge in his pants, pressed a kiss to his lips then rushed from the room. The moment the door opened, he realized his mistake.

"Mr. Maddox. Thanks for coming in so quickly."

Christian sprang from the chair, sending the silver tray clattering against the wall. He bolted to the front of the store and lunged when he saw the immortal male holding his mate.

"Christian—"

His back slammed into the wall, shattering the glass displays as her scream was cut short. The immortal held her by the throat, jerking her off her feet.

"Move and I'll snap her neck."

Christian stilled, despite the compulsion holding him down. Delilah's eyes watered and her legs kicked. "Let her go."

"I think not." He turned his face to Delilah and pressed his nose into her hair. "She's fresh. I can always smell them right before they're ready to be claimed, but nothing holds more of a challenge than a freshly bonded female. Yours?"

Christian seethed and bared his fangs. "I'll kill you."

The immortal laughed. "You're no threat to me, boy. By my calculations, you're still half a decade shy of three centuries old. You're still wet behind the ears."

Christian scowled, struggling to stand to no avail. Delilah's panic was sapping his strength as he tried in vain to gentle her. *Stay calm, pintura.*

Hysteria poured from her thoughts as she struggled to breathe. *Christian, what's happening?*

"You're choking her!"

The male glanced dispassionately at Delilah, then dropped her to the floor. She gasped and coughed. Before she could run, the male fisted her hair and yanked her back. "You don't know who I am, do you?"

She reached for a shard of glass and gasped when the male kicked it away. She fell forward to her hands and knees and he stepped on her fingers, crushing them into the shards on the floor. Delilah whimpered, and Christian struggled to break free of the forces holding him down.

"I won't hesitate to take your fingers, girl."

He's reading your mind, pintura. Be careful of your thoughts. Don't act hastily.

The male jerked Delilah to her feet, and she screamed. Christian growled and snapped, "What do you want?"

The male closed his eyes and sniffed Delilah's throat. Christian's claws elongated and his eyes dilated. He fought the forces that held him down, but the male was much older, his strength and control impenetrable

"I want what's in her blood." The studio light glinted against his long fangs, another marking of an aged immortal. Delilah whimpered, her tear-filled eyes watching Christian, and the male moved her hair to whisper in her ear, "You smell of a girl I once knew." His jaw opened—

"No!" Christian bolted forward only to be hurled back, his body imprinting in the wall

deep enough that the wooden studs broke his fall. Delilah screamed and Christian roared.

The male bit into her throat, tearing open her delicate skin and gripping her roughly as he fed. A ballistic rage took over Christian. The glass in the front windows exploded onto the street and the bulbs in the overhead lights shattered. The walls shook and furniture vibrated as he seethed with uncontainable fury.

"Get off of her!"

The male drew back, jaw open, Delilah's blood coating his sharp fangs and tongue. His eyes rolled closed as he sighed. "There it is. I can taste her in your blood." His eyes snapped to Christian and flashed, his pupils elongated like black diamonds. "What a curious turn of events."

He sensed her intentions too late. *No, Delilah!*

She bit down on the male's hand. The immortal roared and yanked her by the hair, hard enough to rip several strands from her scalp.

"Bitch!" The male jerked her head hard, snapping her neck and her body went limp.

Christian snarled, on his feet, fighting the compulsion that held him to the wall. *"I'll end you!"*

The male hoisted Delilah's limp body over his shoulder and watched him with sinister disregard as he struggled. "You're weak, because a female raised you. It would have been merciful to drown you at birth. Believe me, I would have tried had I had the chance."

Christian stilled. A shiver of disbelief thrummed through him before the truth rocked him to the core. The set of the male's eyes and the cowlick of his hair reminded Christian of himself. He recalled Delilah's greeting. *Maddox.* As in Cerberus Maddox. This male was his sire.

His blood chilled. Delilah was full of Christian's blood which was replete with his mother's unique plasma. "My mother…"

"I plan to hunt her, then I plan to kill her. Slowly." He shifted Delilah's limp body and opened the shattered door, his shoes scraping over the glass. "You can have your mate back once I find mine." He looked into Christian's murderous stare with cold indifference. "Get in my way, and I'll return her to you in pieces."

Christian hissed and lunged, but there was no breaking the invisible restraints that held him. His father was a rogue immortal, full of mortal blood and several centuries his senior. The veins in his neck and arms popped as he strained with all his might, baring his teeth. "You harm her, and I will personally burn you alive."

His father pivoted from outside the shop and laughed, mocking him. "You can try."

CHAPTER 29

reath sucked into Delilah's lungs like water breaking through a dam, pushing out the staleness as her eyes widened and she regained consciousness. *Where was she?*

The ground moved, and her claws extended, digging into the flat, hot surface for grip. Adjusting her sight to the darkness, she searched the sweltering space as the walls and floor rumbled loudly. Dust and grit stuck to her sweaty legs, and the ground rattled and bumped beneath her. *The moving truck.*

Her mind reached for Christian's as she inspected her neck, finding sticky traces of blood and an unclosed puncture wound. "That fuck-er." Breathing fast, she licked her fingers, using her own saliva to close the wound. *Christian, where are you?*

Delilah!

Her body folded forward with relief when his voice reached her mind. Their connection was faint as if he spoke to her from a great distance.

Christian, I'm in the truck.

I'm tracking you, but I'm on foot. I'm moving as fast as I can. You're only a few miles ahead of me.

She looked around the dark, cavernous trailer, a sob working around the lump in her throat as her body swayed and the tires shuddered over the road below. *What's happening, Christian? Who is he and where is he taking me?* When he didn't immediately answer, she panicked. *Christian? Are you there? Don't leave me!*

I'm here. He's taking you back to Lancaster.

What? Why? Still holding her ravaged throat, she glanced nervously at the front of the truck.

He's…my father, pintura. He's after my mother.

Her eyes widened. Christian had been drinking his mother's blood to heal, and Delilah had fed from his vein. That was how he was tracking Adriel. *How did he find us?*

I'm not sure. He's very old, older than my mother, and older than the elders of The Order. He's extremely powerful, Delilah. And dangerous. Do not challenge him. Do you understand?

Drawing in shallow breaths she began to hyperventilate. She was going to die. Of course this would happen right after she found happiness and things started looking up.

Delilah, listen to me. You are not going to die. I won't let anything happen to you.

As if his words couldn't cross the distance, she drew no comfort from his promise. He said it himself, Maddox was old and powerful. He'd already proven he wouldn't hesitate to hurt her.

The sun baked wood of the box truck aggravated her lungs. Or was it her fear of death making it hard to breathe?

Christian, I'm scared.

As you should be... The sinister voice that cut into her mind was not her mate's.

Christian! She gripped her head, unsure how Maddox had done such a thing. "Get out of my head!" *Christian, stay with me!*

She needed to get out of there. Trying to stand, the truck veered and she went careening into the wall, slamming her shoulder hard against one of the wooden beams used for attaching bungie cords.

It was easily a hundred and fifty degrees in the air tight trailer, the sweltering summer heat baking into the metal roof and walls for days with nowhere to escape. Sweat dripped into her eyes. She was already dehydrating and in desperate need of water.

Christian, I can't breathe!

Regulate your body temperature. The return of Christian's voice shook her with relief. Why did he keep disappearing on her?

Her heart beat erratically as she tried to focus through her panic. *It's not working. I'm roasting in here.*

Don't try to cool yourself off. Instead, heat your blood.

She didn't know how to do that. Sweat poured off of her, soaking her clothes and slicking her limbs. She lowered to the floor, the loud rumble of the road rushing by enough to rattle her brain. Her eyes closed as she panted, lowering her cheek to the grimy floor.

Fatigued and dizzy, she fought a wave of motion sickness. The back of her dress glued to her skin, soaked through with sweat. Her pulse was dropping rapidly, and she started to shiver despite the heat.

Delilah, do not fall asleep!

She moaned, rolling to her back. Her clothes were drenched and her hair a damp mess of tangles. She wheezed, taking shallow breaths of the hot air. Her skin dried, her mouth unbearably parched. The arid darkness closed in on her, and she became disoriented, forgetting for a moment where she was.

Delilah... Delilah?

Could she die from heat stroke. She could feel her mind slowing down and her heart struggling to beat. She moaned when her brain started to throb. She needed air. Water. Anything.

Gasping, she tried to move but a sharp pain knifed through her back. The dull throb intensified and she wondered if her organs were shutting down.

Christian...

Delilah, I need you to stay awake. I'm not far behind you. Don't lose our link.

Water...

I forbid you to fall asleep!

The sound of panic in Christian's voice jolted her awake. She crawled toward the back of the truck, rolling as the truck swerved and lurched. Her body slammed into the back door and she weakly searched for the handle. Her palm swiped over flat metal. There was no internal latch or pull.

Listen to me, little one. You are a fighter. You're strong. Delilah, do you hear me? Delilah? Discipline your body to obey your mind.

She squeezed her eyes shut and tried to force her blood to cool. Her body chilled and shivered, going into shock. Her muscles seized. She fell back, shaking violently, her jaw locking and her head knocking against the floor.

Delilah!

The seizure tripped something in her brain, and she lost all sense of Christian. She had no choice but to wait out the fit. Her mind short-circuited as she trembled mindlessly on the filthy floor, half dead from the suffocating heat.

She had no idea how long the seizure went on. Awareness was slow to return. Her heart fluttered with a small murmur as each of her organs pulsed and throbbed, stopping and starting as only her immortal blood kept her alive. Even her skin had wept all the cooling sweat she could produce. Now her flesh was just a dry casing around her dehydrated muscles and bones.

She was dying.

Weak and terrified, unable to reach Christian, she curled onto her side and sobbed. "God, help me…"

A PLAN HAD TAKEN shape before Dane even realized he was moving. Gracie was cooking tonight, so everyone was at Cain and Destiny's. That gave him an open window to find what he needed.

Flipping back the braided carpet in Adam and Anna's den, he found the trap door he'd been looking for. Lifting the latch, he pulled and dust fell into the dark space below.

He dropped into the small chute, feet first, and landed on raw earth, under the house. Every home on the farm had a root cellar, but the Amish also needed a place to keep the weapons they technically used for hunting. Immortals didn't need guns to successfully hunt, so their weapons were mostly stored under the house—forgotten.

The air cooled the moment he was under the earth, ducking through the shadows, searching for the guns. Cobwebs caught in his hair as he felt around. Grit from the stone foundation gathered under his nails, and his shoes pressed into the soft, loose dirt that made up the floor. This was one of the moments he wished he had the night vision of a full-bred immortal.

Metal scraped along the stone and his hand bolted out, catching the barrel of a rifle. Several guns rested against the wall. He felt around, searching for gunpowder and the like, only to knock over a box of modern ammunition.

He reached into the dirt finding the large casings and several other modern weapons hidden beneath a shelf tucked behind a concrete footing. "Hypocrites."

He pocketed several and grabbed the largest gun he could find, then he retraced his steps to the trap door and got on his way.

Rolling the braided rug back into place, he rushed to the front door only to look back and wince at the trail of dirt and footprints he left. He wanted to clean it, but he only had so much time. And it wasn't like they wouldn't realize what he'd done by the end of the night. By tomorrow, they'd all know.

With the gun in his hand, he pulled the door closed. There was no going back now that he was armed with a plan.

THE METAL DOOR rumbled and Delilah stirred, gasping the moment the cool evening air hit her.

"Get up, girl." Maddox grabbed her ankle and dragged her to the opening at the back of the truck. The dirty floor scraping beneath her skin and rubbing it raw.

Delilah was so weak and dehydrated she fell

onto the paved road, slamming her head into blacktop as pain exploded through her skull. She instantly wanted to vomit, but there wasn't time. He shoved her with the toe of his shoe, and she rolled to her hands and knees, her palms scraping along the gravel.

He gripped her hair and she whimpered as he hoisted her to her feet. "Look familiar?"

She blinked at the dark fields. Stars dotted the sky overhead, undisturbed by modern lights. They were there. He'd made it, directed by her blood alone.

A tear rolled from her eye as he shoved her forward. "Take me to her."

Delilah stumbled into the grass and fell to her knees again. She thought of Adriel. The woman was Christian's only family. She couldn't lead this maniac to her door.

The brunt toe of his shoe slammed into her ribs, lifting her off the ground and knocking her to her back. She coughed and sputtered, the wind kicked clean out of her lungs.

"That wasn't a request."

Rolling onto her hands and knees, she pressed her face into the cool grass. *Christian, where are you?*

Her head was yanked back as he fisted her hair. "If you want to see him again, get up and walk. Otherwise, I'm going to rip your eyes from that pretty little head of yours, and you'll never look at sweet Christian again."

She staggered to her feet, her balance off and her hair still knotted around his fist as he shoved her forward. She trudged toward the farm.

Adriel, can you hear—

Her body reeled forward as pain exploded in her skull. He shoved her face into the ground and snarled in her ear. "Don't test my patience, girl. Piss me off again and I'll make sure your mate never finds you."

He yanked her up by the wrist, and she whimpered as his claw dug through her veins, slicing open her skin. She screamed at the sharp burn of his fangs puncturing her tender skin. The intense sting was nothing like the gentle way Christian took her blood.

He held her arm in an unbreakable grip, sucking down several painful gulps of her blood. His fangs released her and he grinned, dark crimson staining his teeth. "We're close."

He shoved her forward, not bothering to close the wound. She licked her fingers, but she was so dehydrated her mouth was too dry. She didn't have the necessary saliva to heal herself.

"I need…water," she rasped.

"Keep walking." He shoved her and she flung forward, tripping over her feet.

She glared back only to quickly drop her gaze. There was no kindness in his soul. He was a cold, merciless, immortal. Nothing like the gentle-mannered ones she'd met through The Order.

He wouldn't hesitate to hurt her if she didn't do exactly what he said.

She led him toward the Schrock property,

still somewhat unsure of the layout of the farm. As they walked, she put pressure on her arm and studied him. By the look of his designer shoes and finely tailored attire, this was not someone inhibited by Amish culture. There would be no pacifying him with thoughts of moral righteousness.

Where was Christian? He should be there by now. Why couldn't she reach him through their mental link?

Maddox jabbed a finger in her back, prodding her forward. "Hurry up."

With no way of warning Christian's mother, she would be caught completely off-guard. What would happen once they found her. Did he plan to kill her?

Delilah stumbled down a hill toward the school house. The land was dark and quiet, hardly any candles glowing in the windows. If someone would see or hear them, Christian's mother might have a fighting chance.

"Why do you want Adriel?"

"She owes me a debt."

Christian said The Order could protect them. She wondered how they would protect Adriel.

Maddox laughed, the sound shooting ice into her veins. "Nothing short of death will stop me from taking back what's mine, little girl."

She looked up at him, her heels sinking into the dirt as she clambered along. He could hear her thoughts, so any attempt she made to warn anyone would have a consequence.

"You're a fast learner." He lifted his nose and scented the air. "We're close."

JUNIPER AWOKE to the rattling of keys. Her heart rate spiked and she swallowed a whimper, her lashes flickering against the tear-stained blindfold that covered her eyes. He'd just left. How could he possibly be back for more?

By the dank smell of the damp musty air, the torches were out. It was late. The sound of the bars opening marked his progress. She struggled to sit up, but her body ached from the earlier assault, and she lacked her usual strength.

"It's me."

She stilled at the sound of Dane's voice, and relief washed over her. What was he doing here at this hour?

"I found the key for the restraints," he whispered, creeping into her cell. "But you have to help me."

He pulled the blindfold off her eyes, and she blinked as her vision adjusted to the shadows. She looked through the heavy metal bridle at him, desperate to have this horrific contraption off of her head.

"Promise you won't make me regret helping you."

She'd do anything to be out of this cell. With no way to speak, she mumbled an incoherent promise and nodded.

"Turn around. The lock's in the back."

She shifted on the cot as he fit the tiny key into the lock at the back of her head. The moment the metal loosened, she opened her mouth and started to cry. Her jaw ached as the piece that depressed her tongue withdrew. She breathed in a full breath and coughed.

Her skin was chapped and raw where the bridle had compressed her face over time. Later, she would fear permanent scarring. For now, she was solely focused on escaping.

"My hands." Pure urgency shook her voice as she feared someone would catch them.

The moment he sliced the rope around her wrists, blood rushed into her fingers. She wrenched the bridle off her neck and threw it onto the ground and stood.

"Wait!" He caught her arm.

Her gaze snagged on the rifle leaning against the wall outside of her cell. She looked up at Dane.

He was strong, at least a foot taller than her. She was weak and injured. He'd catch her if she ran.

"I need a favor."

Her throat was ravaged from disuse. "What do you want?"

"I know you have powers."

Of course he wanted the one thing she couldn't give. "I can't—"

"You can. I saw you use them a few weeks ago. I just..." He glanced to the end of the hall where the chains rattled. She didn't know what was down there but after years of hearing the snarls and screams, she didn't want to find out. "I need you to watch my back."

She hesitated, and looked back at the gun. Dane wasn't like the others. She didn't understand why he was here, aside from the girl he visited each night. She'd gathered it was his sister, but in all the time Juniper had occupied these cells she'd never heard the girl do more than screech and growl like a possessed animal.

"Please, just let me leave." Her bare feet shifted over the dirt floor. "You said you'd help me."

His stare bounced between her, the cellar door, and the far end of the hall. "I am helping you."

She looked past him to the open cell door. "What are you doing with the gun?"

"I'm going to kill that thing in the last cell."

She staggered back. "You'll get us both killed. You can't kill them. Don't you know that? A gun isn't enough."

"I have to try."

"You'll fail. They can only die from decapitation, heart extraction, and fire. Bullets won't do more than hurt them."

"If I aim for his heart, I can blow it clean out of his body."

"Have you ever shot a gun before?"

"No."

They were going to die. "You're more likely

to hit a rib. You're only going to piss him off. What if he gets out?"

"That's where you come in."

"What the hell am I going to do?"

He glanced at the unlit torch on the wall. "You're more powerful when you're afraid."

"That's not true." She'd been terrified and unable to protect herself for two years. "Don't do this, Dane. This place…it's evil. We should both run."

"I have nowhere to go."

"Me neither." She thought about how he took care of her that horrible day when they burned her feet. "We could run together."

He hesitated and, for a moment, she remembered what hope felt like. Then he took it away.

"I need to do this. If I die, I die. All I want you to do is keep him away from my sister."

"How?"

"However you can." He left the cell, leaving the door open wide. "Then you can do whatever you want. I won't tell anyone you escaped." He grabbed the rifle. "Make the blanket and pillow look like you're still asleep."

She quickly did as he asked, afraid he would change his mind and lock her inside. As soon as she had the threadbare quilt and pillow molded in the shape of a body with the bridle peeking out the top, she rushed out of the cell.

Her feet hit the floor on the other side of the bars and another ripple of hope teased through her. *Freedom.*

She almost abandoned him and his foolish

plan, but then she looked in his trusting eyes and cursed under her breath. He freed her. She couldn't betray him.

"I brought you this." He unloaded his pockets, revealing bullets, a feather, matches, a bottle of water, a pouch of salt, and a rock. "Did I forget anything?"

He found her the elements. "*Aether.*" There was no spirit in this place. She'd tried countless times to reach Her.

Dane grinned. "I've been reading. *Aether* is the primordial god of light, born of chaos. I think we can channel Her."

Hesitantly, Juniper looked down at his hands again only to flinch when a malicious growl curdled from the end of the hall. "He knows you're here." Whatever that thing in the last cell was, it hated when other males were around.

"All I need is a little protection spell. Anything to keep me and my sister safe."

She could just run. But if she ran, he'd likely go ahead with this stupid plan and wind up dead. She shouldn't care, but she also couldn't forget how he took care of her when she was in agony.

"Fine. But you have to move quickly, and if things get bad, I'm gone. You should leave too. This place is cursed."

He nodded. "I'll do my best to keep them from following you. Go as far as you can and don't stop until you absolutely have to. They can't track you for long without your blood."

She shivered, and cold dread settled like poison in the pit of her stomach. "They have my blood."

He frowned. "How?"

Her head lowered. She could feel him when her eyes closed. She knew his touch and scent, but not what he looked like. "I don't know his name, but he bites me when he visits."

"Jesus," he hissed. "Okay, then you have to be extra careful."

She looked back at the door to her cell, the sight of her home for the past two years filling her with rage. If she ever did find her powers, she planned on seeking revenge on every single one that trapped her here.

"Ready?"

With a nod, she dropped to the ground and drew a pentacle in the dirt. She set the feather to the right and the water to the left. "I don't know which way's west. This might not work if I have the elements facing the wrong direction."

He looked up at the ceiling then turned. "West is this way."

She shifted the elements. A few pieces were missing for it to be a proper alter. "Hand me a torch." He lifted the torch from the wall and removed a match, but before he could light it, she held out a hand and said, "*Ignisia.*"

The torch blazed to life and Dane jumped back. "Holy shit."

"Don't get too excited. That's all I can really do." She set the torch to the south of the pentacle. Once she had everything in place, she sprinkled a circle of salt around her alter.

Dane looked at her expectantly. "Now what?"

"Now what *what?* I told you not to expect much."

He cocked the gun. "Then let's channel some chaos."

"Dane—"

He paused and looked back. She wanted to remember him just like that, dark hair and bright eyes. Strong and determined. Good. "Be careful."

He nodded, appearing resigned to whatever came next. "You too....Juniper." He tried for a smile, but it didn't reach his eyes.

THE TINY CUP on the nightstand rattled and Adriel's eyes opened, her mind alert and her body ready. He was there. She could sense the shift in the air. It had taken him three centuries, but he finally found her.

She closed off her mind, guarding her thoughts as the pitcher of water on the mantle vibrated. The glass in the windows trembled when the floor began to shake. She dressed quickly, forgoing the trappings of bonnets and pins and opting for functionality.

Closing her eyes, she sent out a forcefield. Her mind instantly recoiled at the sense of her mate's nearness.

It had been ages since she felt him so close. Her blood ran cold at such sharp memories. Fear knocked her knees together, interfering with her self-control.

I'm coming for you, girl...

She slammed down a wall to her thoughts, unsure how he could possibly penetrate her guarded mind without access to her blood. For him to have that sort of power he would have had to—"Christian," she gasped.

Her son was the only one who had access to her blood. Had Cer found him and somehow drank from Christian? Mates shared blood. Fear doubled into stark worry for Christian and his mate.

Did Cer realize Christian was his son? She'd left long before her body had started to show. Did he know? How had he found them?

She grabbed the gun and crept swiftly down the stairs. Her bare feet keeping her steps light and attuned to the slightest vibration.

The shutters slapped shut and the pocket doors of the den slammed. Adriel jumped and spun, but no one was there.

I've got you now, girl.

Every extinguished candle leapt to life, tall flames licking ten inches from the wick, not at her command. Her heart raced as she breathed heavily, keeping her back to the wall.

Her fangs and claws lengthened as she waited in frantic terror. The house wouldn't hold him off for long.

Eleazar... Eleazar, he's here!

Her friend's mind was closed to her. She'd recently given Christian so much of her blood, her link to the bishop wasn't at its usual strength. Taking his blood was a precaution they routinely kept up for three hundred years, but it had been some time since he'd offered. She should have requested more of his blood the moment she started offering hers to her son.

A loud crash shook the front of the house, knocking several needlepoints off the wall. Her breath came fast as Cer's chilling voice called from outside.

"Little pig, little pig, let me in." Claws scraped over the exterior, as planks creaked on the front porch. The front door rattled as he jiggled the lock. "I know you're in there. I can smell you."

Adriel backed further into the shadows, holding the rifle upright, her finger hooked on the trigger and her head pressed into the wall.

"I have a surprise for you, girl. Come to the window and see."

She had no intention of going near the windows until she heard the whimper of a female. Panic gripped her heart as she caught the distinct scent of Delilah. Where was Christian?

"Adriel, don't let him in!" Her warning cut off with a grunt and Adriel winced, certain he'd already hurt the young female.

She panicked, thinking of her son and his newfound happiness. If something happened to

Delilah, it would devastate him. She couldn't let him hurt her.

Heart pounding, she pressed her back into the corner and watched the front door with unblinking eyes. "Where is Christian?"

"Our *son* has been detained. He sends his love and apologizes for not making it back in time to say goodbye."

That meant Christian was still alive. "Let his mate go—"

Delilah screamed and Adriel rushed forward only to draw back in fear. *Eleazar, please! I need help.*

"Yes, Eleazar," Cer yelled. "Come out and play. You and I have a score to settle."

She took a step toward the door then stilled when Delilah yelled, "Stay in there, Adriel!" Another horrific scream.

Eleazar, where are you? Cerberus is here and he has Christian's mate!

"Please don't hurt the girl!" Adriel yelled. "She's innocent and belongs to our son—"

"Our son is weak!" He bellowed, shaking the walls of the house hard enough that the jars on the shelves tremored. "You had no right to keep him from me!"

Her lungs labored as she tried to think of a plan. "Now, we're all here. We can start over. A family."

"You have three seconds to show yourself or our *family* is going to shrink by one. Three. Two."

She hesitated, frozen by panic and indecision.

"One."

Another scream, this one followed by an agonizing broken sob. She could only imagine what he was doing to the poor child.

Eleazar, I need you now!

Then a shot blared in the distance and she flinched. It was too far to involve her and Cer wasn't fazed. Another blast echoed, and then another. What was happening? No one ever used firearms on The Order's land.

The house shook, rattling the windows and building force. The foundation creaked and the shutters clattered.

"Time's up, girl." The candles flared and a curtain blazed when it caught the flame.

She rushed to the kitchen at the back of the house, gathering a pail of water only to double back when the glass burst from the window, the shudders splintering into the house as the flames shot higher, licking up the wall.

Canisters flew from the shelves and shattered against the floor and walls. She ducked when the table flipped on end. He was going to push her out one way or another.

That cold, maniacal laugh cut through the chaos, and she knew she was done. He wasn't leaving without her, and she couldn't go back to that kind of existence.

Ducking low, she raced to the kitchen and ripped open the drawer. Knives and cleavers scattered to the floor. She searched for the sharpest blade and set down the gun. She had to save Delilah. If he couldn't get to her, he had no use for the girl. She lifted the largest cleaver, her reflection glinting across the blade as the flames crawled closer. If she cut fast and hard, she might make it all the way through.

Another window burst and smoke filled the house. Bricks loosened from the hearth and flung into the den, crashing into walls and furniture. Dishes shattered.

She sat on the floor with the gun on her lap and the knife in her trembling hands. She had one chance of getting this right. Aligning the blade with her throat, she lifted her chin and did a slow test swing. She would have to use all of her strength.

A tear fell from her eye. She wanted her son to know how much she loved him and how proud she was of the honorable male he'd become. She wanted to remind him that sometimes joy should come before duty. She wanted to thank Eleazar one last time and remind Dane that he deserved a good life. But she would never have the chance to say any of those things now.

She opened up her mind, letting not just Cerberus in but anyone else. She wanted Delilah to hear her last thoughts as she raised the blade. *Take good care of my boy.*

———

"ROT IN HELL," Dane hissed as his finger tightened on the trigger again, the deafening blast ricocheted off the underground walls as the hard reverberation of the rifle slammed into his shoulder.

Isaiah grunted and staggered back, blood bloomed from another hole, but his heart remained intact. He glared back at Dane with murder in his eyes and let out an unholy roar that shook the air like a nuclear explosion.

Cybil screeched and screamed, her body flinging into the bars like a primate, as she snapped her fangs. Isaiah lunged forward, halted only by the chains that pulled hard enough for dust to crumble from the wall. Dane stumbled back and a shrill howl ripped from his sister's throat as she climbed like a spider up the bars, rattling them in their sockets.

Isaiah was far from dead as he turned into the shadows and yanked the chains, dislodging them from the wall and dragging them toward the bars. The whine of metal bending pierced the air as his blood-red gaze bore into Dane, lethal promise swirling in the muddy depths of his soulless eyes.

He quickly loaded the gun again, his panic making him clumsy as the bullets fell onto the floor.

"Dane!" Juniper yelled. "I think it's time to go."

He looked back at the cell and then to the door on the far end of the hall. If he ran, Isaiah would catch him. It was too late. "Go without me!"

"I'm not leaving you down here—"

A thunderous, blood thirsty roar interrupted her plea. The bars were getting wider apart.

Dane shoved another bullet into the rifle. And aimed it at Isaiah's face. "Get out of here, Juniper! Run!"

Cybil raced to the far side of her cell and lunged at the adjacent wall, hurling herself at the stones and knocking herself to the ground. Like a deviant possessed, she got up and threw herself at the wall again. Dane cocked the gun and steadied his hold, training the muzzle on Isaiah who seemed distracted by Cybil.

"Don't you fucking look at her, you filthy piece of shit."

A low growl vibrated from Isaiah's chest as he glared at him through blood-stained eyes. Mortar loosened in the separating wall, as stones crumbled to the ground of the cell. Isaiah's head slowly turned back toward the connecting wall as a low growl turned into a purr.

Dane's attention snagged on his sister, the scope of the gun angling toward her cell. Isaiah lunged forward, snatching the muzzle and yanking it free from his hands.

Dane sprang back, losing his grip of the rifle and tripping over his feet. "Fuck!"

Isaiah snapped the metal in half, tossing the gun aside like kindling. The separating wall disintegrated as stones fell in a cloud of debris and dust. He coughed and squinted, covering his head as the ceiling crumbled. The slow predatory growl fanned past his ear in a warm breath and he looked into blood-red eyes only inches from his face.

Isaiah was outside of his mangled cell and Cybil was behind him, crouched and panting. The empty cavity of her cell revealed how much their containment had been a joke.

Isaiah bared his fangs and snarled, roaring hard enough to blow the hair back from Dane's eyes.

"*Dane!*" Juniper's desperate voice broke through the chaos. "*Run!*"

Any sudden move and he'd be dead. He looked back at his sister, wishing he could see her one last time as the sweet girl she was.

He breathed through his last moments, certain any life that was this hard wasn't worth living. His vision blurred as he looked up at the ceiling, wondering if his mother and father were somewhere looking down.

"Go now," he said, with little inflection.

The witch stood but hesitated, the flames jumping from torch to torch as she lit up the hall. "Come with me." The torches flickered and a burst of wind syphoned through the hall, distracting Isaiah. "Dane! This is our last chance!"

He scrambled to his feet and raced toward the exit. Juniper rushed toward the door, and Isaiah snarled at his back. Cybil screamed, and frantic energy swirled through the corridor as she sprang free from her cell and scaled the walls, racing along the ceiling only to drop down into a crouch, blocking their only exit.

Then everything stilled, and Juniper turned

to face him, her mouth agape. "Oh my, Goddess."

Every hair on his body stood on end. Cybil's head hung low, wild, blonde hair encircling her youthful face as she seethed with uncontained rage. Her eyes locked on Juniper with murderous intent.

"Cybil, no—" Dane yelled, but it was too late.

She bolted for the witch, jaw snapping and her intent clear. The torches blazed, and Juniper screamed.

Isaiah roared and shoved him aside. Dane's back slammed into the stone wall, and the hall went black. "Juniper!"

Her screams silenced and all sound, save his frantic breathing, stopped. His eyes adjusted and he saw the bishop standing at the doorway, Juniper cowering behind him, covering her head, and Cybil's body crumpled on the floor at his feet.

Isaiah roared and marched forward, crouching to sniff Cybil's hair. He dragged her body close and sprang to his full height, unhinging his jaw and releasing a snarling growl in the bishop's face. He held Cybil's body in his arms when he turned back to Dane, looking so much the way he had in the woods the day he'd killed his mother.

Paralyzed by the sight, Dane could only stare in horror. Was she dead? Had the bishop killed her?

Isaiah's bare feet pounded down the corridor, stomping over the meager alter and scattering salt into the earth. Dane ducked, expecting a mortal blow when Isaiah snarled and threw his weight into the far wall. He clawed at the stones, ripping down the wall until he hit dark earth.

Filthy talons tore into the packed dirt as he snarled and growled. When he broke ground, moonlight seeped from above. He scaled the terrain, Cybil's small lifeless body draped over his shoulder, leaving a trail of dirt and rocks in his wake. Then they were gone.

Jagged breath barely filled his lungs as Dane stared wide-eyed at Eleazar. They were all gone. Juniper too.

"Is she dead?" he asked, now hoping that was the case. When the bishop didn't immediately respond, he shouted, demanding an answer, *"Did you kill my sister?"*

Eleazar scanned the ruined cells, taking in the damage and not missing a single detail. Dane recoiled at the sharp sense of him penetrating his mind without the anesthetic of compulsion. He sorted through his memories, gathering any explanation for the disaster he'd walked into. Dane jerked when he abruptly pulled out of his mind.

"No. I only broke her neck. She'll wake in a few hours."

His breath hitched. That meant Isaiah would have no trouble taking her wherever he desired. And then he could do whatever he wanted to her.

His stomach swilled. They were gone. He'd never find her. She was at the mercy of that monster. This was his fault.

He fell to his knees, a shuddering sob escaping as his shoulders shook.

Dirt ground under the bishop's boots as he approached. A heavy hand rested on Dane's back, but his words were anything but comforting.

"You have until tomorrow night to leave. You disobeyed The Council, and I cannot allow you to stay."

No Cybil. No Grace. Even Juniper was gone. He had no reason to stay. He'd leave Maggie a note and pack his things tonight.

"I'll be off the farm by dawn."

Eleazar stiffened, his head turning abruptly as something caught his attention. "I have to go. See me before you leave."

The dark hall was empty, save the destruction, before Dane had a chance to respond. He collapsed to his hands and knees, defeated in every sense of the word, as he lay his head down in the dirt. What had he done? There was nothing left to do but cry.

DELILAH STRUGGLED to breathe as she lay in a heap on the ground. Her body a mess of deep cuts, gouges, and bruises. He was too strong and far too powerful for her to combat, but she couldn't stop thinking about her own parents.

Losing her mother and father had killed something inside of her that she never got back. She couldn't bear the thought of Christian suffering the same loss and pain. His mother was in that house, and Maddox was going to kill her.

Smoke billowed from the windows as the flames glowed against the dark night. She sensed Adriel inside, but her mind was blocked. Where were the others?

Hands slick with blood, Delilah pushed herself up. She had to stop him. She had to do something to save Adriel.

"Come out, come out, wherever you are," he taunted, enjoying the demonic way he goaded her with his powers. After seeing what he was already capable of, Delilah had no doubt he could have easily caught Adriel by now, but he liked tormenting her the way a cat tortured a mouse before killing it slowly.

She needed strength if she was going to help the other female. Another window exploded, and he laughed. Delilah shut her eyes and spread her senses into the surrounding woods. If she moved, he'd only catch her and hurt her more. She believed he was insane enough to kill her.

Christian, where are you?

A cool nose nudged her limp hand, and she lifted her head, breathing in a sigh of relief when she looked into the eyes of a clever fox. The beautiful creature lowered to its belly, crouching closer.

"Hello there," she whispered, stroking its fur, hoping she could do this.

She'd never fed from an animal before, but necessity demanded it of her now. Careful not to spook the sweet thing, she pulled him closer and continued to pet his back, while parting its fur and searching for a clean area to bite.

She didn't have much time. "I'm sorry." She sank her teeth deep. The fox stilled as she drank.

Her organs were the first to repair. The throbbing pain and what she suspected was a punctured lung healed. Then the tightness of her skin eased. The fox was small and she didn't want to take too much. A few more sips and— her hold broke as the fox yelped, its small body hurled several feet in the distance.

She snapped her head around and bared her fangs at the fucker that kicked it, prepared to go samurai-ninja-don't-fuck-with-my fur-babies-crazy bitch on his bloodsucker ass.

"Did I say you could feed?"

She had enough of this cocksucker. "Did you just kick my fox?"

He raised his hand to strike her and she sprang, latching onto his face and burying her claws in his eyes. Blood poured down his cheeks as he screeched.

He ripped her off him and hurled her through the air. She slammed into the ground hard enough to loosen a few teeth. The wind picked up, and black clouds rolled overhead as she waited for her back to stop spasming.

The crackle of Adriel's house grew louder as beams crumbled inside. The fire had to have alerted the others by now.

Delilah pushed herself to her knees with shaky arms, prepared to fight, and Maddox turned, sensing her rise. Watching her through bleeding eyes, he laughed at her feeble attempt to take him on.

"My son has his work cut out with you." Turning his back to the burning house, he held out his arms, waving her on. "Give it your best shot."

Delilah growled as an enormous bull appeared on the hill. Several other small creatures at its side. Horses and a flock of angry chickens marched toward her like the frontline at the Battle of Falkirk. *This is my army?*

It wasn't looking good. Then the earth pulsed beneath her feet and Maddox turned. She followed his stare and gaped as several silhouetted figures crested the knoll. The long band of immortals stretched across the horizon, armed to the teeth with everything from pitchforks to knitting needles and guns. *This was her posse!*

Lightning flashed overhead and thunder rumbled. The wind swirled in every direction, lifting her hair clean off her shoulders and whipping her dress over her knees. A typhoon of energy pushed into her, and the blaze of the house grew.

Delilah, stay down. The intrusion of Christian's frantic words penetrated her mind.

Christian!

She couldn't bear the extent of her injuries at that moment, so she stayed low like he commanded and searched the horizon for him. Maddox also watched as The Order closed in.

This was her chance. She looked back at the blazing house. *Adriel, run now!*

Maddox tackled her, his fists closing around her throat as he slammed her head into the ground. "Did I not warn you?"

Her airways cut off as he gripped her neck. He laughed and released her, but the choking sensation remained. Clawing at her skin, she struggled to breathe, but no air passed through her throat.

"Delilah!" Christian's shout drifted from the distance as her hearing faded to nothing more than a small hum.

Maddox smirked and narrowed his eyes. "I could kill you over and over again, just to watch you suffer."

Her heels dug into the ground, dragging through the mud as she tried in vain to breathe. Pain exploded in her chest and skull as rain pelted her skin. Her feet kicked aimlessly as her eyes bulged and watered.

Something dark and sinister slammed into Maddox, and air ravaged her lungs. She rolled to her side, gasping and coughing, certain her larynx was destroyed.

Christian towered over Maddox, his expression dark with murderous intent, and a deadly scythe aimed at his father's throat.

BLOOD DRENCHED Adriel's chest as she prepared to swing one last time. Holding the blade in an unbreakable grip, she swung and the back door burst open. Eleazar caught her arm just before the blade hit her neck.

"Adriel, no!"

Her will crumbled as she looked into her friend's hard, disapproving glare and let out a sob. "I can't go back."

He pried the knife out of her grip and threw it across the room, then pulled her into a tight hug. "Death is not the answer, my friend." He rolled up his sleeve. "Hurry. You must drink."

She wept hopelessly. "There's no point. He won't rest until he has me."

Eleazar shook her. "Enough! You've made a mess of yourself, and you're not thinking clearly. Take my blood so you have your wits and your strength."

She bit into his arm, wondering how he would explain such a violation to his mate.

"Let me worry about such things. You just take what you need and listen to me."

The fire crawled closer. They would either burn alive or be forced out by the lethal heat.

"You're going to leave, Adriel. Run as far as you can and lock your mind. I'll be able to track you for a few hundred miles since you have my blood, but that stays between us. I'll tell no one. Not even Christian. For right now, for your survival, secrecy is best. I give you my word, I will watch over your son as if he were my own —and his young mate. If you leave now, you have a chance. Let The Order deal with Cerberus.

Shaking violently, she released his arm. While she appreciated his plan and help, this was one more excuse that allowed a truly dishonorable male to survive at the cost of an innocent female's life. It was too much. "Eleazar, you need to destroy him."

The bishop was a man of God, and as such, he saw murder as a capitol sin, even when a death sentence was warranted by the law. "We could put him before The Council—"

"That is a fantasy and you know it is such. Cerberus would never submit to such authority."

"We can decide his fate later. For now, it's your fate that concerns me."

She grabbed his arm and waited for him to meet her stare. *"Those who rebel against God will bring judgement onto themselves.* You're our bishop, a rightful servant of God and the Good Book declares you His servant, *an agent of wrath to bring punishment on the wrongdoer."* She closed her hand tightly around his. "You must kill him."

"Adriel—"

She shook her head, forbidding one more excuse that allowed Cerberus to live. "This is the horrible truth of your duty, my friend. I don't envy the burden upon your shoulders, but it's what you must do."

He lowered his gaze and released her hand. "You must go." He pulled her toward the back door. "Quickly, Adriel. For now, you must run. Lock your mind and run. Don't come back until the situation has been resolved."

He was hiding truths from her. Sheltering her delicate disposition from the ugly reality of the world. She shoved away his hold and straightened her spine. "I'm not a little girl anymore. You said so yourself. I'm an elder who lacks a title only to comfort the fragile male egos that hold authority over The Order. But I am an elder, Eleazar, and I know what has to be done. I'll run and survive the night, but if Cerberus lives to see the dawn, I'll do what must be done. I'll kill him. So he won't come back."

"Adriel, love or hate him, he is your mate—"

"He is a monster! An evil, immoral male who has terrorized me since I was a young girl. I will not rest until he's put down. And if ending him costs me my own life, so be it."

A large wooden beam whined and creaked as the walls bubbled under the flames. "You have to go now, Adriel, or we're both going to burn alive." He steered her to the back door.

"Wait. *The Book of Confessions*. Show it to my son when this is over. Tell Christian I'm sorry. Had I been stronger, I might have had the courage to explain our family's history to him myself. Tell him how proud I am of the honorable male he's become."

"You'll tell him yourself when you return, but you have to go now."

The ceiling collapsed, and the foundation of the house moaned. "Close your mind, and go as far as you can manage. Wait as long as possible before reaching out. Go now."

The heat of the fire pushed forward as another window shattered. Screams built in the distance as the flames crackled and the wood blazed. This was it.

Smoke billowed and burned her eyes. She met his squinting gaze one last time, unsure if it would be her last chance to stare into the face of a friend. "Thank you. For everything."

He nodded. "Go."

She bolted through the door, running straight for the northern woods.

DELILAH SPUTTERED, her lungs on fire, as Christian's blurry figure loomed over his father's downed form. Maddox's stare turned toward the northern woods, and he sprang to his feet just as The Order closed in.

Thunderous shouts clamored from the hill as a stampede of poorly armed immortals raced forward, closing in from the east, while a herd of mismatched farm animals bleated and brayed, encircling from the west.

Maddox, cornered and trapped, raised both hands and pushed his palms toward the sky. A wave of light burst from the trees, webbing from the black overhead clouds to the wood line below. A deadly bolt of lightning stabbed into the earth. An earsplitting boom blasted overhead, echoing out into the distance. Trees fell to the north as branches and leaves caught fire in a burst of flames and light.

"Cerberus Maddox." The bishop appeared from behind the flaming house. "The Order accuses you of wrongful crimes against your mate, acts of violence that endangered innocent immortals, and the abduction of a claimed female. Surrender now, and we will show you mercy."

Maddox bared his teeth at the bishop, snarling like a predator possessed. "This is a treat. I dreamed of what I might do should I set eyes on you again."

The bishop was unarmed. He was either showing extreme courage or extreme stupidity. The Order held back, waiting for Eleazar's next command.

Maddox tipped his head left then right, the tendons cracking as he pinned the bishop with his ruthless stare and grinned. "There was nothing to dull the pain when you invaded my home, attacked me, stole my mate, and mutilated me. You'd think the body goes numb after the first limb is torn, but no. I remember all of it. Especially you."

Maddox splayed his fingers wide and pushed his energy at Eleazar, but Eleazar was prepared and deflected the push, sending it right back.

The wave knocked several immortals to the ground. The roar of energy blaring like a locomotive running off the tracks. Delilah covered her head and ducked.

Maddox roared and marched forward, shooting out a hand and compelling a sharp stake into his hand from the broken framework of the house. "Let's do this the old way."

The Order marched forward, prepared to protect their bishop. "Lay down your weapon, Cerberus, and we will reach an accord peacefully."

Maddox laughed. "I choose violence." His hand shot out, and Christian's body shot into the flames, propelled by whatever force Maddox possessed.

"No!" Delilah screamed, rushing after her mate, only to stagger back when Christian burst from the burning house with murderous intent darkening his eyes. Scythe at the ready, he roared and charged his father.

The mob echoed Christian's rage and swallowed Maddox. Metal clanked and voices screamed as flesh tore and bones snapped. Delilah covered her mouth in shock at what these Amish would do when evil threatened their peace.

A horrific masculine howl bellowed from the brawl as screams poured from the melee. The earth shook as squalls spun like tops over the fields, ripping up trees and pulling siding off of the houses. The forest fire spread with wild, uncontrolled power. Then everything stilled, and the flames of both the forest and the house dropped to glowing embers.

A young girl Delilah didn't recognize stood several feet away, holding her palms open as if pulling the energy of the fire into herself. She chanted in foreign tongues as the blinding light of the fire throbbed, winking and flickering like a lucent firefly brought to life.

"The witch!" someone shouted. "How did she get free?"

The girl's voice rose with each foreign utterance. Her strength worked like a bubble that trapped and calmed the violent mob, her sorcery strong enough to command obedience of fifty immortals.

A burst of energy rolled forward, knocking them down like pins. Screams and moans cut through the chanting but her intonation never slowed.

"You're hurting them!" Delilah yelled, then doubled over, taking in their pain as several elders fell to their knees and screamed in agony.

"Delilah!" Christian's voice cut through the shrieks and cries. He crawled to her, despite his own suffering.

The suffering was so great, all of their afflictions hitting her at once. A thousand knives seemed to stab into her skull as the unbearable pressure built.

Screams erupted in the distance as the females came rushing out of their homes, pained by their mates' suffering. But Delilah took the brunt, the witch's spell triggering such agony in her presence that a healing naturally followed. Only Delilah wasn't strong enough to heal one of them, let alone all of them.

"You must stop!" Christian screamed. "You're hurting her! The females are innocent!"

One by one, the elders dropped to their knees as their mates shrieked. Delilah lay on the muddy earth, shaking through the onslaught of pain. There was no escaping it. Her mind lacked the discipline to shut off her gifts. Their suffering was too much.

A vicious roar ripped from Christian's throat as he surged forward, teeth snapping and claws extended. He sprang for the witch, tackling her roughly to the ground, and the pain cut off the moment her words silenced.

The dulled flames came back to life, shooting high into the air as the fires roared in chaotic destruction. Delilah twitched and breathed through the remaining tremors, rain soaking through her clothes and mixing with her tears.

Her head turned weakly as she lay in the cold mud. The world slowed. The violence before her would haunt her to her last breath. They were merciless. Clawing. Biting. Tearing chunks of flesh from the bone. Maddox was at the center of their rage, but he seemed the strongest of all.

Screams sounded a hundred miles away. Blood spilled and cries shattered any remaining illusion of beauty. They were ruthless animals, clawing any threat to ruin.

Eleazar went down as Maddox landed a

lethal blow that split the bishop's skull wide. He fell to his knees and looked up with resolute understanding. This was the end. Larissa's scream cut through the night as Maddox raised his claws, prepared to slash his enemy to ribbons.

Overhead, Christian roared as he soared through the air like an angel of mercy, scythe raised and twirling at the precise angle as he spread his legs to land. The clean slice of the blade splitting Maddox's hand from his arm stole her breath in a soundless woosh.

The hewn hand fell to the earth, and Maddox dropped to his knees. Blood sprayed from his wrist. Christian landed in a crouch and quickly rose, angling the blade of the scythe for his father's throat.

A curdling roar ripped through the storm as Maddox turned his possessed fury on his son. His severed hand lay lifeless on the ground and crazed hatred spilled from his eyes. With his good hand, he snatched the scythe, but Christian's grip was unforgivably strong. Claws scraped down Christian's face, fraying his drenched clothing as blood spattered into his father's eyes. They fell to the ground, grappling to the death.

Delilah doubled over, flinching and gasping at her mate's pain. The bishop crawled toward them in a feeble attempt to stop Maddox from murder. It was then Delilah realized this would be the end. Maddox was too powerful. His intent to harm too great. And his hate far darker than any counterpart as subtle as hope or love. He was evil, and he would not rest until all the elders were destroyed.

Suffering the onslaught of too many injuries, she welcomed the pain, letting it swallow her whole. If Christian was going to die, she wanted to go with him. She refused to live in a world where immortals like Cerberus Maddox held absolute power. He would make sure the women suffered and serve only himself. She couldn't keep fighting—would never fight to stay in a world so depraved that only the corrupt survive. The violence was too much. His power too great.

The bishop collapsed and struggled to rise. It was a massacre. Delilah could only look on in horror as blood and mud coated their skin and clothing. If these were in fact holy creatures then the pouring rain could only be God's bereft tears.

Maddox threw Christian's body to the ground and rose. Seething, he held the scythe in his hand, an uncontainable wrath flooding from him as he marched back to the bishop. Eleazar tried to stand, but his injuries were too great.

"No!" Christian roared as Maddox lifted the scythe high over the bishop's head, the moonlight flashing on the blood-soaked blade as it came down with accurate promise.

A furious growl ripped through the air and Maddox was knocked to the ground. Delilah jumped back, as a male—more beast than man

—slammed Maddox into the dirt. The bishop fell back as the scythe landed in the mud at his side, his head still intact.

The flames in the forest blazed as the house crumbled. The males of The Order looked on in shock and awe. Chaos exploded as the beast choked Maddox into the earth.

"Isaiah!" one male shouted, the shock clear in his voice.

"Get the females out of here!"

"How was he freed?" Weapons lifted as they prepared to charge.

"Stay back," the bishop ordered the elders, lifting a shaking hand. The beast turned his eyes on Eleazar.

"Grab him!" someone yelled, followed by more voices encouraging the same.

Maddox lay unconscious on the soaked ground. The beast stood, hunched like a cornered primate, as the others surrounded him. A low growl rumbled from his heaving chest.

"Wait." Christian stepped forward, eyeing the beast with curious perplexity.

"Christian, do not!" the bishop ordered as Christian took a slow step closer.

Delilah held her breath as her mate looked into the beast's bloodred eyes. "Isaiah, do you understand me?"

The beast growled, the low rumble a gentle warning that he would not be trapped.

Lightning flashed, illuminating the drenched fields and something small in the distance. Delilah squinted. The witch was gone, but another figure lay unmoving in the pouring rain. Her eyes strained to identify the small female, noting the way her threadbare shift slicked to her body as she lay…lifeless.

Her breath caught as she recognized the girl. That was Dane's sister, the one The Order kept locked in a cell. What happened to her? Why wasn't she moving?

Her attention snapped back to the beast. This was Isaiah, the thing that lived in the cell beside Cybil. How were they set free?

Isaiah panted and seethed, his bare chest rising and falling under a long, matted knot of hair as his bloodred stare bore into Christian's. The winds lifted the flames shooting a spray of sparks into the sky overhead. The immortals took a step forward and the beast hissed, ordering them back. They were afraid of him.

Suddenly, Isaiah arched and bellowed as Maddox bolted for him, scraping his claws down the beast's exposed flesh. Pain sliced down Delilah's back as her gift absorbed the injury.

The incensed creature turned and hissed, thrusting Maddox back onto the ground. Rather than kill the immortal, Isaiah turned and roared at the elders, then loped off, bleeding and howling as he raced through the rain toward Cybil. The further away he traveled the more Delilah's pain eased.

"He has a female!" an elder shouted as Isaiah scooped Cybil's limp body into his arms. He clutched her slack form to his chest and raced into the burning woods.

"We have to stop him!" Cain yelled. "He has Cybil!" A bolt of lightning forked the sky, knifing into the fields. He rushed toward the flames, but Christian caught his arm.

"No. The woods are burning. It's too dangerous."

Cain shoved off Christian's hold. "*Isaiah* is dangerous!"

"The girl is lost, Cain."

He grabbed Christian, jerking him forward by his shirt. "The *girl* is your sister."

Christian met his cold stare with placid detachment. "She's a casualty."

Cain released him with a hard shove. "You should all be ashamed of yourselves." He scanned the fallen bodies and hobbled mob. "Where is Dane?"

Delilah looked behind Cain, more concerned with Maddox's whereabouts. He was gone. Black puddles covered the ground as rain pelted the earth, kicking up mud. "Christian..." She called, still searching the shadows for his father's form.

"Dane's gone," the bishop announced, pulling himself up at the aid of another elder. "As is Cerberus." He tossed Maddox's lifeless hand into the burning house.

Christian's frantic stare searched the chaos. "Where is he?"

"Christian!" she yelled with great effort.

Her mate rushed to her side, cradling her close. "Are you hurt?"

She weakly clung to him. "I'm not great." She tried to laugh but could only wince. "Their injuries. I need distance. It's too much pain."

He lifted her and they were suddenly racing through the stinging rain. As soon as her pain eased, he sensed her relief. "I should have known. Your gift extracts injuries so others can heal. You must feed, *pintura*. You need your strength."

She weakly nodded, accepting his wrist the moment he pushed back his sleeve. Her body was so battered, she lost consciousness, nursing from his vein as her organs and cells recovered and healed.

"You saved me tonight, Christian."

Delilah's eyes fluttered open as the bishop approached. The chaos and flames at his back illuminated his silhouette as he stood over her and Christian, already recovered from his injuries.

"Your father wanted me dead," he said solemnly. "And you stopped him from getting his wish."

"That monster isn't my father."

Eleazar dropped the scythe into the mud. "It was a difficult choice nonetheless."

"I only acted on instinct." Christian's jaw flexed as he held the bishop's knowing stare. "My true father helped my mother escape tonight. It was my honor to repay the favor."

The bishop eyed him with clear understanding and nodded. "You honor me, Christian. I'm proud to think of you as my son."

She expected Christian to smile, but he only lowered his gaze, the weight of too many worries burdening his shoulders. "How long do you think she has?"

His worry cut through Delilah's returning calm, so familiar to the pain she once suffered at the loss of her own parents. She tried so hard to protect him from this, but Adriel's future was out of their hands. No longer feeding, she hugged his torso tight, so that warm love encircled him.

"Your mother's stronger than she realizes. He'll only be able to track her for so long. He's lost blood. If she continues to run for several days, she stands a chance of evading him."

"And Dane?"

The bishop looked away, his eyes hooded with dark regret. "He disobeyed The Council, freed the witch, and attempted to kill Isaiah."

"Is he in danger?"

"Not from us."

Christian nodded. "Thank you for taking mercy on him. Perhaps his leaving this place is for the best."

"There are consequences for his actions, but he's still your brother. If he ever needs sanctuary, he will find safety and shelter here."

For once, Christian didn't argue.

"Eleazar," Cain snapped, interrupting the delicate moment. "I need to speak with you."

The bishop sighed, and Christian stood,

never once allowing her feet to touch the soggy ground. "I'll leave you to your responsibilities," Christian told the bishop, then turned toward their house, cradling Delilah protectively in his arms. "Come, *pintura,* let's go home."

CHAPTER 30

"Sometimes my body understands my needs more than my heart or mind ever could."

Christian kissed Delilah's throat, teasing her pulse into a rapid flutter as he thrust into her. "Give yourself time, my love."

She playfully scraped a claw down his back, arching into him as he slowly took her. "Says Mr. Impatient."

"He chuckled and groaned, burying himself to the hilt. "I waited three centuries for you. My patience was spent long ago."

She pressed a kiss to his throat. "I prefer you growly and gruff anyway."

"Is that so?" He bit into her throat, and her body exulted, rolling into an exquisite release as he drank from her vein.

It was her favorite time of day, the golden hour just before dusk when the windows let in the most radiant light, and the work on the farm finally slowed until dawn. They had made a habit of using this time to reconnect but usually wound up naked and making love until the sun went down. The moment he touched her, he had to have her, and soon they were in a frenzied tangle of lust, feeding and groping, until they both found the release they so desperately wanted.

Afterwards, they lay in each other's arms reveling in the comfort only such a safe and harmonious coupling could bring. Delilah traced a finger down Christian's muscled arm, savoring the delicious way he clutched her body to his, and wondering if she'd ever think anyone more beautiful than he.

"You're going to find me inside of you again if you keep thinking along that line."

She laughed. "I don't know which you enjoy more, a cock stroking or an ego one."

He growled and thrust his hips. "That's nine. One more and it's going to be your lips stroking me as I teach that filthy mouth of yours a lesson."

"Mmm. Promise?"

Christian was a man who saw to his promises and never made her wait. Once he had his way with her, she was ravenous for something sweet.

"Let me see what I can find for you." He said, always in tune with her needs. A few minutes later, he returned to the bedroom with a tray full of freshly picked berries. "How you manage to keep the rabbits away is beyond me. We're overgrown with ripe fruit in the garden."

She sat up, pulling the sheet with her and grinned. "What can I say, the bunnies and all woodland creatures love me. I'm their greatest ally in this cruel world."

He arched a brow. "And…"

"And I feed them."

"There it is."

He sat beside her and they grazed on the freshly picked berries. "Has anyone heard from your mother or Dane?"

"No."

His willingness to discuss his family dwindled every day. It had been three weeks since his father attacked the farm. The ruins of his mother's home had since been plowed into the ash of the scorched woods and no one had been to Dane's barn save Sister Magdalene and Sister Grace.

The Order had once again started following the English news for devastating traces of Isaiah's existence, but there had been no reports of missing bodies or murders that fit his modus operandi, which she supposed was a relief.

The cells of the Safe House were being rebuilt with modern locks and digital security that would be powered by solar energy and generators. Christian didn't fully understand such things, but when he told Delilah about the monitors and coded entries, she tried explaining how basic that sort of technology was in the modern world. He still couldn't fathom such *'electrical' anomalies,* so Delilah gave up.

His hand smoothed over her shoulder as she leaned into his hard chest. He fed her another berry. She looked down at her bare body, the last of her tattoos gone, and her confidence somehow stronger than ever.

"Are you happy, my love?"

Her finger slowly interlaced with his as she ran her hands over him in unconscious exploration. "You know you make me happy, Christian."

He did more than that. He somehow balanced her. He grounded her in a way nothing else ever could. Her jagged edges smoothed once they moved the remainder of her belongings onto the farm, and she was beyond content to live in such ease by his side. The peaceful way they filled their days was an endless gift. An eternity for them to satisfy however they pleased.

"You miss your friend, don't you?"

She sighed. Destiny had gone with Cain to track down Isaiah and retrieve Cybil. Christian adamantly disagreed with their crusade, as did Adam who worried most for his wife. Apparently, Anna and Cain had a special link that left Anna susceptible to any danger Adam's twin incurred.

"I do. But at least Anna's still here, and so far she's been safe."

"Destiny will return. Cain can't spend his

life searching for things that don't wish to be found."

"Do you think Cybil's alive?"

He hesitated. "Are you seeking the truth or hope?"

"The truth, please."

His arms tightened around her, his first instinct always to protect her, but he was learning not to underestimate her strength. "For the girl's sake, I hope not. Isaiah has done horrendous things. Far too many females have suffered. If God is merciful, she will not face a fate similar to her mother's."

Even the elders hadn't understood the extent of Cybil's condition. No one knew just how broken her mind was in the end, but should she have any awareness left, Delilah agreed that it would be a better fate to die than suffer at the hands of a deranged monster like Isaiah.

"Poor Dane."

"I have an ominous feeling this is just the calm before the storm," Christian murmured, pressing his lips to her shoulder. "We need to start working on your skills, *pintura,* so that you can protect yourself if danger befalls the farm again."

She shifted to look over her shoulder and into his eyes. "I thought you said The Order would protect us."

"The Order will always provide safe refuge and guard the life we hold so dear, but I'm afraid The Council is in danger. The elders have acquired some enemies."

A chill raced over her skin. "You mean Maddox."

Maddox was still alive, and Christian understood one of his parents would have to die before any level of peace would be found. He just hoped it wasn't his mother.

HE NODDED STIFFLY. "My father, yes. But also, the witch, Isaiah, and perhaps even Cybil and Dane. We're approaching a new era, where our location is known by those who wish us harm, and vengeance seemed all they seek."

She thought of her friends out in the wild hunting monsters on their own. They were putting themselves at great risk. If anyone would get severely injured, she might be able to offer her help when they needed healing. But for that to happen, she would have to be strong.

"You're right. We should start training right away so we're prepared for anything."

"We could start by playing the game you mentioned."

"Game?" she searched her memory.

"Manhunt." He cupped her possessively. "Though I prefer to call it Seek—Hunt—Claim."

She slithered out of bed and grinned as she slipped her shift over her bare body. "Then you'll have to catch me first."

He was on his feet and at her back before she saw him move. His fist knotted in her hair, angling her head back so he could look into her eyes. "I always do."

She turned in his grip, plastering her body to his as she licked over his jaw and nipped playfully. "That, my darling mate, is because I let you."

Before he could respond, she was gone, racing over the valleys and into the woods, hiding where her mate would chase her, looking forward to the moment he caught her, dying to experience his claim—again, and again, and again.

DARKNESS SURROUNDED them as they loped through the brush. Pine needles whisked underfoot as each sure step pushed Darius further into the night. His hind muscles warmed beneath his thick pelt as the moon illuminated his path.

His brothers flanked him, only the glow of their green eyes giving their presence away as they raced silently into the night. Always by his side. Always at his back. Together, they were one. Unique from other packs in that they shared one need above all else. Blood.

The river rushed at the banks below as they charged toward the cliffs. Another hiker down. Another source to feed them. But this one, like all the others, was not one from their dreams.

They all saw her. The shared link of a brotherhood like theirs left no space for secrets to hide. But after years of hunting with little success, they lost hope and accepted she was only meant to be a dream.

His brothers refused to discuss her, but she still haunted Darius's dreams after all these years. And lately, a sharp ache of desperation rode him hard. A sense of urgency he couldn't shake, as if time were running out, and she needed to be found.

It nagged like an aching tooth, demanding attention and becoming an unignorable obsession. An ache that would not ease. The lingering sensation of something left unfinished kept him up at night, while his dreams grew more disjointed.

Darkness surrounded her, as did fear. She was running from something that terrified her, something she couldn't control, something she believed would eventually claim her unless he got to her first.

Two nights ago, he entertained the idea of breaking from the pack, a thought that earned him the thrashing of a lifetime when his brothers discovered his intentions. They were one. There was no separating. They hunted together. Always. There was no room for individual ambitions that didn't serve the pack, and no such thing as an isolated claim.

His brothers believed what was his was ultimately theirs.

Their primal need required a pack loyalty that could not be broken. The only brothers that had separated from the clan had done so through death. If Darius wanted to find her, he would need to convince his brothers to do the same. And if he planned to save her from whatever was hunting her down, he needed to persuade them soon.

THE END
Want the next book in
The Order of Vampires series?

Click here to purchase PRIMAL KILL,
The Order of Vampires 5, now!

Want to keep in touch with Lydia Michaels?
Join her VIP mailing list here and receive a free
gift when you subscribe!

SPECIAL THANKS

I'm so grateful for the incredible support group I've found over the years. The eclectic family that forms my "circle" is truly a limitless source of strength for me. You all lift me up in so many ways I'm not sure if thank you is a big enough word to hold all of my gratitude for everything you do.

To my readers, you are my compass and motivation. I aim to entertain you and hope I've succeeded. Thank you for sticking with me, clicking those likes and hearts, leaving your reviews, and sharing my books! I could never do this without you.

To my amazing betas, Darcy, Loren, Perrin, and Claire, your insight is priceless. Thanks for sharing your gifts with me and always making time for my characters in your lives!

SPECIAL THANKS

Thank you, Lucinda Gainey, for your devotion to and enthusiasm for this series. You are the voice of The Order and I have loved working with you on every audiobook we've produced together.

And special thanks to my author besties... Heather, you get me and I love you for that—grace and space, baby. DD, you save me on the worst days with your empathetic soul and bottomless encouragement. Michelle, you feed my evil soul and will forever be the Pennywise to my Joker or vice versa. And Tara, you truly are a beautiful friend and I'm so glad we found each other—you brighten my day.

To my LMB team, Lori, Ivone, and Kim, you are the foundation that keeps me standing. Thanks for never giving up on the dream and reminding me that I'm capable of anything I put my mind to. I love you.

And, finally, to the bitches who teach us lessons... Enjoy the view. We're having too much fun to look back and wave.

BOOKS BY LYDIA MICHAELS

MCCULLOUGH MOUNTAIN

Almost Priest

Beautiful Distraction

Irish Rogue

British Professor

Broken Man

Controlled Chaos

Hard Fix

Intentional Risk

JASPER FALLS

Wake My Heart

The Best Man

Love Me Nots

Pining For You

My Funny Valentine

Side Squeeze

CALAMITY RAYNE

Calamity Rayne Gets a Life

Calamity Rayne Back Again

THE SURRENDER TRILOGY

Falling In

BreakingOut

Coming Home

SURRENDER GAMES

Sacrifice of the Pawn

Queen of the Knight

MASTERMIND

Blind

Untied

NEW CASTLE

First Comes Love

If I Fall

SomethingBorrowed

ADDICTED TO YOU

Crush

Bang

Throb

THE ORDER OF VAMPIRES

Original Sin

Dark Exodus

Prodigal Son

Primal Kill

STAND ALONES
La Vie en Rose
Simple Man
Sugar
Breaking Perfect
Hurt
Protege

WANT TO LEARN MORE ABOUT LYDIA MICHAELS?

When you subscribe to her newsletter, you not only stay in touch but also get a copy of her favorite book, La Vie en Rose!

Click here to subscribe!
Or visit
www.LydiaMichaelsBooks.com

ABOUT THE AUTHOR

Lydia Michaels is the bestselling and award-winning author of more than forty novels. She is the consecutive winner of the *2018 & 2019 Author of the Year Award* from *Happenings Media,* as well as the recipient of the *2014 Best Author Award* from the Courier Times. She has been featured by *USA Today, Romantic Times Magazine,* the *Women in Publishing Summit,* and more. She is the CEO and founder of the *East Coast Author Convention,* the *Behind the Keys Author Retreat,* and *Lydia Michaels Coaching & Consulting.*

Michaels started her author career in 2007 and has become a recognized presence and advocate within the publishing industry. She is an outspoken feminist who is happily married to her childhood sweetheart. Some of her favorite things include cooking Italian cuisine, hosting extravagant dinner parties, sipping espresso martinis, and escaping to her coastal home on the Jersey Shore.